MAYADEEN DAMNED AND THE SISTER KINGS

J. LENDELL WHITE

ISBN: 978-1-7325839-2-4

For my mother, the strongest woman I've ever known.

CONTENTS

Acknowledgments...viii

Part One

I   Rumming Down a Dream 1

II   Guess What's Coming to Dinner?............................16

III Bank Broke...27

IV Witches, Bitches and Tents 39

V   Mayadeen's Chest...52

VI Cheater...66

Part Two

VII   The Day the Earth Stood Up 81

VIII On the Ragged Forest..93

IX   Baubles, Bangles and Birds 105

X   Tempting Fate Then Fucking It...................................118

XI   Lowdown...132

XII City of Lights 143

CONTENTS

Part Three

XIII Damned Blood 157

XIV Threesome ...? 168

XV Of Mice and Bulls 179

XVI The World According to Roe 189

XVII That Desert Cunty 202

XVIII A Promise and a Portent 214

Part Four

XIX Bolora 226

XX Beef 237

XXI Wine Dark Sea, Blood Dark Choice 251

XXII The Captain and the King 264

XXIII Requiem for a Daiquiri 277

About the Author 293

ACKNOWLEDGMENTS

Thank you to my amazing and talented wife, Somer, without whom I could not have seen this project through. I'd like to thank the Burbank Wednesday Night Writers for incinerating this story so that it could rise again from the ashes many times over. They are Steve, Raj, Vanessa, Kathleen, Katherine, Brad, Allison, Holly, Dana, Paul, Robert, Christien, Alexandra, Elizabeth, Tina, Mitch, Bill and the late Mary Delle, our beloved founder. A special thanks to Seth M. Sherwood, Heather Parlato and Zhivko Zhelev.

Part One

I
RUMMING DOWN A DREAM

Offered 'em half a day's catch by a twirl o' my tassel, but they stayed their headings on singular purpose. Even in passing I shuddered at the sight o' those Meridian masts of crimson 'n' pale. Trembled, too, for how many foolhardy opposers they'd be leaving in cold wakes o' blood.

~ Babb, *Recollections of a Fisherman*

Mayadeen plunged her rapier fast and perfect. She penetrated the man, and then withdrew from the bull's bleeding heart.

The flat heel of her boot crunched the nose of another while the steel of her cutlass clanked away pitted iron. She leaped down from the port railing of the enemy's damaged brig onto the main deck. The black smoke from her own ship's bombards clung heavy on the morning breeze. She dodged slightly as a sword slashed wide of her brow just before she sliced her off-hand cutlass into a cage of shallow bone. The enemy grunted as he folded onto the blade. Another hopeful's pommel caught Mayadeen lips-to-teeth on her exposed side, but Mayadeen did not recoil. Instead she wrenched her cutlass free from the butchered rib bone of the first and found quick purchase through the second's neck. The surprised womaner screamed and fell back, clawing to dam up her life blood in a levee of flesh.

"To me, my trumps! Cut 'em all down to pay the price of ghosts."

The boarding party that now swarmed from behind Mayadeen comprised the greater part of her seventy-two proven scalawags of the *Sea Licker*. They'd have to pass harsh judgment on those who dared challenge a Daughter born's war galleon of the Meridian Isles.

Mayadeen eyed the captain's quarters on the afterdeck. But before she'd have the privilege of breaking down its door, two more of the enemy looked to try their luck. A skinny womaner with a shaved head came at Mayadeen first with a three-pronged pole hook. Skinny swiped then pulled, hoping to catch Mayadeen's rapier. Skinny missed, only to be blindsided and run through by a short sword to the back. The blade belonged to Teague, one of Mayadeen's sturdiest mates. She'd be sure to make the assist worth his while the next time she needed a good rough 'n' tumble.

Mayadeen flashed Teague a grin before focusing her contest on the second womaner. This one, much larger and covered in floral tattoos from head to hand, clutched a hefty club. Mayadeen lunged slightly forward with a feint of her rapier. Always best to see how jittery her opponent would be. Flower didn't take the bait. Instead, she turned and clubbed Teague over the head as he removed his sword from Skinny. The bull went down cold, and Mayadeen thought she heard his skull crack.

Apparently, Flower wanted to die slowly.

Mayadeen drove her rapier for the big womaner's leg. Flower barely avoided the thrust and stepped into Mayadeen with a downward swing of her club. Mayadeen sidestepped—always moving in to close the space, like the turn of a screw—and caught the outside of Flower's hand with a slash from her cutlass.

Flower growled. "Ye Meridian horse fucker!" Her elbow mirrored her frustration and jabbed Mayadeen's bad eye.

Although that patched-over memory was numb as a rock, the blunt shock still rattled Mayadeen's head. She reeled for a moment before darting up her rapier to lodge beneath Flower's chin. The scalawag shrieked and let go of her club. Mayadeen spun the gagging bitch around. When certain nobody else was about to ambush, Mayadeen drove the blade further upward into Flower's wasted mush. Her eyes crossed and rolled over to nothing but the whites. Mayadeen withdrew her dripping rapier even before Flower could collapse to the deck.

Her curiosity as to who was captaining this vessel was growing with each gory second. It was not unusual for splitties and bulls to cohabit a pirate ship. Mayadeen always preferred to crew her vessels with the latter, though that preference was a rare and known exception amongst the bitch barges on the Nine Seas.

The three-masted enemy brig with neither sigil nor colors had emerged out of nowhere in the morning fog that shrouded the shoals of High Island. But as the gods would will it, not that Mayadeen had any use for them, the surprise incursion proved shoddy. Once the ships were on top of each other, the failed offenders must have been more chagrined to find Mayadeen's *Sea Licker* housed six bombards—three on a broadside—new and expensive weapons capable of launching iron balls through cast iron tubes with the use of fire and black powder. Only the finest and most prized ships in all of Tabor possessed such devices, and Mayadeen's custom galleon recently joined their ranks.

The bombards fired a round apiece taking out a large portion of the brig's quarterdeck and severing several chains off his port quarter mizzen. The fantastic sound and blackening smoke in tandem with a volley from the *Licker's* archers had stunned the opposing crew, affording Mayadeen the preemptive hijack.

"Hook the rest of them cunties alive, damn ye," she now commanded over the receding din of clinking and yelling and grunting. Her mates were quickly gaining the whip hand. She finally strutted aft toward the small cabin. The brig was a decent ship, despite inferior size and capacity to the *Licker*, so whoever captained him had a right jolly reason to cross wakes. That bog hag Cutter, maybe? Bellcroak? Bon Rock?

The thick-slatted cabin door threw open. Out scuttled a half-size man with one hand clutching a strange device and the other massaging an open wound on his bald head.

Lil' pint o' piss ...

He rushed, stopping short before pointing the miniature cylinder. "Die, Mayadeen Damned!"

The device combusted with a puff of black smoke. And that was that.

The little man cursed incoherently and threw the smoking metal to the deck.

Mayadeen flipped up her diamond-shaped padded leather patch. The breeze cooled the sweat on her partial eye. She recognized the sea dog as Minnow Baels. His stones had always been his largest attribute, and his days of privateering with worthless mercenaries to stab old chums in the backs had come to a blundering end.

#

What she really needed was a drink. The balm and brine of midmorning on the Jeweled Sea already threatened a long, hot summer.

"May as well let me fall, heh. Ye'll get nothin' from me, ye one-eyed monster!"

Parched is what she was. Parched as a beached jellyfish at high noon. Her tongue ran across the crusty terrain of her lips to the now scabbed over lump.

She'd be sure to make it three drinks.

Mayadeen held Minnow Baels by both of his worn leather boots, dangling him off the starboard railing of his own vessel. If nothing else, he had a good view of the salty roll several heads below. He'd imbibe soon enough, though his swill wasn't going to be rum, sugar and lime.

"Laddy, make sure those belly sharks are good and frothing," Mayadeen ordered aside to a wiry young deck hand. The ravenous fish, so named for stomachs that could expand to hold five grown women at once, had yet to call. Considering the twenty dead, blood-soaked unfortunates already thrown overboard, Mayadeen was surprised they hadn't attracted every cursed thing with teeth from there to Torperand.

She watched as Laddy tossed the final bucket of chum made from hacked limbs to the coppery water. Laddy was a good sea pup for no other reason than he had a cute arse and matching chin. He'd do just fine so long as he preferred the tit to the trunk.

Mayadeen again licked her lips, this time over the edges of a smirk. After those drinks, she'd be sure to muster her fill of something else entirely.

"'Twas a time ye sailed for the Island Realm, Baels," declared Mayadeen loud enough for the fish to hear. "How a shriveled lil' leg humper like yerself could've pulled off as much as ye have, only gods and devils would know. Should've kept ye to running down shit sloops and lost sea monkeys. Half a traitor's a traitor still."

That brought a good chorus of laughs from the jeering victors crowded at the gunwales and main deck. Her hand-picked crew of bulls and gelds glistened in the morning sunshine—a sweaty mix of brown and white, skin and cloth, hair and hairless—like a busy oil painting still wet on the canvas. After the day's excitement, she'd lost four of her own. Not bad for an impromptu deck battle, though Mayadeen was never thrilled about losing any of her mates. She didn't believe in dead weight, and every one of her trumps was worth the space of his berth.

"Fie to that 'n' the lot of ye! I may be half everything else, but I'm a captain complete." Baels wagged his arms and attempted to spit into the breeze at Mayadeen. "Ye Meridian devil womaners have pissed yer blood on the waters for too long. The Nine Seas belong to ye no more than to any. I'll give ye my seed, Captain ... right in yer great white arse!"

Baels hailed from the backwards land of Edenvane, where bulls were gaining some headway in ruling themselves. Mayadeen had to give the little man credit. Edish pirates had been trying for years to cobble their reputations by either joining Meridians or sinking Meridians. Minnow Baels was one of the few sailors still living who'd managed to do plenty of both. His was the rare ilk that wouldn't be missed by either side.

"I'll say nay to that, Baels. But yer face'd make a fine saddle for a tired splitty." Mayadeen snickered as she plunged him up and down in the air. The wee bastard was starting to get heavy.

"Ye're as lucky as ye're arrogant," growled Baels. "Ye'll grow another eyeball 'fore ye reach the Southern Isles, heh."

Now *this* was of interest. "And yet ye seem to be helping me to get there, bringing fresh maps right to my threshold. Retrieved 'em from that rat's nest ye call a cabin. Who sent ye, Baels? What do ye know 'bout the Southern Isles?"

Baels flashed a devilish grin, or frown since it was upside down. "Heh, heh. Like to know, wouldn't ye?"

Then he shouted to his captors once more. "Almost ended ye all, I did." He stuck out his chin at Mayadeen. "This one's too big for her soppin' breeches. Follow her to the bottom soon enough—" Baels screamed all the way to the water.

Mayadeen still squeezed the two boots out of which he'd accidentally slipped.

A hush fell over the onlookers for a suprised moment until laughter again filled in the blanks.

"Ah, bugger a broken bottle," growled Mayadeen. After a subdued splash, her prisoner seemed to have disappeared in the reddened waves. "Laddy, go fetch the lil' shit bird."

"Aye, Cap'n ... but ... but what 'bout them sharks?"

Mayadeen almost acknowledged Laddy's logic when Baels appeared again, severed at his spine, bobbing like a baby turnip in a tomato soup.

And so was the fate of Minnow Baels.

Mayadeen sighed and tossed away the child-size boots. Despite the heat, distant thunderheads moved like sagging ink blots over the horizon. A storm was on the march and moving fast. The *Licker* had weathered countless tempests throughout six of the nine seas, and under Mayadeen's command his seafaring constitution knew no equal. Mayadeen also wasn't about to let some undesirable weather avert her line of thought. She wanted some answers in light of the day's hijinks. And her crew needed a good break, besides.

She turned to Jagger, her First Mate, one of the few gelds on her ship. Though drenched in sweat with blood on his sleeves, Jagger always managed to look as though he was from some higher order. But rather than merely intimidating others with his aplomb, he forced them to take some of it on themselves.

"Half their stores and all of their weapons now belong to us, Captain," said Jagger.

Mayadeen studied the thirty two survivors of Baels' former crew, all on their knees in two rows and bound with a single rope.

"Then let 'em loose and cut away the brig," she ordered.

"Aye, Captain," said Jagger. "Cut 'em loose! Away those tethers!"

Thirty-two scalawags were less than a skeleton crew, even for a smaller vessel. Provided they didn't run into too much of the elements or otherwise along the way, they could manage a return to their strange little homeland beyond the Sea of Cats.

The Edish whelps would have quite the sad story, something along the lines of how they'd survived a one-eyed madwoman and her all-male crew. Of course, they'd shade it a bit more to their favor. Perhaps the madwoman stood seven feet tall with snakes thrashing out of her head and the crew an army of frenzied cannibals. They might as well make a decent bedtime yarn out of it for their young ones.

"We'll all sup well tonight," Mayadeen shouted before a rally of cheers as she climbed back onto the gunwales of her slightly taller galleon.

"We hold a southerly course then, Captain?" asked Jagger from over her shoulder.

"Aye, windward as it flies to beat the storm," she assured him. "Put Yolton on the wheel and meet me in my cabin."

Jagger nodded and repeated his orders up to the forecastle of the *Licker*. "Smartly, now! Haul the wind as it flies!"

Another crewman echoed the words, while yet another started up a familiar lyric. After half of the first verse nearly every hand on deck caught the contagion of song.

> *"Shimmering, shimmering, five fathoms deep*
> *Booty in the brine, hauling up the keep ..."*

Mayadeen gave pause as her sea dogs busied their backs once again into bringing the *Licker* to life. They sallied forth as if reinvigorated—true scalawags riding high from the rush of adventure and the taste of violence. They handled their floating fortress like bees managed a hive, caressing and nurturing him with every climb, knot, tug and furl. They kept his hardwood deck swabbed, the natural peach-colored grain almost golden with stain still fresh from his last anchorage. The wood on his hull waxed darker, but with red and gold gilt adorning his gunwales, masts and yards.

> *"... Carried me sure, 'n' carried me far*
> *Anchor on the shoals, 'n' diving off the spars ..."*

The *Sea Licker*'s sixteen square sails on four masts—lateen-rigged on the mizzen—dominated the sky overhead. Their beige canvases were interrupted by a single faded red sigil on the main top, nine serpents fanning out from a terraced pyramid. The Jeweled Sea, along with the three other oceans in the northern hemisphere of Tabor, was Meridian waters. But regardless of territory, in the reaving nets of the Island Realm, all nine seas of the sphere belonged to the Daughter born.

Mayadeen watched with approval as Yolton, the ship's Second and Bosun, took the rudder. Bosun was the highest rank a bull by law could achieve on a ship, but Mayadeen took liberty to combine Yolton's role with Second Mate. He kept long, grayish hair with a scruffy beard to match, and he could growl orders meaner than even Mayadeen was capable. He was also her most trusted mate next to Jagger, and the perfect instrument to ensure the other bulls were kept in line. Yolton had reminded Mayadeen of her own dear Pap, besides the fact she'd invited the former to her bed on more than a few occasions.

Not that her Pap hadn't pearled his pecker every chance he could muster. It was why he'd remained a bull—a long life of fishing and fucking—and he was famous for it. Mayadeen's mother chose good seed, and every splitty from Cleft Rock to Point Watch wanted to partake in the sowing. Mayadeen figured she'd all kinds of bastard half-sisters running around, although her Pap's half didn't mean stewed shit in the Meridian Isles. A woman was her mother's namesake, and the Damned moniker ensured Mayadeen a place in the pantheon of maritime masters.

A dark blur crossed high behind a fluttering topsail above. Mayadeen whistled in three short bursts. They were answered by a squawk; and a red-winged, black bird the size and shape of a small chicken swooped around into view.

"Prick, to me, damn ye."

The redgull made another circle before braking and spiraling to find Mayadeen's shoulder. As usual, he had a trinket in his clutches. Redgulls were master navigators—they could track a quarry halfway around Tabor—and they also had a penchant for scavenging. It hadn't taken long for Mayadeen to train the bird to lift just about any piece of jewelry, usually off of corpses.

"What a pretty have ye?" She pried a ring from his talons, silver with amethysts from the looks of it.

Prick thrust his beak into Mayadeen's hair, no doubt hoping to find something living. She was happy not to oblige the evil creature on this occasion. Prick had earned his name by once having pecked a hole the size of a copper tail into Mayadeen's neck while she was giving her crew instructions for an island raid. As she cursed and tried to slash the insufferable bird out of the air with her cutlass, the scalawags laughed themselves into stupors.

"Ye're a fine trump, Prick." She tossed the swag to Yolton who snatched it from the air. Though the ring obviously fit a womaner's finger, Yolton was big for a bull and could fill it out. He grinned and held the ring to the sky for a better look.

Mayadeen strode aft to her cabin with Prick in tow. She felt the hungry leers of her bulls upon her, though she never did mind the attention. She figured she wasn't too sore on the peepers should a sailor happen to have two of them. She thought briefly how she had lost her left eye on her sixteenth birthday—a mess of a memory that only she and her own dear mother knew the truth about. Nevertheless, not having two made the one all the keener.

"What're ye gawking at but yer own dear Captain, ye greasy sea apes?" shouted Yolton as he stepped to the wheel on the poop's riser. "Ready yerselves to tack or swim home, damn ye …"

#

Yolton's rebukes trailed off as Mayadeen entered her tidy cabin and kicked the door shut behind. Prick squawked and launched off her shoulder to perch on one of three open porticoes at the center rear of the mahogany room.

Even the cursed bird knew where she was headed.

She crossed to a jade and alabaster credenza beneath the portico. The furnishing alone was worth more than the price of a small ship. There sat her private stash of bottled spirits secured against the wall by a net.

"Bloody fucking hell," she grumbled when she discovered her silver bowl of limes was empty. Just four months at sea and her sugar reserve had depleted to half a finger as well. She could only hope her latest victory resupplied these urgent shortages.

She turned to hear Yolton's shouts from the deck for a brief moment more as the door to the room swung open and closed again. Jagger was the culprit. Mayadeen watched her unassuming friend enter and toss a large map onto the knotty pine slate in the room's center.

"The map you requested, Captain."

Mayadeen leaned over and spread the papyrus map about the table. She pointed to a cluster of islands in the southwest.

"See here? The Southern Isles at Fire Hoof drawn anew. The lil' shit was worth the trouble after all."

"Minnow Baels had one of Captain Bon Shemble's maps? But ... how?"

"'Cause sure as a pig shits its own happiness, the biddy bitch survived, is how. I'll wager Bon Shemble scoured every puddled crevice of those islands not a year past. As to how Baels got his lil' pinchers on it, who's to say?"

"No map will help us in those lands, Captain."

"Won't be needle accurate, nay, but they're a start."

Disappearing landscapes or not, the Sarasatha ruins in the Southern Isles had yet to be plundered, and Mayadeen would succeed where Bon Shemble failed.

She had mixed feelings about her former teacher and patron, Captain Sonner Bon Shemble. Last Mayadeen heard the ornery old crone had sailed the Southern Isles in search of the very same riches Mayadeen was after. Though the reports and sightings differed on whether or not she returned, Bon Shemble had supposedly been the sole Nine Master to drop anchor within the Isles themselves. The last of an ancient civilization had finally expired there, and for several years since, every pirate and smuggler on the Nine Seas was vying to loot the ruins.

The first problem they all had in common was getting to the Southern Isles, as the encompassing waters were anything but inviting. The storms in that region raged the better portion of every season, and the fathomless depths of the Fire Hoof bred leviathans few scalawags lived to tell about. Three out of every five ships to venture there never returned. And when a ship did get through the tempests and terrors, the islands themselves were said to harbor dark magics so powerful that entire mountains, bays and reefs would shift to appear someplace else.

"What more did we plunder from Half-Bull Baels?"

"His stores had plenty of citrus for you, Captain. I sent for a bucket. We've also three dozen steel blades, ten pairs of breeches, four jugs of wine, two barrels of rum, and salted mutton. Baels had other fresh maps, and we took all but what his lot needed to find their way back, should the gods be generous."

"Any sugar?" Her eye briefly shifted to Jagger.

"Not a pinch."

"Aye, so remember the gods are never fucking generous." Mayadeen focused back on the map. "Every feather cock south of the Spread will be out to stop us or race us," she said while tracing vectors with her finger on the map.

"You'd be right then, Captain. Nine Master Bon Shemble must've survived."

"I wouldn't lose a flagon of piss over the old coot either way."

"If she made it, there would be no chance of these maps going to Edenvane, certainly not into the hands of Minnow Baels," Jagger continued. "She'd take them to her pillow at night, and not even the most ambitious cutthroat would cross Old Bon Shemble."

"Ye speak true enough."

"Except one."

"Fuck a god in her starry arse, Jagger, out with it."

"Creyland Fenn."

Mayadeen finally looked up. Fenn's was a name she hadn't heard in a long while.

"So what of 'im? Ye think Crey Fenn sent Baels our way?" Mayadeen considered that Jagger might be onto something. Nobody was better at turning enemies into friends, or friends into enemies, than Creyland Fenn. After all, the pretty bull had gotten Mayadeen out of her boots. What's to say he hadn't coaxed old Bon Shemble out of hers? Mayadeen cringed at the thought.

"Nay, not even Fenn could pull that off," she continued. "'N'

Baels was out for blood, not plunder or parlay."

"Then I guess Baels must've snatched the maps on his own," sighed Jagger. "Maybe he cracked Bon Shemble's hull before having a go at ours?"

"Humph. Unlikely, that." Mayadeen hated being nonplussed by details that didn't make a damn bit of difference, and she resented Jagger for planting the seed about Creyland Fenn.

"We claimed his Captain's chest—Baels, I mean," said Jagger.

Mayadeen was relieved to change the subject.

"According to one of his lads," Jagger went on, "the key went swimming with him. Riles said he could probably charm the lock, though it looks to be of Aterian make."

"I'd not let him spend much effort to it. Like as not, Minnow Baels' lockbox is filled with copper tails, shit-stained diapers and his mother's mummified tit."

"Well, every man needs a taste of home," said Jagger.

The cabin door swung open. It was Tyker who carried in a large bucket of limes. He was a surly old bull cock, but a tried and trusted scalawag. He also happened to be the only crewmate to have once sailed under Mayadeen's notorious mother.

Now those drinks were imminent. Mayadeen grabbed a lime from the bucket and stepped over to her netted shelf. She chose a dark bottle, pried the cork with her teeth and spat it into a bowl with twenty others. She took up two golden jewel-encrusted goblets. Two pinches of sugar went into each cup—would have been three on a more bountiful day. She unsheathed a dagger from her belt, drove it through the center of the lime and twisted it back and forth on the skewer held above one goblet and then above the other. She poured three fingers of darkest rum into each goblet and stirred with the dagger's dripping point still skewering the fruit. Then she retracted the dagger, wiped the blade clean on the edge of her trousers and replaced it at her belt.

"Tyker, ye ol' chum cock. Have a dram with us?"

"Nay, nay, Cap'n. I don't take to sweets 'n' lemons in my rum."

"Then take to getting out," said Mayadeen. "And they ain't fucking lemons."

Tyker cackled before exiting as Mayadeen's stare seared through his old, wrinkled head.

Jagger, too, stifled a laugh. "Captain, I realize that bottle ain't the good stuff, but have you ever tried it without the lime and sugar?"

"Aye, Jagger. I have at that."

Mayadeen pulled another, less fancy cup from her netted particulars. She set the cup on the floor of the room. Then she unfastened her trousers, pulled them down and squatted over the cup. After a solid, resonate stream, she pulled up her pants and placed the warm cup on the table in front of Jagger next to the other goblets.

"Here's yer drink without lime and sugar."

Jagger smiled. "I'll take the daiquiri."

Mayadeen threw the cup of piss out the portico.

"Now cease fillin' the room with tidings of shit and let's drink." Mayadeen handed Jagger one of the jeweled goblets and plopped down into a rattan half-seat at the slab table. She held up her cup. "To buggering what may come to pass for it ain't come yet."

Jagger nodded and smiled.

Both took generous sips. Mayadeen smacked her lips and relished the richness of the rum's molasses over the faint tinge of citrusy sweet.

"How many chests of the like have you and I won over the years? Fifteen? Twenty?"

"Twenty-two."

"Twenty-two? Well, that's keen to a point! And could there be more to this life than the glisten of gold or the cut of a gem?"

"For me ... no," answered Jagger. "But for you, aye, there is one more thing."

"There is, indeed, ye balless letch. A crew of cocks is a crew for me, says I and always will!" Mayadeen grinned wide. She liked Jagger. The hairless man made her laugh. If he hadn't chosen to have his stones snipped off at adolescence, she would've enjoyed hearty pleasures with him in the berth. But like many gelds, Jagger had no taste for such adventures.

After a good tip of the cup, Mayadeen rose and turned towards Prick's portico to take in the air. The bird must have flown off during their palaver. Mayadeen let the light breeze dance across her cheeks. Her nostrils flared as the savory smells of roasting fowl, boiling stew and baking bread wafted in. Curdly, the ship's cook, was already at work. It would be a welcome change from more than a week of moldy biscuits dipped in vinegar, dried fish, and rotten cabbage.

Jagger quaffed his grog with a couple more swallows. "That storm still threatens from the northeast. It came and went on the far and now it's back. Yolton agrees it's a hasty one."

"Strange," said Mayadeen. "As if the cursed thing's toying with us." They'd already lost half a day's progress from the business with Baels. She didn't want to batten down until it was absolutely necessary, and they'd maintained the downwind since resuming their course. "Well, it'll have to wait 'til aft we sup."

Mayadeen finished the rest of her daiquiri and began to prepare another. All she needed now was a hard shaft and an enduring tongue. Teague, one of her favorites in that regard, survived his thumping in the skirmish but would be recovering for several moons.

"Send me Laddy," she added over her shoulder while Jagger made well to take his leave. "But not before he takes a dive and scrubs himself."

II
GUESS WHAT'S COMING TO DINNER?

When you make a plan, plan on being fucked bloody in the arse with your own dagger, and then your plan will have a greater chance of feeling successful no matter what the outcome.
~ Nine Master Mabelia Damned

The last of the grog felt good as it coursed across Mayadeen's palate. She sat up on her mattress with trousers off, boots crossed, and shirt unbuttoned. The fine wood in her cabin creaked with the gentle lull of the ship while the glow of the room's single lantern cast an encircling shadow.

Without a bumbling word, young and supple Laddy closed the cabin door behind him.

She'd make a sea dog of him yet.

At best, the whole business of using her bulls for pleasure portrayed a dubious morality, and Mayadeen was reminded early on that she needed to quell her appetites. In her first foray captaining a vessel she'd tried taking the rough and tumble with every bull on the ship. Under the laws of the Meridian Isles, a captain was sanctioned to use her own crew any way she saw fit. A ship meant a throne of sorts, and its captain a king. Sex with impunity offered scintillating temptation for anybody that could receive pleasure from the deed, and anybody who said otherwise was either gelded or lying. Just the same, even a floating kingdom could capsize.

On that first voyage, three of the bulls refused her indiscretions, and whether out of ego or simple disappointment, Mayadeen threatened to kill the third man for disobedience. Once word got around the ship that the captain would slit a man's throat for not returning carnal comforts, several bulls and even a few gelds banded together to support their cause for retaliation. It could have ended with Mayadeen thrown overboard and a mutinous escape to Edenvane if she hadn't made a plea and apology to the entire crew that she'd been *too much under the grog*. It was a humbling experience, and its ramifications on the morale of her ship forced her to port and replace most of the crew.

A precarious start, indeed, that nearly cost Mayadeen her reputation as a Daughter born Captain and hopeful Master of the Nine Seas; for a woman of the salt and sword who could not command a vessel could not command the sea, and so by rights would command no place amongst the elite of the Island Realm. Had she not been the daughter of Mabelia Damned, one of the most revered Nine Masters in all of the Isles, she might have been exiled from the Meridian Isles.

But Mayadeen since learned to better gauge the sensibilities of her prey, and judging by the grin on his face and the shank in his breeches when she removed her breast wrap, Laddy had been anxious enough to pacify her weakness.

She finally yanked off her boots and leaned back against the corner of her bed chamber. She always wore her boots during a petting—she felt naked without them. A tepid breeze entered from the starboard portico just above her knees, gently chilling the sweat beads across her flesh and well-sated jolly parts. Now her mind raced at least forty leagues ahead of the *Licker*, although the custom war galleon she purchased three years prior with a cargo of uncut jewels plundered from merchant wreckage was making good progress. The *Sea Licker* was much slower than her previous vessel, but he was also steadfast and could take on any competing ships they might encounter in the trade runs that crossed his southerly course.

Their first major challenge would be steering the Spread, nigh more than a week's journey if they could maintain a leeward line. Mayadeen was the best pilot and navigator on her ship. She could, however, rely on Yolton to second the rudder between measurement and counsel with Jagger. Once beyond the straights, her path would turn south by southeast into the Fire Hoof—where neither island nor main took sight for three weeks on any line. If she could hold south for the duration of that treacherous void, the Southern Isles lay but a few days west according to the charts. The Isle of Pelins was the largest if Bon Shemble's maps were accurate, and that's where Mayadeen would seek anchorage, provided the island itself wasn't some devil's disappearing act.

Where Bon Shemble failed, Mayadeen would succeed, laying claim to riches enough to buy her own holdfast, perhaps even two or three. That wasn't asking for much, considering some womaners from the Isles owned entire coastlines. Mayadeen thought she might even fancy having her own fishing village, complete with harbor and a fleet of perrygill trawlers. The big blue fish was her favorite delicacy and it always fetched a good price at market. That, in addition to all of the horny bull fishermen she could practically call her own, would give her something worth coming home to.

And if Crey Fenn and his latest tub of Edish swineherds wanted a piece of her action, then let the puffed-up peacock meet her on the swells. Mayadeen had sent plenty to the cold, black depths when necessary, enemies and old friends alike. Fenn was just another competitor in the end, and of late the competition needed some diluting.

#

By the time Mayadeen and her crew assembled main deck for a victory banquet, the taste of storm permeated the air. The dark tempest on the horizon shifted its course twice within a ten-hour period and now was lapping at the *Licker's* wake. But a storm was no more a stranger than the *Licker* was a virgin bull on Seedus, and the brisk gales and intermittent sting of sea spray weren't about to curb the appetites of the scalawags celebrating atop of him.

Four loading ramps each set on eight barrels across the waist of the main deck served side-by-side as makeshift tables for the lot. Mutton stew stole the menu with bountiful rolls of bread to soak it up. Roasted fowl, grease-cooked parsnips, pungent cheese, savory wine, and biting rum rounded off the meal.

At the head of the first table sat Mayadeen, immediately flanked by Jagger and Yolton. The three of them presided over the four columns of crewmen. Mayadeen primped a bit for the occasion, tying back her limitless hair, which she usually kept in several small pigtails, and sporting a black and gold-cuffed broadcloth frock coat over her traditional jerkin. She even pulled over her fancy eye patch with the emerald studs. Though she'd not inherited the handsome angles of her mother, she fancied to look half the moon strumpet from time to time. It also worked to give the bulls something to desire when she needed a fix.

Mayadeen nudged Yolton with her elbow and the bearded Second and Bosun stood up.

"Settle now, ye mongrels," he said with minimal effort across the cursing and laughter. "Settle now, damn ye. Yer own dear Captain has a missive."

The group quieted gradually to some elongated chuckles and smiling murmurs. Mayadeen guessed that half the grog rationed for the occasion had already been drank, though she'd played her own part in educating that estimate. And it was just as well, for she was never a pigeon for speeches.

She hoisted herself with a fist to the table. "As ye know well enough, we now bear a heading to beyond the Spread to the Fire Hoof direct."

Some mixed affirmations and groans at that one. Even though

most of her crew were veterans, exactly none of them had ever ventured close to the lower latitudes of the Seraphim Sea, the dangerous waters that held the pinnacle of their journey.

"When ye took up with me and my vessel, ye took up a promise and a portent—a promise of life high with a portent of death low. As for myself, I'd have it no other way."

The silence grew heavy but for the growing winds at sea and the rhythmic creaks of the ship.

"But I tell ye true just the same that once we hit the shores we seek, ye'll be sharing in riches enough so even the gods will piss rains of envy."

That brought them out of it with a cheer and clanking cups all around.

"We're not to be diverted, damn ye. Ye're *my* men—Meridian men—and ye cut the nine waters with the finest ship in all of Tabor."

More agreement and a couple of whistles sang out.

"The sea is ours, my trump-hards, along with any and all that glistens above or beneath it."

She really had them going now. She touched her own cup to Jagger's while the eunuch smiled up at her, his eyes twinkling like torch lanterns.

"We'll send them that say otherwise beneath ... but them, *they* won't be glistening. Why for ye ask won't they be glistening?" Mayadeen liked to end a good speech with a jest of provocation. Old Bon Shemble had always done it, and such humor was a traditional way to end a song or story in the rowdy taverns back home.

Several men at once repeated the question, but then young Laddy shouted out the bait winner, "Whyn't they be glistening, Cap'n?"

The men again grew quiet, their eyes magnets of anticipation.

Mayadeen grinned at Laddy and licked the sharp of her silver tooth. "Well, because we'll be taking all their shiny trinkets, of course!"

The pirates roared with laughter.

Mayadeen thrust her cup out high before dropping back into her seat. Thunder grumbled in the distance.

Jagger toasted her cup then leaned into her ear. "That storm's nigh upon us. We'd better start clewing down and getting these bulls alow."

"Well, aye, aye, Captain Jagger." That the bloody storm followed them windward and leeward alike for a hundred leagues as some needy old cur annoyed Mayadeen to no end. But the fact remained they needed to be ready for it, and a good seawoman always knew that any dark on the horizon could spell certain doom. "Send ten to reef the main and mizzens. As for the rest, we've got us some time yet. Let 'em finish a final round of rum. They need a taste of the good stuff."

Jagger nodded and quickly removed himself.

Mayadeen squinted around at her bulls. They were a worthy lot. At last, a crew she could boast about. With these men she would scribe her page in legend. She would best her peers. She would best her insufferable mother. She would best them all.

#

Some minutes and another round of rum later, the wind and spume lashed out from the surrounding darkness. The wooden Captain's chest lifted from Baels' conquered ship was brought out with much fanfare to be formally presented to Mayadeen, even though her best thieves still had yet to crack the confounded thing. But it would have to wait. Mayadeen spied lightning skitter at the end of a starless sky. For the rest that were drinking too much or laughing too hard, a subsequent thunder so loud it made tuning forks out of every plank on the main deck grabbed their attention alas. Mayadeen stood up with both hands this time, feeling the rum a bit more than before the speech.

"That concludes supper then ye sated triggle ticks. Time to hunker ye down—"

Some of the men laughed as a platter of cheese and marmalade was blown from a table.

Mayadeen was about to speak again when the next flash of lightning made her eye go wide. A swell the size of a small mountain towered above the *Licker* at starboard. The trench of the swell pulled the ship into a sudden free fall, and a mighty heave rolled it into a wall of sea. Everything on deck at once upended, including Mayadeen. She fumbled through air to fold over a jutting rope post. The breath snatched from her lungs, she glimpsed several of the men perform questionable somersaults over the tables. The loading slabs lifted from the barrels, pinning those who'd been seated on the less fortunate ends to the deck and forecastle risers.

Thunder boomed louder than the fire from a hundred bombards.

In little more than an instant, the great tempest at last held the *Sea Licker* firm, rolling and dipping him like a god might a ladle through the well of a world. Waves with fifty foot crests ensured every ebb felt like a descent into oblivion. Just as the ship righted itself to weather the next pull, Mayadeen scraped her way astern to gather the wheel. Directly in her path two men crashed into one another only to topple each over the gunwales. Sig and Melder they might have been, but she wasn't sure. At least Dobbs and Tyker it appeared were able to make for the lower deck and take comfortless refuge into the churning belly of their wooden home. Those that Jagger had sent to the masts still manned their posts, lashing down the shifting yards with extra twine. It had to be done should the ship survive the drowning.

Mayadeen reached the rudder which spun to and fro. She slammed herself into the wheel column and grabbed the pegs with an angry yell. She'd never known a storm to hit so fast and with such stealth. A great spray of cold water threatened to undo her grip, but somehow she held on and found another hand clutching a peg below her own. It belonged to Yolton. Their yells to each other were barely audible shoulder to shoulder through the deafening bedlam. Several times the wheel nearly escaped them, which would have sent the ship into a whirling frenzy.

After the next squall of white foam receded, several dark presents appeared scattered about the decks. When the storm first began to call, Mayadeen thought she'd recognized a bellow in the distance. Now it was confirmed. Just once in all her career at sea did Mayadeen ever have to tangle with a krode beast, a great kraken of the deep. As a child, she knew them only in legend from wild tales her Pap would whisper at bedtime. But unlike she, her father had never actually *seen* a krode beast—the old fool probably hadn't even believed they existed. Well, she'd have news for him on the other side, perhaps before the night was through.

Mayadeen glanced at Yolton. His jaw firmed as he watched the capstan. The dark pod-like clusters began to scurry about on short spidery legs.

"Krellusks!" This time Mayadeen's yell was heard.

It was said that the parasitic crustaceans were like pilot fish to a krode beast, which had been known to warden hundreds of them. Vicious creatures each about the size of a fox hound, krellusks would swarm their prey, paralyze it, and drag it seaward to the awaiting behemoth. Such was already the case with Stromm, a sturdy young bull and a hard worker, who was being carried off by a cluster. The poor scalawag flailed for his life, so Mayadeen surmised that the paralysis hadn't quite taken effect. In the next instant he vanished into the chaos. Mayadeen hoped he let himself drown before reaching his final destination.

She grabbed Yolton by his jerkin and gestured up to the men aloft who clung to whatever was close. "Hail 'em down! They're of no more use up there!"

Yolton nodded and unsheathed his cutlass while still keeping the wheel with one bulging arm. He let go, and Mayadeen leaned in with all of her weight to hold the line. The old bull was as stalwart as any Mayadeen had known, and she was glad to have sailed with him. A single krellusk scuttled its way up the poop. Yolton batted it so hard with his blade that a good third of the creature flew off into the darkness. The rest contorted sideways into a mess of its own fluids.

"There's naught for this, Cap'n! We should get us—"

A concussion of thunder swallowed his words.

The storm's savagery knew no equal in Mayadeen's recollections. As the rolls turned more and more to whirling tilts, it had become obvious the ship was caught in the thralls of a tremendous maelstrom. It explained the surfacing of the krode beast, itself subdued in the vortex just the same.

Mayadeen's heart skipped as a lightning flash betrayed the monster's silhouette swaying just twelve span or less from the *Licker's* starboard bow. The bowsprit snapped under the weight of a giant tentacle. The entire ship cracked and submerged beneath the next wave. For a brief spell Mayadeen was pooped—a drowning blind woman on a giant seesaw. The cries of her crewmen seemed a league away through the torrent. Letting go of the wheel, she took a stinging blow to her shoulder that sent her sprawling forward. On all fours, she choked and gasped on sea water. The *Licker* tottered and another spar snapped followed by halyards and stays whipping through the darkness aloft. Something large and fishy landed inches from Mayadeen's feet. It squirmed and squished as she struggled to grab hold of the nearest railing. She went for her cutlass still secured just below her ribs—a beautiful weapon given to her by the Elders of Corolon replete with a bejeweled silver hilt and clouded steel blade. But the ship again upended, and Mayadeen went head first over the poop deck balustrades. She splashed to the main deck already flooded waist deep in chill water.

Raw and battered, Mayadeen surfaced to glimpse the origin of the fifty foot tentacles. The krode beast loomed close enough for her to behold even in the stormy darkness. More krellusks rolled down from the slopes of its conical head, instinctively negotiating the gaping hole lined with spiraling rows of teeth, if teeth they could be called. Mayadeen wondered how such weapons found root in what looked like an amorphous mouth of tar and jelly.

A great moan escaped the krode beast's ever-shifting maw as the *Licker's* stern spun into its massive head. This time its fetid flesh breached the hull, and ship and kraken were one. The vessel broached from the force, now exposing a broadside to the pulverizing waves.

As the watery darkness whirled around her, Mayadeen fought to keep hold of a single iron shackle holding dual lines from somewhere abeam with the main mast impossibly below her. At the trench of the next swell, a large blinding light revealed itself, half submerged in the water, and then it was gone. Her vision must have played tricks, for it was as though a star decided to settle from the night sky to the sea. Illusion or not made little difference as the four hundred ton *Sea Licker* refused to capsize and righted once again.

A hand grabbed Mayadeen's shoulder. It was Jagger. Half of his vested shirt had been torn and hung sopping from his waist. "Captain," he yelled as he braced himself against Mayadeen and the main deck gunwales.

Mayadeen smiled in spite of all. Just the sight of Jagger's face tempted her to laugh louder than the godsforsaken krode beast, though she also didn't want the geld to mistake temporary joy for permanent insanity.

"Captain, there's land" Jagger continued. "Rocks ahoy, I say!"

Mayadeen looked to where he pointed on the black, undulating horizon. When next the lightning flashed, there were in fact rocks ahoy, or perhaps half a dozen more krode beasts. Either way, it made not a rasher of sense unless she and Jagger had already perished and crossed into the Bone Reef.

Yet there was no mistaking the crags in the breakers. "We're aground! Rocks ahoy!" echoed Mayadeen more out of instinct than warning. She reckoned half her crew was pooped by now and the rest drowned in the stores. Had any taken to the yawls? When she turned again Jagger was gone. Perchance she'd only imagined him.

Mayadeen watched the main fore sail stab the water as the *Licker* again canted ninety degrees. That looked real enough. She thought she heard more screaming from somewhere beyond the spume and din. The krode beast, close enough that she could smell its ancient content, bawled a bass so deep that Mayadeen's bladder gave way to add a patch of warmth to the stinging deluge. All at once, wooden planks splintered upward with a deafening crack. The ship was breaking in half.

Mayadeen closed her eye and readied for the end.

III
BANK BROKE

"What beasts are these that stand before me?"
"The two-legged kind, Your Majesty."
~ Balern, The Conquests of Elocinda

Mayadeen roused to an allied assault on her senses—white flood, wind's caress, piercing squawks, stinky kelp, creeping bile—and she promptly retched.

"Aye, the Cap'n's alive, she is," started a familiar voice.

"That much we gathered, ye cursed idiot. Out of slumber is what she's now. Give her some ploughin' space."

"Just wanting to be sure she's well and her own, s'all. Mayhap she's lost some of her noggin?" replied the first.

"Like as yer own, ye fucking halfwit? Just 'cause she coddled yer tolliver don't make her blood and kin."

"That's not what I—"

"Shut yer bone traps! Damn yer bloody corpses to the bowels of the fucking ..." Mayadeen's words croaked into a fit of coughs. She raised her head enough to eye her company, the long, dumb faces of Laddy and Jord.

She peered around the bright beach head. Every muscle in her body felt weighted down by hot irons. The sands were painted from a palette of bone whites and desert browns. The shore was rocky here, with a smattering of crags out to sea. Mayadeen guessed the *Sea Licker* must have hit one of the large ones at least half a league out, with some detritus now visible in the breaking waves. There was no sign of land prior to the storm, and their course had carried five days east of the nearest main. *'Twas Minnow Baels. Those cursed maps of his were to blame. Sham charts they were.* But she knew better, and her course was already set prior to the little bull's incursion.

She had to face it—the once great and promising Mayadeen Damned screwed up. Except this time, it wasn't some morally questionable act or a misjudgment of character. This time it was a disaster.

"How long have I been out?" Mayadeen asked. She found her voice and leveled it at her Master at Arms. Jord proved a hearty seaman for the short time he'd been under Mayadeen's masts. But the pudgy bull was Aterian, and hadn't come aboard by his own accord. Mayadeen never quite trusted him just as she hadn't trusted his metallic implements of powder and fire. Then again, both he and Laddy could've had their way with her and been dining on her roasted flesh by now if they'd the mind. So either Jord's loyalty extended beyond her celebrity, or else he had a more practical reason to keep his captain unbowed and unmolested—unarmed, too, apparently. Mayadeen glanced at her sword belt sitting in the sand next to Jord.

"Missing these, good Captain?" Jord snorted a chuckle before reaching down and tossing her belt and scabbards, still housing the cutlass for a high left draw and the ornate rapier for a low right.

Mayadeen stiffened, but now wasn't the time to invite suspicion to breakfast. She tugged the hilts of her weapons slightly to ensure the blades hadn't been swapped for a wedge of tar or a tassle of rocks. It was an old trick that had probably led to many a mutiny. All appeared to be intact.

"How long, damn ye," she repeated.

Laddy chimed in this time. "Just the eve and half a day, Cap'n.

The First found ye caught on a piece of the *Licker.*"

Jagger was alive? A resilient geld. Now her situation made more sense. "Who else then?" Mayadeen added. She spied no other crewmates in the immediate vicinity. Not even footprints fanning out.

"Well, Cap'n, we lost more 'n' a few ... we, uh ... we, err ... besides yerself and me and Jord—"

Mayadeen shot up her hand in a gesture for him to cease talking. She shifted her attention to Jord. He just smiled, either at Laddy's bumbling or Mayadeen's irritation, the latter having difficulty telling which.

"Just Tyker," said Jord. "He's the only other made it here. Him 'n' Jagger took to scout the place nigh two hours past. Figure they ain't back by evenfall, they ain't coming back."

Mayadeen got to her haunches. Though her body throbbed with pain, she did her best not to show it. Jord and Laddy both watched her closely, as if any second they were ready to forsake her as incapable—no longer valid to run a pack of hungry wolves. Yet none were more starved than her since the thought crossed her mind. For a moment she thought she might turn cannibal on *them.*

She finally found her feet, which both still bore her boots. She was happy for that, at least. "How long's the fire been going?" she asked. It took her until now to really notice it. Scalawags were ever resourceful. Stupid, too, since they hadn't moved off the beach to a more defensible position and were using wet wood that smoked like a pipe stuffed with hackleaf.

"Had it going since the First left," said Laddy.

That much Mayadeen had figured. Unlike these two, Jagger was not an idiot.

"Put it out, damn ye." Mayadeen looked at Laddy and then switched to Jord. "If we're where I think we are, the longer we go unnoticed the better."

That smug look returned to Jord's face. The fat bastard came as a package deal with the bombards after she'd purchased the fancy weapons for the untried voyage of her at-the-time new vessel. She shuddered to think it was now all at the bottom of the sea. It would be appropriate then for Jord to join them, should Mayadeen have to make a quick example of him. With each passing second her strength gained along with her ire.

"Where in fuck's sake are we then, Captain?" asked Jord. "Or do ye even know? Thought ye Meridians could chart the ploughin' waves themselves." Jord guffawed and turned to Laddy for a reaction.

Mayadeen moved like a cat, and what Jord got instead was a fist so hard to his face that he tumbled off the box he was sitting on and into the sand. When he looked up, Mayadeen stood over him. She hadn't drawn her cutlass. If she had, he would have been no more, for she never produced her steel merely to threaten.

"Any more to say on that? I'll gut ye here and break my fast proper, ye bloated bag of Aterian shit. This Meridian knows exactly where we've landed ... where they've no use for balls and cocks, especially those with trouble shooting straight. Where were yer puny cannons with that krode beast? Lodged up yer own twat hole?"

Jord managed to answer with sand, spittle and blood dribbling from his lip. "The ship was in too much of a frenzy ... couldn't get a clean shot. Couldn't even see—"

"Then what bloody good were they?" shouted Mayadeen with enough fire in her voice to smelt iron. She suddenly felt her aches again as the rush subsided. Her throbbing eye found Laddy, then the campfire.

Laddy immediately began throwing sand on the flames.

Mayadeen looked back down at Jord. "Get up and gather any rations washed ashore ... if ye haven't eaten 'em already," she spat, wringing out the final drop of venom and kicking him in the leg.

Without looking at her, Jord got himself up and sulked off down the beach. After making sure the fire had more than a shallow grave, Laddy turned to follow him.

"Ye stay with me, Laddy," said Mayadeen, already seating herself back into the sand. She felt like she had just swum all the way from the Meridian Isles. "We'll await Jagger's return." The last thing she wanted was Laddy commiserating with Jord, or more likely the other way around. Co-misery could lead quickly to conspiracy. She needed Jagger back, and soon if she was to maintain any order and keep the remnants of her crew together.

Now that Jord's fat arse was off of it, Mayadeen noticed Baels' locked captain's chest somehow survived the wreckage with hardly a scratch. As for her own captain's chest, the eight gold ingots that weighted its base at nigh three stone in sum would have ensured it a permanent new home with the coral. Suddenly she wanted to retch again.

Instead, she focused on the locker in front of her. "Baels' lockbox … ye crack it?"

"Nay, Cap'n," replied Laddy. "Jord tried … said he could charm any hole from here to Torantance, on legs or otherwise. But not that'on."

"Then get to it. Might hold something we can use."

Laddy nodded and pulled a small dagger from his belt.

"Not with that," said Mayadeen. "You'll fuss it up." She fished into the pockets of her damp trousers but came up with nothing more than sand and lint. "Fates be fucked … lost my pickers, too." She wanted to scream at the top of her lungs and jump up and down, but that might have simply confused her present company. Instead, she kicked the chest and took another scan of her surroundings. There bloody well had to have been more survivors from her crew. Perhaps they'd cobbled a raft and paddled in further up or down the coastline.

"So Cap'n … ye pretty sure where we landed then, aye?" Laddy sounded hopeful.

He shouldn't have been. Provided a large uncharted island hadn't sneaked up on them, of which there were none in these waters, they would have to have hit a mainland. There was but one such coastline flanking thousands of leagues west of the Meridian Isles—a barren, isolated realm having served merely as a buffer for over a hundred years.

"The Warlands, Laddy. The Warlands Main is where we've fallen."

#

Just before the sun readied to make its final descent beyond the deserted sand dunes, Mayadeen spied two horses approaching up the beach from the south.

"They're back," announced Laddy. He'd spent the past few hours separating out the rations Jord had been able to recover. Potatoes, limes, cabbages, strips of dried mutton and even a couple uncut loaves of soggy bread were segregated into tidy little piles. All three pirates had been disappointed to find no salvaged bottles of wine or rum, although Mayadeen suspected Jord was holding out on them.

"Looks like 'em enough," said Jord. "But where'd they get the horses?"

Where, indeed, thought Mayadeen. She clocked her squint to the west and then to the north. No sign of any other riders. Of course, with the sounds of the ocean and the breaking surf, she could only rely on her eye and not her ears, though often times one could *feel* the approach of multiple hooves if that was to be the grand reveal.

As the two horses came between trotting and loping, it seemed Laddy was only partly right. Jagger and Tyker were indeed back, propped and tied to the saddles—arms detached from their torsos and gaping holes in their chests— with the wet, shriveling hearts of each decorating the necks of their respective mounts.

Laddy and Jord grabbed the reins of each passing horse. Laddy's, the chestnut stallion that bore what was left of Tyker, stopped without a fuss. Jord jogged for several steps with the other, a grey nag well past its prime. Jagger's rigid corpse teetered on the saddle.

Mayadeen breathed deep. Whoever had done this would pay the price of ghosts. But there was no time to wallow in the horror of it.

A plume of dust and sand became visible on the horizon.

"Ready yerselves, damn ye," shouted Mayadeen while drawing her rapier and then her cutlass.

Laddy produced his short sword. "What if they've an army? What then, Cap'n?"

Before Mayadeen could answer, the horsemen appeared at the crest of the dunes and halted, blocking the low sun like a line of exotic statues. Though they seemed two hundred, Mayadeen gathered a quick count of around twenty.

"Bugger this," grumbled Jord, yanking Jagger's corpse from the saddle and climbing atop the nag.

"Jord, damn ye. To me," yelled Mayadeen.

Ignoring her, Jord turned the nag and kicked her several times into a gallop. The dirty coward knew how to ride a pony, Mayadeen would give him that.

"Jord ...where ...ye can't ..." Laddy called after.

Mayadeen thought the young bull looked as though his own pecker had just upped and pissed in his face. "That's it for 'im," she said to Laddy through gritted teeth.

Five riders broke forward from the line, yet only one bolted in Jord's direction. Armed with spear, the rider took aim and launched the javelin with a follow-through so uncanny that even from fifty yards it skewered Jord to the back of the nag's neck. The two fugitives went down in an explosion of wet sand. The rider turned her mount sharply to join the other four that now trotted towards Mayadeen and Laddy.

"Lower yer weapon and keep ye calm," Mayadeen said to Laddy without taking her eye off the riders. She, too, lowered her blades to be ready at her side. "And keep yer pusing mouth shut."

Mayadeen's mother taught her the two most important things to bear in mind when overwhelmed by interlocutors were to observe and reserve. The first had always come natural to Mayadeen, her eye ever reconnoitering the immediate environment. She was at a grave disadvantage here, however, with the riders' backs to the sun, though she had still been able to recognize several details amid the excitement. Her initial count of twenty riders was accurate. Their steeds were made for war, all of them painted in pattern or glyph, some with armor and trophies at the head and breast. The riders themselves were mostly adorned with leathers and hides suggesting they traveled from higher, colder lands, certainly not from the desert. Half also wore some fashion of helm, and none of the riders displayed uniforms. This latter observation was perhaps most important because it meant these warriors belonged to no formal military. They were tribal. Perhaps even reavers in their own right—pirates of the land rather than the sea.

And, as far as Mayadeen could parse, they were all women.

Four of the five nearly upon her were *big* womaners. The largest sat in the center, and she donned a serpent-faced helm over pauldrons of sun-bleached bone with a long cape of stitched hide or skin that flapped in the gales. She stood out as the Leader. To her immediate left lounged the smallest of the group. She wore no mask or helm, though light blue war paint caked her face and a circlet headpiece lent her a false, flowing mane of blood red hair. Her finer garbs, a mash up of exotic linens and rough-woven leather, revealed the flat belly and firm bust of a woman in her prime, perhaps only slightly younger than Mayadeen. Red was definitely the non-warrior of the group. The others were all fighters, or at least really efficient killers given how quickly they handled Jord.

Mayadeen balanced her attention between the Leader and Red. Now it was time to implement that second part of her mother's sage advice, the part with which Mayadeen had a much more difficult time. She had to *reserve*. She had to show them she was in control. Fear would tempt her to speak just as much as it coaxed Jord to run and Laddy to want to shit himself. Just the same, stupidity—some called it courage—would make her want to attack. Mayadeen wasn't quite ready to concede to stupidity, although a good part of her was still trying to figure how she'd come from commanding a full crew of bulls and the most successful ship on the Nine Seas to present predicament. Stupidity, therefore, could stake a valid claim.

She glanced sideways at Laddy, whose mouth moved up and down yet no sounds escaped.

Red spoke first.

"Ulaktak owgana ara ulak."

Mayadeen had encountered dozens of different languages during her career, and she could speak and understand exactly one of them. Though it took on myriad dialects, the most pervasive language heard from the Meridian Isles all the way to the south of Torantance was Corish, and so it was simply referred to as the common or folk tongue.

Two of the warrior lackeys snickered with devilish grins. Mayadeen hoped to the souls of her drowned mates she'd be able to deal with those bitches first.

The Leader, however, was not amused and mumbled some more foreign sounds to her red-maned emissary. After a moment, Red spoke again.

"Are you deaf? Slow of wit? Or do you simply not understand the language of kings?"

"Nay to any of those," replied Mayadeen now granting Red her full attention. "Though I ken it well the language of cunts."

Mayadeen had observed and reserved to the best of her abilities, and those had finally been trumped by weariness, hunger, sorrow, despair, and time-honored indiscretion.

Red smirked. "Aren't you the bold one? Perhaps you've found your country." The smirk left as fast as it came. "Or perhaps not."

Red mouthed more unfamiliar words to the Leader, whose deep-set helmet formed the face of a horned asp or dragon and never strayed from Mayadeen's direction. She'd rather take on a hundred faces she could see for every one she could not.

"Ye can tell her I didn't start this quarrel, Red." Mayadeen again addressed the one who could speak the common tongue. "But by the gods high and low I'll end it now if that's what's to be done."

Mayadeen glanced sideways at Laddy whose eyes bulged with all the anxiety of a cat about to hit water. Before he could speak, one of the mounted soldiers flung a well-placed set of bolas around his arms and torso. Laddy yelped, and the force of the weighted ropes placed him butt-to-sand.

Mayadeen readied herself as another soldier, one with red and purple war paint and a shoddy leather cuirass, dismounted with an axe-like weapon in hand. She approached with a growl, and stood about seven inches over six feet, giving her only a slight height advantage over Mayadeen. This She-beast was thick, both in bone and muscle, and all Mayadeen could hope was to use the warrior's own heft against her.

The first attack came slow and lumbering, almost as if a test. Mayadeen easily side-stepped, but nearly lost balance while forgetting she was in damp sand not ten feet from the tidewater's edge. Her rapier returned a quick counter thrust, which the She-beast reached out to block. Mayadeen made another feint of thrust, and her opponent once again went out of her way to block it. *Twitchy, this one.* After dodging a faster and more vicious attack from the axe, Mayadeen riposted with a good slice to the She-beast's exposed triceps, this time utilizing her off-hand's stout cutlass. The warrior yelled in fury, and Mayadeen feint another cutlass strike to her face. The She-beast took the bait and blocked high. Mayadeen kicked her hard in the groin. The larger woman wailed, this time in agony, and the next slash from Mayadeen's cutlass severed her jugular. A pint of hot, sticky blood leapt forth and the muscle-bound womaner dropped to her knees, then to her face.

The warrior that had pinned Laddy with the bolas now took a couple steps toward Mayadeen, hand on the leather wrapped haft of her sheathed weapon.

"Baltaka." The word boomed from beneath the mask of the Leader.

The other warrior halted.

Still regaining her breath, Mayadeen watched as the Leader dismounted her destrier. An enormous womaner, she towered over seven feet from hide-covered toe to crest of helm. Her shoulders, even without the garish pauldrons, set as wide as a crown bear, and those rare beasts weighed a ton. The Leader removed her helmet, tossing it to the sand where it landed with a thud. The swell of her cheekbones slightly obscured flat, grey eyes. Her head was shaved bald but for a tuft of loose orange curls dangling from the top. A faded tattoo of patterns discolored her face from upper lip to forehead. The Leader was by no means hideous, though her hardened and exaggerated features now covered any youthful beauty that may once have been. Either way, Mayadeen still preferred her without the cursed helmet—overcast eyes she could deal with, even though she was looking up at them.

Mayadeen staggered a few steps back as the heels of her boots sank into the sand. Her chest burned and her legs now felt like gelatinous globs. She gulped in more air and assumed her two-weapon stance.

The Leader started mumbling something under her breath while drawing a great sword from her back. Although she had impressive pieces of individual armor, she wore less than half plate, leaving many of her vitals exposed. Of course, such would also mean she'd survived countless battles in light cuirass, confirming her abilities as a fighter and, more importantly, a leader amongst fighters.

If Mayadeen was to have one final dance, at least it would be at the salt water's edge.

The Leader struck first. Her sword, an exotic and more specialized version of a bastard, swept over Mayadeen's head with a scream of air. Mayadeen ducked the swing, but didn't dodge in close enough to counter with her rapier at little more than half the length of the great sword. Instead, she stumbled forward and found the Leader's foot as it kicked sand in her face—an old trick easy to employ on the shorter combatant. Lucky for Mayadeen, the bulk of the sand hit her patched eye. With a guttural yell, Mayadeen thrust forward with a series of her own combination blows—cutlass for slashing, rapier for piercing—each one unable to breach the Leader's wide yet impenetrable guard.

Mayadeen wobbled delirious with fatigue. Her next stab glanced off the Leader's right pauldron, and it was countered with the great sword's pommel finding Mayadeen's face. This time, it was her own blood that leaped forth. She reeled only to glean the great sword's shining arc. Mayadeen parried to prevent the giant blade from hewing her in two, but the force sent the cutlass spinning from her numbed fingers. She drew up her rapier to block the next attack, and the much thinner blade shattered just inches from its dazzling, bejeweled hilt. Mayadeen fell to her knees in the wet sand, the reaching tide nipping at her trousers. It felt cool and oddly comforting.

And then her world went black.

IV
WITCHES, BITCHES AND TENTS

Proud and mighty are they, and yet smallish and stunted in so many ways.

~ High Vicar Gwethol

Mayadeen grew sick of waking up in strange places. She twisted from stomach to back beneath a large pelt blanket on a bed stack of soft leather. It was nighttime as she could tell from the dancing orange shadows on the stitched-hide veneer of surrounding tent, which billowed intermittently from outside gales. It was a large tent, more like a pavilion, decorated with plush pillows, streamers of colorful and exotic weaves, hanging brass torch urns, and a large fire pit over which spread a strange stone or metal contraption with four arms jutting inward to a node.

She arose to her elbows, but grew dizzy when trying to rise further. When she'd awoken on the beach, her body merely felt sore and depleted. Now nearly every part of her felt limp and useless, and her head throbbed to the aural thrum of her heartbeat. A great pain shot through her right hand. She winced and fell back onto the pillow when the blurry shape of a figure loomed over.

"You need more rest. But first, let me look at that hand."

The person above Mayadeen shrank into focus. It took a moment, but Mayadeen recognized her as the one who had done all the talking on the beach. *Red*. Except now, sans war paint and ridiculous circlet with scarlet mane, the womaner peering down actually had tightly braided brown hair, pulled back to above the ear. She was a petite one, lacking any of the womanly attributes of her towering companions—Red looked more like she hailed from Edenvane or Thresnare. The swollen giants on the beach, however, were something else entirely, and seemed to have sprung from the mountain soil rather than any birthing pool.

"Bugger my hand, damn ye," rasped Mayadeen. Again, she tried to prop herself up, this time favoring her left side. She noticed a water skin next to the bed.

Red scooped up the misshapen blob in both hands and offered it.

Just as it was to her lips, Mayadeen refused.

Red only smiled and stole a small sip herself, not the least reassuring since she could be some kind of witch immune to poisons. But then Mayadeen considered her current situation and the futility of such a suspicion. Red offered again and Mayadeen sucked out some of the cool water.

"Where 'n' fuck are my clothes?" asked Mayadeen. She was naked as the sea was green. Worse still, her boots had been removed.

"Your vestments were filthy with every substance known to the Nine Gods, not the least of which was poor Yudrid's life blood," replied Red. "I'm having them scrubbed."

Mayadeen did all she could to sit up further. She peered around the pavilion. From beyond the fluttering tent sang a gradual chorus of cracking wood, clinking metal and laboring voices. Red's love nest must have shared part of a larger encampment, surrounded by however many of those grunting behemoths were fresh about their daily duties. Or perhaps those bitches on the beach were just an elite few and Mayadeen had been brought back to their nomadic, domestic core. Either way, more pressing matters took the vanguard.

"I'm yer prisoner, that it?"

"You are here against your will, yes. But Lusul would rather consider you her ... guest."

"Then ye best put me in chains 'cause when I'm able I'll slit every overgrown throat in this outfit, starting with yer grunting leader."

"Naturally. If she expected anything less, then she would never have let you live. Lusul admired your courage and it's not often we get visitors from the Meridian Isles."

Mayadeen again tried to move too fast and winced in pain. She growled her next words through a slit eye. "That monster bitch butchered three of my crew, and they were of the Isles all."

Red averted her own gaze briefly. "Indeed. I'm afraid men have no province here. Lusul has no use for gelds, and the bulls were beyond their youth ... but for one. Laddy, is his name?"

"They were all good mates, still," said Mayadeen, though she immediately thought of the fist of shit Jord turned out to be. "Where's Laddy then?"

"Alive and well, I promise you. He will serve a use or two."

"And who might ye be? The Court Cuntlicker? Or do ye have 'em duped into thinking ye're some sort of magician with yer fancy head ornaments and contraptions and the like? Ye're a young one to have yer splitty sewn shut either way."

"I would suspect you and I are around the same age, Mayadeen. And I assure you that my 'splitty' has not been sewn shut." Red seemed annoyed at the jab. "You do know that's a myth created by your people?"

"My people?" Mayadeen guffawed even though it hurt. "So ye are a soddin' Thresnary magician."

"You're clever if not perceptive. But like you, I was born in the Isles. And like you..." Red paused for a moment. "Like you, fate brought me here."

"Enough about our likes, damn ye. And I ain't even certain where here is." Mayadeen knew the Warlands were split into four vast territories, and she suspected she'd landed on Rul, the largest of the four. It was the how her ship had arrived there that evaded her.

"A pirate who doesn't know where she is? Perhaps *you'd* serve better as a cuntlicker."

Mayadeen didn't like to be bested, least of all with words. But she was too tired and in too much pain to be effectively plotting Red's demise. At least she was getting some answers, as clever and unctuous as they came.

"You're in Rul, part of the lands north of the Tair—the Warlands Main as referred to by the rest of the world. Here they're known as the Four Kingdoms, wherein that 'monster bitch' rules the largest of the four. She is a King. Her name is Lusul, and she has crushed every force that's ever opposed her. Of course, even Lusul is kept in check by her sisters, who each sit upon the other three thrones."

Mayadeen fell back to the pillow. "Bloody hell ... Rul it is then. S'pose I needed to land in the dung heap sooner or later."

"Your ship, the rest of your crew—what happened to them?"

"Ah ... on my lee, nymph! Ye'd like to know, wouldn't ye? Mayhap they'll be coming for me. Steal into the night to loosen a few Rullite throats." The thought of that fantasy made her laugh. "Just be done with it, sorcerer. Strike me dead with the power of yer god and take my ashes to the sea." Her cackling turned to coughing, which prompted another assisted drink from the water skin. Mayadeen batted it away.

"You were feverish last night, but that's been taken care of," said Red as she placed the water skin aside. "Now, your hand, please."

Mayadeen could hardly feel her right hand, which lay at her side beneath the blanket. Even with a useless limb and half her life force, she was confident she could strangle the cleverness from this dainty plum flower faster than it could raise an alarm. But there was Laddy to consider, if the blathering bull idiot really was alive, and nothing life preserving could come from hasty decisions in their current predicament. Mayadeen peered down at her right hand and wrist—the appendage now resembling some sort of beached fish carcass instead of a hand—at twice the size of its counterpart.

"Well, that doesn't look terribly pleasant," said Red. "Good thing I'm a magician."

Mayadeen didn't miss the sarcasm. Her hand looked much worse than it felt. She remembered when she lost her eyeball and had been forced to view the immediate aftermath in a mirror. That, by contrast, had felt every bit as bad as it had looked.

Red momentarily stepped away from the bed and returned with a bowl and some cloth wrappings. This time she didn't ask for Mayadeen's hand but simply took it, and began applying a thick salve from the bowl.

Mayadeen cringed. "What're ye slathering me with? More of yer devilry? Smells like a rotting foot."

Red ignored the jeer. She delicately wrapped Mayadeen's hand and wrist with the linen to form a poultice.

"Three days, and you might be able to grasp a sword once again. I'll change it out each night."

"Don't ye trouble, Red. Won't be staying. And ye'll get no thanks and kind regards, nymph."

"Of course." Red turned and crossed to the pavilion's exit. As she lifted the tent flap to the night's darkness, two very large women like the ones that had been on the beach entered and took their place on either side of the door. They were sentries, obviously there to keep Mayadeen in and perhaps anyone else out. Both carried axes and glowered through blotchy and faded face paint. One even snarled.

The sorcerer turned back. "Red?"

Mayadeen was fiddling with the poultice. "Aye. On account of that stupid fucking monkey that adorned yer head."

Red's brow crested and she smiled. "My name is Elona. You may be Lusul's guest, but you're my ward, at least until you're better. I apologize for your friends. There was ... nothing that could be done for them."

Mayadeen glared. "There's always something can be done."

Elona looked down and gave a slight nod. It made it more unsettling that the witch actually seemed sincere. Why couldn't she just proclaim her evil intentions and submit Mayadeen to some unnatural torture or death? Vengeance was so much clearer without cursed kindness and understanding getting in the way. At least there remained the two vicious beasts at the vestibule. Nothing misleading about their intentions.

"And you must be hungry," Elona peeked back in. "I'll have food sent."

Now *that*, Mayadeen thought, was the best thing Red had uttered since she'd started flapping her fancy trap. Food at this point would be the greatest exotic treasure ever stumbled upon, rich beyond even the Southern Isles. What she wouldn't do for a succulent capon or a meaty leg of goat. Her stomach instantly turned acrobat and her mouth watered.

Elona exited, leaving only the Rullite guards.

After Mayadeen filled her belly and let the foul shit on her hand work its promised magic, she'd be sure to relieve them of their duty. But the night passed more quickly than she'd planned. The throbbing in her hand subsided somewhat. And the promised meal of wine and venison—no rooster or goat, although she suspected those wild womaners probably had an abundance of both, leaving the arse end of a deer to their captive—was satisfying enough to allow her to succumb to sleep once again.

#

She awoke the morning of the second day to a bustle of activity from outside the large tent, the taut hide walls again slightly aglow with early morning azure. Elona was nowhere to be seen. The two sentries from the night before had been replaced by two others, and Mayadeen found them to look and smell just as unpleasant. She was used to every body odor capable of clinging to flesh. These cunties, however, reeked like the fetid leftovers from some carnivorous animal's den.

Mayadeen ignored their feral scowls while she withdrew her naked self from the thick hide blanket. She slowly stretched her legs over the side of the bed stack. She, too, needed a good bathing and began to wonder if it wasn't her own stench that assailed her. The morning chill gave her goose bumps, and she noticed for the first time the air was thinner here. Beyond the body odor and exotic scents that filled Elona's abode, a hint of birch wood also lingered. That scent Mayadeen knew well. They must have made it to higher ground rather quickly.

Either way, Mayadeen's yearning to step outside to gauge just where in the hell she was trumped all. Her jerkin, breast wrap, light rough-spun shirt, trousers, sop rag and boots sat neatly atop some crates just a few feet from the bed. Just as Elona had promised, they'd been scrubbed to a vibrant finish.

Her hand still ached when she tried to move it, but the poultice seemed to be working fast on the swelling. She just hoped the next time she had to face the one they called Lusul, it would be on Mayadeen's own terms, which didn't translate to one-on-one sword combat with a giant. No, next time she'd be certain to even the battlefield. Slow-working poison sprang to mind.

Her feet found the grassy floor, which to her surprise hadn't been covered by colorful rugs or linens in the sorcerer's private quarters. Of course, Elona had probably grown accustomed to the rustic ways of her company, though judging by the rest of the pavilion's lavish decor, only some of those ways.

Mayadeen folded her arms over her chest, not out of coyness, but rather to fend off the chill even though a nice size fire crackled beneath the spidery stone apparatus.

"What're ye overgrown rock apes looking at?"

The two guards had been staring at her. They even seemed to understand some of the question. Mayadeen pulled on her trousers and boots first, and then snatched up the rest of her sorry clothes which still smelled faintly of the sea. It was somehow comforting to know that one could not merely scrub the sea from the scalawag. She'd lost her good broadcloth coat during the wreck—a shame considering its warmth and the fact it had a vial of dray root nectar sewn to its inner pocket. A couple drops of the rare and notorious extract on a blade would turn a few nicks and scrapes into mortal wounds. A couple drops on the tongue would end things even quicker.

Mayadeen was saving it for a day when either death was imminent or all was lost. Two such days already came and went.

She hadn't had a chance to ask either Jord or Laddy about the frock coat, though its parting had probably been necessary when Jagger pulled her from the drink. It was sort of pathetic that so many details from such a pivotal night of her existence would forever be up for speculation.

Once her garments were in place, Mayadeen again addressed her feral-faced jailers with the big axes. "Where's yer witch? Ye know, the one who makes ye all experience those rare moments of joy during the cannibal orgies."

The guard on the left of the flap entrance snarled something under her breath, gripped her axe a little tighter and took a step forward.

"Ah, to me then." Mayadeen picked up a heavy silver urn from the table beside her bed. "I'll put that axe where it fits."

The urn might have registered a decent blow, but disarming the guard to gain an axe that weighed as much as a small ship anchor was an empty threat. Just when Mayadeen thought her end would come at last, Elona entered the pavilion.

"Olatak," she commanded, then reached up and slapped the guard square across the jaw. The larger guard recoiled and hesitated— poised to strike a blow that would have cloven Elona in two. But it was already too late. The Rullite warrior's fists ignited into flaming stumps. With a wild shriek, she dropped her axe and ran out of the tent.

Mayadeen could hear the guard's howling outside, which was quickly joined by roars of laughter. The second Rullite guard, much plainer and less crazed in appearance than her fiery sister-in-arms and who up until now had shown indifference to the three-way confrontation, leveled her own axe and threw accusatory gibberish at

Elona. After the second guard had her say, Elona mumbled something back in Rullite words. The second guard stood down and quickly exited the pavilion.

Elona glanced at the urn.

Mayadeen had nearly forgotten it was still raised above her head. She tossed it aside. "Lusul lets ye treat her pets like that? Makes me wonder whether *ye're* not the king around here, Red. Something ye ain't telling me?"

"If you live to see the morrow, Mayadeen Damned, then maybe I'll entertain that question," returned Elona. She picked up a sack near the entrance and tossed it to Mayadeen. "You'll walk with me. But first you'll need some proper garments for the cold."

#

By mid-morning, Mayadeen had reconnoitered a good portion of the Rullite encampment with Elona. Endless tents, looms, sharpening stones, spits, cauldrons, foot bellows, workbenches and fire pits festooned the pine and birch-strewn woodland. Hammers clinked, axes chopped and wheels ground. Only the elderly toiled with the weaving and cooking, sometimes accompanied by one or two of the very young, who were always hard to recognize due to their impressive prepubescent sizes. The warriors, consisting of everyone else, took care of the more physical labors, which ranged from hoisting heavy loads to shaping hot metals.

Those not engaged in actual work either ate, slept, laughed, fought, or a combination thereof. Mayadeen appreciated that all of the wood and metal burning helped to counter the stench of ten thousand filthy vaginas. She supposed most of them to be on similar cycles, and rued the thought of being around when nature again purged the unwanted mix. As to that notion, she'd not seen a single bull on her two hour excursion, and Laddy's specific whereabouts continued to vex her. She needed to find him before making any plans to escape, and with any luck towards that purpose, hoped to steal out by nightfall.

She had been able to muster a few answers from her clandestine host. Elona estimated they were at least twenty-five leagues from the nearest coastline, and less than three leagues in from where the desert lands swiftly gave way to the high country. Mayadeen, and what was left of her crew, had been discovered by a patrol who then warned a nearby hunting party that just happened to be led by King Lusul herself. After the brief fight on the beach, Mayadeen was transported to the base camp, which was already on the move just a couple leagues inland. In essence, an army of ten thousand moved themselves and an entire encampment twenty three leagues in less than a single sun and moon. Mayadeen thought it little wonder then that Lusul had been so successful, for to mobilize such a mass that quickly would have confounded even the most seasoned generals of the Meridian Isles.

The Rullites, as Elona pointed out, were an unmatched juggernaut. It was fortunate for the rest of the world that the ambitions of these women thus far wanted no stake in the lands beyond the seas. Lusul's people had no interest in any lands other than their own vast region, with two of the Nine Seas forming natural boundaries to the east and to the north, and three great mountain ranges providing barriers to the south and to the west. Although the other three kingdoms—Leth, Sundvane and Drost—also fell within those borders, Lusul, at least for the time, perceived no threat from the much smaller realms ruled by her sisters. Indeed, the nomadic would-be King who won her first battle at age seventeen had intended on such a perimeter of blood relations, tenuous though two of the three may have proven.

Mayadeen stayed close to Elona during the tour. She had at least two heads on the sorcerer, rendering silly the whole idea of captive and captor. But considering how Elona had handled that axe-wielding ogre, the visual might be deceiving. Elona donned what Mayadeen assumed to be her typical garb when she wasn't trying to look like Lusul's little pidgeon emissary: light black hide cuirass over black and crimson velvet doublet, but now with a white fox fur travel cloak draped from her shoulders and her pulled back brown hair without the maned monkey tiara. Mayadeen begrudgingly sported the garments given her, a similar hide cuirass over a faded blue doublet with an oversize bear hide wrap. She felt like a walking bed stack. If they wanted her to look like an invalid amongst sweaty titans, then she fulfilled the role. Of course, her eye patch was ever a bonus in that regard. A well-used thick wool shirt and trousers would have been preferable. For the time being, she'd just have to adapt to the landlubber fashion. At least she had her boots.

"Don't suppose ye could have given me a blade. Mayhap even my own," Mayadeen accused as they passed a rather hard looking group of Rullites. The four soldiers stood up while still gnawing on their lunch of a roasted critter that Mayadeen couldn't identify.

"If I had, you'd be dead already," Elona replied.

Mayadeen paused to meet eyes with her ravenous audience. Every Rullite she'd seen thus far looked as though they'd been sculpted by hammers with no chisels.

Elona grabbed her by the arm and pulled her along. "Just keep walking, Captain." After a few more paces she continued. "These women are always looking for a challenge to outdo one another. The right posturing could even secure a place in Lusul's elite guard. In their eyes if you're armed, then you're both ready and willing for a fight."

"Thought I was Lusul's *guest*."

"You are indeed, which is exactly why any one of them would want to replace you. Only blood matters in Rul. If you're not kin, then you're only part of the food chain."

"That so? Then where does that place the witch foreigner?"

"I've no weapon."

"Don't ye be fucking clever. I spied ye turn a set of hands into torch lamps."

Elona shrugged. "Like anybody, they fear what they don't understand. The fact is I've had several attempts on my life since joining them five years past, and any one of those attempts might have prevailed."

"Well ain't ye just the humble butterfly," said Mayadeen with a sideglance at Elona. They continued by some children at play, probably quite young considering they actually resembled children. A rusty-haired freckle face acted like a bear as she growled and lumbered after three other girls, each wielding sharpened sticks. Mayadeen wondered what might happen to freckle face when the others gathered their courage enough to slay the bear. It appeared the Rullites started them young.

Mayadeen kept talking. "This dumb bunch of axe-wielding ogres ought be afraid of ye. In the Isles we hang yer kind, Red. Ain't natural the shit ye magicians conjure."

"What I do is as natural as the wind that brought you here," said Elona.

"Nothing natural about that, neither," returned Mayadeen with a suspicious glare. She was about to ask Elona just how far her magic could reach when something pulled Mayadeen's attention a few tents ahead. Two Rullites carried a large box. Mayadeen at once recognized it. "Yonder chest ..."

"What about it?"

"That's ours, damn ye. We earned it."

"Are you sure?"

"Sure's a witch pisses potions ... or in yer case foul jellies. 'Twas on the beach, damn ye."

"Ah ... then it definitely would have been scavenged."

Mayadeen started forward. Elona caught her by the arm. This time, the landlocked pirate captain shrugged her off.

"I'll have them bring it to my tent," assured Elona. She hailed the two Rullites, both of whom were a little older and shorter in stature than the typical seven foot, wild-eyed bone crusher variety. They paused and seemed to recognize instantly their interlocutor. "Vasa ul duranak al gokala," commanded Elona.

The Rullites nodded and then looked at one another. They searched across the encampment in the direction where resided

Elona's pavilion, and sighed in unison.

Elona turned to Mayadeen. "Before we go back, there's something else that you'll want to see."

V
MAYADEEN'S CHEST

If it be the last thing ye'd ever need and the first thing ye'd ever want,
then thrice and more should it be in yer lockbox.
                    ~ Nine Master Tar Cutter, *So Ye Can Fucking Read*

The smell overwhelmed Mayadeen long before she reached the pens. Even Elona appeared to be affected. As they got closer, Mayadeen scrunched her nose and covered her mouth with the side of her good hand.

"By the gods 'n' their demon offspring, what in bloody—"

The trees opened into a large clearing that parked fifty or more wheeled carriage cells. Each of the iron box cages were packed full with the naked, filthy, emaciated bodies of men.

Arms and legs dangled through the bars, some motionless while others swayed or flicked beneath a busy blanket of flies. Gaunt faces lolled their blank stares toward Mayadeen—eyes with nothing behind them but shadows of misery.

One or two such cages would have been expected, while three or four understandable. Mayadeen had seen prisoners and slaves in every sort of woe circumstance all over Tabor, especially during times of war. But *this* was different. She had spotted no males anywhere in the sprawling encampment, and she remembered well how the

Rullites had dealt with her own bulls. The legends surrounding these territories rang true. Her Pap mentioned the wild womaners of the Warlands in a story once, but to a child's mind they were a people far away and of no consequence to the Island Realm.

Mayadeen remained motionless.

"I'm sorry if this offends you," said Elona. "But it has been the way of Rul for centuries. The men here serve two purposes only: breeding and labor, both of which usually lead to their deaths."

"Just ye tell me where's Laddy."

"Well ... rather unusually, I believe he's been taken to the pit."

"The pit?"

"Where they prepare the combatants for the evening's entertainment. Lusul has something special planned for him—"

Mayadeen grabbed Elona by the throat. She glanced around, already knowing the two Rullite guards that had been pacing that side of the perimeter were currently out of sight. But it was merely a warning hold, and Mayadeen released her.

Elona snatched a breath.

"Could've squeezed the magic right out of ye just then," said Mayadeen. "These Rullite bitches scare far too easy from the likes of a skinny little nymph."

"I didn't bring you here to fight with you," returned Elona with tears in her eyes while she massaged her throat.

Mayadeen couldn't tell whether the chokehold or hurt feelings brought the tears. The conundrum just roiled her more.

"I, too, was captured by Lusul," said Elona. "I never stayed by my own choosing."

"A guest yerself, huh? Fancy fucking that."

"I belong to the Order of Prenn. Her Eminence Ursade, High Vicar of the Order, is my only king. She sits at Valindrost."

"Ursade? I've heard of the bitch. Didn't know she was another bloody king."

"She's Lusul's sister, one of three others. The four of them rule the Warlands Main. I was gifted ..." Elona sighed and put a hand to her forehead. "It's more than we need to get into right now. Just know that I want out of this place, same as you. Now that I have an ally in that regard, perhaps I can finally start preparing my exit in earnest."

More lies wrapped in half truths. If she didn't know any better, Mayadeen would've thought the little woman to be of Meridian rather than Thresnary blood.

Mayadeen glanced at the caged bulls then back at Elona. "So why haven't ye just set the whole place ablaze with a wave of yer magic hand? Or at least burn King Bitch to ashes whilst she's giving ye the arse rod?"

"Don't be crass," said Elona. "It was never like that. Lusul prefers neither men nor women."

"That so? Horses then? Pigs?"

Elona rolled her eyes. "Even if I had set twenty fires and made my escape, where would I have gone? I can't go back to Valindrost. The only practical way out of the Four Kingdoms is by ship, and there are no ports in Rul."

This was news. Although every pirate knew the trade routes within a thousand leagues of Rul's barren shores had ceased to exist for decades, Mayadeen hadn't considered the total absence of a coastal civilization. "What do ye mean no ports? I figured these halfwits to lack a naval force, but no fishing vessels? No skiffs to cross the bays?"

"No. None of that. They've been done away with over the years, and the Rullites as you find them have no use for the sea."

"But there may still be ships, aye?"

They both stopped as the two nearby guards observed their exchange. One of the guards, a grotesque with a halved squash for a nose and a wall-fountain under bite, held her bulging pregnant belly up with one hand while carrying a spear in the other. Mayadeen felt for the poor bull that had been forced to give the woman seed. She peered at one of the bull slaves, his near skeletal legs thinner than his arms. She wondered how many of their cocks had been broken along with their spirits.

"Piss on Rul," Mayadeen spat while shifting her gaze back to the pregnant guard. "And their buggered ways, beside. What do I care 'bout any of it? Luck of the dung heaps I'm even here."

Elona took a couple breaths and lowered her voice, perhaps in case the guards could parse any of the common tongue. "There might be a ship far to the north in White Bay. But Leth is a desolate realm and, like Rul, there is no outside trade to speak of."

"Then drown the north. What about Tyrport? New Scorprince? The trade runs muster again to the south with the Sharbantine." That much she knew from fellow scalawags who had both raided and traded on the Sharbantine Sea with the queer peoples of Sundvane, a realm that was considered to be part of the Warlands but that lay far south.

"Yes, there is Sundvane," replied Elona. "But we'd never make it through the endless deserts of the Bone Veil to reach its harbors."

Mayadeen sighed deeply. It seemed there'd be no simple way off or out of the Warlands Main, same as there would be no simple way to be rid of Elona.

"Well ain't that just convenient and pretty, Red. Now ye've got yer captain and a quest for a soddin' ship."

Elona smiled and seemed quite smug with herself, though Mayadeen wasn't ready to return the appreciation. There was still the matter of Laddy, and making any sort of an escape undetected long enough to gain some ground seemed doubtful, if not impossible. Lusul would hunt them down swift and sure. Perhaps that lent truth to Elona's own suspicious tale of captivity.

"We go north," continued Mayadeen. "All I need is a vessel worthy enough to get me to the Jeweled Sea. But I ain't leaving without Laddy, and so ye better start gathering how to get him back."

#

Two more hours passed before they returned to Elona's tent, in part due to Mayadeen wanting to see where the Rullites kept their horses. Only Lusul's Elite Guard and a handful of warriors rode them. Elona assured Mayadeen that although the Rullites were not exactly known for their horsemanship, they could move like prairie wolves on foot. Indeed, they'd been known to chase down mounted riders. This didn't encourage Mayadeen's confidence that flight to the north would succeed, even with a mount, but she knew she had to try. Laddy would not last the week, and maybe not even the night based on Elona's tidings of *the evening's entertainment.*

They arrived at Elona's pavilion by mid-afternoon, the temperature having already dropped another ten degrees in the forest shade. A different duo of guards flanked the entrance. They ignored Elona and sneered at Mayadeen, the latter growing bored of the tiresome hostility. It was as if the Rullites possessed a collective mentality—a hive mind allowing for near inhuman efficiency yet stagnant predictability—all to appease their biggest and strongest, the blood-soaked calling currently held by Lusul. Ironic then that the King had no heirs as Mayadeen was fairly certain a horse could not fill a woman with child. Then again, considering how Mayadeen had somehow magically wrecked on the Warlands Main, perhaps she couldn't be certain of a godsdamned thing.

As they entered the tent, Elona muttered some words under her breath to one of the guards, a particularly mean looking cunty with a cataract-infested eye and three long braids over a shaved head. The guard grunted and gestured to her shorter and stockier compatriot for both of them to remain stationed outside. Elona tied the tent flaps closed behind her.

"What were ye whispering about?"

"For them to give us some privacy," replied Elona.

"Ye could've given us some of that before," said Mayadeen.

"First, I didn't trust you before, and felt safer with guards in the room. Second, I was able to convince Gorla that you'd be giving me pleasure for the next couple of hours."

"Heh. Sorry to dash yer dreams, Red ... but I don't do nymphs, or horses."

Elona sighed and feigned a smile. "We need to talk about how we plan on getting far away from Lusul."

Mayadeen brought the bear skin wrap down tighter around her shoulders. Hardly a single ember glowed in the fire pit. She found a couple logs and pitched them in. "Can't think when I'm freezing my tits off. Ye got any vittles in yer tongue 'n' fist abode?"

Elona seated herself on a cushioned lounger. With an upward flip of her hand, the fire sparked to life in a way that otherwise would have taken some kindling and a stoking to achieve.

Mayadeen flinched back. "Fancy tricks. Now what about the food, damn ye?" Before Elona could respond, Mayadeen shifted her attention to something the firelight revealed next to the lounger. "Ah ... Minnow Baels' locker."

Although Mayadeen would not have given a copper tail for the chest two days earlier while aboard the *Sea Licker*, breaking into a locked box now was like she was getting a rare taste of home. She glided to the chest and knelt beside it, caressing the rusted iron lining and rough hard wood until she came to the gilded clasp lock, Aterian-made by what Jagger had reckoned. As Torantance was known for its rum, so was Ateria known for its mechanical devices.

"A tough lock to charm," said Mayadeen. "Lost my picks, besides."

Elona perked up. "Well now ... I hadn't realized it remains unopened. That *is* interesting. What do you think it holds? Money? Valuables?"

Mayadeen frowned while still admiring the chest. *Mayhap a mother's mummified tit. Mayhap sapphires and rubies.* Either way, she wasn't about to let Red spoil the beautiful moment, though the sorcerer seemed as sincere.

"Would you like *me* to open it?" asked Elona.

Mayadeen whipped around. "I'd like ye to get us some food, damn ye. Next ye'll be asking me to split the profits. We earned this—" She broke off. Everything had been lost. Her magnificent ship, her crew, her friends—even her cursed bird. Her chest swelled and her face went numb. But she wasn't about to let a single tear fall in present company. No, tears were for the sea, and she'd save every last one for her return.

Mayadeen couldn't remember the last time she'd allowed real self-pity to set sail from a harbor of pride, happiness and minimal regret. Perhaps it had been a sham life up until this point—one destined for a headlong dive into a landlubber's hell of witches, withered cocks and murderous cunts. Of course, marauding wasn't all daiquiris, boodle and bliss. But Mayadeen was born upon on the tide, and to have the sea was to have sanctuary. Whether rain, sun, storm or krode beast, she knew the sea—peering out from her wooden cradle where the future called in every direction and where life and death were eager playmates. The mainland was a prison, and she had to break free.

"Do you need some time alone?"

"Nay to that." Mayadeen rose and turned to face her enigmatic host. She thought it all too convenient that this sorcerer, herself supposedly from the Island Realm, claimed a similar cause, but it was neither the time nor the place to try and cipher the angle. For now, she would believe the alliance true, however temporary it might prove to play out. "As ye spoke, we need to plot an escape."

Elona nodded, unable to conceal her giddiness.

"But first, I need ye bound."

"Bound?"

"Aye, *bound*." Mayadeen grabbed the bottom half of her rapier that she noticed now sat on her bed stack. A lovely reminder of her defeat, Lusul had shattered it like an icicle, but the nub of jagged blade protruding from the hilt was still keen enough to slice paper or pierce iron. No sign of her equally valuable cutlass. One of those snarling gorillas was probably using it as a meat knife, and the missing end of her rapier as a toothpick.

Mayadeen made a fist around the blade and pulled it through.

"What are you doing?" Elona said while wincing. "Isn't one injured hand enough?"

Mayadeen crossed to Elona and offered the blade. Blood trickled from her cut palm. "Take this as I took it."

"Oh... no. No, I can't do that."

"Then ye'll take it through the neck, damn ye." Mayadeen gestured again.

Elona recoiled at first, but then took the blade by its impressive bejeweled, silver handle. She looked away and mouthed a silent yelp while quickly running the broken blade across her open palm. She gave the hilt back to Mayadeen, still cringing. "Could not we have just shook on it?"

Mayadeen grinned and placed her bloody palm into Elona's same. "Aye. And we shall."

Elona shrank back.

"Shy of a lil' blood are ye? These fucking savages ye live amongst paint themselves with it."

Elona swallowed and nodded hastily.

"By the blood of our mothers, a promise and a portent, Red. That's what this is, ken that do ye?"

"Yes, I think I understand," replied Elona.

"A promise that we do this in pair," continued Mayadeen.

"Under what portent?"

"That we're likely to fail and die."

Again Elona nodded, albeit this time more slowly. Mayadeen let go of her hand. In a way they were sisters now, the blood having co-mingled, bound to one another as Mayadeen was bound to only a few, though certainly never to a witch.

"Now charm that ploughin' lock," said Mayadeen.

Elona strode to a small table and took some swaddling from a bowl. She wrapped her own wound and handed a strip of cloth to Mayadeen who simply clutched it in a wad. A click came from the Captain's chest. "It's open," assured Elona.

A witch indeed. Mayadeen smirked and knelt to the solved latch. She flipped it up and the chest top opened with an exaggerated creak. Mayadeen's smirk turned into a grin that halved her face. "Mayhap my luck is changing, Red."

It was a good day to be a pirate.

#

Nightfall came crisp, and Mayadeen and Elona once again crossed the bivouac as the dry air fostered cold breaths. They were not alone, however, this time escorted by four of Lusul's battle-hardened Elite Guard. These Rullites were much more disciplined than the pugnacious minions assigned to guard Elona's tent. The four towering killers hadn't even glanced in Mayadeen's downward direction the entire walk. Elona ordered two of them to carry the chest, which would be presented to Lusul as a rare gift.

Mayadeen thought the encampment akin to some magical city with thousands of flickering firelights spread throughout the forest's pine pillars as far as the eye could see. She'd witnessed whole cities smaller than what the Rullites had been able to make migrant. Some of the womaners still toiled—the clangor of hammer and anvil yet to cease—though most now either retired to their tents or huddled around their fires feasting on flat bread and roasted meats.

As they got closer to their destination slightly beyond the camp's perimeter, Mayadeen heard the robust cheering, laughter and yelling of a ravenous crowd.

"Sounds like the show's already begun," quipped Elona, half sarcastic and half uneasy.

They crested a knoll and the ruckus exploded into view. A crowd of a few hundred heads encircled the stands of a small arena, peering down into a gladiator pit. Like everything else in Lusul's traveling empire, Mayadeen assumed the arena had only been erected within the last couple days, with fresh cut pine logs, mud and whatever else. Though it appeared sturdy, she sort of hoped the godsforsaken thing would collapse beneath all the heavy hips.

Not that Mayadeen didn't enjoy the occasional pit fight, especially when the bloodshed involved betting. But such sport in the Island

Realm was usually relegated to cocks, dogs, bulls and young splitties. Since no slaves existed in the Isles, all were usually willing participants, although the occasional penal punishment had also been employed in the combat arenas. Many argued that the poor cocks and curs weren't willing participants, but in every fight Mayadeen had ever put tails on, the animals sure as snot seemed willing enough. She once even placed some action on Prick, when half her crew thought it false that the redgull could best a greytail, the latter known for its size and ferocity amongst ocean fowl. The little black bastard won her some coin on that day.

Mayadeen half expected to see Lusul sitting on some throne elevated slightly above everyone else, laughing and carrying on with an arse cheek in one hand—horse or otherwise—and a barrel of mead in the other. However, the Rullite King was nowhere to be found.

"Pit fighting," said Mayadeen the same as if she were yawning. "Big soddin' surprise for these snatch heathens. Let me guess ... they've their skeleton bull-slaves swallowing one another while bleeding to death?"

"Not exactly," said Elona. "Slaves aren't usually considered for this sort of thing, since they're made better use of in other capacities. Besides, most of them are useless fighters."

"Tend to be when half-starved and sleeping in shit."

"In Rul, the arena is primarily used to settle vendettas and to exhibit might. It's where Kings are eventually named."

As they neared the base of the arena, two new guards greeted them. Mayadeen thought it more of an admonishment than a greeting, as every grunted word out of their stunted language threatened like a branding iron threatened an arse. The two guards carrying the chest were beckoned onward.

Mayadeen started after them. "That's for Lusul, ye gorilla humpers." All four guards ignored her.

Elona followed with a few words in Rullite which seemed to reach the guards better than Mayadeen's name calling, though only slightly.

They didn't seem to think much of the sorcerer, either. "Don't worry," she turned to Mayadeen, "that chest won't be touched before it's presented to Lusul."

"Then they're dumber than I pegged 'em for." The irony encouraged Mayadeen that their plan might actually work. It seemed the underlying thread of militant order amongst the Rullites was the one thing that had kept her alive. Any other group of savages would have already eaten her and offered their shit to the god of dirt. As for an unopened chest, it would have been scattered to the four winds by now. "Where they keeping Laddy?" she continued.

Elona pointed to a dark area beneath the arena. "The cages are over there."

More cheering surged from the crowd. The escorts now seemed more interested in what was happening from the pit than watching over Mayadeen or Elona. One even seemed irritated with the duty. After a quick glance at Mayadeen, Elona huddled the two guards forward and started conspiring.

Mayadeen took the cue and slipped away unseen. The slave pens were tucked away in the darkness behind some support beams, with the pounding and grunting of the audience directly above.

"Laddy? Laddy, damn ye ... Laddy ..."

"Aye, here I am." Laddy's face appeared at the bars right next to Mayadeen. Startled to a grin, she quickly put a finger to her lips.

"Shhh ye ... for the sake of sin."

"I knew ye'd be back, Cap'n. Ye wouldn't leave me to die ..."

"That so? Shut it and listen." Mayadeen looked back toward Elona and the guards. They were still engaged for the moment, exchanging what looked to be some sort of coins. She guessed even nomadic warlords had an occasional use for money. She turned back to Laddy. "Don't know what they've in mind for ye, but it ain't a cock rub 'n' a daiquiri." Mayadeen pulled a small vial from beneath her travel cloak, just one of the useful treasures she'd gathered from the cracked captain's chest. She slipped it to Laddy through the cage. "If they give ye a blade, then ye put this to its edge. One cut will slow even a whale enough to finish the job."

Laddy clasped the vial and nodded. The young seaman looked like he hadn't eaten for a week, let alone a couple days.

"We're stealin' away tonight. Stay alive and I'll suss ye out," said Mayadeen. "Mayhap then we'll see to that cock," she added with half a grin. Mayadeen knew the young bull fancied her, and to him she now felt an obligation much stronger than before. Not only because she had allowed him to share her bed, but because he was the last of her priceless possessions—a sea dog in the making, and one who would as soon die for her as lay with her. That kind of loyalty was never for sale, and she needed it now more than ever.

Mayadeen slunk back to Elona and the guards as if she'd never left them. Elona reproached her tardiness with a sideglance, but the two smiling Rullites seemed none the wiser. There was no denying that Elona had proved resourceful in a pinch, and Mayadeen wondered if she wouldn't make a scalawag of the pretty little witch yet.

After more words from Elona, the guards led them up some wooden steps ascending to the stands. As the crowd parted, Mayadeen could view the show at last. Two large Rullites stood in the pit, one moaning and clutching the hilt of a double-axe protruding from her clavicle like a defiled grave marker. The titan fell to her knees—nearly six feet tall even at that disadvantage—seconds before another axe, smaller with a single edge, plummeted into the top of her skull. She toppled, blood bubbling and cascading like some sinister hot spring. The crowd roared, and Mayadeen recognized the victor as none other than King Lusul herself.

"What in watery hell's *she* doing in the pit?" Mayadeen shouted for Elona to hear.

"She must have been challenged," replied Elona. "It's customary amongst the Rullites, and far from unusual, even with a leader as strong as Lusul." Elona pointed with her eyes. "Appears she had two challengers."

Mayadeen hadn't noticed, but a second dead warrior lay in a heap to one side of the pit. At least that one had been smart enough to wear half plate, though little good it did in the end against a monster capable of breaking cold steel—no tall tale as the throbbing in Mayadeen's hand reminded. She wanted to put a dagger through Lusul's swollen face so bad she could almost feel the pressure of the hilt as blade penetrated fat and bone. But such satisfaction at this point in time would come at an impossible price. Only survival could eventually afford vengeance, and perhaps Mayadeen needed to refrain from any further trifling with fate—a loathsome concept that she'd no use for until quite recently. It was *just the way of it*, as Mayadeen's Pap always said. For the first time in her life she was beginning to understand her father's seemingly pathetic words. *Damn the gods high and low.*

As with the last, the body of the fallen challenger was dragged to the side by two sturdy pit guards. Lusul dislodged her double-axe from the corpse and walked up a set of steps leading directly from the dirt to her throne-like chair on a platform raised a few heads above the stands. Mayadeen likened it to an ascent from hell, wherein some demon lord had but only to climb a few steps to and from her domain of horrors.

Lusul took her seat and scanned the crowd wherein Elona and Mayadeen must have resembled children amongst adults. She wiped some blood from a gash on her cheek and settled her gaze on Mayadeen.

"Let's go to her," said Elona. "She knows some of the common tongue so be careful what you say. She'll want you seated closest to her. It's a sign of power to show she's not afraid of a conquered pet."

Mayadeen's eye patch suddenly seemed to serve the purpose of holding back all of the blood in her face.

Elona began to speak but was stopped before her lips even opened.

"Not another fuckin' word, Red." Mayadeen looked back towards Lusul, the latter now devouring a leg of roasted fowl off the bone and gulping wine.

"On my lee, I'll kill that woman. I'll kill her ... and by the gods' bleedin' twats I'll make time forget she was ever a king."

Elona sighed as if it were her last.

"This is going to be a long night."

VI
CHEATER

A drop o' this'll make her drowsy. Two'll shut her up like a clam with air in its eye. Three ... well, that's when we move on from medicinal application.

~ An apothecary to her apprentice

Their plan progressed perfectly. Once at Lusul's side, Mayadeen personally presented the King with the contents of the late Minnow Baels' chest: eight rope-wrapped, wax-sealed bottles of Torentantian black rum—the *good stuff.* Every pirate on the Nine Seas was familiar with the Anxiety Rum, so called because it always made one anxious about choosing whether to drink it or sell it. Mayadeen wasn't exactly sure which Captain Baels had planned on choosing, but she sure as shells knew what *she* was going to do with the stash.

After Elona translated the contents to Lusul, Mayadeen uncorked a bottle and imbibed the first long swig. She then passed the potent molasses water to Lusul, who tipped back a slug longer than Mayadeen's. Lusul lurched forward in her seat with her eyes squeezed shut. When she opened them back up, a smile cracked across her face like a fissure to hell.

Over the next few hours, Lusul and six of her closest Elite Guard drank themselves into stumbling bliss. Normally eight bottles of fine rum would have lasted for an entire crew, getting the majority tipsy besides. These beasts of womankind, however, took a bottle each, with Mayadeen sharing some warm nips in between.

The shade flower poison that Mayadeen slipped to Laddy was also procured from the chest, along with a vial each of tarryseed oil and kernsenic, themselves slow-working poisons often used by scalawags to quietly remove rival or even mutinous shipmates. And, as Mayadeen hoped, Laddy put the shade flower to good use in the arena. He was given an axe half his size, which elicited a lot of laughs considering he could hardly pick it up, and a rusty, yet much lighter, scimitar. He was also afforded some shabby light armor. Mayadeen found that amusing since pirates were notorious for wearing naught but their trousers and the occasional shirt. She guessed Laddy had opted for the safer bet, although the idiot would find out rather quick that even light raiment made it twice as difficult to move.

To round out the comedy, the Rullites pitted Laddy against a seven-footer named Shar. The goliath looked as though she had fought one too many battles, cross-eyed with a severe limp. And yet for her the crowd roared in exultation. Shar carried a steel axe with dual blades that bore some craftsmanship, and she donned a crude, scaled iron plate across the upper portion of her favored right side.

Lusul, appearing quite happy with her new drink of choice, shot Mayadeen several looks of proud confidence in light of her champion.

"Shar has never been beaten," Elona whispered to Mayadeen's other side. "Please tell me that your bull has the poison."

Mayadeen grinned, although she wouldn't bet another chest of rum that Laddy could go the distance. His only chance would be to administer the poison right at the outset, and then endure as long as he could while the shade flower worked its hindering effects. Mayadeen only witnessed Laddy in combat during Baels' boarding party. He may not have been the brightest algae in the waves, but the young bull wasn't a coward. Laddy knew how to dance with a sword. However, just one blow from the vital side of Shar's axe could end the fight, and Laddy wasn't exactly in sporting shape since the shipwreck and his subsequent captivity.

The fight started out well enough. Shar did the one thing Laddy needed for her to do, which was overcompensate a strike. She went for a gusting lateral swing to the head that Laddy ducked and countered with a scrape to Shar's inner thigh. As the hulking Rullite had nearly two feet of height on Laddy, it seemed negligent that Shar bothered not to armor her mid-section and leading leg. Laddy couldn't reach anything above her ribcage if he'd leaped. That oversight alone made Mayadeen think the match-up remiss. Either way, Laddy had executed the critical strike. But it would still take at least another two or three minutes for the poison to sail to the innards, perhaps even longer considering the size of those particular innards.

Shar didn't flinch from the graze to her leg, and her next strike Laddy wasn't able to dodge. Her left fist came down so hard and fast on the top of his head that he probably didn't see the dirt before he was snorting it. Shar lifted her axe to finish the job.

Mayadeen grabbed the first thing she could reach, a silver chalice filled to the brim with an assortment of nuts, and flung it into the pit at Shar's back where it registered with a clink. "Ye big, dumb, cunty bitch," she yelled while leaning over the pit railing. "Fuckin' cheat, are ye!"

The crowd booed and yelled in response, some at Mayadeen, some at Shar, and some at each other.

Two of the Elite guards started towards Mayadeen, but Lusul only laughed and gestured them to stand down.

Mayadeen pulled Elona to her. "How do ye say 'cheat' in their grunting tongue?"

Elona thought for a moment. "Lak ulu."

"Lack aloo! Lack aloo! She's a bloody lack aloo," accused Mayadeen above the crowd's shouts while pointing down at Shar.

The seasoned warrior seemed to understand Mayadeen enough to look up and snarl something back, although it was lost in the cacophony. Laddy had recovered to all fours in a daze, and somehow, Mayadeen was able to lean down over the pit railing far enough to grab his attention. She pointed to what lay behind him. Laddy crawled to grab his scimitar and rolled onto his back to again face his towering challenger.

Despite Mayadeen's insult, Shar was able to pry more cheers from her fellow Rullites. Then Shar hesitated and shook her head. Mayadeen's hope swelled. The poison was swimming fast.

Laddy regained his feet. The crowd rejoiced and readied itself for another exciting clash between the resilient little man and the veteran killer. Shar came at Laddy with a couple short swipes with the top of her great axe. Laddy kept back, forcing Shar to work to close the gap. As soon as she gave another slight shake of her head, Laddy lunged in for a sword thrust. Shar barely parried it away from her stomach as Laddy pivoted, spun and registered a reverse slice across her unprotected left arm. Shar grunted in pain. She bashed Laddy's shoulder with the flat of her axe. The blow made him stumble, but he quickly recovered and landed another slice to Shar's upper thigh. The great warrior buckled with a knee to the ground.

The onlookers quieted.

Mayadeen glanced sideways at Lusul. Though quite drunk, the King looked as though she was ready to jump up and slaughter everyone in the place.

Laddy pivoted and with both hands sunk his blade deep into the hollow between Shar's shoulder and clavicle. Her gasp swept over the entire arena like a chill wind, and more red flowed onto the already blood-soaked soil.

Whispers and grumblings abounded across confused faces. All eyes went to Lusul. She descended the steep dais a couple steps in an effort so sloppy that she nearly descended the rest with her head.

Mayadeen's heart raced. She risked the entire escape plan to spare Laddy, and it all might end before it barely began.

Elona remained seated and silent. Now could be the moment when the little witch proved her bound oath ... or not.

"Lak ulu," boomed Lusul while scowling down at Laddy. "Asook tem ur lak ulu." She then turned to Mayadeen. Lusul smiled. "Lak ulu." She gestured a large hand to Laddy and addressed her warrior audience. "Lak ulu. Lak ulu."

Soon the Rullites broke into the chant. "*Lak ulu. Lak ulu.*"

Cheater. Did Lusul somehow surmise the poison? Mayadeen leaned into Elona's ear, "She's calling Laddy a cheater, aye? Can't be fucking good, Red."

"Because he cheated *Death*," said Elona with a smirk.

Mayadeen sighed with relief. She peered down at Laddy. *If they only knew.* Never again would she underestimate the resilience of youth. She raised her rum-filled goblet to Lusul. But there remained the question of how to get Laddy out ....

"I must go and prepare," said Elona into Mayadeen's ear.

Mayadeen grabbed her by the shoulder. "What about him?" She pointed down to Laddy, who was still catching his breath as the unlikely victor. His eye swole to the size of a lime with a good amount of blood from a gash. Mayadeen couldn't help but think that Lusul was just setting the bull up for a harder fall—maybe next have him fight Shar's twin sister, if the gods would allow twice such a creature.

"He'll be fine. I already secured his release."

Mayadeen raised a brow. Elona was just full of surprises.

"I won my bet with the Slavemaster." Elona winked and disappeared into the sea of reeking onlookers.

#

Elona had told Mayadeen the story of how Lusul came to rule the entire region, while allowing her sisters dominion over the surrounding kingdoms. She was the eldest daughter of Lubid, a Chieftain of a much smaller band of warriors. Lusul proved herself formidable at just fifteen years of age when she led a victorious raid against a rival Rullite tribe. Within just a few years Lusul stood as her mother's greatest champion and their tribe had tripled in size. Then Lubid fell ill. Before any would-be leaders could vie for Lubid's seat, Lusul ended her mother's increasingly frail life. Mayadeen imagined Lubid was very much awake when Lusul loomed over her—mother and daughter exchanging glowers of fear, regret, and betrayal. It forced Mayadeen to wonder whether she could ever do the same to her own wretched mother.

Lusul had been grabbing and pawing Mayadeen for a good part of the evening, so it came as no surprise when Mayadeen was invited back to the King's cozy pavilion along with the Elite entourage, once the arena carnage subsided. Mayadeen never thought the Rullites could be in such good spirits until, of course, they imbibed in the spirits. The six of them laughed and pushed and slapped all the way back to the tents while passing between them the last rum bottle.

Mayadeen pretended to be drunker than what she was and remained careful not to expose the two particulars, both hidden beneath her bearskin travel cloak. Once inside Lusul's spacious animal den, she found a place behind one of the two blazing fire pits. She quickly removed the cloak along with the contraband. The Elites were already beginning to rip away each other's belted hides and raiment. They licked and bit and wrestled in a mess of sloppy drunkenness. One of the larger Elites, not altogether unattractive, whom Mayadeen thought was called Ora, spotted Mayadeen on the other side of the fire. Ora could hardly stand up straight, yet she grinned with half her tongue hanging over her lip and managed her way over.

"Well, ain't ye a full specimen," said Mayadeen through gritted teeth.

Until the rum and exhaustion took their final tolls, she would have no choice but to play along.

#

The wee hours grew brisk. The soft glow of embers from the fire pit in the center of the pavilion made shadow play of Mayadeen on the wall of tanned hides. After slipping back into her button-down jerkin, she sneaked over to her bearskin travel cloak heaped in a corner. From it she withdrew the broken rapier, strung behind her shoulder to hang at her armpit, and a single rolled-up piece of parchment. Ora lied flat on her back while snoring so loud and hard that it made ripples on the side of the tent. Mayadeen used the bestial cadence to skulk around Ora toward Lusul's sleeping mound.

Her head jerked as Ora ceased her snoring and nestled deeper into some fur pelts strung about her bed stack. The powerful Elite had been surprisingly gentle in her petting, and Mayadeen ensured Ora didn't climax before passing out. Mayadeen was seldom a fan of the tit, but once or twice in her day had indulged to gain the windward advantage. Ora wasn't so bad, and at least her splitty didn't smell like the freshly gutted innards of a wild boar.

Between Lusul and another naked Elite did Mayadeen place the rolled parchment. Earlier in the day she'd filched the sheet from Elona's tent and quickly scrawled the note using the witch's writing implements. The note was a gamble, but it might act as warrant later on should they get far enough to meet Lusul's supposedly estranged sister, Ursade.

Mayadeen brought the jagged edge of the broken rapier to Lusul's neck—the sweet spot just under the ear and behind the jaw. Lusul slept sprawled out on her stomach atop a palette of cushions with three other splitties wheezing in awkward positions around her. Even while vulnerable she exhibited a power unlike anything Mayadeen had ever seen, save for maybe a krode beast. The long sinew and bulging muscle rippled across her back like the topography of some vast mountain region viewed from the eyes of a bird. The scars of many close calls formed roads and tributaries weaving in and out of freckles, blemishes, and faded tattoos, all part of a landscape surely exposed to ice and wind as much as sun and sand.

Mayadeen knew she shouldn't linger, for everything up until now had followed the plan. Killing Lusul would be a bonus. It would render the note useless, but better to quell a problem when the solution was at hand than to wait for one that may or may not spring from inspired design.

Her left hand squeezed the custom-fitted hilt of her broken weapon of piercing. Though the pain still lingered in her wrist, it had regressed to merely a dull throbbing by the strange healing powers of Elona's reeking poultice. It would be the left hand—the hand that suffered defeat—that would drive the blade that suffered the same to a final resolution between Captain and King. *Just stick this bitch and be done with it.* She thought of their battle on the beach. It was by no means a fair fight, to be sure, but Lusul could just as well have ended Mayadeen. Instead, the barbarian spared her and even gave her quarter. Of course, such mercy—or pity—could have been Elona's doing, but that didn't make murdering a King in her bed taste any better.

Indeed, Mayadeen had never stooped to an assassin's work, though pirate, mercenary and poisoner would almost qualify. *Poison*, now that might have made things easier. Lusul, however, having exhibited a larger brain than the rest of the herd, stuck to drinking from one rum bottle at a time while filling Mayadeen's own goblet from the same bottle. Mayadeen had considered the tarryseed oil and kernsenic, but like the shade flower used by Laddy, they were only non-lethal inhibitors. But they would make a good killing that much easier, though the potent rum had worked well enough to achieve the same effect.

Funny that Mayadeen now thought of this blood-thirsty nomad as a king, although Lusul would be considered a chieftain amongst savages by the rest of the world's standards, at best. Then again, the rest of the world was lucky the Rullites weren't interested in it because those standards would be torn limb from bloody limb.

Mayadeen's mother once told her that feelings seldom belie the hand that forces them, but that *decisions* do all of the time. The science of dilemma, she went on to say, always then comes down to the greater good. Mayadeen's gut told her not to kill Lusul—at least not this way. Her noggin, however, told her that if she didn't end Lusul now, then three lives would be constantly at risk for the rest of their time in the Warlands. She was already responsible for Laddy, and so too was she now bound to Elona. Then there were the slaves and the never-ending war that Lusul was waging against the other natives of Rul. But none of that was Mayadeen's problem. If Lusul was cast adrift, it didn't mean her ship would sink with her. There'd stand ten other would-be captains in line to take the helm, some perhaps even less benevolent than Lusul. Then there was the matter of Lusul's siblings ...

As the cursed logic piled up in her thoughts, Mayadeen heard soft hoof clops and the sputtering of horses from outside the tent.

She hesitated. The blade now trembled in her hand. One simple throat cutting could spare her a whole host of potential future troubles ...

Mayadeen retracted the broken blade's edge from Lusul's neck. *Logic be damned.* This time she'd go with her gut. She glanced at the rolled parchment. The note would have to serve its purpose.

Elona's head popped through the flaps at the pavilion's entrance. The night was quiet, and no sentries were posted at present, probably because they were in the tent sleeping with everyone else. "Mayadeen," she whispered with urgency, "we have to go *now.*"

Mayadeen peered down one last time at Lusul. "Ye'll never know yer fortune, ye big stupid ..."

"Bitch," finished Lusul as her hand darted up to catch Mayadeen's left wrist.

Lusul squeezed so tight that the broken rapier's hilt easily fell away. Mayadeen cried out, but at the same time grabbed an empty rum bottle with her right and cracked it across Lusul's temple, glass imploding within the rope-wrapped carapace. Lusul's grasp immediately gave, and for a second Mayadeen thought that perhaps she'd completed the aborted assassination after all. But Lusul only groaned and rolled to her side.

Mayadeen made a dash for the exit where Elona remained wide-eyed. Two of the slumbering Elites sprang from their makeshift nests, one with hand already on axe, while the other stiff-armed the first in her confusion. Both Elites, naked as cliffs against the sea, groveled to all fours and cursed loud enough to wake twenty of the closest surrounding tents. The other guards now also came to, one after the other. Soon it would be like a hundred rabid curs running down a few squirrel cats.

Mayadeen reached Elona and saw that the sorcerer had more than come through with her end of the bargain. Three tacked horses awaited with Laddy perched in the saddle of the smallest, a white peppered roan. Laddy held the reins to another horse which he offered to Mayadeen. Elona hopped back up onto her own mount like she'd done it before.

No, the only utter failure here belonged to Mayadeen—but denial and deflection was all about timing.

"Red, damn ye. Arrived too soon!"

"You're lucky I arrived at all. Mount up and follow Laddy," shouted Elona. "I'll create a diversion ..." Elona's hand curled into the air and within seconds three surrounding tents caught fire.

Mayadeen threw a leg over the saddle of her horse, a rather runty piebald, which remained stalwart. Runty or not, these animals weren't battle shy. Mayadeen glanced back long enough to see Elona maneuver her horse through a group of confused Rullites. The barbarians choked and grunted from the smoke and flame.

With a kick of her heels into its side, Mayadeen's warhorse bolted forward.

Laddy kept a few paces ahead at barely a canter. "This way, Cap'n," he called back to Mayadeen. "Five throws nor'west."

The stars were visible in the clear night, so Mayadeen trusted the bearing, even if Laddy's skills as a navigator were less than experienced. But he'd at least been seafaring long enough to know his constellations, and Arrin's Arrow always pointed to the north.

Mayadeen felt something blow on her ear as a spear soared out in front of her. Several Rullites now gave chase, and she and Laddy both would be breakfast in a matter of seconds if they didn't make a run for whatever it was they were supposed to find.

Mayadeen kicked her horse from a canter to a gallop. "Haul yer stinking arse, damn ye!" She slapped Laddy's roan on its flanks as she caught up and passed them.

Both Laddy and his pony took the cue, launching forward to keep up with Mayadeen. A couple warriors tried cutting them off but failed to get close enough for a leaping tackle. Another projectile, something smaller than a spear but probably every bit as lethal, sailed past Mayadeen's one-sided periphery.

They cleared the camp's perimeter at last, with what seemed like at least a hundred war cries close behind. As they rode into a field not far from the makeshift arena that played host to the night's events only a few hours before, Mayadeen thought that anything less than a mythological dragon swooping in and picking them up would mean a death sentence. She cursed Elona under her breath. Then the field lit up with much more than that granted by star and moon, accompanied by a strange humming.

At the crest of a grassy drumlin she saw it. A great ovular rainbow of light danced and spun at the far edge of the next field, just before the trees dominated once again. Its brilliance pulsed, waxing and waning, while the colors coiled around it like exotic snakes on a charmer's extremities.

Mayadeen's mount slowed its approach, until she pulled it to a circling stammer. Laddy's did something similar. As inviting as the unnatural presence looked, the horses wanted no part of it.

"Cap'n, we have to go into it, aye?"

"Yer asking me, ye bilge whore?" snapped Mayadeen while trying to calm her animal.

"The sorcerer said as much. She said to enter it."

The whooping and hollering from their pursuers was growing louder, and the patter of hooves joined the encroaching chorus. With no sign of Elona, Mayadeen again looked to the pulsating rift. The long grass seemed to be getting pulled towards it, and to confirm her suspicions, a fallen tree branch emerged from the edge of the forest and was sucked into the trilling light.

Damning the constant dilemmas, Mayadeen didn't want to leave Elona behind, but also knew that the witch had risked all for their escape. Such sacrifice demanded to be honored, whether by the bound blood of a scalawag or just common gratitude, the latter for which Mayadeen never thought she'd have much use.

"Then get yer bony arse in there," she shouted to Laddy.

He nodded, but when he tried to spur the roan onward, the beast refused and reared up.

"On foot then, damn ye. Smartly now," Mayadeen commanded.

Laddy rolled off the horse, but maintained his feet. As he came within ten yards of the rift, Mayadeen watched as he toppled forward. The pull of the thing had him.

Mayadeen tried spurring her own mount, but the piebald only sputtered and held its ground. As she dismounted with a volley of expletives, she spied half a dozen horsemen coming fast over the hill. Elona wasn't with them.

Mayadeen turned and ran toward the light.

Part Two

VII
THE DAY THE EARTH STOOD UP

Even I'll admit sometimes seeing is believing, and I thank the Nine
there's still plenty I don't believe.
~ The Bard Sigga Leval

This time Mayadeen awoke first. She must have ejected into a roll
or slide, for the nettle was torn and matted for several feet across the
cold forest floor where she'd found herself. Grey light fanned
through the gnarled thicket, suggesting morning arrived, though
Mayadeen wasn't exactly sure which morning. Her surroundings
looked and felt similar to Lusul's camp—cold, dry and drab—so she
figured she'd been transported somewhere still within Rul.

Once she had mustered her bearings and taken inventory—
relieved that she'd grabbed her bear skin travel cloak, pissed that
she'd forgotten anything else of use—Mayadeen began her search for
the others. Ten paces out she nearly tripped over Laddy, his skin and
rags so filthy he blended into the ground. A couple slaps to his sallow
cheek and he was awake. She was careful to avoid his swollen eye,
now blacker than Mayadeen's patch.

"Cap'n?"

Mayadeen chortled and slapped her hand down onto Laddy's
stomach, forcing him to sit up. Laddy gasped but it served its purpose.

"Aye. 'N' we ain't found the Bone Reef," said Mayadeen while glancing about the brown, sullen forest. "Though mayhap the Bone Yard."

Laddy looked to be in one battered piece, so Mayadeen left him to his own pondering and continued her comb for whatever else might have followed them through the beacon. First she came upon one of Lusul's Elites, her body mangled and crushed by a large horse which the warrior must have forced through Elona's magic trick. That much weight hurled from the void probably wasn't going to end in a processional trot. Mayadeen snickered. The big dumb cunties lacked no resolve, she gave them that much.

Laddy limped up to the scene while clutching his leg with one hand.

Mayadeen gleaned his black eye to be a gift from the late Shar, but she'd just noticed the limp.

"Yer draggin' the weeds with that leg. Flesh, bone or the both?"

"Neither. Just stiff 'ith pain," replied Laddy with no sign of concern in his eyes.

Mayadeen nodded. The young were always so stupid when it came to knowing their own bodies, but anything short of a broken bone or open gash was manageable. She reached down and untied a water skin from the tangled mess of horse and Rullite. The crude leather bag felt about half full. At least it was something, and there was no telling how far they'd go before they found more water. She tossed it to Laddy who caught it in the crook of his arm.

"See what else can be salvaged. Keep a watch for more carcasses or otherwise."

After scouring another hundred or so paces of brush and stepping in a large pile of something foul, Mayadeen found Red face down with her head next to a tree. At first glance, the sorcerer appeared to have met her end with a broken neck. But then Mayadeen heard a groan. She knelt down and rolled Elona onto her back.

"Red. Red, wake up, damn ye. By the cold, black depths I'll have the pleasure of killing ye before some tree." Perchance she was injured, Mayadeen refrained from slapping her—she wouldn't want to knock the dainty flower's head off. Instead, she gave Red a shoulder and hoisted her onto her feet.

Elona put a hand to her brow while her other hand steadied against Mayadeen. Elona's nose scrunched.

"What's that smell?"

"The smell o' shit," quipped Mayadeen. "Ain't ye familiar? 'Cause it's a fine mess ye got us into."

Elona pushed Mayadeen away.

"Me? I'm the one who got us out of the camp. You're the one who decided to play assassin and raise the alarm. That was never part of the plan."

"The plan, eh? The plan where ye failed to let me know I'd be stepping into a giant splitty of light? I might well've been fucked bloody by rainbows."

"I didn't have time to explain it to you in certain detail," snarled Elona.

"So ye take me for some blathering fool, do ye?"

"About things you don't understand ... yes, Mayadeen, I *do* take you for a fool."

"Watch it, Red ..."

"We escaped. I gave us the opportunity and you took it. You of all people shouldn't give a damn as to how or why."

Mayadeen's reply crumbled to a mutter. The arrogant little witch had a point. They'd escaped with their lives and that was really all that mattered. To a scalawag, seeing the next sunrise was known as Pride of the Day. One of the first lessons in command that Mayadeen learned under her brief yet intense tutelage with Captain Bon Shemble was there was a marked difference between strategy and tactics. One focused on the war while the other focused on the battle. Strategy was the plan. Tactics were the execution. *Leave the maps to the admirals and the generals*, old Bon Shemble would say. *To us leave only the wind, the waves and the ship in our sights.*

Like Bon Shemble, Mayadeen was a tactician. She excelled in the battle and never gave a squid's black piss about the war. Perhaps now wasn't the time or place to change philosophies, although since running aground, Mayadeen started to think about the grander scheme. Maybe it had something to do with no longer having the waves or a ship in her sights? At least she still had the wind.

"Where are we now then?" asked Mayadeen. "Seems I've been leaping across all of Tabor of late like a touched compass. Not exactly becoming for a sea captain."

"I tried to get us as far away from Lusul as possible," said Elona while peering around at the ancient trees. "We should be at least four days west of the low plains as the horse rides, halfway across Rul."

"West," grumbled Mayadeen. "North to Leth is where we should have landed. I need to be heading to a port, not further inland."

"I never agreed to go north. Once King Bolora gets word of our treachery we won't want to be anywhere near that evil woman's stronghold. Our chances of getting help now fare better with High Vicar Ursade and my Order in Valindrost. She won't be pleased, but I'll make her understand."

"*Ursade and my Order. Ursade and my Order,*" Mayadeen mocked under her breath. She felt the blood ready to erupt from her head again. "All these bitch kings are blood 'n' kin. What makes ye think they ain't all in league together?"

"Because I know they're not. Bolora is unpredictable but still answers to Lusul, whereas Ursade broke her alliance long ago. Lusul and the Rullites are no supporters of magicians or magic—"

"Well I've *one* thing in common with 'em."

"—and Ursade re-established the Order of Prenn."

Mayadeen took a step forward causing Elona to flinch.

"Sisters they be still. And blood is blood. Ye'd do well to remember it." She wasn't quite sure how Red could be so naive, and wondered whether it was her intention all along to simply take refuge west in magic splitty land. But then Mayadeen had another thought. "Why can't ye just keep conjuring lights and take us there faster? We could get across the realm with just a couple more of yer tricks—"

"It doesn't work that way. Not only does the spell take hours to prepare, but I no longer have a projector, which allows travel across much vaster distances. The most I could do on my own would afford a few miles at a time, and the energy required would deplete me. No, we need to get to Valindrost, three days west of here or less if we make good pace. There, with the Order's combined power ... they might even be able to send us straight to the Meridian Isles in a single ritual."

"Heh. That so? They'd be sending us straight to the dirt with a single ritual, to be true." Mayadeen saw Laddy out of the corner of her eye. She wondered how long his skin and bones had been standing there.

"Find anything, ye filthy bilge cock?"

Laddy stood with a tightly rolled pelt under his arm and a leather satchel slung over his shoulder. He also hefted a sturdy cleaver-like weapon that was half his size. His hands and wrists were almost black with blood and guts as if he'd rummaged right through the corpse of the unfortunate Rullite.

"Aye, Cap'n. Other'n the clothes on her body ... and a mess those were ... the big womaner had her a bedroll, some jerked meat and this here axe." Laddy looked as though he could barely hold up that last item.

"S'all we've stowed then," said Mayadeen. "Just hope there's some running liquid somewhere in this shriveled hell." She reached down and snatched the cleaver from Laddy's hand. "Better let me have that."

Even for Mayadeen, who had at least four stone of meat and frame over Laddy, the garish war implement boasted some heft. It was little wonder the opposite sex never had a chance in the Warlands. These Rullites seemed like giants, even compared to the tall, broad-shouldered daughters of the Island Realm.

"We should be on our way," said Elona while glancing at Mayadeen's new toy. "I don't like the looks of this forest either ..." she trailed off with a pensive pause. "I feel as if ... as if ..."

"*What*, damn ye?"

Elona threw Mayadeen a sharp glance.

"As if we're losing daylight."

Mayadeen lifted the cleaver to rest its squared haft against her shoulder. "Seems we agree on something."

Elona, who now resembled a cheap whore with hair frazzled and a ripped doublet exposing the upper half of her pitiful bust, was starting to grow on Mayadeen, the latter admiring her pluck. At the very least with Red along, they'd have no trouble building a campfire.

Mayadeen just hoped they would make it to nightfall.

#

After five hours of walking the lifeless wood through biting brambles and lashing chaparral, Mayadeen finally recognized the sound of trickling water. Elona was in charge of carrying the water skin. It was down to half a sip with plenty of backwash, compliments of Laddy, to which slobbering over everything he put his fuzzy lips on Mayadeen could already attest.

The sun grew angry by mid-afternoon, and the thicket seemed to covet and trap the heat within its fluttering shadows. It made for a sultry, heavy ambling, and Mayadeen almost allowed herself to cheer when the rippling creek finally came into view.

"Oh, sweet Xinixelica," Elona sighed. Her voice cracked and she seemed one held breath away from blubbering like a child. She all but threw herself down to the creek's crusty carve-out and submerged the water skin.

"Zinna who?" Mayadeen had heard some long handles in her life but never that one. Although something about it sounded familiar.

Elona answered from over her shoulder. "Xinixelica, the great provider of mysticism and magic. She is my god. You Meridians know her as Zilcara." Elona let a handful of water spill from her cupped hand.

"Aye, aye ... I know Zilcara and her soddin' Sirens. Another bitch god from nowhere and everywhere. Why not stick to what's flesh and blood? Even if yer Zinna-licks-a-clit is eyeing from above, she wouldn't waste a cloud's piss on any of us, Red."

"Tell me, Mayadeen. Why is it the Island Realm fears magic so?"

"We don't fear it, damn ye. We forbid it."

"Yes, but why? You yourself have acknowledged its practical application," Elona glanced down at Mayadeen's left hand, "and you've only received a small taste of its potential."

Mayadeen brought her hand up and made a fist. Magic or not, whatever Elona slathered on two days prior had indeed nursed her appendage anew.

"'Tis unnatural, s'why. Belongs to the gods, should the everlasting cunts actually exist. Magic ... fie. It shouldn't be. Makes kings of cowards and cowards of kings." Mayadeen glared. "Just as I suspect it makes fools of sea captains."

"And yet magic is the province of women, for the Sinbalak rarely flows through men. Surely the Meridian Isles would see the advantage in that."

The Sinbalak. Mayadeen hadn't heard the reference in years. It was what a large part of the world believed to hold the key to wielding magic, although Mayadeen's homeland still considered it an elaborate myth designed to legitimize magic as a natural right. It was a fiendish privilege at best, and unlawful either way.

"We see the advantage of what we can do with our own flesh and wits. 'Tis why we dominate the Nine Seas, gods or no gods. When I come about to sink ye, take ye or fuck ye, I do so with naught but the wind at my sails. The rest's by my own devices, keen or dull as they be at the hour."

Elona tipped the water skin's spout and squeezed out a swallow. Laddy now joined her at the creek's edge, splashing water on his face and slurping up mouthfuls. Elona tossed Mayadeen the swollen skin.

"Well, then it's a good thing we found this stream. Wouldn't want to quench our thirsts *unnaturally.*"

Mayadeen scowled and briefly considered drowning her in it. One less thirst to quench. But then she remembered the campfire, and dusk wasn't far off. Who knew how many nights they'd be staying amongst this endless dead forest? They'd walked for hours and the weaving trees never once broke for a clearing. Mayadeen now noticed that even the rushing creek nurtured no surrounding greenery, and she'd not heard so much as a bird's chirp since her excretion from the rift.

She wondered how Prick was faring. The ornery redgull always did possess a fine sense of direction. But there wasn't a worm to be had in this godsforsaken place, and Mayadeen wouldn't hold it against her pet if he decided to stay clear of it.

Just as she was about to gulp down half the dripping water skin, Elona toppled onto the bank.

Mayadeen started forward and then heard a flopping splash.

Laddy lay face-first in the stream.

Mayadeen swapped priorities and ran over to the young bull, who was making no effort to pick himself out of the foot of creek. She grabbed him by the scruff of his ratty wool vest and pulled him ashore.

"Hell's the matter with ye?" Though breathing and eyes wide open, Laddy didn't respond. Or *couldn't* respond, Mayadeen thought. Her eye got big as the creek water began to change to a brackish green, beguiling its former fresh and crystalline appearance.

"What sort of devilry ...?" Mayadeen looked over to Elona, who also wasn't moving. "Red. Red, get—"

A snarling grunt echoed through the copse followed by the crackling of underbrush.

Whatever it was, it was big.

Mayadeen readied the great cleaver with both hands. Unlike on the beach with King Lusul, here she could exploit the element of surprise. She dashed up the small embankment to the trees and hid behind one of the wider trunks that must have been leafless for an eternity. Though a bit of a retreat, her position was such that five long strides could propel her cleaver to lodge into the head of what would soon be hunched over Laddy. Two more strides would get her to Elona.

The sounds of more disturbed twigs and a thump now revealed the interloper on the far side of the creek opposite of Laddy, although Mayadeen wasn't sure exactly what she espied. The creature resembled an extension of the landscape itself. Rock, bark and soil covered its misshapen form, and even a few tree branches protruded from its humanoid arms and squat legs. Its head seemed to reside level with its shoulders, lending a spherical form to the whole of its upper half. Whatever served as the face lay hidden beneath a natural mask of hanging roots and mosses. The eyes, however, blazed a bluish glow from beneath the tangled mess.

The sweat dripped into Mayadeen's eye and she felt a shiver rake from the tip of her arse to the back of her neck. She'dbattled fell monstrosities before, the krode beast not excepted, but whether she could destroy this thing—this *dweller*—with what amounted to an oversize cleaver was doubtful at best.

Mayadeen peeked around the trunk to watch the Forest Dweller as it lumbered across the murky water to loom above Laddy. From where she hid, Mayadeen could hear the raspy reverberation of its sucking breaths as if she a large conch shell lifted to and from her ear in rhythmic succession. With its back now to her, she could probably rush in to get one good hack, although finding anything less than vital would leave Mayadeen with just a few harsh words before her doom.

There had to be another way. Mayadeen surveyed once more the immediate area. Just withered trees, brown brush and some small rock clusters. Everything here was as dry as desert bones.

And it would all burn.

But first, she would see if the cursed creature had any wits. She guessed it did, considering it almost ensnared all three of them in some sort of illusory or magical trap. Mayadeen herself had been ready to go diving for oysters in the disguised creek water. If she'd done so, then all three of them would have been living parcels for the whims of something evil.

If she could distract the Forest Dweller, then she might be able to get to Elona to tell the paralyzed witch they needed fire. Mayadeen picked up a fist-sized stone and threw it into the thicket on the other side of the creek. The stone hit with a thwack, and the monster seemed to shift its mangled mass just enough to register the noise.

Mayadeen willed herself from her hiding place. As she stepped forward she noticed Laddy beginning to stir. The Forest Dweller wheezed out something like a hiss and turned its attention back to Laddy. With another wheeze and a grumble, it reached down and placed a large fingerless appendage on Laddy's chest. The young scalawag choked out a yelp and began to flail his arms and legs. Mayadeen lifted the cleaver and with four lunging strides swung the blade down onto the Forest Dweller's back. The force of the blow sent a spike of pain through Mayadeen's bad wrist causing her to squeal in fury and let go of the haft. The cleaver sunk deep into something; that much she knew.

A deafening mix of scream and roar came from somewhere out of the Forest Dweller, its blue slits now blazing on Mayadeen.

"Laddy, get up, damn ye!" Mayadeen stumbled back. "Red ... we need fire!"

The Forest Dweller's arm became one with the dirt, and a fissure of living roots shot forward like an army of subterranean spiders. Mayadeen leaped sideways into a shoulder roll as the lashing roots streaked past her and disappeared back into the ground.

Mayadeen glanced at Elona who appeared as though her paralysis was wearing off.

"Red, set it ablaze! Burn it all, says I!"

As if it understood, the Forest Dweller turned its attention onto Elona and extended its left arm towards her a like a worm doubling its own length. Mayadeen vaulted from her position and threw herself onto the elemental appendage, knocking it from Elona's path. The arm now formed a three-pronged hand around Mayadeen, switching from subdued to subduer. She yelled as the rocky vise began to squeeze her. Just as the Forest Dweller's other arm was about to finish her with a bash, the arm burst into flame. The Forest Dweller screamed in a pitch so high and shrill that Mayadeen's ears rang even as she was thrown several feet to the creek's opposite bank. She lifted her head from the dirt to see Laddy jump onto the creature and pry the cleaver from its back.

The ground shook for a brief moment and Mayadeen thought she heard a great voice vibrate from all around, the words only gibberish.

Flames began to blanket the branches and brush on both sides of the creek. Elona must have gone wild with her sorcery, similar to how she handled Lusul's camp the night before. But sometimes to get rid of a dweller you had to burn the house down.

"Cap'n!" Laddy's voice came from somewhere beyond the screaming beast and the thickening smoke.

Mayadeen scrambled to her feet. She couldn't see Laddy, but spotted Elona. She held a fist over her nose and mouth as she ran back across the creek to where Elona stood doubled over and coughing.

Mayadeen grabbed her by the arm. "Find yer legs, Red. Smartly, now." Elona moaned something but followed the command. Mayadeen smiled when Laddy emerged from the haze to flank her support of Elona. There was no sign of the Forest Dweller, whose screams subsided, but the larger matter at hand was to escape the impending flames and stifling smoke.

The three of them climbed the small embankment back to the thicket, a portion of which had not yet caught fire. Mayadeen motioned with her throbbing hand and they stumbled through some stiff brush until the air cleared enough to breathe again. She fell to her knees as did Elona. Laddy was the only one still capable of standing. Mayadeen couldn't gather from where the skinny little bull drew his energy. She decided it was just sea green youth. All three took a moment to catch their breaths.

"Where'd that rock fucker get off to?" said Mayadeen looking back at the wall of smoke.

"Upstream, he did," replied Laddy. "Screechin' all the while, that wood fucker." Laddy had recovered the war cleaver, its stout blade rippled with black ooze.

"Then we head downstream," said Mayadeen.

"We've got to get out of these woods," joined Elona between a fit of coughing. "I know where we are now. It's the Ragged Forest." A frightened look came over Elona's face, one that Mayadeen hadn't yet glimpsed during their brief yet varied time together. There presaged much more to this place, and the witch was hiding something. Big surprise, that.

"What if it comes back, Cap'n?" Laddy asked as if he hoped the Forest Dweller *would* come back so that he could finish it off proper.

Mayadeen was glad the young bull was a survivor. He was proving his mettle in fathoms rather than feet, and he'd make a fine scalawag once Mayadeen got their chapped arses back on a poop deck. She glanced again at the sullied war cleaver.

"The dirt fucker bleeds, aye?"

"Aye, Cap'n. Aye," Laddy grinned.

"And it will burn, too," added Elona, "... that ... that rock, wood and dirt ... *thing*."

But Mayadeen couldn't shake the feeling that the creature would prove the least of their worries.

VIII
ON THE RAGGED FOREST

"Then I have found death?"
"Nay ... You have found fate, young one. Those who do not find fate
find folly, for only fate serves the gods."
         ~ Xaven, *Tindris and the Fire*

Before dusk fell like tar over a hull, Mayadeen estimated they'd gained at least another league downstream of the day's sinister events. The fire they'd started must have blown in the other direction—either that or petered out entirely—for its traces quickly dwindled despite the faint smell of charred wood and a thin haze on the air.

Not too far into their hike, Mayadeen had decided it was time to give the only water source another try. Like every other damnable thing, she'd forgotten the water skin on the bank where they had encountered the Dweller, leaving them little choice but to stay with the creek on their journey westward toward the city called Valindrost. Although sticking to the creek could invite another meeting with their abhorrent host, at least it would prevent them from ambling in circles.

Once again, the water appeared inviting enough, but this time Mayadeen had Laddy drink first. After she was sure he wasn't going to choke or fall on his face, Mayadeen went next, followed by Elona.

The new moon steeped the forest blacker than good rum, and the comparison only made Mayadeen resent ever having wasted six precious bottles on Lusul's half-witted savages. She'd be lucky to ever get a taste of grog again, let alone the good stuff. It was woe to believe she'd not had a splash of the daiquiri in four days, hardly a benchmark to be proud of.

Now the three of them sat and ate and watched the crackling campfire lick at the night's crisp zephyr. Elona sat propped against a tree across the fire. She'd no trouble starting it, of course, and Mayadeen couldn't help but wonder what sort of devil's pact a magician would engender to possess such destructive abilities. Not that she had any complaints. Red could burn her way to the next life for all Mayadeen cared. Nevertheless, there was a cost for everything, especially for something that came from nothing.

Mayadeen flicked her eye sideways to Laddy, who, unlike herself, proved responsible enough to keep hold of his satchel of dried rations, upon which the three of them now ravenously dined. Even though he looked like he'd been dragged across a desert whilst clubbed and stoned, the resilient young bull still kept his chin up with a glint in his eyes.

Mayadeen swallowed down her last piece of salty jerked venison. She peered up into the evening sky and a few of the brighter star clusters revealed themselves through the interwoven treetops. "Ah, now there's a thing familiar," she said aloud.

"What is?" asked Elona.

"Pyre's Piss Hole for one," Mayadeen pointed up with her finger. "Bright as brass this time of year and on the western reach by the flutter o' my luffs. Here it's nigh straight above."

Just as there were nine oceans were there nine major constellations and nine gods attached to each. Murgast's Orchid constellation, which wasn't really an orchid but rather a woman squatting, hosted Pyre's Piss Hole as the brightest star where the name would suggest. Pyre herself was a demigod of spite and vengeance, and one of Murgast's many daughters. Mayadeen knew the pantheon well only because she was forced to learn it as the daughter of an Elder and Ninemaster. If she had to choose a side with any of the cosmic cunties, it would probably be Murgast, the god of wealth and pleasure, because what else would one do with omnipotent immortality?

"You must know all of the constellations," said Elona.

"Aye," Laddy interjected. "The Cap'n knows er' last one of 'em. Find a fly on the waves by 'em, she could."

"And yet, Laddy, you are here," said Elona.

"Aye—"

"Just what in fuck's fortune is yer meaning, Red?" Mayadeen was almost too tired to fight.

"It was only a jest, Mayadeen, I didn't ..."

"I told ye it weren't natural the way we arrived at this godsforsaken main of eternal shits. I ain't never had a lick o' business here, and as far as we're concerned we've still no business here. The last thing in the whole of Tabor we should be doing is escorting yer honeyed arse to the kingdom of fire-conjuring twats."

Mayadeen supposed that was the end of it after an awkward silence. She didn't need to be reminded of her misadventure, and the incredible fashion in which her ship went down smelled of magic all over. She wondered whether Red knew anything about *that*.

"Captain Damned, I could teach you how to conjure fire out of *your* twat," said Elona in a voice meek but loud enough to hear.

Mayadeen scowled across the campfire. Elona put a hand to her mouth to muffle a giggle. Then a snort and a chuckle slipped from Laddy.

Pretty soon both Elona and Laddy were laughing themselves to tears.

Mayadeen bristled. On any other evening she probably would have joined them, but considering she spent the past twelve hours fleeing a barbarian horde, battling a dirt monster and avoiding a forest fire, her general wherewithal didn't quite lend itself to the mood. A belly full of water and lousy dried venison didn't tickle her toward the bard's show, either.

"Aye, all mates and merriment, ain't it?" Mayadeen stood up. "How 'bout the two of ye butterflies cozy up proper? The nymph there is pining for the pole, Laddy. Spill yer reeking virginities all over each other."

That shut them up, and both were blushing brighter than the campfire.

"Fuck me all the fish in the sea at once," Mayadeen said with an exaggerated frown. "Ye truly are a couple o' saplings." Mayadeen laughed under her breath. "Now then," she went on as she hunkered back down by the campfire, "what were ye goin' on about earlier, Red? 'Bout why we shouldn't be in these here particular woods?"

"I could tell ye why, Cap'n," said Laddy.

Mayadeen chuckled. "So could we all, Laddy." Her eye again found Elona. "But something portends there's more to it than the beast."

Elona smiled but hesitated.

"Yes, there is a reason why even Lusul won't step foot in this forest."

"Ye don't say? Thought mayhap that moss fucker would be Lusul's type." Mayadeen shared another jeer with Laddy.

Elona rolled her eyes. "Could we stop referring to the *elemental* as something that copulates with everything the landscape has to offer?"

"'Twas a dweller," returned Mayadeen. "All the same, Red. Mayhap I'd have taken my chances with Lusul if I'd known about this god's twat of a thicket."

Elona sighed and stared into the fire.

"There is a greater legend that surrounds this place. *Shorsas.*" Elona glanced nervously around the darkness after saying the name.

Mayadeen also scanned the darkness. "So? Who is the bitch?"

"She was one of the founders of my Order more than a thousand years ago. I only know what I've read in books. She's not spoken of beyond what's written."

"Well, now ye've got my heed, Red." Mayadeen clapped her hands and rubbed them together. "Always treasure attached to things so old and unspoken of."

"Treasure or a curse, Cap'n," said Laddy while peering around the still night. "Mayhap we shouldn't goad it."

"Mayhap ye should piss yerself by another fire," snapped Mayadeen.

Laddy brought his arms up around his knees and averted his gaze.

"Go on, Red," she continued. "Tell it true."

"It's quite simple, really. There were three founding sorcerers: Gwethol, Torberan and Shorsas. The Four Kingdoms were all part of the same realm at that time, ruled by one King for whom the Order of Prenn was formed to serve. It is written that Shorsas felt her own talents and mastery of magic along with those of her fellow sorcerers did not warrant such servitude. In a short time her skills surpassed even those of Gwethol and Torberan, and she tried to take control of the Order to defy the King. Although Shorsas failed in her coup, her powers had become so great that she could not be defeated by hand or sword."

"That so?" Mayadeen interrupted. "I've known an assassin or two that could've strangled that silly nymph with her own hair." She ran a finger through her matted locks and sniffed them. They smelled a combination of blood and fish.

"Yes, and I'm sure there were those who tried," Elona continued. "But in the end, only Gwethol and Torberan together could stop Shorsas, and they were able to do so by separating her life force into five runic shards—pelitite crystals imbued with her spirit."

"Ah. Ye see, Laddy? Pelitite's worth a tidy sum." Mayadeen cackled. Like as not, there was hardly a story in all of Tabor that didn't end with some sort of prize attached to it. She'd once witnessed Captain Bon Shemble stumble upon a small load of pelitite crystals after boarding a merchant dhow. The boodle valued enough to afford the old crone a new ship.

"You'd never get to *this* pelitite, Mayadeen," assured Elona. "The five shards were scattered across Tabor, each buried deep beneath the ground in places that carried special significance for Shorsas. They were separately entombed and hallowed shrines were erected upon them, though any such markers would be probably all in ruins at this point."

"Sounds like a perfect plot to dissuade certain scalawags. Them who believe in curses." Mayadeen regarded Laddy.

Laddy only swallowed and scanned Elona. "Wha, wha ... where did ye say them crystals were buried, 'Lona?"

Elona smiled. "I didn't say, Laddy. But since you asked, one of the shards, the first, was written to have been buried right here beneath the Ragged Forest."

Mayadeen scoffed. "Oh, fie. So what're ye saying, Red? That cursed beast was this same witch of old ... Shorsas?"

"It is known this forest once thrived before Shorsas' imprisonment. It was called the Valinwood. The legend says that Xinixelica did not approve of Shorsas' defeat and within just a fortnight of the first shard's burial, the soil became fallow and the entire forest shriveled up into what it is today. But Shorsas' power was so great that, even in death, her spirit could reap life within reach of the shards even where there was none. Over the centuries, perhaps that power has grown, and that fell creature might be a manifestation of it."

Mayadeen stood up. "I'll give ye all the feathers off my twat if that legend were true. That *fell creature* is just another one of Lusul's sisters. Ain't ye saw the likeness?"

There was still the matter of the echoing voice Mayadeen heard during the battle with the Dweller. But since she couldn't decipher whether Laddy or Red had heard it, she thought best to keep that part to herself. She didn't want to go validating Red's gossip. Not when they were in the thick of it.

"Where are you going?" asked Elona.

Mayadeen reached into her own trousers and after tooling around for a moment, produced a wadded cotton cloth.

"Had me the cramps all night," said Mayadeen over the fire to Elona. She kicked some of the dirt beneath her. "Seems I've bled all over yer founder. Heh." She held up the freshly soaked linen.

Laddy inhaled with a smile. Mayadeen would have let him have it if it weren't her only sop rag. Some bulls fancied that sort of thing.

"I'll be scrubbin' down in the creek mayhap there're any real animals as opposed to mythical ones about these woods. Ye'd be wise to do the same." Mayadeen whiffed Elona's blood windward a few times and so she knew the sorcerer didn't have some clever magical means to stop the flow of creation. They'd both be bleeding for the next few days.

Elona reached beneath her own doublet but then glanced at Laddy.

Mayadeen guffawed and stomped off into the darkness.

#

That night the campfire offered no comfort from the cold embrace of the Ragged Forest. On first watch, Mayadeen fed and stoked the flames several times to no avail in an effort to ward off the clinging chill. She thought more than once that perhaps the fire wasn't real, its licking and popping a sham performance. It was ignited of Red's magic after all. But she remembered the fire from earlier in the day, the one that had engulfed the Dweller, and the blazing heat and smells of smoldering wood it produced. *That* fire had been real enough.

Mayadeen pulled her travel cloak closer around her shoulders. She sat with the leather-gripped handle of the Rullite cleaver across her lap, her back against a thick tree root protruding from the ground in a small arc. The surrounding darkness loomed heavy and opaque, with not so much as a cricket's chirp from beyond its gossamer. Mayadeen detested total silence. She missed the creaks and groans of her former ship just as she yearned for the roll of the sea and the gentle sway of her berth. Most of the sleep she'd mustered since being stranded in the Warlands came only out of sheer exhaustion so that she hadn't the time to be uncomfortable. Yet now that she'd gained some of her old strength anew, Mayadeen likened a landlubber's respite to curling up in an open-air grave.

Laddy looked to have no trouble adapting. He'd been singing to the lions off and on for the past hour. Indeed, his snoring was the one thing that helped break the unbearable silence.

But now even Laddy breathed softly.

Mayadeen heard a whimper from the other side of the fire. Elona stirred as she slept atop the fur hide bedroll that Laddy recovered. The horny scalawag no doubt had hoped to be invited to it. Instead he got a dirt sward with a wad of weeds for a pillow.

Suddenly Elona shot up to a sitting position.

Mayadeen smirked. "Sour dreams, Red?"

Elona didn't respond, her eyes still shut.

"Just when I thought ye could irk me no more, ye're a bloody sleepwalker." Whenever Mayadeen found out that one of her crewmen walked in his sleep, she would leave him at the next sea port. There were enough cursed variables to deal with on a pirate ship than to have some damaged halfwit skulking about with his eyes shut while pissing himself and unsettling the entire crew.

Elona whimpered again and then mumbled something.

Just as Mayadeen was about to rise and put an end to Red's torpor, a chain of words leaped from the magician's lips that were not her own.

"Rah selekavon tah vorath."

It was the same voice from earlier in the day, unmistakable in its alto, and again it resonated in some ancient and foreboding dialect. Elona's rolled back eyes opened, the whites streaked red with blood vessels. Her irises rolled forward, not the golden brown like Elona's own, but rather a silvery blue unlike any pair Mayadeen had ever met.

Elona inhaled deeply and stretched her arms out above. A thin smile crept across her face and she arose.

Mayadeen rose quicker with axe in hand. She hesitated while side glancing to Laddy who remained asleep.

"Let him sleep," said Elona. She spoke the folk tongue this time, but the *voice* was still older and richer with a commanding resonance.

"He will not be disturbed."

"And just who might I be talking to?" Mayadeen suspected it was not Red, but who could tell for sure? Yet another reason why she despised magic. One couldn't be sure of anything.

The impostor laughed as if she'd known exactly what Mayadeen was thinking.

"It's been so long since I've peered through eyes." Again she inhaled with flaring nostrils. She waved her hand above the dwindling campfire. It at once reached twice as high and the impostor allowed the flames to lap at her hand. Those empyrean eyes glinted in the firelight. Mayadeen flinched momentarily from their glare.

"Everything is so ... focused."

"Ye've me at a disadvantage still, womaner. A devil, a witch or a ghost are ye? Mayhap all three?"

The impostor's lips turned down. "Elona knows much about you, Mayadeen Damned of the Meridian Isles. I wonder how much *you* know about *her*?"

Not much at that, was what Mayadeen wanted to say. But she decided not to offer up any more knowledge than was necessary. If this was the same Shorsas of Red's legend, then perhaps her powers did not extend to those of an all-knowing oracle or god. Anything she knew about Mayadeen was obviously being filched from Elona's head. Or so it seemed.

"Why don't ye tell me all about her, Shorsas, if that is yer handle?"

"You speak my namesake, and yet you do not believe that I am she. Or perhaps I am Elona, tapped into the vast yet latent reserve of my true power?"

"Heh. Ye certainly goad me like Red would. But a puffed up sense of yerself betrays ye, nymph. Take it from one who knows."

Shorsas again forced Elona's pale pink lips into a smile and began to circle the campfire. Mayadeen circled with her, keeping the dancing flames between them. Fighting the witch would be futile as any attack with the axe or otherwise would result in injury to the real Elona. It would seem possession came with an assortment of advantages for the possessor.

"Enough riddles and pretense, witch. Name yer want."

Again those silver eyes pulsed with the understanding of alternate worlds.

"I want my realm back."

"That so? Along with every other inbred sister ogre in the Warlands. Tell me, what's here that ye're all fighting over? For I sure as slime on a Jelly Tip ain't seen it yet."

Shorsas ignored this and kept up her circling amble.

"Too long have I been trapped between worlds—'twixt the living and the dead."

"Mayhap I can help ye get all the way to that latter one."

Shorsas lingered when she arrived at where Laddy slept. Mayadeen stood ready to close the distance. If forced to choose between Laddy and Red, it would have to be one of her own.

"Hobbled. Broken. I yearn to be whole. I yearn for the flesh." Shorsas put her hands to her breasts and felt down the slight curvature of Elona's thin frame. "Mine was taken from me ... too soon, you see."

"Looks as though ye claimed some flesh, though I'd say ye could do better. So what's more?"

The smile finally fled Elona's borrowed countenance.

"Alas I am still weak. I cannot assume this body for much longer. But *you*, Mayadeen Damned, could help me," Shorsas said with more enthusiasm. "And in return, I could give you riches and power beyond that ever afforded a Daughter born of Corolon. This I can promise."

Corolon was what the Meridian Isles were called hundreds of years before they were conquered by Mayadeen's own ancestors. The Elders of Corolon, the highest ranking authorities of the Isles and of which Mayadeen's mother was one, had kept the original namesake. Only a very old bag of bones indeed would refer to the Island Realm as *Corolon*.

"And just why would I trust ye?" Mayadeen didn't like where the conversation was going, so she'd bluff her way to a swift end if that's how the hooks set.

"A fair question ... if we both were fools. You and your friends are my prisoners. Only I can allow you your escape."

Shorsas paused while dirt crumbled from somewhere closeby. More crumbling and popping from all over joined the chorus. Suddenly there hovered several sets of glowing blue eyes in the surrounding darkness.

"And only *they* can allow you your lives."

Mayadeen spun with her back to the fire. It was the Dweller—*lots* of Dwellers—as if beckoned by the ancient witch. Even though they remained in the shadows Mayadeen remembered well the misshapen beast from earlier in the day. They must have emerged from the ground itself—Shorsas' own personal army of lumbering monsters.

Mayadeen flinched away from Shorsas who now stood beside her.

Shorsas coughed and gasped as her head went back. She staggered, and for a moment Mayadeen thought the silver faded from her eyes. But the silver returned, and with it a more urgent expression.

"There's no time," said Shorsas. "By your blood and oath as a Daughter born of the Meridian Isles, Mayadeen Damned, name me as thine ally or name me as thine enemy."

"Damn ye, spirit bitch—"

"Choose."

The floating eyes encroached, their hosts' hulking masses now visible at the edge of the firelight.

"Ally ... ally, damn ye!"

"By your blood?"

That was a strange request considering Mayadeen couldn't exactly exchange blood with a ghost. But she figured she'd go along with it.

"Aye, by my blood."

"By the blood that you already gave me," Shorsas' brow raised. "The blood of your loins?"

The cursed witch must have referred to her business in creek.

Hardly the same as being bound by mutual blood, but Shorsas didn't seem to be caught up in the details. Mayadeen sighed and shook her head. *Clever spirit ...*

"Aye, aye."

"By your oath?"

Mayadeen was many things, but an oath breaker was not one of them, which is precisely why she didn't take many of them. Yet again a conniving magician, not to mention a dead one, had her by the tit. She only wished she could start charging for her services as every sorcerer's personal escort.

"By ... by my oath. Fie, ye wicked harpy!"

The few more moments that Shorsas stared seemed to Mayadeen like an eternity. Then with an exhale Elona collapsed to the ground. Mayadeen rushed to her lifeless body. The glowing blue eyes encircling the darkness now vanished. Mayadeen spoke out to nothing and everything.

"What do ye want then? What do ye want from me? What am *I* to do—"

The voice of Shorsas boomed from the darkness. "By and by, Mayadeen Damned. By ... and ... by."

The last of her words faded into an echo.

IX
BAUBLES, BANGLES AND BIRDS

Magic is not an abstract concept—it either floweth from within or floweth not at all. Only if the former can one learn to wield it. That is the nature of the Sinbalak.
~ High Vicar Gwethol, *Practical Blood*

The nudge translated to an unseen presence in Mayadeen's dream, kicking her in the arse as she watched the belly sharks circle her cockleboat adrift in the middle of a crimson sea. A voice descended somewhere from beyond the amber clouds that morphed into sun-soaked trees above her. Then came Laddy's stench.

"Cap'n ... Elona's gone."

"By all the salted shit ever to crawl ashore ..." Mayadeen adjusted her eye patch, which had the uncomfortable tendency to stick on the encrusted pus from her bad eye. Her back popped, a welcome relief each morning since her youth, while she sat up from the pile of bark and leaves that served well as a hair-tangling pillow. She was starting to feel like one of those Dwellers. If Laddy and Elona only knew there was an army of them.

Mayadeen got the first watch of the night, followed by Laddy and then, supposedly, Red. Mayadeen thought the skinny nymph to be dead as driftwood, but only moments after the encounter with

Shorsas did Elona snap back to the world of the living. She had no perceivable memory as to the possession, and Mayadeen decided it best to remain mum about it, at least for the time.

"Ain't a sign of her, Cap'n," said Laddy.

"Aye, aye, damn ye. Heard ye the first screeching time. Mayhap she's loose in a bush or awash in the creek." She gave Laddy an extra scowl on that last suggestion.

"Or might be the Dweller got her," said Laddy while scanning the forest floor.

Mayadeen picked up the Rullite cleaver, grateful they carried some sort of weapon, clumsy and rudimentary though it was.

"We'll rally and search a perimeter that borders the creek. Anything beyond that—"

Elona stomped out of a thicket, disheveled and disagreeable as ever. Mayadeen thought she was even starting to resemble a scalawag.

"What happened last night?" Elona asked in her usual high-pitched snobbery.

Mayadeen had half-hoped for the *other* voice.

"Where were ye just now, ye lil' devil brat?"

"We thought mayhap the Dirt—" Laddy checked himself. "The, um, Dweller got ye."

"Shut it, Laddy," snapped Elona.

Laddy obeyed.

"I was relieving myself," she continued to Mayadeen. "Answer *my* question, you big, vulgar ... pirate woman!"

"Heh," Mayadeen snorted. "Well, Red, ye were carrying on and moaning and grunting in yer drippin' dreams. At one point ye rubbed yerself up and down and squeezed those nubs ye call boobies."

Elona turned pink.

"You can jest and mock all you want. We're in a very dangerous situation and—"

"Who says I jest?" Mayadeen interrupted. "By bound blood I speak true. And I know well the situation." Mayadeen stepped closer to Elona. "We'll be leaving this here ragged fuckin' forest today. On my lee, Red, I'd say ye're the one still harboring secrets."

They glared at each other, Mayadeen satisfied with the impasse for now. Next time she spoke with Shorsas, she'd be sure to get all the hard facts on Elona, although a part of Mayadeen still wondered if the entire drama from the previous night actually happened. Maybe Elona was just crazy? Or perhaps Mayadeen herself was starting to lose a few jewels from the fruit bowl. Either way she felt something different about the forest, as if an invisible pall of death and emptiness had been lifted. A breeze now rustled through the complex weave of old branches that canopied the copse. And for the first time, the songs and chirping of birds could be heard from not too far.

"Wish we'd something to eat," said Laddy.

Mayadeen looked at him, relieved this time for the subject changer.

"Aye. We're out of rations and we won't be breaking our fast 'til we find greener ground. So long as we've the creek, we've plenty of refreshment."

"Yes," said Elona with a belated sigh. "We're all hungry. I apologize for my behavior, Laddy. I ... I mean you didn't deserve that."

Mayadeen was about to laugh and say something clever about the fact that the apology didn't include *her*, when a caw resonated from the sky above the trees, followed by two more. Her spine tingled. Never in a thousand suns did she think she'd be so happy to hear that distinctive cry again—a single scratchy long caw followed by two short ones.

"Prick, to me," Mayadeen called with a chuckle while glancing above.

Prick squawked a few more times and swooped down through the high canopy of ancient branches. The bird clutched something in its small talons that it dropped at Mayadeen's feet. He circled the group first before resting with a series of flaps onto her shoulder. His beak dove promptly into her hair.

"Cut that, damn ye, Prick," said Mayadeen. "Ye bring me presents?" The redgull squawked and flapped its wings some more. Mayadeen gestured to Laddy and he scooped up what appeared to be a bracelet. He handed it to Mayadeen and Prick launched away with another piercing caw.

Elona watched the bird fly off into the trees.

"That's quite a pet you have there to find you this far inland. Is that a redgull?"

Mayadeen smirked. She raised the bracelet for a better look.

"Now what a lil' pretty have we?"

Two serpents, one made of silver and one made of bronze, wove around to form the bauble's circumference until each fanged head faced one another. The fangs themselves curved oddly inward which probably rendered it not the most comfortable piece of jewelry.

"Wonder where he lifted this. Red?"

Elona gave the curious bracelet a once over, then handed it back.

"It looks familiar, but I can't say where I've seen it. Perhaps it belonged to a Rullite? They're always scavenging trinkets off corpses and captives."

"Mayhap, though I didn't figure them bitches to have naught worth stealing." She was only slightly exaggerating, as she hadn't spied so much as a polished stone during her short time in Rullite custody, even while frisking around in the King's tent.

Mayadeen pitched the strange serpent bracelet to Laddy who seemed altogether taken by the trinket. He caught it in both hands and looked surprised to even be holding it again.

"The silver in it might fetch some tails," assured Mayadeen with a nod.

Laddy quickly pocketed his prize. Then his eyes went wide over something else.

"Cap'n—"

Mayadeen turned to find two new faces nearly upon her.

"Mayadeen, wait—" Elona charged forward.

Though she didn't need Elona to stay her hand, Mayadeen also didn't appreciate being sneaked up on. Never mind that her thirty pound cleaver wouldn't have provided the quickest defense.

"Ye're a bold one, Red." She shot her eye back and forth between the two yellow-robed figures now at Elona's flanks. Both wore hoods low over their brows and appeared to be womaners around the same size and stature as Elona—certainly not native to the Warlands Main. They each shouldered large satchels and kept their heads down.

"Who're they?" She growled it and saw the nervousness in Elona's eyes.

"Friends ... they ... they've been sent to help," said Elona. "I was going to tell you ... I thought they would have warned me before arriving."

Elona whispered some admonishment to the two strangers in yet another foreign tongue. But this one was vaguely familiar, and Mayadeen thought it the language spoken around the Sea of Cats and the Thresnare—the language of magicians.

"Ye can say to us what ye said to them," shot Mayadeen. It wasn't an offer.

Laddy joined Mayadeen's side as riled and confused as ever. His cock might now have four ports of call if he rolled his bones right.

"So now ye're pulling fellow nymphs outta the bushes, huh, Red?" continued Mayadeen. "No end to yer tricks, and yet here we remain amblin' about like peasants and starving besides."

"Which is exactly why Her Reverence, Ursade, has sent us help," replied Elona, the rouge rising in her cheeks.

Ursade. Mayadeen figured that Sister King Cunty Number Two was more involved than Red had originally let on. Kings and rulers of their realms were always three steps ahead of everybody else, which was exactly why they were kings.

"Send them two back to the bushes, then we'll talk."

Elona sighed and mumbled some more gibberish under her breath to the robed witches. Giving slight nods each obeyed without hesitation and stepped lightly around some trees and out of sight.

"That wasn't necessary," shot back Elona. "They brought food.

They're here to *help*."

"That so? Then how 'bout ye have 'em sprout glittering wings and fly Laddy and me back to the Meridian Isles?"

"Don't be absurd. After ... whatever happened last night ... I was finally able to reach the Order at Valindrost. They conjured a portal to travel here."

"Why ain't we using one to go *there*, Elona?" Laddy stole the words right from Mayadeen's lips, but a furl of his captain's brow was enough to let the sea pup know to remain quiet. Laddy could take his cue from the two mutes in the bushes.

"What've ye been plotting, Red?" Mayadeen returned her focus.

"There's no plot. Early this morning, during my watch, I communed with Her Reverence, Ursade. I let her know our predicament and she sent help. Senna and Reen will accompany us the rest of the way, and they'll do exactly as they're told. To answer Laddy's question, it's always a great risk to cross through a portal unprotected. We're lucky we all survived the first time. Those of the Order are practiced in such forms of travel. As was evident back at Lusul's camp, I am quite out of practice."

Mayadeen took a moment to consider her next words. Not in all her days did she need to make as many concessions as she had with Elona, whose bound blood Mayadeen was supposed to be able to trust. Magicians were ever a tricky lot. On a ship, if Elona proved any kind of a threat, her throat would have been cut in her sleep and her body tossed to sea. In the Isles, she would've been wrangled by individuals who specialized in dealing with witches and then either banished or publicly executed. But in this provincial land with no ocean to dominate or politics to manipulate, the options were few. It was akin to following a friendly snake back to its den, venomous though it might be, in an effort to get away from much bigger snakes that would simply devour anything that moved.

"No more surprises, damn ye magician. Or else Laddy and I make a go of it ourselves, and I won't give a piss in the four winds who I have to cut down to get us back to the brine. Ken that well do ye?"

Elona nodded, though Mayadeen could see it was all the sorcerer could muster to hold her tongue. That was wise as Mayadeen had no desire to knock out Red's pearly teeth in front of her subordinates.

"Now, let's have at those victuals."

#

They continued following the creek for more than an hour before the gnarled gray woods and brown nettle gave way to a ripened glade with lush and verdant underbrush. Senna and Reen hadn't uttered a word since briefly conspiring with Elona, and their feet hardly seemed to hit the ground when they walked. Perhaps they weren't even human. The rations they'd brought were simple enough—a variety of berries, nuts, smallish turnips and bread—and did nothing to stop the groans and growls of three deprived stomachs. Mayadeen did her best not to think about a proper meal, but then her thoughts would only turn to rum.

Food and drink weren't the only cravings battling for space in her noggin. She'd not enjoyed a proper petting since before the shipwreck, and Lusul's snatch heathens certainly didn't surrogate for the ol' high and hearty. Laddy used to be one of her favorites to satisfy such urges, but the bull was affecting her a different way of late. She couldn't quite figure out why. After all, Laddy was young, willing and well-equipped. All the damnable landstriding had her as mixed as a daiquiri.

"Red, I'll have me another fist of those berries. And another biscuit."

"We just ate."

"Aye, and we'll eat again. I'll die sober as a fallow crone 'fore I wither at the flesh to join the ranks of ye waifish nymphs."

Elona huffed and summoned over Senna and Reen. Without question Senna, the one with a nose that made Mayadeen wonder whether she could catch fish with it, rummaged into her satchel and withdrew a terrycloth pouch. She handed the whole pouch to

Mayadeen along with a rather fresh biscuit.

"Now," Mayadeen continued with a tone more serious while having a seat in the grass with her snacks, "start telling me about these cursed Sister Kings and how they ain't yet ripped each other to pieces over these so-called Warlands."

"We don't have time for this—"

"Everyone needs a breath, even yer magical constructs over there." Mayadeen snubbed her nose in the direction of Senna and Reen.

Elona rolled her eyes and seated herself in the soft grass opposite Mayadeen.

"Well, I don't know everything," she said. "Lusul is the eldest—"

Mayadeen scoffed. "Of that mad cunty I've heard and seen enough. What of the others?"

"You may be surprised to know that Lusul isn't exactly the mad one. That honor would go to the youngest sister, Bolora. Of the four siblings, those two are closest. Lusul handed Bolora the whole of Leth, and baby sister now rules the entire North. With Lusul protecting her from the south and the Shadowmurk Mountains forming a natural barrier to the west, Bolora claim to power remains safe, if not entirely isolated."

"Ye know the mad one then?"

"I met Bolora once, though it was very brief. She almost never leaves her stronghold at Crinmarr Spire. Lusul visits her whenever she's collecting slaves from that region. Bolora is wary of magic, and she insisted I reside away from the castle the one time I accompanied Lusul on a visit." Elona stared for a moment in thought. "The once great kingdom of Leth had been reduced to squalor and misery. Anyway, Bolora struck me as quite odd, beyond her distrust of me. Rumor has it she carries a taste for human flesh, though that almost seemed unlikely considering how waifish she was." Elona made a bit of a face.

"Runt of the litter, eh? Yet this Bolora is my best hope for a ship."

"She's not your best hope for anything. But, yes, Leth has the one sea port on White Bay. At least it did when I visited."

"Tell me more about the desert cunty. What was her name?"

"That would be Leweln. She's the sister I know least about. I know that Lusul carries a tenuous pact with Leweln, and that the two have been at war in the past. But there's a respect there as well, one that Lusul doesn't share with her other sisters. Next to Lusul's, Leweln's is the most formidable army, and unlike Bolora and Ursade, Leweln wasn't handed a kingdom. She usurped her throne at Sundvane and has been estranged from her sisters ever since." Elona sighed and lounged back on her elbows. "And so Lusul has somehow managed to maintain an accord between all of them. It's only a matter of time before something snaps."

"Then why aren't we headed south, damn ye? At least Sundvane has ties to the outside world. They've ships and merchant runs to Ateria besides. Ne'er crossed wakes with 'em myself, but I've known them that have. That desert cunty seems like the only sane one of the brood."

"I believe I mentioned it's a five day journey through the Bone Veil, an expanse of desert so hellish not even Lusul has attempted to cross it. It would only prove a death sentence for all of us. Besides, King Leweln and Her Reverence Ursade hate each other most of all, which wouldn't have bode well for me. They're closest in age and had a terrible falling out when they were young."

"That so?"

"Yes, but I don't know the details. All Lusul would say about it is that Ursade and Bolora were lucky that she was around to maintain the peace or else Leweln would have at them both."

"Maintain the peace," Laddy repeated with a huff from under his breath. He and Mayadeen exchanged a glance and the two laughed.

"I gotta say, Red, I ain't been in such a nest of fucking vipers through all my days, and I've been in some nests. Seems our splitties are buggered raw whichever way we choose, eh?"

"No, Her Reverence Ursade will help us."

"Ye sure are sweet on this King of the Fire Twats, even after she cast ye out to a colony of ogres. Something you ain't telling us, Red?"

"I've told you everything, Mayadeen, and I'm tired of talking. What I'd like to do right now is to move on from this uncertain—"

Mayadeen's finger flew into the hush position while she heard something disturb the nearby brush. She found her feet and readied her cleaver. Elona and Laddy both froze. The witches, too, were suddenly aware.

A familiar crumbling sound of dirt and sod resonated softly and then grew louder. The ground popped and pressed upward to form a humanoid mass that was one of the Dwellers. Laddy cried out. Elona did the same while Senna and Reen threw up the sleeves of their robes to reveal glowing blue energy surging from their hands.

"Belay," warned Mayadeen to the two witch soldiers. They didn't flinch, so Mayadeen used a sweeping hand motion. "Stand down, damn ye bitches," she repeated. They acknowledged but only looked to Elona for counsel.

The Dweller stood still as a tree, eight feet tall and five feet wide, its blue orbs visible within the concave of its opaque visage. The eyes were not obscured by clinging landscape this time, lending the creature an even more chilling presence. It smelled only of the sod, nettle, wood and rock that created its form—no different than if one had inhaled the forest floor. And yet it breathed the same hollow wheeze as all the ones before it.

Elona whispered, "Mayadeen, what are you doing?"

Mayadeen didn't answer, but only stared into the eyes of the beast. Soon there was nothing else around her save for a languid warmth and a gentle sway not unlike a ship caressed by the rolling swells. For the briefest moment she felt the wind in her hair and the sting in her nostrils. On that same gale sailed the voice, "Take this, Mayadeen. Take this and beckon me when you require but a fragment of my power. *Take this.*"

Mayadeen gazed down as the Dweller's great hand-like appendage unfurled to reveal a crystal of deep violet, about the size of an inkwell. *Pelitite.* No other rock in all of Tabor reflected such a hue.

She leaned forward and reached out to take the crystal—that which could only be one of the five crystals from Elona's telling of the legend of Shorsas and, therefore, a piece of Shorsas herself.

Mayadeen turned to face the others. Her secret was out, or was it? Elona, Laddy, Senna and Reen were all transfixed on the crystal with dazed and stupefied expressions.

Mayadeen herself lingered halfway in a trance—halfway only as she was vaguely aware of it. She placed the crystal in the top hidden pocket of her trousers, usually reserved for coin.

The Dweller lumbered away and Mayadeen instinctively began to follow it, almost as if something else was willing her legs to progress.

Laddy's voice came from behind, sounding more cautious than befuddled. "Follow *it*, Cap'n?"

Mayadeen turned to regard him while Elona and the witches continued to follow the Dweller in a slow, yet unfettered cadence.

"Aye, Laddy," she said with some effort as her legs started to move. "It's time to leave this cursed place."

#

They followed the creature for what seemed like half a league before finally reaching the edge of the woodland. It was difficult for Mayadeen to decide whether they would have eventually arrived there without guidance, although the whole business seemed to pass like a lucid dream. No doubt a devilish beguiling or enchantment was involved in the exodus, for even Shorsas herself had admitted to entrapping them in that endless Ragged Forest the night she manifested herself to Mayadeen. They gained exit from the woods at last, however, and Mayadeen failed to recall exactly when the Dweller had left them. The disorienting magic seemed to have affected the memories of all, especially Elona and her obedient sisterhood.

None of them spoke during the long hike once the grasslands opened up to far-reaching foothills. Senna and Reen took the lead until they finally reached a wide dirt road which, although partly covered with patches of weed grass, had obviously been well-travelled at one time.

"When we left the Ragged Forest we also left Rul and entered Drost. This is the Murr Path," said Elona. "It will lead us all the way to the gates of Valindrost."

"How far?" asked Mayadeen.

Elona turned to her fellow witches. After some low muttering, she turned back to Mayadeen.

"Less than a day."

"Less than a day feels like three in this hellish outland, and my feet like bloody stumps. We'll rest here away from the road and shove off again at dawn." Mayadeen lifted her eye patch to allow some breeze to cool the sweat. At least the Ragged Forest had offered shade.

"I don't understand what happened back there," said Elona while holding her head. "You held something but I don't—"

"Ye don't what?" Mayadeen felt for the crystal in her pocket, reassuring herself it was still there. Her own memory of receiving it was hazy at best, but she did remember those cerulean eyes. And that voice.

Elona concentrated. But she only exhaled with a sputter. "It's ... nothing," she said while shaking her head. "But I think all of us now know first hand the stories surrounding that forest are true. I was a fool to have taken us there. I'm sorry."

Mayadeen's lips drooped, and she saw that Laddy was watching her. The bull might have been less affected by the enchantments of the forest than the rest of them. She hailed him over as Elona had already moved ahead to consult with Senna and Reen.

"Laddy, we rest here for the night and shove off for the city on the morrow." Then she said in a lowered tone, "Tell me what ye saw on the morn 'fore we gathered out of those woods."

Laddy hesitated and looked to see if the others were listening.

Mayadeen pulled back his attention. "On my lee, tell it true."

Laddy glanced at Mayadeen's trousers pocket.

"That Dweller came back ... gave ye a gem the size o' my fist, it did. Then we followed it on yer own command, Cap'n."

Well at least one of them hadn't been confused. "That all?"

"My head was swimmin' the whole time but, aye, Cap'n ... methinks 'twas what I saw."

"Aye, and so ye did." She whispered even lower. "'Twas pelitite. But keep it 'twixt us for the time. Wouldn't want the witches gatherin' any greedy ideas."

Laddy searched Mayadeen's eye while some of the color left his cheeks.

"A cursed gift from a cursed place, methinks."

"Nay, my able young trump. A *valuable* gift from a cursed place," returned Mayadeen. She grinned and patted the lump in her pocket.

X
TEMPTING FATE THEN FUCKING IT

I'd trade a thousand intricate lies for one decent half-truth.
                    ~ Nine Master Sonner Bon Shemble

The arid yet tepid first night in Drost passed without event, and with Senna and Reen to help keep watch, Mayadeen decided to sleep the whole of it through. After breaking their fast with the remaining rations the next morning and setting out three hours on the Murr Path, Mayadeen and company at last espied the walled city of Valindrost at the base of the Shadowmurk Mountains. It was a small city by most comparisons, although the several high reddish-brown towers with ocher spires that jutted from its interior were an impressive sight. The only other structures Mayadeen saw since arriving in Warlands Main were hide-stitched tents.

Valindrost boasted scale similar to Cleft Rock, Mayadeen's childhood home on the Isles, except no great bulwark served to confine that city. Of course, plenty of Valindrost's populace appeared to live outside the protection of the wall, with a hundred shoddy hovels spread before it, finally reaching out to a few farmsteads and scattered cottages. She decided those unprotected claims must have been where the witches lived who couldn't yet shoot fire from their twats. Funny that they'd be the first to burn should Lusul decide to call on her estranged nymph of a sister, Ursade.

Mayadeen assumed Lusul was tracking them ever since the escape—indeed she was counting on it—and half expected the barbarian king and her painted splitties to be camped out in front of the city waiting for them. But such was not the case, at least not yet. The magical jump Elona had performed probably contributed to confounding a tracking party's efforts, and passage through a burning forest stalked by earth monsters and haunted by a vengeful spirit didn't help Lusul's cause, either. But due to Elona's supposed affiliations with High Vicar Ursade and her cult, Lusul would have little trouble deciphering their destination. All roads led to Valindrost and Mayadeen had to be prepared for the worst.

The best way to escape a nest of vipers is to disturb the nest.

Elona grew quieter and quieter as they approached the city through outlying farmland. Mayadeen knew something treaded on the prissy little witch's conscience, though it was tough to determine the details. If Elona wanted Mayadeen dead, then she'd already had plenty of opportunities to carry out the deed long before Valindrost. But if somebody *else* wanted her dead or captured...

Mayadeen pondered her options as they reached the first farmhouse. A familiar trill came from the sky above. Prick found them again and now circled over a wheat field, ready to snatch a plump worm from the soil to be sure. They could all use a hearty meal, and a bottle of something spirited to help it down. Even the raw odors of livestock now coaxed Mayadeen's palate. She was just relieved to find Prick hadn't ended up a meal himself or worse for one of those Dwellers. Her insufferable bird had an important role to play in her backup plan should their meeting with Ursade threaten to capsize.

"Let's get something cooked down our gullets 'fore going any further," Mayadeen said after taking note of her pet and sucking in some saliva. "Any nays on that?"

"Not even the sight o' sails could've me wanting more right now, Cap'n," Laddy replied.

Mayadeen nodded. Elona had yet to answer. The two escorts remained deaf and dumb as always.

"Red?"

"Yes ... yes, we should eat something. It will probably be another hour before we reach the gates." Elona looked as though she was about to fall over. Perhaps Mayadeen mistook guilt for emotional and physical exhaustion.

"Aye, well and good. Beyond that I'm going to need weapons, supplies and two ponies. From here we'll be heading north, Laddy and I."

Elona frowned. "Mayadeen, you'll never make it. Even if you did, Leth is even more remote and treacherous than Rul."

"Mayhap the treachery is right here, beyond those gates," snapped Mayadeen. "If ye're gonna tell me different, better tell me now."

Whether out of surprise or fear, Elona hesitated. "The Leader of my Order, and King of this Realm, is the most powerful person I know. And she's on our side, Mayadeen. Her Reverence Ursade is our only hope ... *your* only hope ... if you want to get home."

Mayadeen watched Elona for a long moment. This time, the plucky nymph didn't demur. If she was holding something back, Mayadeen suspected that it wasn't an immediate threat.

"All right, damn ye. We'll give this next Sister King a bonny 'hello.' And whatever happens aft's on *yer* head."

There was no point in pressing the matter further, and Mayadeen figured her chances with Ursade were far better than her chances of surviving a journey north, anyway, especially without Red. But the sorcerer wasn't telling her something, and Mayadeen hoped to finally get it out of her before having to resort to extreme tactics. Alas it would just have to play out. They were bound in blood and had defied certain death nearly every step of the way since Lusul's camp, so whatever was to happen next would happen to the three of them.

Mayadeen started for the farm house. Smoke billowed from its chimney peeking from a thatched roof.

"But I'll tell ye this, Red," said Mayadeen from over her shoulder.

"By the gods high and low and their ceaseless hungers, I ain't dying on an empty stomach."

#

Never in all her days had she walked so far for so little. Indeed, Mayadeen had never walked so far for anything. From a distance with its reaching towers and impressive outer wall, Valindrost promised to be a rich and bustling anomaly of activity in the Warlands. What Mayadeen got instead was the austere shell of a city devoid of anything but scattered clusters of yellow-robed waifs moving solemnly about. It almost made her want to run back to Lusul's tent land, though her blistered feet probably wouldn't have lasted ten steps out the main gate.

"Fuck's this, Red?"

Elona's smile would hardly fit on her puny little face.

"Blessed sanctuary and my home for many years. Not what you expected?"

"Ye mean an open air crypt? Nay."

"I suppose it's very different from the Meridian Isles," returned Elona.

"Ye suppose, do ye? Very different? 'Tis very different from everything. No merchants? No inns? No reek o' shit in the streets? Ain't any kind of city, this. What are we to steal?"

Laddy chuckled. At least *he* understood the strangeness of it.

"How nice all that either of you can think about is marauding."

Mayadeen pretended to ignore such an asinine remark and began a series of flute-like whistles through her fingers. She peered above to the rooftops and the cloudy sky. After a moment, she repeated the call.

"How could that bird possibly hear you?" asked Elona while also looking up.

The redgull answered Mayadeen's third call and landed on the archway of a nearby structure. Most of the buildings as they got nearer the main citadel resembled small temples or shrines. It was all as solemn as it was cold and uninviting. Mayadeen smiled up at Prick.

"Ah, a good pet, that one is. Never know when I'll need his wings." Mayadeen turned her grin onto Elona.

"That silly bird should be the least of your concerns right now." Elona squared off to stop them. "You're about to meet a very powerful woman, and not just in name and title."

Mayadeen felt certain that was a slight to her own status, but decided to let it go.

"She is to be addressed as 'your Reverence' and you should only speak when spoken to," continued Elona.

"Ye mean she actually speaks?" Mayadeen ran her tongue across her teeth to loosen some wedged gristle. "Don't ye worry none, Red. Mayhap I'll just let Laddy do all the jawing."

Elona's eyes widened and she looked at Laddy. "No... I mean, Laddy, there are no men within the city walls, you understand? You'll be an exception because you're a guest."

Laddy appeared nonplussed. "Ain't a bull here?" He peered around at the possibilities.

"Gelds?" added Mayadeen.

"As I said," repeated Elona, "no *men*."

Mayadeen stepped in close.

"Well no wonder ye all look so melancholy and lacking for conversation." With that she laughed, spun around and swaggered towards the looming citadel.

#

Her Reverence Ursade of Valindrost and High Vicar of the Order of Prenn descended the steps of the dais almost as if she didn't have feet, and perhaps such was the truth considering Mayadeen couldn't see them beneath all the garments. She was striking with steely grey eyes and every bit as tall and broad as her sister, Lusul, yet without the swollen face and permanent frown. She was obviously of a religious cult or priesthood, with her dark finery layered and flowing like some demigod of old paintings and lore. Mayadeen had seen womaners like her in the Thresnare, a tiny realm on Ateria's southern border, where magicians and their strange religions were known to thrive. Those cunties always wrapped themselves from head to toe like their bodies were buried treasures. Apparently, they all shared the same blood, which might have accounted for them hiding their inbred faces.

After sizing up Ursade, Mayadeen realized that both Elona and Laddy were kneeling with their heads bowed. She did the same in spite of herself.

"There's no need for that here," assured Ursade with a wave of her hand. "For a woman who wouldn't kneel, shouldn't kneel."

Mayadeen couldn't agree more. She glanced at Elona who was now beaming at their host as a swabby lass would at a Daughter born. Elona was already right at home. For Mayadeen, it was just another painful reminder that this wasn't the Meridian Isles.

"Ye speak the common at least," said Mayadeen to Ursade as the latter stepped gingerly to their level. As with Lusul, Mayadeen still needed to look up to her.

"Every time yer sister opened her jaw she sounded like she was squeezing out a—"

"Your Reverence, forgive my companion," Elona interrupted. "She's not from here."

Ursade smiled and looked from Elona back to Mayadeen.

"Yes, Captain Mayadeen Damned of the great Island Realm."

Mayadeen turned to Elona with an exaggerated smirk. A little vindication could coat the palate sweeter than a daiquiri.

"Lusul knows well the common tongue, she just refuses to utter it," continued Ursade. "Foreigners that gain the unique pleasure of her company usually find that out too late."

"Well, eh, yer Reverent… sorry to say yer gorilla kin and I were ill-met after she cut down three of my crew and made slave and sport of Laddy here." Mayadeen saw Laddy turn four shades of red when she gestured to him. Her intent wasn't to demean him, but rather to make sure the Witch King had her facts straight.

"Entire peoples are ill-met with Lusul, so don't feel that with you she set any precedence. I've already dispatched emissaries to clear up any confusion with my sister as to why Elona left her so abruptly. Believe it or not, Lusul can at times be reasonable."

Mayadeen was about to tell her that sending emissaries probably wasn't the best idea in this particular situation, but decided instead to wait and see what the next moments unfolded. Her instincts told her since arriving in Valindrost that a plot was about to be sprung, and the time was nigh.

"But you're a long way from home, Captain," Ursade continued, "and I'm sorry for your losses. You must be weary from your extraordinary plight."

"Her plight has only just begun," sailed in a man's voice from the entrance of the great hall. "And, trust me, she doesn't tire very easily."

Mayadeen's mother once told her that if she was prepared for anything, then very little would surprise her. The words seemed true enough as uttered, and although Mayadeen suffered her share of surprises, she'd also constructed a gradual cynicism over the years that had indeed prepared her for most designs. But not all of them. The key, however, was to never *appear* surprised.

Captain Creyland Fenn of Edenvane was suspect from the beginning, even before Mayadeen's late First and friend, Jagger, had suggested as much that fateful day on the Jeweled Sea. But now as the devil himself walked in, Mayadeen still couldn't help the flutter in her heart. She turned her good eye onto Elona. If Mayadeen herself revealed any alarm, it was trumped now by Elona's own wide-eyed visage.

Laddy took a step forward, but Mayadeen stayed him with a gesture. The young bull didn't even have a weapon and was willing to rush to his death to honor his Captain. And against the cheeky bull who now approached, his death probably would have been swift.

Captain Creyland Fenn boasted all the sculpted beauty of the finest clouded steel blade from a master smithee. If a golden carafe encrusted with all the jewels from the crowns of Tabor was filled with rum and could smile, it might be as desirable a sight. Fenn stood close to Mayadeen's height, just over six feet, and tendrils of his rusted yellow hair clawed over his brow just before obscuring eyes of a blue not found in nature. Unfortunately, this bulging bull actually had a brain to go along with his more desirable traits. Mayadeen always thought he would have made a far better womaner.

"Your Reverence ... who ... who is this man?" whimpered Elona to Ursade whilst avoiding Mayadeen's glower.

"Your employer, Elona," returned Creyland still waltzing forward. "I'm not usually *that* forgettable, even by a magician's standards."

He entered with his entourage, two hearty womaners posing as pirates. As Mayadeen preferred to stock her crews with men, Creyland preferred to stock his with whatever back alley cunties he could muster for the charade. These two oblong gorillas looked to be Marbanian, and so his carnal tastes finally appeared to be lowering to the depths of his reputation. Creyland stopped just far enough away that Mayadeen could suffer the always mischievous gleam in his eyes and smirk of his lips. He was wearing a scruffy goatee now, which only served to solidify his villainy; perchance anybody found themselves confounded as to his intentions. He was a scoundrel that Mayadeen desired even now, but his countdown to demise had begun, and Mayadeen would make sure her hands had the final squeeze.

"I'm sorry, Elona," said Ursade, "but Captain Fenn had discovered your ploy and came to me with his concerns. He has other business with your quarry, and we are not to intervene."

"But ... I don't understand ... you—"

"We will discuss this at another time, Elona." Ursade grew stern. "As it would seem you and me do have much to discuss."

Elona cowered, and for a brief moment Mayadeen thought she saw her own mother in Ursade's unwavering eyes.

"Captain Damned is to accompany Captain Fenn on a most challenging journey," continued Ursade as glib as she'd been before. "I'm sure she'll be in like company on terms she can understand."

Mayadeen glanced back at Creyland. He smiled ear to ear. The interminable arse expected her to go with him to the Southern Isles—indeed to get him there—after having been the instigator for this entire mess. Seemed his pluck far exceeded his wit. That part wasn't a surprise. She wanted his blood so bad that for a moment she understood what it would be like to frenzy as a shark.

As for Red, Mayadeen could only focus her disdain on one treacherous, arse-fucking backstabber at a time.

And now she'd empty a bottle of piss in their collective pudding.

Mayadeen began to laugh. Her cackles echoed throughout the great hall. She laughed so hard her head throbbed and she needed to adjust her eye patch betwixt the tears. She noticed that several of Ursade's robed, female minions were starting to flank from darkened alcoves at either side of the tremendous space. Confusion and apprehension broke their icy calms. Nothing like the ravings of a madwoman to shake the general confidence of a room.

"Ye think me the fool in all this, do ye? Aye? Try to out-fox the fox?" Mayadeen's eye found Creyland. "Out-snake the snake? Heh." She turned sharply on Elona. "I knew this was a scheme from the moment ye created that cursed portal at Lusul's camp. I remember seeing a light where there should've been naught but darkness the night my ship was swept in the maelstrom. 'Twas a portal the size o' this castle brought my vessel to the Warlands Main. Quarry, indeed, ye buggerin' lil' nymph."

Elona only averted her eyes with quivering lips.

Mayadeen grinned and moved closer to her. "Aye, so I decided to do something about it. To hedge my bets, ken that do ye? Just like I hedged my bets with Laddy and his fight with that big ugly bitch in Lusul's death pit. I hedged my bets, Red. 'Cause I'm a rogue cheat to the bloody end, and ne'er has there been one better."

"Explain to us your meaning, Captain Damned," said Ursade

sounding more curious than annoyed. "How exactly have you 'hedged your bets?'"

Mayadeen gave a reassuring glance at Laddy whose head moved back and forth between Creyland Fenn and the slowly encroaching witch minions.

It was time to work on Ursade.

"Yer sisters, Lusul and Leweln, both converge on Valindrost even now."

That invited a murmur from all, including the witch guards who halted for the moment.

Ursade took in the information. "That's absurd ... and quite desperate even for one of your reputation." She smirked, but Mayadeen sensed a forced smirk this time around.

"You causing trouble again, Mayadeen?" quipped Creyland Fenn from behind. "Mayhap we should be on our way before entirely squandering the generosity of our host?"

Mayadeen spun around. "Ye ain't seen trouble, Fenn. On my lee, but it's coming." She made sure the words dripped venom, and was satisfied when she saw that Creyland understood their import.

She turned back to Ursade.

"Ye think I'm a stranger to these lands? Fie! I've sailed every depth of drink from Ice Claw to the Arse of Pinethel and charted a few new ones besides. I know King Leweln like a boon matey since she's the only one of yer four splitties keen enough to trade outside 'n' abroad. Tyrport's a fine anchorage for fencing goods, always has been."

Ursade kept her taut smirk. But her lines were about to be cut.

Elona urged, "Mayadeen, you don't fully understand the situation. I was going to—"

"What possible reason would Leweln have to come *here*?" interrupted Ursade who had not taken her eyes off Mayadeen.

Mayadeen grinned wide and rolled her tongue across her teeth. "Ah ... I'm just getting to that part. Before leaving yer sister Lusul's crotch-rotting hospitalities, I tried cutting the bitch's throat. Invited me to her bed she did, ye see." Mayadeen threw a nod towards Elona. "She can attest to that much."

Ursade's eyes shifted to Elona.

"It's true, Your Reverence. She tried to assassinate King Lusul on her own accord."

"Right as rainin' rum it's true," said Mayadeen still focused on Ursade. "And right before botching the job I made sure to leave a single note on parchment: 'Yer beloved sister Ursade sends her regards.'"

Mayadeen's heart raced as she awaited Ursade's response. The High Vicar again reminded Mayadeen of her mother—not a quick one to agitate, but beware when the threshold was reached. *To infernal hell with the both of them.*

"Mayadeen, what have you done?" Elona imputed to almost a whisper.

"Her lies are bouncing off the back of that eye patch," assured Creyland. "It's the oldest strut on the stage ... she's just trying to stall our deal, Your Reverence. Mayadeen can spin yarns to rival the loom mills in Marbane. Don't believe a word."

Ursade had at last lost the smirk, but still tempered her ire.

"Implicating me with Lusul was bold but plausible, and is already in the process of being assuaged. What, however, does any of this have to do with Leweln?" Ursade asked with significantly more urgency in her voice.

"Well, now. I wrote yet another message. As of four days past, Leweln was informed that ye tried to bugger Lusul and had sent the same witch assassins to take care of yer other crazed sister ... Bolora is it? All in defiance of yer sisterly accord and a grand scheme to take the Warlands Main for yerself."

"Nonsense. And how could you ever have informed Leweln of such a ridiculous web of lies? Sundvane is nearly a fortnight away, beyond even my own magics." Ursade turned her gaze onto Elona.

Elona, now looking very confused, just shrugged.

Mayadeen chuckled. "Yer lil' helper there had naught to do with sending the message, nay. No showy spectacle with that one, like she did with my ship. Magic doors and mind tricks ain't the only means of sending the dispatch."

Placing two fingers between her teeth, Mayadeen blew out the same whistling call that she used on the thoroughfare of the barren city.

Ursade took a step back.

Mayadeen peered up to just below the beamed ceilings where the open arched windows allowed a flood of natural light. She whistled once more, and the redgull appeared at one of the stone sills.

"Prick, to me, damn ye!"

The bird swooped down to find Mayadeen's shoulder and buried its beak in her hair.

Mayadeen smiled at Ursade while stroking Prick's shiny red and black wing.

"'Tis a good pet, Prick. Thief. Tracker. *Messenger*."

Ursade's cheeks flushed purple.

"You lie. It's what you're obviously very good at. All lies. And even if any of it were true, what would possibly be in it for you, pirate, other than your head on a pike?"

Mayadeen darkened. "Not a pissin' thing was in it for me except revenge. Revenge for ever having washed up on yer cursed shores. Revenge for my crew, my ship and my friend, Jagger, butchered for no reason by yer monster kin. I knew Elona was up to something— fucking Fenn, too—and I'll dive to the cold, black depths myself 'fore allowing either of 'em the treasure trove. 'N' if I'm to be sunk, then I'm taking ye magic-spewing monkey worshipers and a few kingdoms in tow. That, Yer Reverence, is the Meridian way."

Ursade's eyes bulged.

Prick cawed and took flight back to the open-topped walls of the great hall. He'd played his part well. Of course, the bird could no more carry a message than Mayadeen could summon a portal. But she wasn't about to be outflanked by Creyland Fenn or play some sacrificial lamb for Red, whatever their game. At least having the last laugh would be better than nothing. A shame it would be a short one.

Mayadeen glanced at Laddy. He was probably sorry he had ever taken up with his Captain. Then again, the life of a scalawag never promised anything but adventure, no matter where it ended up. He could have spent his days fishing and his nights screwing, but he chose to be a pirate on the Nine, which granted a bit of those and a whole lot more.

A witch minion in yellow robes pattered rapidly from beyond the dais to Ursade. She carried a hide sack soaked brown with blood.

"Selentina fasal, Ibali," said the minion. "Imalatin!"

Ursade responded under her breath in the same language of the Thresnare. The witch minion bowed her head and upturned the sack, out from which tumbled three severed heads.

"Impossible!" Ursade recoiled from Mayadeen as if the latter was some feared and reviled demigod sent to destroy all things sacred to the sorcerer community.

Mayadeen guessed the heads belonged to Ursade's emissaries. It was the one variable that could have destroyed the con, but instead paid off in rubies. Lusul was ever out for blood and predictable as the sunrise. Her own sister might have underestimated her, but Mayadeen had not.

The other witch minions closed the gap. Two of them had taken Laddy down during the excitement. He was on the floor struggling as if bound by invisible restraints.

"Mayadeen—" Elona made some sort of strange hand motion that propelled a witch minion away from Mayadeen's path. Then Elona was subdued by three other witches also employing nothing but straining faces and hand motions. Elona's arms and chest constricted as she yelped and crumpled to the polished, marble floor.

Mayadeen heard the scraping draw of a sword, no doubt Creyland Fenn's, just before a grunt and a clank on the floor. She could not turn as something held her body in place, gripping her neck.

Ursade hesitated as her hand mimed the neck grip from three arm's lengths away, and a look of uncertainty fell across the High

Vicar's face. The invisible hand choked Mayadeen and held her stalwart like a force she'd never encountered.

"Something isn't right," said Ursade. "Something about you is ... different."

Maydeen struggled through a veil of tears. "Ye mean ... I ... prefer to take it in the splitty ... rather than ... the ... the arse?"

"You filthy Meridian whore," seethed Ursade while scowling once again. The pantomime seemed to physically tax her. "You think you're clever, but I'll rid this world of you right here and now. I don't care *what* you are."

Mayadeen's vision blurred and a reddish black closed over her. She felt her tongue licking either at the air or the back of her teeth, she didn't know which. Her hands pawed at her own throat and yet there was nothing there to grasp.

"Wait! I need her alive ... we had a deal." Creyland's taxed and slightly muffled voice came from behind.

The grip on Mayadeen's throat desisted. She curled to the floor gasping for breath on all fours.

"Telbalense iy curana al abansa," said Ursade, reestablishing her calm. "Including Captain Fenn." Her next words seethed out begrudgingly. "Secure the gates and double the watch."

Hidden beneath a curtain of hair on the cool floor, Mayadeen smiled.

XI
LOWDOWN

The next time you betray me, just make sure there's nothing left that you hold dear in this world. This way as you bleed out with my eyes on your final horizon, you can do so with peace of mind.
~ Crowla Syn, *Black Nectar*

The walls around Mayadeen shook. She sneezed as more flecks of stone and dust trickled down onto her nose.

The first dull thuds and cracks from above started sooner than she'd expected. During her tour of King Lusul's encampment six days past, she noticed just one wheeled catapult, and that siege engine was now most likely employed along with a dozen others against the bulwark and ancient stone structures of High Vicar Ursade's magical witch haven.

Mayadeen always thought it a good bet she'd meet her final days in a dungeon. When captured, pirates from the Meridian Isles were rarely executed in public for their captor's fear of retaliation from the rest of the Island Realm. This is why many defeated pirates, especially Daughter born Captains, would simply go missing, never to be heard from again.

Now she sat in the sour, hey-strewn dirt of her own cell, reclined against a wall of moldy old masonry.

"A fine mess this is," grumbled Creyland Fenn to Mayadeen from his barred cell across the way in the low-lit jailer's block. Laddy had been thrown in with him since there were only three cells. "Could've been halfway to the Southern Isles, you and me."

"Trust me, ye pretty bastard ... it'd only been *one* of us, and not we together hand in fucking hand." Her throat still felt like rope coiled in sand since Ursade's abuse, and it hurt to talk above a raspy whisper. That icy bitch reminded Mayadeen way too much of her mother.

"Cap'n, say the word 'n' I'll strangle this Edish pigfucker, I will." Laddy peered toward Mayadeen through the rusted iron bars. With the wild look in his eyes, she half believed he could do it. One less Creyland Fenn would be a peerless gift to the world.

"Ye're not strangling anyone until we get out of here, damn ye. Now the both of ye shut up and let me think."

"Why'd they keep this little shit bird alive, anyway?" Creyland spoke to Mayadeen while regarding Laddy. "They slit the throats of my two mates, who each had a hell of a lot more to offer."

Laddy shot up and curled his fists. As he did so, another great smash from above rocked every wall in the jail block, forcing him back down on his bottom.

"Makes little difference now." Creyland half chuckled, waving off Laddy. "Instead we'll all be buried alive beneath a city that may as well not even exist." He lounged against the front corner of his cell where the archaic masonry swallowed the thick iron bars. "They'll sing about your lies from here to Hope's Horn should one of us live to tell the drunkards, Mayadeen."

True, Mayadeen fudged the truth about the whole business of sending a letter to Leweln that framed Ursade as Lusul's would-be assassin, embroiling the three sisters in a precarious state of political confusion. She'd also manufactured any personal connection to the Sister King in the south, Leweln, although that yarn was the easiest to spin since any pirate on the Nine could have pulled into Tyrport or New Scorprince if they'd the clots enough to do so. Mayadeen came up with most of it during the quiet feast at the farmhouse, based entirely, of course, on what Elona had gossiped of the longstanding animus between the sisters. Those machinations coupled with the *actual* note she had left for Lusul blossomed into a terrific conspiracy against Ursade, with Mayadeen as the sole conspirator. Of course, she couldn't diminish Prick's little role in the whole affair. She smirked to herself until Creyland's voice again interrupted her cheery thoughts.

"But I have to question ... how did you know Ursade would send emissaries to Lusul? And then for them to return without their heads?"

Mayadeen sighed. Her brain felt like it may as well have been a flaming boulder flung from one of those catapults. "I didn't. But I knew bloody well they'd not be coming back breathing. Wasn't expecting the theatrics, s'all."

"Ha, ha! You've the luck of legend, Mayadeen. You were my talisman then and by the gods you're my talisman now. A bonny trump if ever there was one!"

Another hollow smack penetrated from the beyond. Mayadeen began to wonder whether the city had any sort of magical defenses as there was no mistaking the sounds of stone hitting stone. Even bulwarks as old and stalwart as Valindrost's could only withstand so much punishment.

"And yet here we are," continued Creyland against all that was decent and considerate in the universe. "Though I'm not rightly sure which lies to blame, yours or our lovely Elona's? Funny that the nymph there turned out to be more treacherous than the two of us combined." He peered into the cell adjacent to Mayadeen's.

Although a wall divided them, Mayadeen knew Elona was housed there, and unlike the rest of them, Elona was shackled in clanking chains.

"You used me and I used you," came Elona's voice. It cracked at first, suggesting she was in extreme discomfort or even pain. "It was no more treacherous than that, you dirty thug."

"Oh, I'm the thug? You conniving little strumpet," accused Creyland. "I paid you to do a job and you didn't fucking do it."

"Which is likely the only reason you remain alive, Captain Fenn," returned Elona.

"So I should be thanking you?"

"We'll draw each other's blood anon, damn ye to the nine watery hells! By rights I should be clutchin' both yer drippin' gizzards." Mayadeen coughed and kicked the bars with her boot. She couldn't remember the last time she craved a murder more than she wanted a drink.

In truth, she'd hadn't much time to think about Elona's half-hearted betrayal. At the moment, it made nary a consequence. She felt for the pelitite crystal which still formed a lump at the top of her trousers. The witch guards had in fact searched her, and one had even grabbed the crystal and held it in a gloved hand. But like the strange business before in the Ragged Forest, the guard gave it back to Mayadeen almost as if not having found it in the first place. So much for being rid of the thing. She could try calling on the ancient bitch that lived in it, but she knew neither how to perform such a summons nor whether it would even work.

Mayadeen growled a sigh and let her back thud against the cool stone. "What we need is to get us out of here else we'll be accusing each other's ghosts from the grave," she said at last.

"Now see there? That's the Mayadeen I know well and wish I'd met in Ursade's great hall. A pragmatist. A leader of logic. A survivor!"

"And a killer that doesn't soon forget, ye preening cock whore," added Mayadeen.

She was done palavering with the likes of Creyland for the moment and shifted her attention to the hinged gate on her cell. It used a skeleton lock, so the pins would be rather simple to bypass. Unfortunately, there didn't appear to be a cursed thing within reach from which she could muster makeshift tension and lever picks.

"Mayadeen?" The voice was Elona's. "Mayadeen, you must know that I never meant for this to happen. I took Captain Fenn's offer only as a way of getting to you—"

"Red, no more on that. Not now."

Mayadeen glanced at Creyland who was laughing under his breath. The smug bastard never did know when to quit. Neither did Mayadeen when they were together, and it was those qualities that had dug a well of love filled with the water of hate. She curled her lip and clutched the iron bars so tightly that a searing pain shot through her bad hand. It had healed well enough, but the scar tissue would forever serve as a reminder of the misbegotten adventure, sort of like her history with Fenn.

Mayadeen shook away the past to focus on the present. The one witch guard standing at the mouth of the adjoining corridor seemed indifferent to their banter. They'd started with three of Ursade's witches watching over them, but two were summoned from their posts when the pummeling outside commenced.

"Red, can that one cipher the common tongue?"

"Some of it," replied Elona with a shortness of breath. "But she's in a contemplative state."

"Fuck are ye saying?"

"She ... she's holding my magic at bay."

"That so? With her gone could ye get us out of here? Melt away the bars or the like?"

"I wouldn't give her that much credit, Mayadeen," said Creyland. "You should see her, chained up like a marionette—"

A shockwave from above registered through the whole chamber. This time, several chunks of brick the size of grapefruits fell from the ceiling like hail.

Mayadeen assumed an awkward position face down with one arm protruding from the cell bars. She screamed and wailed as if in acute agony, all the while keeping her eye on the witch guard.

"Mayadeen?" shrieked Elona.

The guard snapped out of her white-eyed trance and started towards Mayadeen's little fit. "Levast ... levast ental?" said the blue-eyed witch with a pixie face.

She knelt down to Mayadeen who was now pretending to whimper.

"Vezla sikk, levast—"

Mayadeen's hand darted to the witch's throat and squeezed with the might of a krode beast's tentacle. She got to her haunches and then to her feet, bringing the flailing witch up with her. With a single and vicious motion, she used her free hand to dart out behind the witch's head only to smash that pixie face against the space between the bars.

Some blood trickled down the iron as she made sure the witch's breath was no more. Mayadeen felt the hair on her arms rise followed by a shudder down her spine. Perhaps the witch conjured some final magical defense only for it to be extinguished with the very life force that beckoned it. She released her stranglehold and the smaller woman flopped to the dirt floor. Mayadeen quickly groped at the yellow robes for a set of keys. Nothing.

"No keys on her?" marveled Creyland while dropping his head back. "By the gods—"

"Mayadeen? Mayadeen, what happened?" The voice was Elona's.

"The guard is no longer a problem," cut in Creyland who was now standing with his arms dangling through the bars of his own cell. "So it's time to do whatever it is you do before somebody remembers we're down here while the city's being razed."

Laddy, too, was up against the bars.

"Mayhap she'll surprise ye, feather cock," said Laddy to Creyland with a scowl. How the two hadn't yet come to fists escaped Mayadeen, but it was probably best considering Fenn knew some dirty tricks.

"Red," said Mayadeen at last. "Do what ye will. Smartly now."

There was a long exhale followed by a couple more deep breaths.

"Stand away from the cell doors," droned Elona as if her confidence was shackled alongside her.

Another clobbering came from above, but this time it sounded more distant, perhaps focused on the opposite side of the city.

Mayadeen's cell bars vibrated with a low buzzing. And then they shook within their centuries old iron joints. Creyland's and Laddy's did the same as both men back-stepped to the darkness of their ten square space.

Then whatever was happening stopped just as fast.

An exasperated groan carried from Elona's cell. "It's no use. I'm too ... I'm sorry."

Mayadeen placed her forehead against the bars. Something in her pocket seethed and simmered. It was the pelitite shard. Shorsas the Horny Ghost had probably been watching and listening the whole time. She might have considered coming to Mayadeen's aid when Ursade was choking the life from her. A real guardian angel was that Shorsas.

The iron bars on each cell contorted, shriveled and compressed like a snail doused with salt. The metal creaked and groaned and with a single deafening clang, the cage doors exploded outward off their hinges and slid to rest at the center of the prison chamber in a cloud of dust.

Mayadeen sprang from her confinement and whirled around to Elona's adjacent cell. The sorcerer hung limply from the chains and manacles supporting her arms on either side. Shorsas must have only possessed her long enough to perform the powerful sorcery. Mayadeen wanted to kill Elona as much as she wanted to embrace her. Perchance she'd do both.

Creyland and Laddy shuffled up from behind.

"Didn't think the nymph had anything like that in her," said Creyland.

"Find the key to these chains," Mayadeen growled to them without turning.

"Oh, for pity's sake, leave her."

Mayadeen moved fast and low enough to lodge her shoulder into Creyland's stomach with a bull rush, lifting him off his feet and delivering him to the dirt just inches from the pile of twisted metal behind.

"If I'd a blade, we'd be trudging through a swamp of yer guts presently, Crey Fenn. Pray to yer useless gods I don't find me one."

Laddy, scouring the cell block for a key, guffawed.

Flat on his back, Creyland snatched for the breath knocked out of him and slowly lifted himself to his elbows.

"Things should never have gone awry between us, Mayadeen. I should've never let it happen. You're more womaner than every overgrown galley in the Warlands combined."

Mayadeen smiled and walked over to pick up a piece of sharp iron severed from the pile of broken cage doors.

"Won't be needing a blade after all." In an instant she stood over Creyland with the jagged edge of the bar pointed at his unshaven neck.

"Wait," Creyland croaked, the sneer now absent from his voice. "You'll be finding nothing at the Southern Isles without *me*."

Mayadeen simpered. "I've Bon Shemble's maps to memory, ye conceited monkey. Don't need ye for bilge swabbin'."

"You mean the maps from Minnow Baels?"

Mayadeen gritted her teeth. Seemed there really was no end to Creyland's machinations. More important, however, was where his ended and Elona's began. Pirates were always trying to outdo each other after all. But the sorcerer's intentions were yet to be fully disclosed.

"Aye, aye, the maps from Baels, damn ye. So ye sent that stunted lil' grotesque after me?"

"Well, yes and no—"

"Fuck ye say?" Mayadeen wrung her grips over the bar doing everything in her power not to kill him too soon. She needed answers.

"What ... what I mean is, yes, I sent him your way at High Island. But I knew for a bloody fact he wasn't going to come back from it." Creyland thought for a moment. "Then again I'm surprised he didn't just take the false maps I gave him and run."

"False maps?"

"Those maps I gave Minnow Baels were sham, Mayadeen. I've got the true ones."

"Of course ye do, Fenn. Ever and all to save yer pretty skin. One thing I'll say for ol' Minnow Baels is *he* paid the price of ghosts—a price ye've been dodging for decades, ye dirty bilge rat."

"Now I did us both a favor with Baels—"

Mayadeen pressed the edge into his neck enough to draw a trickle of blood.

"The winds with that cursed runt and yer maps!" She looked back at Elona. Laddy, having somehow sussed out a key ring, removed her shackles and was trying to gently slap her awake. "What was *her* role in yer ploy, damn ye? Or have ye been behind the whole ploughin' affair yerself?" She pressed the edge even harder and Creyland's tongue hung out for a moment.

"No, no ... hear me out ... She ... She brought your ship here through a magician's means ... a ... a ... portal," stammered Creyland. "I found her in the Thresnare over a year ago. Or rather ... she found me."

A great rumble from above shook the prison walls once more.

"Cap'n, we should leave," urged Laddy while cradling Elona. "I can tow Elona, methinks."

Mayadeen nodded at Laddy and then focused back on Creyland. How she wanted to drive his brains into the dirt. But if what he said about the maps were true, she could very well have problems navigating the Southern Isles once back on course. If nothing else, Creyland was resourceful, and Mayadeen's chances at procuring a vessel and finally bidding the Warlands Main a fond "fuck ye and die" could increase twenty-fold if she played the practical companion.

Her hands squeezed and twisted on the bar. She saw the fear in Creyland's eyes, and it was just as well. For if it hadn't been there, Mayadeen would have skewered him where he lay.

"Jagger, Yolton ... my entire crew! All drowned or worse. Was that yer plan, damn ye? Tell me true, Fenn, or I'll fuck yer wits with this iron—"

"No! No, that all ... all happened by chance. The plan was to displace your ship to the coast of Rul ... much ... much farther south than where you landed. I ... I was to meet you there with my offer. I fully expected your ship and crew intact ... is why I brought three of my own schooners for the parlay ... I swear it. That cursed magician ... Elona ... did everything else herself. That's why I came to Valindrost ... no easy task as you could attest to yourself."

"What deal did ye strike up with Ursade then?"

Creyland hesitated. "The ... the beginning of an alliance with Edenvane. I spoke for Stitwell and his pathetic rebellion and was paid nicely for every word. Edenvane would send Ursade fresh recruits from the Thresnare and Ursade would provide gradual access to the mainland of Rul. The intent was to start a ground war with Lusul and the Rullites. Of course, thanks to you, Emerald Eye, things have now changed a bit."

Emerald Eye. That was one she hadn't heard for a long time. And yet she remembered when that endearment once meant something to her.

"Ye're a fool for trustin' these magicians, Fenn—a sad excuse for a scalawag."

"You trusted one yourself."

"Never by my own choosing, ye blight fish. And ye've buggered me rougher'n that bull shaft of yers could ever have done."

Mayadeen saw the frown in his eyes. Creyland wasn't a man of regrets, but this botched betrayal he would take to his grave.

"If Baels' maps were sham, then tell me where I might be finding the real maps."

"I stashed them," replied Creyland.

Mayadeen again pierced his neck with the point.

"I ... I burned them. My first mate was an ambitious little shitbird. The other two captains were mercenaries—cowards wouldn't step foot ashore Rul but would bound off for the Southern Isles in a fart and a wink. Couldn't risk it." Creyland grinned halfway. "You know well I committed every line of those maps to memory, Mayadeen, just like you would. Only difference is what I've got is exactly what ol' Bon Shemble inked with her own hands."

Mayadeen retracted the sharp metal point from Creyland's neck and watched the relief wash over him.

"Let's get back to the brine and put all of this to our lee," said Creyland while propping up again on his elbows. "The Southern Isles have been calling us for years, Emerald Eye. We were fools to have waited even this long. We'll assemble a new crew, me and you. Meridians, like before. To hell with Stitwell and my people."

Tarn Stitwell had proclaimed himself *King* of his people in direct opposition to the Island Realm and every other politically recognized trade power in the world. Beyond that absurd and pitiful fact, Mayadeen had given exactly zero thought to him. Fenn really was lost.

"If ever I see ye alive again, Crey Fenn, mayhap we'll finish this talk. And don't ye fucking call me Emerald Eye." She batted him in the temple with the blunt end of the bar.

Creyland fell back limp to the dirt.

Mayadeen crossed to Laddy. Elona was still out. The pounding above hadn't ceased.

"Sling her over a shoulder. We push off before the city is sacked."

XII
CITY OF LIGHTS

*The smallest of our covens could match a thousand of your fighters,
unless of course they were Rullite fighters.*
~ Gramms the War Witch

Mayadeen took the sulfurous night air first, slapdash weapon in hand. Laddy followed with Elona draped over his shoulder—she was small enough for him to carry with little trouble. They exited the prison by way of a guard tower at the interior base of the city's forty foot retaining wall. Most of the sconces and torchlights had been quenched, likely to give the witches the added cover of darkness should the wall be breached. Many voices called out through the adjoining yard and the feral din of Lusul's savages could be heard from beyond the bulwark.

Though they surfaced from a different exit than how they entered the dungeon prison earlier in the day, Mayadeen had taken note of the way Valindrost was classically situated: back to the mountainside with Ursade's castle aft of the interior and everything else on a gradual declining sprawl to the main gate.

The sky was clear, despite an intermittent haze of dust and black smoke. Mayadeen ciphered from the stars they were on the north east side, which placed them within half a mile's hike to the main gate. Why a dungeon jail would have been positioned so close to the wall remained a mystery, and Mayadeen decided magic would mitigate such an oversight in security.

She peered straight up the high battlements, but couldn't see much activity from her angle. Every now and then something would flash and light up the night, followed by a rush of yells from the outside. All of the individual pieces of a siege were here, but none of them fit into the same puzzle. Indeed, despite the occasional pounding from Lusul's catapults, there was something strange in general about this attack Mayadeen couldn't quite lash down.

"I need to get a better eye from aloft," she said to Laddy. "Ye stay with Red and try to wake her. We need a way out of the city. A couple ponies would do us well, or mayhap she can conjure one o' her gyrating light doors."

Laddy nodded. "Aye, Cap'n." He carefully set Elona down and propped her backfirst against the cool stone. "If ye ain't back in half a wind, I'll be sussing ye out, I will."

"That so?" Mayadeen scowled in the darkness, but her brow softened just as fast. Laddy found his courage these past days, and he'd follow his Captain to the cold, black depths if that's where she'd take him. He was as resilient and loyal as he was thick and ignorant. He also happened to be the last remaining member of her former crew. The thought of it still hadn't entirely made anchorage in Mayadeen's head. And, yet again, there was no time to deal with such an unprecedented loss.

"Just ye get her awake, and mind ye keep to the shadows," continued Mayadeen. She placed a hand on Laddy's knotty shoulder. "We'll be outta this yet, Laddy my trump."

With that she crept back to the guard tower entrance while keeping close to the wall. Just when she started to question why she was skulking, four of Ursade's witches scuttled right by her from around a jutting buttress. They were in a hurry, though one would never guess it with their ever saturnine faces and seeming inability to turn a patter into a run. That's what made the whole damn business so strange, whereby Lusul's army of blood-thirsty heathens may as well have been laying siege to a monastery occupied by walking emotionless constructs. If Lusul sacked Valindrost, it might not prove as rewarding as she would hope.

After the witches passed, Mayadeen skirted to the large wooden door and slipped inside. She assumed the spiraling steps at the vestibule ascended to the top of the wall, and so she proceeded.

Provided she hadn't cuffed Crey Fenn too hard for any permanent damage, Mayadeen reckoned the pretty scoundrel would soon be returning to his senses. She might have ended him if it were not for that damnable seed he planted discrediting Baels' maps. No different from herself, Fenn always knew how to leverage the bluff when it meant securing his next sunrise. But the salt in the bleeding arse was the fact that this time the conniving cockcrab may not have been bluffing.

It felt as though she'd climbed five stories before reaching another door that finally led to the battlements. The thuds, clanks and yells from outside sounded clearer from this vantage point, and Mayadeen cracked the inward opening door just enough to gather a glimpse. The wall ran for well over a hundred feet before bobbing shadows danced with hurried purpose to great bursts of bluish light.

Mayadeen stepped out and peered over the merlons of the battlements. Lusul's bitch horde swarmed the open farmland leading into the city, the hollering heathens easily recognizable by their scant yet varied armor and costuming, even under cloak of night. Mayadeen suddenly felt for the witch peasants who had cooked them all that delicious meal earlier in the day. Now those poor women were likely themselves being cooked to feed Rullite cannibals.

She may have brought disaster to Ursade's little magical utopia, it was true, but by the gods high and low, this was war, and so far it seemed to be the only language the Sister Kings of Warlands Main truly shared.

Her thoughts were interrupted by a streak of lingering lightning that lashed out from the battlements to the rushing army below. Two others followed in rapid succession while a cluster of Rullite warriors were scattered about into the sky from the spot where the bolts exploded beneath them.

"Haha! Fie ye charging monkeys," exclaimed Mayadeen. Now she understood why Lusul's ladder teams failed to claim the parapets. Who needed gunpowder and fancy bombards when you had weather-wielding witches to rain their fury on the vanguard? Perhaps Ursade didn't even need archers, although the mere thought of not having them for a city's defenses seemed remiss.

Mayadeen crept further along the battlements when something else caught her eye.

"What devilry—"

A glowing amber mist began to envelop one of the high spires of Ursade's monolithic keep in Valindrost's upper interior. Soon most of the city was aglow with its ghostly beacon. Mixed with the bursts of unnatural blues from the conjurers on the wall along with the occasional arcing fireball from Lusul's catapults, the whole scene resembled something one would hallucinate upon while fuming a chaw of expensive pipe leaf.

An object clattered on the stone scarps just feet ahead of Mayadeen. It was a ladder, and a growling head emerged from its crest. Almost instinctively Mayadeen met the helmet with a downward swing of her iron. The loud crunch was followed by a few shouts from further below, and the Rullite who just absorbed the blow kept coming and fumbled a bloodstained hand over the squared precipice.

Mayadeen brought her iron back for another go.

"Ye big ... dumb ... bitch!" This time the iron came sideways and smashed the womaner right between the eyes. Her head jerked backward. She paused mid-air as if levitating at the wall before falling out of sight. There was another clank and angry shouts from whoever else was making their way up from below her.

Mayadeen could have stood there splitting noggins all night as two more ladders found the battlements. But she'd seen enough, and it was time to get back to Laddy and Elona.

When she ran back to the guard tower door, the amber mist enshrouding the castle tower grew much larger and brighter, now with smaller orbs of light spiraling around it and rising like bubbles in a bottle of ale. Mayadeen flung open the door with little care this time and hurried down the winding steps. She came again to the empty yard and scanned the shadows closest the wall.

Before she could open her mouth to call Laddy's name, a massive ball of flame careened directly overhead and crashed into a small tower on the far side of the courtyard. Mayadeen shielded herself as wood and stone embers showered in her direction. The yard and adjacent wall were now lit up orange by the aftermath.

Laddy lay curled against the stone with no sign of Elona.

#

"What happened, damn ye?"

Minutes passed before Mayadeen was able to bring Laddy from his simple dreams.

He blinked a few times and rubbed the back of his head.

"Fenn ... Fenn, it was. Edish bastard came back, Cap'n."

Mayadeen reckoned Fenn would continue to be a thorn in her pale arse, but she didn't think he would recover so quickly. Curse him for ever having slithered back into her game.

"Where's the nymph then?" she asked.

"Fenn found us just as Elona was coming to. I took a swing at 'im and he rapped me on my head. The bloody coward was armed."

And yet Fenn hadn't killed him. The relentless scoundrel must have still held out hopes for Mayadeen's alliance. Now he held a ransom besides, although Mayadeen was seriously considering cutting her losses with Elona, with or without answers to so many course-altering questions.

"Get up, smartly now. We need to gather an exit."

A splintering crash could be heard from further down the wall.

"Lusul's made it to the gates," said Mayadeen as she scooped Laddy to his feet with her free hand. "With me, damn ye, and stay close."

Valindrost was ready to fall, and Mayadeen could smell its fate on the burning night air. But short of climbing down one of the enemy's ladders on the other side of the wall or walking through the main gate, she knew no other way out of the city. She wasn't even certain whether the witches maintained a stables. After all, their spectacular methods of transport didn't require horses.

She turned sharp to notice the first Rullite ape making her way from the guard tower. Two more followed, and they all carried their favored axe-like weapons. For them, the bolted plank door at the top of the tower must have been like a curtain of dried leaves.

The first Rullite spotted her and yelled out.

Mayadeen readied her iron bar. The Rullite started into a sprint and raised her axe while a single horseman rode up fast from behind her. A sword reflected in the firelight and slashed the back of the charging Rullite's neck. With a surprised howl her hulking frame pitched forward into the dirt. Mayadeen handed her iron bar to Laddy and picked up the fallen Rullite's double-bladed axe that landed a mere span from her boots. The horseman turned for another pass.

Mayadeen recognized his smug features.

"Fenn, ye bloody fiend!" Somehow he'd procured a horse, which meant she would just have to pluck him off it.

But the next Rullite already closed the distance and swung her large maul. Mayadeen flinched back, feeling the wind of the thing on her forehead. The counter blow came from Laddy, who smashed the Rullite's kneecap with the iron bar. The warrior grunted and folded just long enough for Mayadeen to sink the heavy axe into her ribcage.

The third Rullite, wearing some sparse plate armor and wielding two crudely shaped scimitars, held her ground, probably waiting for reinforcements. Mayadeen kept an eye on her while trying to dislodge the axe from the other. She succeeded at last only to be spattered by a smelly glob of blood.

"Emerald Eye," called out Fenn. "This way."

He was too far out of reach for Mayadeen to attempt to dismount him.

"Laddy, let's follow the bastard," she growled over her shoulder.

"Follow 'im, Cap'n? Him?"

"Aye, aye, damn ye. We haven't a pusing choice. Move!" She kicked Laddy with the side of her boot and he stumbled begrudgingly in Creyland's direction.

Mayadeen hadn't taken her eyes off of the second Rullite and took several steps backward. When she was satisfied the other wouldn't pursue, she dashed towards where Fenn awaited, his small stallion dancing in circles.

"First smart choice you've made all night," cracked Creyland before winking and moving his horse to little more than a trot.

That blow to his head must have damaged his brain, for Mayadeen's arch nemesis was even more persistent than she could have anticipated. But she knew he was only out to save his own soft hide, although the deranged scalawag was merely decreasing his chances of survival while in her company.

The three of them made their way across the blazing courtyard; Mayadeen glancing back over her shoulder several times to discern whether or not any enemies gave chase. The sounds of battle and panic blared less on that far side of the city's interior, and the tremendous light emanating from the citadel cast harsh shadows over the dwellings and ancient structures below. Creyland's route kept them close to the wall, though they needed to cross at least two thoroughfares, both of which granted spectacular views of the violence down the grade to the main gates.

After running what seemed like half a league, Mayadeen noticed Creyland cut his steed sharply around a buttress. The slippery snake kept a good berth ahead of them, so at no point had there been a chance to snatch Creyland from his saddle. Almost completely out of breath, Mayadeen at last heard the sounds of neighing and nervous stammering. Never was she so grateful for the stench of hay and manure to assault her nostrils.

Creyland stopped his horse and turned to face them.

"Off that pony, ye fucking peacock," challenged Laddy before Mayadeen could get a word through catching breaths.

Creyland smirked. "You know, I could have ended you, boy."

"So let's end it!" Laddy postured forward and Mayadeen pushed him back with a swat of her arm.

"Where's Elona, Fenn? I'll cut that pony in two with ye on it." With the axe she held she felt she could've carried through on the threat.

"I'm here," came Elona's voice as she stepped out from behind a wooden partition. She had donned padded black leather armor in place of the skimpy cuirass worn in Lusul's custody, with a crimson hooded cloak thrown over. Sleek metallic gauntlets now covered both of her hands, the craftsmanship detailed enough to allow for segments down each of her slender fingers whilst honing to talons for added effect.

"Where'd ye get those?" grumbled Mayadeen.

"From exactly where I left them. I used to spend a lot of time here and knew well the hostler."

"Ye look like a leather-wrapped candlestick."

"Thanks." Elona pointed to an equipment rack. "Will those do?"

Mayadeen's scowl softened to see a rack loaded with swords and daggers of all shapes and sizes. They were in fact the first civilized weapons she'd seen since washing ashore. Laddy, whose blood had rushed right out of his face to his pecker upon Elona's dramatic entrance, was still gawking.

"Reef yer tongue," said Mayadeen to Laddy while nudging him in the gut. She pointed him to the weapons rack then spun back around to Creyland. "We ain't done, Fenn."

"We will be if you don't haul fucking wind," said Creyland. He wiped a nice trickle of blood from above his eye.

Mayadeen's lips turned up into a snarl. If she was fast, she could have the Edish prickhard off of his horse and under her boot...

"He's right that we have to hurry," urged Elona.

Creyland Fenn wasn't worth them all dying over. Mayadeen breathed deep. "Linger at yer peril then."

"Valindrost wasn't always a closed city," explained Elona while moving to one of the horse stalls. "It used to play host to merchants and tradesmen from beyond the western mountain ranges. Weapons were never allowed and would be confiscated. Genevaise, who ran these stables, collected quite a cache over the years."

"Laddy, get ye a blade." Mayadeen crossed to the rack. "Or two." She quickly scanned the weapons, many of them hanging from their own belts and scabbards. One rig that caught her interest held a rather plain rapier with twin daggers holstered at the small of the back. She withdrew the rapier and judged its balance and temper. It wasn't clouded steel, but steel nonetheless.

"Mayadeen," called Elona who brought her chosen horse forward while stroking its nose. "I suggest you choose your mounts."

Mayadeen fit the holster rig in place and cinched the belt strap around her hips. She'd lost at least an inch in her time aground and was beginning to feel like a moon strumpet. A flat belly was a wasted belly.

"Yer always in such a hurry, Red." She sideglanced at Creyland, who now rubbed the purple egg forming on the side of his head. "Why did ye run off with Fenn?" she said in a lower tone, her hand now clutching the hilt of the holstered rapier.

Elona gulped. Apparently, she didn't miss the threat. "Fenn ran off with me. We're not working together, Mayadeen. Please believe that much." She moved her gaze to Creyland. "He was going to take me back to Ursade until I informed him that I know a way out of this city other than the main gates through a secret smuggler's tunnel. Then I told him I'd burn him alive if he didn't take a horse back to find and retrieve both you and Laddy."

"Well ain't ye just the charitable one." Mayadeen relaxed her grip. She at least would need Elona alive to escape the city. Even Fenn knew that much. She pulled some errant strands of her straight black hair away from her face. Yet again she hadn't inherited one of her mother's nicer traits that was the coarse, wavy hair more conducive to the elements. She was never a fan of ponytails but didn't mind the occasional head rag to keep the thin black stuff out of the way during high winds at sea. She tied one off now using a faded red cloth, probably used for wiping the horses' arses.

"Why are we wasting time?" Creyland didn't look amused at having been blackmailed by a witch; just as Mayadeen wasn't amused the haughty bastard was in their presence with sword and horse.

She was trying to think quickly about how to do something about that fact when one of Elona's palms shot up in Creyland's direction. With a melting sigh, Creyland dropped his long sword and slumped over in the saddle.

Mayadeen glanced back at Elona. "New trick, have ye?"

"No, but that's the first time I've gotten it to work." Elona scrutinized her fancy gauntlets.

Mayadeen walked over and grabbed a coil of rope from a stable door hook.

"Laddy," she tossed it over to him. "Tie 'im up good and well to his saddle. We'll take Fenn with us."

"Aye, Cap'n," returned Laddy with a frown. "And then what?"

"I ain't yet decided and ain't in the mood for fucking questions. Just get it done. Truss him up like a pig for all I care."

Mayadeen strode to the stalls and looked the horses over. They appeared to be well cared for, but unlike the hearty mounts from Lusul's camp, these nervous creatures were not war hardened. Her Pap, a skilled rider, taught her to always take geldings over stallions or mares for even temperament. Funny that same counsel would apply largely to crewing her ships. She found one grey gelding already with tack and settled for a chestnut mare for Laddy's mount. She figured he was already accustomed to dealing with irritable women.

Mayadeen handed the gelding's reins to Elona and then grabbed a plain saddle off the wall for Laddy's mare.

"What about food and drink?" Mayadeen asked Elona while throwing the seat over the chestnut and tightening the belt twice.

"I grabbed what I could from the storeroom, and it's not much. Some bread, cheese and tinklenuts are all we've got along with three water jugs. We'll be traversing grasslands mainly. We're on our own now, Mayadeen."

An explosion rocked the stables from somewhere further down the wall. A distant cheer sounded followed by war cries and scattered screams.

"Lusul's made it through," warned Mayadeen.

"That was the plan," returned Elona. "It's time for us to go."

#

They emerged from the underground tunnel along a spur nearly a hundred feet up the mountain's south face. The beacon rising from Valindrost's tallest tower was a familiar sight—a pulsating rainbow of colors slithering around a brilliant yet soft core of white light.

Mayadeen shielded her eye while the beacon suddenly grew to engulf the entire city. The low hum became an ear shattering buzz. Mayadeen's mount reared up to resist the pull from the great rift, even from that distance.

For a brief moment the night turned to day, and then day back to night.

No light. No sound.

No Valindrost.

Part Three

XIII
DAMNED BLOOD

Call it what ye will, but the magicians' blood is a curse. Only devilry
and fell tidings can come of it. 'Tis why the witches made such a mess
o' things in the old tales. 'Tis why the Isles got rid of 'em.
> ~ A Meridian fisherman to a foreigner

"Crabs. Fucking crabs." Mayadeen stomped her boot on one of the little devils and it cracked like an egg. For some odd reason, the mountain pass they'd been crossing for the past two days was infested with the eight-legged crawlers no bigger than common field rats. Most unsettling, however, was they resembled crabs found on the seashore.

"How can there be crabs with not an ocean for a thousand leagues?"

"I've found them rather savory, myself," said Creyland as he stretched out his bound wrists over his head.

"That so?" snapped Mayadeen. "Well, why don't ye tell 'em to crawl back into yer breeches, Fenn?"

Laddy laughed before picking up and tossing one of the crabs at Creyland.

Creyland slapped it away. "Don't think these cuffs would keep me from throwing you off this mountain, boy."

"And don't think ye wouldn't be following 'im," said Mayadeen.

Creyland sulked.

It gave Mayadeen satisfaction to know she was finally rankling his rudder. She'd supposed on the first day of their crossing the Shadowmurk Mountains it wasn't necessary to keep him tied stomach-first over horse and saddle. So instead she shackled Creyland's wrists in front so he could walk and piss but would have trouble doing much else. They traveled single file with Elona on point, followed by Laddy, Creyland and Mayadeen on anchor.

Now on day three of their meandering where the mountain's ascent plateaued, Mayadeen wondered whether escaping Valindrost had been the best course of action. Maybe Ursade and her capable brood of fallow followers moved the city to a coastal region? Or perhaps it was moved straight to eternal hell. Either would have been better than the crab-infested, craggy, cold terrain they'd been negotiating—the majority on foot since they didn't want to risk injury to their mounts. Seemed even when Mayadeen had a pony she couldn't use the reeking thing for all it was intended.

"Here's as good a place to rest for the night as any," said Elona, who for the better part of the journey was quieter than Laddy.

Elona had a lot to account for since her treachery in Ursade's court, and it was high time she paid for her passage. Indeed, Mayadeen watched closely her routine as a magician. In the early mornings Elona would start fresh out of her strange meditative states. As the day progressed, she would grow weary at random intervals, as if something unseen was sucking her breath and draining her vitality. Then came the lighting of the evening's campfire. Elona would have no trouble performing the trick which would instantly and unwaveringly bring flame to wood or grass. But the unnatural act would fatigue her, and she would just as instantly and unwaveringly refresh with water and snack. Mayadeen had witnessed it often enough, such as when Elona had set the Forest Dweller ablaze and after she had put Creyland to sleep—the act of magic, no matter how small, would tax Elona to her very core.

"Aye. We'll bed here tonight," replied Mayadeen, trying to keep her lips from turning up into a smile. She clutched the pelitite crystal that now dangled from her neck. She'd found ample time to fashion a necklace out of it using rawhide strings removed from one of her saddle bags. She wrapped it well on both ends so that it wouldn't slip from its leather carriage while lying horizontal on the low part of her chest. Although Mayadeen had yet to reveal the truth about the relic, she figured Elona gathered her own suspicions of what happened that night in the Ragged Forest, and again in the dungeons of Valindrost. Yet Mayadeen remained determined not to call upon the ancient power unless the need arose and spared no other choice.

"Laddy," she continued while still watching Elona. "Fetch us more of them cursed crabs for sup." She turned to the scalawag and gave him a nod.

Laddy frowned and glanced back at Creyland. "Aye, Cap'n."

#

As the sun sank behind the farthest reaching peak to the west, part of yet another mountain range known as the Sky Pass, Mayadeen's plans for the night's events were already in motion. Everyone was exhausted, which made sense in light of all of the walking as opposed to riding during the day's journey. As was routine, Elona gestured the campfire into being, and just as the previous two nights, they'd dined on the small yet bountiful mountain crabs.

"Red," whispered Mayadeen into Elona's ear after their supper and the night grew cold and dark, "I think ye should put Laddy to slumber tonight along with Fenn."

Elona's brow shot up. "Do you feel that's necessary?"

"Aye. The bull's had trouble sleeping. He's told me as much."

Elona looked in Laddy's direction and sighed. "Well, if he's approved, then I'll help."

"He's approved if I've approved," assured Mayadeen.

"Be wary, Laddy, as the women conspire," said Creyland from the other end of the campfire. Mayadeen thought watching him bring the cooked crab to his mouth with shackled hands was akin to watching a sea otter play with a clam.

Laddy looked back and forth between them. Mayadeen was certain neither of them could make out her whispers.

"Ah, but Laddy knows well I don't conspire," Mayadeen said with a wink at Laddy.

To Creyland she said, "No need for secrets when I just tell ye fuckin' bilge whores how it'll be."

Laddy chuckled while Creyland scoffed.

"If old Stitswell back in Edenvane could only have met you, Emerald Eye. Ha! He'd be thinking twice before sending a fleet into the Island Realm."

"A fleet says ye? A fleet of painted turds? Shitswell has no call putting boats in the brine. We should've crushed yer pathetic homeland years ago when we were puking all over it from the bad rum. Humph. Bulls and gelds placing crowns on each other's heads. Yer womeners have grown soft and senseless to allow it."

Creyland shook his head. "No gelds in Edenvane. All of the men keep their stones. And our females appreciate a man for what he can do, not just what seed he can offer for making babies."

"Well ain't that sweet," said Mayadeen. "Sounds like one big festival of cock goop. Might even be fun for a day or two, until the bulls start using their tongues to speak."

Creyland snickered. Then he suddenly slumped over to the ground. Laddy was already out cold. Sometimes Elona would work her magic without so much as a sound or gesture. Unnerving as that sorcery was, Mayadeen knew it took everything out of Elona.

Now all she had to to do was to watch and to wait.

#

The frigid night grew tense and the horses sputtered restlessly. Laddy slept with his head propped sideways on the small seat of his brown leather saddle. Mayadeen situated him that way after Elona's instant spell took effect. Creyland, however, was left to slump with his cheek in the dirt and his arse held skyward. He'd have a gnarled crick in his neck come morning.

Elona lounged next to the fire, her eyes half open.

Mayadeen stood up. She walked over to the petite sorcerer who claimed the Meridian Isles as her place of birth.

"Need ye on the crow's nest, Red. On the uptake, bright and savvy now."

"Oh. Can't I take the twilight watch?"

Mayadeen took last watch into morning each night since they'd attempted the mountain pass. She'd shuffled the duty so as to watch over Creyland in case he got it in his head to run.

"Nay," said Mayadeen while extending her hand.

Elona placed her hand in Mayadeen's with a sigh. Mayadeen's other hand wrapped around her throat. She lifted Elona to slam her into an abutting rock face.

Elona's hands went up as if to cast a spell, but Mayadeen saw the fear and hesitation in her eyes.

"Don't ye devise it, Red," growled Mayadeen through gritted teeth. "Ye put me to flame and we burn together. Ye put me to slumber, well then ye best kill me where I lay 'cause I'll run ye through when I wake."

Elona struggled. "Pl-please—"

"Please yerself! Not many have crossed me, and even fewer've lived long enough to forget it. Here and now ye tell all with not a lie amidst." Mayadeen brought Elona's panicked face closer to her own. "Damn ye, I'll know, too." She clutched the crystal around her neck and shook it. "I'll know by the power of this pelitite."

Elona flinched. "What is that? What do you—"

"The ancient witch ye spoke of during our bonny frolic through the Ragged Forest. None other than yer own dear Shorsas!"

Elona's eyes widened.

"No. No, you can't use that—"

Mayadeen firmed her grip on Elona's throat and pressed her harder against the rock. The latter shuddered and began to choke.

"I can and will, ye haughty strumpet. Better speak true, Red ... I'll be wringin' naught but yer spine in seconds."

"Sister ..." Elona gurgled the word. "I ... I'm your—"

"Sister? Sister to me?" Mayadeen chortled. She eased her grip but kept her arm as taut as a pry bar. "I've so many bastard sisters I mayhap drowned one along the way without e'er knowing it. Sister, says ye—"

"Not by your father's half." Elona gasped for a breath and slit her eyes. "But by your mother's."

Mayadeen felt her mouth open, but nothing came out right away. By her Pap's seed it never mattered, for his strong bloodline was chosen to commingle with as many Daughter born lineages of the Island Realm as possible, including that of the great Mabelia Damned. To give birth to a boy was forgiven, two boys tolerated. But only the daughter, the first daughter, was allowed to carry her mother's name. With the rare exception of twin daughters— considered a divine dispensation—a second daughter was not allowed, especially by an Elder. Such was known in the Isles as heir not the second, whereby if the first heir to a lineage died on her way to fulfill that lineage, then the lineage itself ceased to be worthy to continue. The Damned lineage had lasted 127 years and counting.

"Ain't possible," said Mayadeen while trying not to sound unsure. "Yer a bloody sorcerer for one!"

"Yes ..." Elona stuttered, "Yes, my father was Edish but hailed from the Thresnare."

"Name, damn ye."

"Tolis. Tolis of Ranmir."

"Talos, Tellis ... never heard of the peacock." Mayadeen thought for a moment. "How many years have ye?"

"Thirty two ... Thirty three in little more than a fortnight."

"Aha! I've thirty four years myself. By the gods high and low and damn them all, ye think I'd not known if my own serpent mother was with child?"

"At two years old?"

"Fie ye, galley! Ye wrecked my entire vessel. I've weathered a thousand storms. I thought for days how that one was any different. 'Twas yer own devilry that brought me here!"

"It should have worked," said Elona. "Your ship should have made it through that portal intact."

"Aye, the ship got through, fool of a lousy nymph. 'N' so did the bloody krode beast yer magic lured from the depths!"

Elona averted her gaze. Tears streamed clean rivulets down her dusty cheeks.

"Seems Fenn was tellin' the truth 'bout something. Why, Red? Why all the deceit? Why'd ye bring me here ashore? Here beyond all salt and sea?" Mayadeen pursed her lips. She just wanted to squeeze Elona's reed-hollow neck until she could make a fist.

"Because there was no other way," croaked Elona. "You'd have laughed me off of your ship even if I could have gotten an audience with the feared and fearless Captain Mayadeen Damned. By your own account you probably would have drowned me. You think it was easy all of those years I spent in Edenvane and the Thresnare? Whoring myself out for food in the one and being spat on as an impurity in the other?"

If Elona was telling the truth about her plight, then being known as an impurity in the Thresnare would not have gone well for her. Those who claimed to have the Sinbalak but could not prove their claim to the exotic bloodline through family heritage were shunned as impostors and labeled as impurities. Mayadeen's concern, however, was the much larger implication that there would be only one way Elona could have such an unfortunate lineage.

Mayadeen released her choke hold and Elona slunk to her knees.

"So that's what ye're about, Elona, or whatever mayhap ye're called. Out to accuse my mother a witch and me a witch's brood? Ye've salt I'll give ye. But ye've proof of naught."

Mayadeen's hand moved to the hilt of one of the daggers holstered at the small of her back.

"And now, for yer own part in sinking my vessel, scattering my crew and killing my friend, Jagger, I'm gonna to spill yer cursed blood all over this waste of a main."

"But I do have proof ... please."

Mayadeen hesitated.

"It was with Ursade at Valindrost. I have the proof," whimpered Elona.

Mayadeen never did see such a pathetic sight as the desperate and determined womaner who now groveled before her. And yet this sorcerer who'd risked her own life as well as the lives of so many others seemed to plead her mission in earnest.

"What proof? On my lee, tell it smart and tell it true. Or else I'll gut ye, Red. I'll gut ye and call it even."

"A letter ... a scroll ... written by our mother's hand and sealed by her crest. I was to be sent to Valindrost as soon as I was named. There's more to all of it, Mayadeen, and I'll tell you everything I know. But trust me when I say that our mother knew her secret would be forever untouched in the Warlands Main. Perhaps it's the only reason she allowed me to live."

This information, whether the truth or an intricate lie, landed like a direct hit by one of those flaring metal balls on a forecastle poop. It was all too much to grapple, and suddenly Mayadeen felt exhausted. The answer to one question opened the floodgate to a thousand more. Confound this cursed little fool of a nymph for ever having pursued such a treacherous and impossible course of birthright. She should've kept to wetting bull shanks and telling fortunes on the streets of Thresnare, or at the very least been satisfied with her better fortunes among the witches of Valindrost.

Mayadeen pushed the dagger back into its sheath, the blade having been halfway revealed. Instead, her hand went to the rawhide strap around her neck and produced the pelitite shard from beneath her jerkin.

Elona's eyes widened to allow another pool of tears to spill.

"Shorsas," grumbled Mayadeen while rubbing the crystal betwixt her fingers.

"No. No, please, Mayadeen. Can't you see? That crystal shard is dangerous. The soul within it will continue to—"

"Shorsas." Mayadeen glared at Elona.

Elona sniveled and began to weep. "Mayadeen, listen to me! Ursade sensed its power ... I ... no, I can—"

"Shorsas, damn ye!"

On the third calling of the ancient's moniker, Elona collapsed at Mayadeen's feet. Whether she'd done so out of her own hysterics or by possession would remain to be witnessed. Mayadeen hadn't yet willingly called upon the fabled stone that was given her by one of those creatures from the Ragged Forest, and she'd continued to wonder whether her experience in those haunted woods was entirely lucid—as if those three days and two nights of her abstract journey were one long rum holiday.

Elona's eyes opened, and this time the silvery orbs were already present. Indeed, the magic of the violet crystal glowed and rang sure as the clink from a clouded steel blade.

"Ah, yes," Shorsas gasped, her eyes closing and opening again.

Mayadeen likened the reaction to breaching a water's surface after having been under for as long as the breath would allow.

Shorsas turned onto her elbows in a lounging position. "You should speak quickly, child, for I've not the strength to linger."

Mayadeen's fists clenched. Perhaps she'd just be done with both of them—Elona and Shorsas—with one swift crack of the neck.

"If ye're so bloody weak, then what good are ye? Decrepit nymph!"

Shorsas's face grew dark and her brow furled beyond anything Elona herself could have exhibited.

The rock face next to Mayadeen exploded, forcing her sideways to the dirt. She took the fall with her shoulder, but what was spared her head was taken from her lungs. She pushed to all fours while catching her breath. Her right side stung from the pelting with bits of granite protruding from her arm.

Mayadeen's heart raced as Shorsas now loomed over her.

"Forgive me. You mustn't test me, pirate. For are we not beyond introductions?"

Mayadeen scrambled backward and settled on her rump. She watched a drop of blood trickle from Elona's nose. Shorsas wiped it away.

"Just tell me whether Red speaks true, damn ye."

Shorsas smiled. Any trace of anger now vanished.

"Elona speaks her own truth, yes."

Mayadeen snorted. "What's that mean?"

"It means she believes she speaks true."

It wasn't the answer Mayadeen was hoping for, but it still didn't mean they shared a mother.

"Then she's vexed, and a fool besides," said Mayadeen.

"Perhaps." Shorsas scanned her. "The truth frightens you?"

"This ain't about me ..." Mayadeen drew a breath and frowned. "She says she has proof of her claim."

Shorsas peered around the camp and settled her gaze on Creyland who slept in an awkward position on his side.

"Your slaves are quite loyal."

Mayadeen reeled. "The proof. The scroll, ye lousy ... Shorsas ... does she have it?"

"She has beheld the truth. Scroll or no scroll, Elona is sibling to you by your mother's half."

Shorsas didn't seem to understand the import of such a statement, and Mayadeen wasn't about to bring her current on a thousand years of wars and politics. Either way, she felt nauseous.

"I see this upsets you. The Sinbalak is a gift from those that were beyond ancient ... perhaps even from the gods themselves. You should rejoice that it flows within you."

"How 'bout I puke instead?" Mayadeen bent over and put her hands on her knees. The cursed Sinbalak had flowed right out of her head.

Shorsas knelt to run a finger over Creyland's temple and down his whiskered cheek. Her hand continued down the cold bend of his steel-plated chest piece and further to where his shackled hands rested over his pleasure mound.

Mayadeen scowled while still clutching the pelitite crystal. "So how do I get ye back into this thing?"

Shorsas turned to face her, the irritation building again in her cosmic eyes. But she relented, and once again only smiled.

"Do not tarry with this new information, for it matters not. You must continue to the North and find a way out of the Four Kingdoms."

"Aye, ye old witch, 'tis what I'm aiming for." Mayadeen wanted to laugh at the irony but found she couldn't even bring herself to a smirk. "Mayhap now ye'll tell me what's in it for ye. What's yer price for all this?"

"I must go now," said Shorsas. "I've entrusted the shard to you as was our deal. Do not part with it. That is all I require at this time."

"'By and by'," scoffed Mayadeen. "Ain't that what ye told me?" She spat into the dirt. The dizzy spell passed. "Jump back into yer crystal. I've had enough of ye." She winced as she plucked another piece of rock from her abraded arm.

When she looked up again, Elona's own eyes stared back at her.

And those were the last things Mayadeen saw before her world went dark.

XIV
THREESOME ...?

If she be one, and she be won, too, then two like her would be two won, too, and three for three won.
> ~ Wydla, *A Book of Vexing Jests*

"Cap'n. Cap'n."

"For the love of hard fucking, just wake her up."

Mayadeen rolled herself onto her back while shielding her eye from the blaring sun. Her whole body felt sore and depleted with a slight ringing in the ears. Perhaps she'd been used as a bell hammer.

"Cap'n," urged Laddy with relief in his voice. "We've been out for hours, methinks. All of us."

"That so?" Dirt covered Mayadeen's chapped lips as the words came forth from her hoarse throat. She cracked her neck and back and slowly found her feet. "Hours, says ye?" She recalled her frustrating palaver with Shorsas, and Elona had returned to her own shell without so much as a swoon. Mayadeen would not soon forget the anguished look in Red's eyes.

"I'd gather two days," said Creyland. He sat by the remnants of a campfire, his hands still shackled in front. "Laddy and I awoke starved and parched. The mounts were chewing on sage."

He gestured at a small pile of charred shells.

"Of course, there's always those cursed crabs." Creyland handed Mayadeen a water jug. "Be sparing. It's all we've got left."

Mayadeen snatched the jug with a sneer and gave it a couple quick sips. She coughed, wiped the morning grime from her mouth and picked up one of the mountain crabs. She sucked out a morsel of tasteless, half-cooked meat and went for another.

"That little witch whore left for good this time," continued Creyland.

"Ye don't know that, ye Edish keel cock," snarled Laddy.

Creyland huffed.

"She cast sleep charms on us," said Mayadeen. The situation with Elona was too complicated to explain, and Mayadeen didn't reckon how to convince either Laddy or Creyland that the sorcerer hadn't abandoned them out of betrayal or some sinister purpose. Disappointment, shame and regret were probably closer to order.

Mayadeen glanced at Laddy. She couldn't hide the misgiving in her voice. "I don't gather she'll be coming back."

After a prolonged silence, Creyland was the first to open his mouth.

"I suppose that's all you have to tell us then?" He grinned and licked his teeth after saying it.

"Nay, I've plenty more to tell ye, Fenn. But first, how fares that bump on yer head?"

Creyland grimaced and gently put a hand to where his skin was still a purplish hue.

Mayadeen had always thought it a safe bet she'd never see Fenn again. He'd survived many a beating, a few of which started and ended with Mayadeen's boot. They partook in a tumultuous go of it at one time, as exciting and pleasurable as it was cruel and vindictive.

"You can threaten and posture all you like, Emerald Eye. I spared your life perchance you'd forgotten."

"And I yers."

"Mine? When?"

"Every day I ain't opened yer throat. So I reckon ye owe me."

Creyland shot up to his feet. "Well, you could at least remove these sodding shackles."

Laddy stood in turn and his hand went to the hilt of his recently procured dagger.

"You produce that, sea pup, you best be ready to use it," said Creyland.

"Heh." Mayadeen thought this was turning out to be a lovely morning indeed. "Ain't had me a good cock fight in two winters. Laddy, keep yer blade in yer breeches. There won't be a lick o' that today, or by yer swollen bull stones I'll spill ye both.

"Now that it's settled ..." she reached into her pocket and produced a rusty key. She tossed it to Creyland who clapped it in both palms.

Laddy couldn't have looked as flummoxed if he'd glanced down to find his arse where his pecker should be. "Cap'n, I—"

"We ain't privy to what could befall us from here to the northern coast, and we'll need an extra pair of able hands now that Elona's fled."

"We can still find her, Cap'n," assured Laddy. "She couldn't be further than—"

"We ain't hauling in pursuit o' that one, damn ye," Mayadeen interrupted.

"She could be halfway to one of her silly witch covens by now," said Creyland.

Laddy again clutched his dagger hilt. "Shut yer skull, ye Edish kelp fucker!"

Mayadeen stepped forward and placed a hand on Laddy's shoulder. She gave it a little squeeze and patted his cheek. "Don't ye concern yerself with Fenn," she conspired while glancing in Creyland's direction, the latter now busy again trying to unlock himself. "He aims to get to the coast same as us. And that's where we'll dump him."

The fact remained that Mayadeen really didn't know what she was going to do with Creyland, but the scoundrel could prove useful in the interim. Besides, Fenn was the least of their problems.

Laddy sighed and smote another side glance at Creyland. "Aye, Cap'n. I'll see 'im to the coast."

"Yer a fine pinch of salt, shipmate. Now get ye to watering those ponies but be sparse with it. We'll need it for ourselves. We push off readily."

Laddy nodded and ambled off. Creyland gloated in triumph, his manacles jangling to the ground.

"Laddy," Mayadeen added forcing him to stop and turn. "I know ye were fond of her ... Elona, I mean. She and I had our outs, but for her own part she'd something she needed doing. And there ain't nothing more o' less to it."

"She'll be back, methinks," said Laddy. "I know she'll be back, Cap'n."

Mayadeen sighed, but gave him nod.

Laddy lowered his sea-green eyes and continued to the horses.

#

"Ha, ha. I knew you'd find your savvy senses, Captain," said Creyland moments later while stretching his arms in every direction.

"That so?" Mayadeen curdled a good ball of snot from the back of her throat and jettisoned it to the embers. She thought the resulting mess resembled a beached jellyfish as it sizzled in a hell it had never known.

Creyland reached around the side of his head and gently pulled. "Ugh. Can hardly move my neck." He winced and groaned with what sounded like both pain and relief. "Emerald Eye, there's naught you and I can't do while standing on the same forecastle."

"Don't recall much standing."

Creyland leered. "And you'd be right as foam on ale with a cheery clink besides." He approached Mayadeen while adjusting himself. He rubbed up against her, hard as a mizzen post beneath his trousers. His gaze never strayed from her own. Creyland was tall for a bull and

Mayadeen had him bettered by a few inches.

She grabbed him by the rim of his thin steel chest plate and brought him within breath. Creyland had always preferred to armor his heart. A lot of good it would have done him should a blade have aimed for the neck.

"Yer damned words mean nothing to me," whispered Mayadeen. Her mouth lunged at Creyland's own to gently bite his upper lip and tease his tongue to her palate. He followed eagerly as she felt his tongue swirl around her own. It was brief yet savory, while her hand cupped the bottom of his stones. She squeezed just enough to make him grunt and flinch.

"Heh." Mayadeen shoved him back with the same hand that gripped his armor. "Ye couldn't be stiffer if ye were dead." She licked her lips with a half grin. "Mayhap for the better I spared yer pearly skin."

Creyland riled. "If you're worried about the guppy spying us rolling in the dirt, I'll make it painless for him. It could be like old times."

Mayadeen got serious. "Or mayhap for the worse."

"I only jest," Creyland recanted. "Laddy seems a loyal scalawag."

"Aye, and the last of the best crew I ever had, us and ours included, Fenn."

"Now you're just being cruel," said Creyland.

"When a swabby saw the *Sea Licker* on the horizon, a swabby started paddlin'."

"And paddling s'all it would take to outpace a floating castle, Emerald Eye. Nay, your *Licker* had nothing on our *Swallow*. The *Foam Swallow* was the finest, fastest schooner on the white. Would be today if not for your intrepid mother. I cried me a bottle when that vessel was dismantled."

"Ye always were a crier." Mayadeen smirked in spite of herself.

Creyland grinned. "Well, one of us had to be."

Mayadeen dithered. They'd quite the high time on the schooner, it was true. They had cut the waters with a small crew, just twenty hands with Mayadeen at the helm and Creyland her first. Mayadeen took three Daughter born under her charge in those days, two of them now captains themselves, with the rest of the crew gelds and one or two bulls to keep the action interesting. The Foam Swallow was swift and could tack on a bottle, making him perfect for stealthy night raids on rival scalawags from Marbane or merchant lines on the Edish coasts. One time they'd outrun an entire fleet of privateers after filling half their stores with diamonds and velveteen intended for a noble's wedding, an absurd ceremony wherein a womaner and a bull swore monogamy with one another.

Marriage in the Island Realm was as simple as one choosing to bind a bull's blood with her own, and a womaner could strike several such accords if she so desired. Marriage was just another form of binding, although the majority of coupling didn't concern itself with labels in the Meridian Isles. The one thread weaving its way through all forms of binding was commitment—the blood pact had to be honored. Either way, the particular binding of marriage wasn't a thing to be celebrated. It was just another mutually beneficial alliance, sometimes more and never less. Creyland had been Mayadeen's third marriage and sixth binding. Her two other husbands, the useless arse twats that they were, still worked the quay back in Cleft Rock.

"Where are your thoughts, Emerald Eye?" asked Creyland. "Hopefully in a warm place without breeches or boots."

"Aye, but neither my boots nor yer breeches."

It was a lie. She wanted him at that moment. She'd thought about being with him—naked and dripping within the soft-lit, mahogany womb of their own ocean fortress—since he first strode into that Witch King's great hall. But the only way to quell her desperation was to keep moving. She couldn't let Elona's departure, quickly becoming a void of guilt and regret, seize the last bastions of her resolve. No, if they were to survive the next uncertain leg of their journey, then she would have to make sure the measures outbid the pleasures to fill that void.

"Just mount yer pony, Fenn. We've lost enough light for one day."

#

The next morning, Mayadeen opened her eye to blurry surroundings. It took a few rubs and a tap on her noggin to finally bring Creyland into focus. How she'd taken so suddenly to becoming a heavy sleeper—on a lubber's slumber, no less—gave cause for concern.

They hauled more wind the previous day than on all the days combined of ambling through Rul and Drost since escaping Lusul's camp. They at last exited the steep, jagged mountain pass to the open grasslands, and the horses immediately gained a marked enthusiasm in their walking and trotting, with plenty of newfound pasture for grazing.

Indeed, for the pirates, finding food and water never fell from the top of the short list. Mayadeen was no huntsman, but she could have kicked herself silly for not having grabbed a bow and quiver from the Valindrost stables when they had their pick. At least then she could have pretended to pursue the abundant game herding about the open prairies. Fortune put the feather to the foot, however, and Creyland and Laddy were able to run down an injured fawn at the edge of a small oasis. The result was a decent supper without the strange native crab on the menu, although it had taken the three of them over an hour to ignite a simple campfire.

Perhaps they'd come to rely on Red's sorcery a bit too much.

"A finer morning couldn't be had on the Jeweled Sea in springtime. Wouldn't you say, Laddy?" Creyland stretched next to the kindled campfire and started buckling the straps on his chest plate. Another leg of venison was set to roasting above the flame.

"Um. Aye." Laddy glanced at Mayadeen. The young bull hadn't waned so apprehensive since first witnessing King Lusul and her gorillas ride in on that beach.

Mayadeen's head swam like a school of frightened perrygills. The night before, she devoured a good meal of the venison and plenty of water to wash it down. They'd refilled their jugs at the pond, the water deemed potable after Creyland was handed the honor of testing it. Mayadeen even held the first watch so as to digest her food properly. After that, she'd slept the night through. Yet she ached all over. Her neck, back, arms, legs and all the crevices between them—

She shot up and fell back to her hands as her trousers were bunched to just below her knees. She pulled them back to her hips with a single motion and jumped to her feet.

Mayadeen grabbed Laddy by his vest. "Tell me true or I'll twist yer sodding head off," she growled.

"Whoa, whoa, Emerald Eye," came Creyland's voice.

She placed her free hand on one of her back daggers with a quick glance at Creyland. If either of them tried to sleight, she'd plant a knife in Laddy and toss his flapping carcass at the other.

"Cap'n," pleaded Laddy, "I told 'im it weren't ye ... I ... I told 'im something was afoul, I did."

"What're ye blathering about? Out with it!"

"Ye weren't yerself," said Laddy, eyes wide.

"Not herself? She was herself and then some," added Creyland. "I think we all needed a good—"

"Oh, belay yer pissin' tongue, damn ye." Mayadeen kept her glower on Laddy. From him at least she could extract the truth.

The reek of lust was unmistakable, and it was obvious they'd all wrestled like sea turtles sometime during the night. She'd slept arse-to-air with half of her clothes on, her shirt unbuttoned to her belly, and although she still wore her holster rig, at least two of the belts were unbuckled.

Poisoned. Creyland must've had a vial of something hidden all along ...

But then she'd another thought as her hand went to the necklace beneath her shirt.

"What color was my eye?" Mayadeen brought her straining orb closer to Laddy's dismayed countenance.

Again Creyland interjected. "Green as ocean grass, of course.

Though I was on your stern and it was very dark—"

"'Twasn't green," said Laddy. "'Twas a shimmerin' silver."

And so there it was exposed. Mayadeen let go of Laddy's vest. A great numbness washed over her like she was being dragged by a ship's hawser through icy waters. *Shorsas.* The ancient, horny bitch had told Mayadeen that the Sinbalak flowed through her veins, and it was all Shorsas needed to commandeer the vessel of Mayadeen's essence. This, however, was more akin to mutiny.

She grabbed the pelitite crystal and yanked the rawhide from her neck.

"Noticed that dangling from your beautiful chest last night," said Creyland. "Only such a fine piece of pelitite indeed would be worthy to quarter between those magnificent twin keeps."

Laddy turned on him. "This here ain't naught to be laughing at. The Cap'n's got a curse, she does."

Creyland chortled. "A curse?"

"Nay, nay, ye sons of seeping swab whores," said Mayadeen. "Not a curse. The both of ye be my curse!" She turned the crystal over and over betwixt her fingers. "'Twas a pact ... though a devil's pact to be sure."

"By the gods high and low and on my lee and up my arse," said Creyland while shaking his head. "I've never known a creature to harbor more secrets in all my fruitless life. You knew about this, Laddy?"

"He knew as much as I bloody wanted 'im to know," said Mayadeen before Laddy could open his jaw. "As for yerself, Fenn, I'd have been fine as flotsam without ye gleaning fucking naught."

"Well, then how could you make a pact with a crystal? What sort of magician's stone do you keep?"

"The sort possessed by an insufferable old cunty. Such a one that would be wise to never again fill my head with her own petty appetites."

Laddy and Creyland only exchanged stupid looks after Mayadeen realized she'd been speaking directly to the crystal. No matter, as she couldn't think of a worthwhile pirate captain that hadn't gained from being perceived as at least a little crazed.

Creyland scratched his head. "So you're saying you were under the control of a ghost that lives in the pelitite?"

"Aye, aye, damn ye!" Mayadeen squeezed the shard with all her might. She wanted the thing to bleed, cry out or simply crumple in her fist. It did none of those.

"Perhaps one of us should guard your trinket?" asked Creyland.

"Aye," Laddy seconded, "mayhap Cap'n Fenn should guard it."

It was a notion Mayadeen hadn't yet considered. Shorsas bound herself and entrusted her care to Mayadeen, so it only made sense to keep the old harpy close. Besides, she liked having a secret weapon to call on when absolutely needed. With Elona's absence, however, such was no longer a boon. Indeed, the blasted shard of legend was turning out to be a liability.

"Mayhap." She addressed Laddy. "It's yer charge then. Gather yer fucking stones. Ye really are a halfwit if ye think I'd let Fenn bugger me raw again." With that she tossed Laddy the crystal.

Laddy caught it in his chest. After only a moment in his hands it flashed an unnatural color. He yelped and dropped it to the ground.

Mayadeen flinched, but immediately ran to Laddy's aid. The young bull winced in pain while a bit of smoke cleared from his palms. The enchanted shard singed his flesh.

"A magician's stone indeed," quipped Creyland with a chuckle. "I suppose your precious Elona had something to do with this?"

Ignoring Creyland, Mayadeen swiped up the pelitite. "Damn ye wretched, whorish, ol' maggot fucking ..." She made ready to throw it into the center of the nearby watering hole. But something stayed her arm. Perhaps a thread of her own honor remained tethered to it? Or perhaps Shorsas already held a power over her that she could not entirely deny? Either way they were bound.

With Elona it had been different as it was not Mayadeen's choice to have parted with her half-sister. *Sister*. It was strange to entertain the word in her head. Of course, she'd heard of several sisters and bulls by half in the past. But those worthless peacocks hailed from her Pap's side of the helm—the side that made not a damn bit of difference to anybody, anywhere. She never imagined her mother, the very picture of Meridian tradition, would have named a bastard. To not have drowned it in the nearest tide pool was stranger still. And to round off the miasma of shit, there remained the tainted bloodline. Mabelia Damned, at one point in her celebrated career as a Master of the Nine and before taking her chair with the Elders, had been severely remiss.

Mayadeen sighed and shoved the infernal piece of Shorsas into her trousers pocket. "For now I'm bound to the bitch. 'Tis all ye sink-cocks need to know, damn ye. And by the gods what happened last night won't happen twice. Or I'll bury this crystal high in the first arse to boast otherwise."

She turned away from them as she tucked in her shirt and buttoned and buckled up her vestments. In spite of the treachery, a smile tried to creep up her face. A thousand years apart and she shared something in common with Shorsas after all. The old biddy might have been steering, but it was still Mayadeen's ship.

She'd be damned, drowned and dead if she didn't feel like a pirate captain again.

XV
OF MICE AND BULLS

Just as both weep from pain and are helplessly attracted to my
nipples, so is there little difference between babies and men.
~ Trilan, *All of Her Wives*

Again Mayadeen held the first watch, and again the night lingered like so many others before it. They were six days out of the strange, ancient city of Valindrost, or at least out of where Valindrost once stood. When they reached the open grasslands Mayadeen maintained a northerly course to the best of her ability. Unfortunately, she had no accurate reckoning of how far north they'd have to go before reaching the coast. She did know from various charts she'd eyed during her career that the Warlands Main covered a tremendous amount of land. Bolora's isolated kingdom could be well over a thousand leagues from where they now camped.

Food and water were also an ongoing problem. They'd received a cut of good fortune with the injured fawn, but with no salt on hand they had to cook it all the first night rendering it consumable for about a week. Mayadeen was no stranger to rationing, especially when it came to fresh water. She'd had over seventy mouths to feed and quench while captaining the *Sea Licker*, and there would sometimes be weeks of maggot-infested meat and bread so hard it could only be consumed in a hot stew or soup. It was why one of the sternest demands she'd placed on her hand-picked crewmen was that they could fish off a trawl. Both the *Licker* and the *Foam Swallow* before it had been outfitted with trawl lines, something lesser pirates on the Nine Seas would scoff at because of the extra weight. But a good catch of perrygill or club fish for a few days' work of netting and curing could fill the stores for a month or more. Any scalawags who considered themselves above such toil were usually not of Meridian blood, and Mayadeen enjoyed nothing more than sending such unworthy bilge bandits and their dung barges to the cold, black depths.

Something yowled and cackled out in the blackness. Soon a chorus of similar cries followed. Mayadeen tossed another bundle of sticks onto the fire. She'd instructed Laddy to gather as many as he could find from the minimal tree clusters that festooned the savanna.

Each night during their watches on the plains they'd also kept a lit torch stuck in the ground to have at the ready. Considering the monstrosities she'd already encountered in the Warlands, she carried no more cynical thoughts about what packs of fell beasts were out to eat the three of them whole. A lone bear was spotted during their descent from the north face of the Shadowmurks, but it ambled far in the distance and appeared not a second time. The only bear Mayadeen wished to intimately encounter was the one she wore wrapped around her shoulders, for even summertime in the northern climates could chill the bones on a breezy night.

But now all Mayadeen could think about was her little sister.

She missed Elona. Not only had Red proved capable in almost every sort of situation—igniting campfires with a gesture was one magician's trick Mayadeen might attempt to acquire—but for some reason beyond the wisdom of women and gods, Mayadeen *trusted* her. She reckoned that didn't appear to be so on the night of Elona's grand revelation. Yet how was she supposed to have responded to such accusations?

It was hard at first to accept the small womaner who hailed from the Thresnare as her half-sister. However, a part of Mayadeen knew it to be so even before Elona gifted her the scandal. Indeed, Elona had exhibited unrivaled moxie with her flawed and risky plan to bring Mayadeen to the Warlands through uncertain magic. That cursed portal proved devastating to her ship and crew. Only Mayadeen had been somewhat protected, but even that could have failed. It was a desperate and foolish maneuver that could never be forgiven allowing for its reckless and selfish motives.

If Elona only knew how much their mother would have approved.

More yowling from the void. The horses stammered restless. The warhorse that Mayadeen named Fucker, then somewhere along the journey started calling Scurvy, threw up its head and took a couple steps back. Mayadeen stood up and peered around the firelight. She reached for the torch as all grew quiet again except for the light wind, which only served to mask and muddle the approach of potential stalkers. Creyland shifted in his sleep while his silly chest armor creaked and rattled. Laddy, as usual, slept like an anchor on a shoal.

Mayadeen threw some more sticks into the dancing flames and turned back to her thoughts. *Shorsas.* The bitch in the rock was threatening to become a problem. And yet Mayadeen still had not a sprout of an idea as to what the ancient ghost was really after, unless it involved two cocks and a ferocious petting. Perhaps that had been the old witch's twisted way of letting Mayadeen know the Sinbalak truly did flow through her veins? It only made Mayadeen feel lower for having used Elona as the devil's instrument.

Scurvy neighed.

Mayadeen sprang up and grabbed the torch. All three horses sputtered and bolted. She caught a mere lump of a shadow atop Scurvy that steered the beast to lead the others.

"Avast, damn ye!"

Creyland rolled awake with sword in hand. Two more shadowy figures ran to catch up to the horses. Mayadeen darted to intercept them. They were two bulls draped in furs and hides. The first stumbled in his effort to mount Laddy's horse and slid into the tall grass.

The other bull was able to climb onto the bare back of Creyland's mount, but not before Mayadeen reached his side. She snatched the man's ankle and, with both hands, yanked him from the trotting horse. The man thumped against the ground with a gasp.

Creyland and Laddy could deal with those two.

Mayadeen continued running until she grabbed the horse's blond mane and vaulted onto its back. She could make out her own horse not very far ahead, its rider much smaller than she'd expected. Whoever it was, the thief was having trouble getting Scurvy to break into a gallop from an intermittent canter. The trick to these horses, as Elona had instructed, was to squeeze instead of kick. Mayadeen urged hers into a gallop although riding without a saddle and reins proved clumsier than striding a wet deck in a squall.

With a cloudy night and a sliver of moon, the darkness covered all but a few feet at a time. But she came upon Scurvy fast with a gallop to his begrudged jog, and a mere boy of eight years or less clung to the horse's withers.

She reached out to grab him when Scurvy decided to dash into a gallop. Mayadeen pulled one of her daggers and flipped it around to its point. She wasn't about to lose another horse in the Warlands Main.

The dagger toppled through the pitch of night and struck its mark.

#

Mayadeen returned to the campfire with a skinny child slung over her shoulder and Scurvy in tow. Fortunately for the boy, he'd received the handle of the dagger instead of the blade.

Creyland and Laddy hovered above the two older intruders, each of them having been beaten, bound and forced to his knees. One of them had long, shaggy hair with a weather-beaten beard to match. The other fashioned a shaved head and as much facial hair as his companion.

Mayadeen set the unconscious boy gently on the ground and

propped his head against her saddle and bear fur travel coat.

Shaggy cried out something in a foreign tongue and tried to get to his feet when he saw the child. Laddy cuffed him across the face and the prisoner went back down.

Creyland laughed. "Well, that younglet got a lot further than these two."

"We'd a'been buggered for sure if they'd got away 'ith it," snarled Laddy. "Oughtta cut their—"

"Stop yer rattling teeth," snapped Mayadeen. "These two peacock savages ain't a threat to their babes. Question is, where are the splitties?"

Creyland glanced around the darkness. "That is a question."

"They went on a hunt and never came back."

Mayadeen spun. The little voice with the heavy accent came from the boy. He could speak the folk tongue though, and that much was a blessing from the tides.

"Laddy, give the little beast some water."

The boy watched with cautious brown eyes as Laddy retrieved the water jug. He gave the boy a brief tip of trickling water.

"Now," said Mayadeen to the boy, "ye speak our words which bodes well for ye. These two bootless shit pigs," she pointed back to the bound men, "what are they to ye?"

The boy looked up at Laddy, who hovered close in case the former took a notion to run for it.

"He's my Pap." He nodded at Shaggy. "The other's my sister's Pap. Never much cared for him." Roe focused again on Mayadeen.

The boy showed no fear in his gaze, a rare find among bulls and gelds, especially the young. Mayadeen guessed this one would be keeping his stones if given the choice. "What's yer name, boy?"

"Roe's my name. And yours?"

"Her name's Cap'n, ye thieving lil' rodent," threw in Laddy.

"We're thieves all of us here," said Mayadeen. "Though some of us better than others, mayhap. Thing ye gotta gather 'bout thieves, Roe, is that our failures come rife with consequence." Mayadeen glanced at Creyland, the smirk off his face for once. She knew he had a pretty good idea as to what was coming next.

Mayadeen crossed to Shaved Head and helped him to his feet. The man's eyes dripped with fear, unlike young Roe. Mayadeen remembered being much the same way as the boy—fearless and invincible when it came to getting what she desired. But like herself in those early years the boy lacked wisdom, and a good gill or two of it would cure fearlessness faster than a worm would dry in the sun.

She addressed Roe without taking her focus from the man in front of her. "Tell 'im he's through with this world. And on my lee, boy, tell it true."

Roe hesitated, but then spoke in words that sounded similar to those grunted by the Rullites, though likely of a different dialect. Shaved Head's gaze rolled up to meet Mayadeen's. She nodded and her dagger planted upward, scraping beneath the bull's ribcage to find his heart. She brought his head to her breasts—a tradition of old when executing offenders in the Island Realm—and he exhaled with a slight curdle. His body became twice its weight as Mayadeen bolstered him to the ground.

She retracted the slick blade and crossed back to Roe.

The boy tried to break, but Laddy caught him by the scruff of his animal hide vestment. Mayadeen knelt down to Roe with the dagger held out in front. The beveled steel was slightly longer than the boy's neck was wide.

She heard Shaggy cry out from behind her, his gibberish quickly squelched by another fist.

Roe frowned and his lower lip twitched. He remained quiet, but his dark irises now shone with tears. In a single moment Roe had grown wiser.

Mayadeen grinned. She wiped the blood from the dagger clean on Roe's lapel. She replaced the blade to its sheath at the small of her back.

"Ye were right to be afraid."

Mayadeen stood up. Her display for the evening, though not easy, was enough to both uphold her reputation as a pirate captain and to teach the boy an important lesson. Fear was one's connection to the rest of the world. Without it, one was doomed to a fiend's sort of darkness. It may have already been too late for this hardened young bull, but knowing his limits early on might save his life in a land ravaged by womaners thirsty only for his seed and blood.

"Now that we're mates, younglet, with that business all settled, we crave food and water to continue our wanderings. Ye and yer Pap will make sure we've what we need. Take us to yer people."

Roe wiped the wetness from his dark eyes and nodded.

#

They'd saddled the horses and set out fast to find Roe's home in the dead of night. Mayadeen kept him close between lap and pommel as she rode. Shaggy, Roe's father, whose name was something along the lines of Sard, remained bound and tethered while walking beside Creyland's mount. Sard said very little and mostly kept his eyes to the ground. If not for the child, Mayadeen would have eliminated Sard as swift and sure as the other.

Roe's people were known as the Nahana to outsiders from the West, and Roe told how he had learned the common tongue from a warrior of the Soldrons, a land that lay halfway around the world from the Island Realm. He stood by his original claim that the strongest womaners of his tribe were out on a hunt. He assured only the crones, bulls and children remained. He could be lying through his shiny little teeth, of course, but Mayadeen had no reason to believe that Roe would doubt his throat being severed as soon as such a lie confessed.

The real problem, as Creyland was so smug to point out, was how they should approach an encampment of around thirty shelters with a few easily rattled archers on watch—again, according to Roe. So as not to come upon them too unexpectedly, Mayadeen decided to carry lit torches. If any of them were cast from the same forge as Roe, they might prove formidable, although for any sort of negotiations to proceed with Roe and his father as ransom, Mayadeen would take a confident group over a pack of shifty cowards. There was also the matter of Shaved Head who hadn't survived his mission. His body was tied over the rear of Laddy's horse to be offered back to the Nahana as a show of strength, although that, too, might not go as planned.

"We're almost there, Captain Damned," said Roe while looking up at her. His hair smelled a combination of wild animal and ginger root. Mayadeen supposed the latter was rubbed on him between long stretches of not bathing. Either way, he smelled like sodding spring flowers next to a scalawag at sea. On a ship Mayadeen would have her crew scrub down with a mixture of whale blubber and dried mint—twice a week for her and her officers, once a week for the rest—with a dive overboard to finish the duty.

"Cap'n ..." It was Laddy. "Better have an eye at this."

The three horses walked side by side in a skirmish formation, with Mayadeen and Roe on one end, Creyland and Sard in the center, and Laddy on the far. Mayadeen broke out of formation and trotted over to Laddy. They must have been at an escarpment, for his vantage point suddenly overlooked a distant stretch of flickering fire lights in the darkness. The hollering of combat and the clicks and clanks of metal on metal were barely audible. Many of the lights came from fires much bigger than torches or campfires. The entire village was being razed.

Roe gasped, and Mayadeen felt his heart starting to beat rapidly through his back pressed against her bosom.

"That yer home?" she asked Roe, unable to hide the urgency in her voice.

"Yes." His voice cracked.

Mayadeen gave him a little squeeze on his shoulder for what good it would do. The boy had certainly weathered a rough night.

Creyland trotted his horse up to join them while his captive-in-tow almost tripped. "What in bloody hell—"

Shaggy-haired Sard cried out when he saw the situation. He held up his binds while assailing Creyland and Mayadeen and gesturing to Roe.

"What's he saying?" Mayadeen asked Roe.

"He ... he wants to go and ... and help."

"If those are Lusul's gallies," said Creyland, "then his people are already a bonny memory."

Mayadeen searched Sard. The bull obviously wasn't thinking clearly. "He wants to run to his death, does he?" But there was something in the man's eyes that went beyond tomfoolery or even pride. It was something that demanded to be honored.

"Cut him loose," said Mayadeen to Creyland.

"So he can fly and give us away?" Creyland took in some of the slack on Sard's rope.

"Laddy." Mayadeen had her hands full, otherwise she'd cut the cursed rope herself.

Laddy pulled his short sword and obliged to sawing the rope from his mount.

Creyland rolled his eyes but held the rope taught. "What of the boy, then?"

"Let me worry 'bout the boy, damn ye. Just let that fucking bull charge to oblivion if he means to. And unload the other. That plan's been stymied, and we can't be hauling around a corpse."

"I want to go with my Pap," said Roe. He tried to wriggle free from Mayadeen's grip but she held firm.

Roe exchanged some words in his native tongue with Sard. The bull shook his head and seemed to be demanding that Roe stay put. The boy struggled and reached out to take his Pap's hand one last time.

"I suppose you want to give him a bloody blade besides?" cracked Creyland.

"No," answered Mayadeen, annoyed the miserable shit could be so terse in such a moment. She should have run a *bloody blade* through Fenn a long time ago. "We can't spare any weapons." She said it more to Sard than to Creyland.

Sard looked Mayadeen in the eye. She nodded and he nodded slightly in return. He beheld his son once more. And then he was off.

Roe yelled something after him and sniveled.

"Yer a younglet to be running to yer death or worse," said Mayadeen while holding him to her. "Yer Pap knew that much. That's just the way of it."

The child tensed with a heave and a twist. He was strong for his small size and young age. If Mayadeen ever decided to bear a daughter, she could only hope for the same qualities. She used both arms to hold him while he twisted to peer over her shoulder. Mayadeen felt the fight leave his little body, and she only held him tighter.

XVI
THE WORLD ACCORDING TO ROE

Sons aren't so bad in Rul, especially if you name a passel of them.
At least you'll never starve and they're quite tender.
~ Chela the Bard,
An Unfortunate Stowaway's Guide to the Four Kingdoms

They rode hard for the better part of an hour before a clear twilight began to open up the endless plains. Mayadeen wanted to gain as much distance as possible from Lusul's army, and it vexed her how the relentless cunty had mobilized northward so fast—she was fairly certain Lusul wasn't using magic and lights. Although after witnessing the spectacular business at Valindrost, she had to keep in mind that the traditional laws of time and space didn't apply to this barren realm.

Mayadeen trotted her horse in a tight skirmish line with Creyland in the center and Laddy on her starboard far. Roe slept for most of the ride and now awoke as Scurvy slowed from a trot to a walk. Mayadeen would run the horses at intervals—gallop, cantor, trot, repeat—but they all were looking quite exhausted, especially Laddy's smaller roan. Roe reached out to stroke Scurvy on his blonde mane and then swiveled his head up and around to Mayadeen. He was a lithe one, Roe, and Mayadeen readied herself to make sure he wasn't planning on squirming his way to freedom in the tall prairie grass.

"It wasn't a dream," he said after turning forward again. "I miss my Pap and Mum. Will I see them again?"

"Mayhap," assured Mayadeen, trying to mask her doubt. "I'm sure yer people have seen plenty o' trouble, Roe. But ye'll be with us for a spell or longer." She took a deep breath. Words were seldom her weakness. "As to yer Pap and Mum, well, they would've wanted ye safe and unbridled. On my lee, I know that much."

"I think I'll see them again," said Roe.

Mayadeen gave his leg a little squeeze. He was shivering. "Cold, are ye?"

"A little," mumbled Roe.

The early evening had been tepid, but the wee hours' chill served as a healthy reminder they weren't on a tropical island.

"Unless ye'd fancy half a bear on top of ye, I'm afraid we've not much in the way of jackets and wraps."

"No, I'll be fine."

"That's a sturdy trump. Ye hungry?"

Roe nodded with an enthusiastic smile.

"Heh. Yer in like company then," said Mayadeen with a grin. "The sun will be rising before long and we'll find a place to make camp and break our fast."

"Where are we going?"

"North ... to a great castle." Mayadeen figured it an even bet that would turn out to be the truth. King Bolora lived either in one of those or in some infernal spider's lair.

"What's a castle?"

"Well, eh, let's see. It's a dwelling with lots of rooms and big walls. If ye took a couple hundred of yer tents and stacked 'em all atop each the other, ye'd have something like a castle." Mayadeen glanced over to see if Creyland had caught her ridiculous description. Fortunately he seemed too busy picking something out of his teeth, the vainglorious arse.

"Not sure if I want to go to a place like that," said Roe. "I might get lost or trapped."

Mayadeen chortled. "Mayhap. But it'll have roaring fires, silky beds 'n' savory vittles. Ye might fancy being trapped for an eve or two in such a berth."

"Is that what it's like on a boat in the ocean?"

"Ah, ye know about them, do ye?"

"Only from drawings and what my Dad told me. He said he saw real boats when he was young and journeyed all the way to the ocean."

All the way to the ocean, indeed. Mayadeen thought of her former magnificent vessel. It would take a lot of plunder and otherwise good fortune to earn that sort of a ship again, and she might be starting with little more than a raft out of White Bay. "Ye stick with me, Roe, and earn yer keep, I'll show ye ships unlike any yer Pap would have beheld."

"I think I'd like that," said Roe with a nod. "Do you have a home, Captain Damned?"

"Aye, I've a home," she said as if the idea hadn't occurred to her for a long while. "That warrior teacher of yers ... she ever tell ye of the Meridian Isles?"

"Yes."

"Well, I hail from those rock-infested islands. What do ye know of my home?"

"She said your people are scarier than the Rullites. That the pirates from the center of the world will come and take us for slaves and pets."

Mayadeen frowned. "Ye say that bitch was from the Soldrons?" It only figured a rogue from that part of the world would poison Roe's people against the Island Realm. The Soldrons and their surrounding territories had been conquered numerous times by just about everybody, each time with the Soldrons pledging their allegiance to the latest victor. Politically, they were a mess, but they were also known to produce soldiers, rangers and even sailors formidable as any on the Nine Seas. "Don't be so fast to believe everything ye hear," she continued.

"Very well," said Roe. "Should I believe you?"

Creyland guffawed from his mount. Apparently, now he was listening. "He's a learner, that one."

Mayadeen shot him a look but didn't bother with insult. The bastard always did have ears like a cur in heat, and he would eavesdrop on his own funeral.

She turned back to Roe. "Nay. Ye shouldn't believe a cursed thing I say, except for one: I'll look after ye from now until ye're of age, and beyond should ye prove a worthy bull. The two of us, we're bound by circumstance. On my lee, don't ye take it for naught." She scowled again in Creyland's direction on that last warning. She'd been bound to him as well at one time. But he'd betrayed that blood pact for better or for worse.

"Then I'll look after you, too, Captain Damned," said Roe.

A smile crept to Mayadeen's lips, but receded when she thought of all those that she herself should have looked out for. Perhaps the boy would be better off without her. After all, he'd survived the whole of his life in these barbarian wilds.

Mayadeen and her dwindling band of miscreants had yet to survive a fortnight.

#

As the first light of dawn cast blue, Mayadeen circled her mount to join Creyland and Laddy, their visages just visible in the low grey light. The torches lost their flames, and only Laddy still held his stick wrapped in grass and cloth.

"We're losing cover," said Mayadeen to both of them, "and we'll need to find a place to drowse. From here out we'll move by night. Laddy, how fare we on water?"

Laddy untied one of the jugs dangling from the rear of his saddle rig. The other was already empty. "Mayhap 'nuff for a couple drams between us, Cap'n."

"Then save it 'til we're dying," returned Mayadeen, although she was fairly certain that none of them stole so much as as sip for at least a day, so in a sense they already were dying. Her own throat was parched and her head ached. "Our first order is to muster water." The grassland turned more barren as they moved north, although there still appeared a few clusters of trees and denser foliage sprinkled about. The nearest was silhouetted against the horizon perhaps half a league to the east. "There," Mayadeen pointed to it. "That's where we'll rest and fall about in shifts to suss out water."

"The guppy there knows this land better than we," said Laddy. "Why don't ye have 'im look?"

"Laddy's right," said Creyland. "The younglet could sniff it out quicker than any of us."

The seconded motion irritated Mayadeen, but she couldn't deny they both had a point. She gave Roe a pat on his thigh and peered down at him.

"Just follow the Clawbacks," blurted Roe. "They're always thirsty. And hungry."

Mayadeen, Creyland and Laddy exchanged glances. Mayadeen scanned the open terrain. With only a word Roe had suddenly made her feel quite vulnerable.

"Clawbacks?" repeated Mayadeen.

"Aye, aye," said Roe with a smile toward Laddy.

Laddy twisted to nearly fall from his saddle, his eyes darting everywhere at once. "Fuck are 'em? Why didn't ye mention 'em earlier, ye lil' bilge rat?"

Creyland, too, appeared unsettled yet stayed his tongue for once.

Mayadeen saw Roe was enjoying his little flex of power, and her hand became firm on his thigh. "Better explain yerself, lubber pup. What are Clawbacks and how would ye follow 'em?"

Roe giggled. "Oh, they won't hurt us, Captain Damned. They're just dumb grass gobblers." He laughed again.

Creyland snorted. "Seems we have ourselves a scalawag after all."

"I noticed their tracks right over there." Roe pointed to some grass that looked the same as all the other grass.

"A tracker are ye, shipmate?" asked Mayadeen.

Laddy harrumphed. "He ain't no ploughin' tracker. The sun ain't up yet and he's spyin' tracks?"

Roe craned back to Mayadeen. "I can follow them, Captain Damned. But not from a horse."

Mayadeen glanced at Fenn and then at Laddy. They were all tired, hungry, and above all, parched. If the boy could find water, then by the gods high and low their fates would have to be left to his juvenile devices.

"Aye, and so ye'll track on foot," said Mayadeen. "But we wait until there's more light as we wouldn't want to lose ye, now would we?" She didn't suspect the boy would fly, yet she also wanted to be able to find him should her trust prove misplaced.

"The trail is fresh," sighed Roe. "We should go now."

"The lil' shit monkey's fibbin'," said Laddy. "He'll run off to his next tribe of savages. Or lead us to 'em, mayhap."

Mayadeen glowered. "I'll be the one to decide if he's fibbin', damn ye. Any more to say on it, Laddy, I'll drown ye right here in a puddle of yer own pissing tears."

Mayadeen let Roe hop down from the saddle. She thought Laddy averted his eyes, but couldn't quite tell in the lowest light of morning.

"The boy's our only hope of finding water, Laddy," said Creyland with a tired sigh. "Surely even you can glean that fucking much."

Laddy dismounted and ran to Creyland's side. "Off that pony, ye Edish prick whore."

Creyland scoffed just as Laddy grabbed for his leg. Creyland came off of his horse, found purchase on Laddy's head, and two merged silhouettes went tumbling and grunting into the dark grass.

Although just one of Laddy's stones was bigger than his brain, his stubbornness trumped even Mayadeen's at his age. Fenn would have to teach him an earned lesson, though the thought of either bull taking injury at this stage in their journey made Mayadeen want to leave them rolling in the weeds and to start anew with little Roe. She walked Scurvy to grab the reins of the abandoned mounts. No use trying to intervene this time around. But they'd have to observe her limits.

"No blades, damn ye insufferables," said Mayadeen as she was pretty sure Laddy just got pounded a couple good ones. "Or I'll skewer ye both 'n' bury ye together, cock to arse in the same soddin' grave."

After plenty of grunting, winded cursing and even a yelp, the wrestling match ended with a clear victor.

"Had enough, boy?"

"Aye, aye ..."

Creyland came to his feet and pulled Laddy up with him. Both panted heavily while inspecting their wounds.

"Now take yer cursed ponies," said Mayadeen before tossing away their reins. She squinted around the shadows of the tall grass where they'd been standing. "After that lil' love exercise, ye both better hope we find water even sooner."

Creyland grabbed the jug with the remaining water from Laddy's saddle and gave it a good tip into his mouth. He then thrust it into Laddy's chest. "May as well take your last drink."

"Where's the younglet?" Mayadeen asked more to herself than to the preoccupied bulls. "Roe, to me, damn ye, pup!"

A great roar vibrated across the meadow, followed by a low grumble.

"That came from something big," said Creyland as he grabbed hold of his horse's reins.

Roe was nowhere to be seen.

#

Several intense moments passed without another calling from whatever was out there. As Creyland and Laddy retook their saddles, Mayadeen heard a rustling.

Roe at last appeared from the wavy straw. "I think I found them, Captain Damned."

Mayadeen sighed. She was glad the child had not flown. That would have been disastrous for all them.

She grinned wide at Creyland and Laddy. "What's that ye found now, Roe?"

"The clawbacks, along with a big fuzzback."

"Aye, boy," said Creyland while licking away some blood from his lower lip. "But did you find water?"

Roe nodded. "We'll have to wait until the fuzzback is done drinking."

The basso growl came again from somewhere not too far. This time the horses stammered with nervous jerks of their heads.

"That the fuzzback?" asked Mayadeen.

"Yes, err ... aye," answered Roe, perhaps a bit too enthusiastically.

As to why harmless critters would be labeled *clawbacks* and a ferocious beast, *fuzzback*, eluded Mayadeen like the stars eluded the day.

"I hate this horrible place, I do," said Laddy as Mayadeen thought the same sentiment. He'd received the worse end of the scuffle with Creyland, with incipient swelling on one side of his face and a bloody nose to match a bloody lip.

Mayadeen thought for a moment, which wasn't easy considering her current state of fatigue and general duress. They might have to risk being eaten to get a drink. It was a vicious and pitiless sort of irony.

"I'll need to get a peep at this cursed monster." She dismounted Scurvy, who for the first time seemed even more nervous than the other two horses. She stroked away some of the cold sweat from his hide. "Roe, ye'll take me to this watering hole."

"You really think that's the best strategy here, Emerald Eye?" asked Creyland. His own horse, which he'd named Roy, reared up but Creyland maintained control. "I'm ready to drink my own piss, but it's nothing a couple more hours is going to change."

"Ye know as well as I the beast ain't leaving that drink, Fenn. Not today, mayhap not even tomorrow. But we've still the strength now to try and filch some for ourselves. Then be on our merry way."

"Or find another watering hole," returned Creyland with some urgency in his voice.

"This water was cool and tasted good," said Roe.

"By the drowned gods, you're not helping, kid." Creyland frowned and licked his lips.

Mayadeen walked to Laddy's horse and untied the water jugs, both of them now empty. "I'm done palaverin', damn ye." She patted Laddy on the leg, and it was one of the few times she would ever have to look up at him. "Stay here with Fenn and the horses. Ye hear another roar and some bloody yells, then off with the both of ye to find another oasis with bonny fuckin' luck and good portents."

With that she nodded to Creyland and pointed for Roe to show the way. They ambled through the thick grass for several minutes before Roe got low and began to crawl. Mayadeen hunkered down as her knees popped and back creaked. She felt older than the ground she was pawing over, yet somehow followed Roe's lead on one hand while her other pressed the dangling rapier firmly against her hip to muffle any extra sound.

The morning sun now bled over the horizon, turning the bluish grays to yellows and ambers.

Before Mayadeen espied any sort of oasis, the wild, acrid stench of a carnivorous beast invaded the air. Roe kept low and subtle in the grass. When Mayadeen bent aside a large thatch of willow weed, she saw the source of their potential trouble. The fuzzback was a monster of a crown bear, a predator whose gargantuan head and appendages Mayadeen had only ever seen up close nailed to the plaques of trophy hunters at Marbanian night markets. This must have been the same they'd glimpsed far out on the plains when coming off the mountain range. The bear stooped on the opposite bank of a small pond twenty feet across and half as wide, its snout submerged in the glistening water as it gurgled and lapped up the refreshment. It was nearly as wide from shoulder to shoulder as the pond, and even while hunched over the fuzzback's withers reached fifteen hands, taller than most riding animals let alone a lumbering flesh eater.

Mayadeen carefully dipped her jug into the shallow water and motioned for Roe to do the same. Surely the beast had already sensed their presence, but perhaps its need for hydration trumped any less immediate need for fresh meat. With her jug filled to the brim, Mayadeen gave the cue for them to leave back the way they came. But when Roe went to lift his jug from the water, its new heft must have surprised him for he dropped it halfway up and it made a good splash.

The bear's black and grey muzzle—easily the same girth as the gallon water jugs—came up slowly from the pond. Its nostrils flared and sniffed the air, an intake that could be felt as much as heard across the oasis. The fuzzback grunted, brought its rusty brown-furred head up to meet its shoulders, and roared so deep and dreadful that the ripples sent out by Roe's jug doubled back on themselves.

Mayadeen's first instinct was to grab the boy and run. With the pond as a buffer, they might have had the briefest of head starts.

Instead, Roe grabbed Mayadeen's hand and urged, "Don't move, Captain Damned. We can't run. We have to stay where it can see us."

Mayadeen took a breath. The boy was right. There was naught they could do against such a foe if it decided to make them its quarry. They could only hope it decided to the contrary.

"Yer a mate and a trump, Roe," said Mayadeen without taking her eyes off of the Crown Bear. "That big fuzz fucker comes at us, ye run back to Captain Fenn and Laddy and don't stop."

The great bear took a few steps back from the water's edge, the fat stores in its ample limbs jiggling with each movement. It sniffed the air again, almost as if it sensed something else within its mobile domain. With an awesome heave, the beast stood up on two legs, its massive head rising well over twelve feet into the sky. Mayadeen withdrew her rapier. The blade would do little good against the fuzzback's thick hide, and only the bear's own weight could allow any vulnerability to the long blade's piercing of throat or heart. For that, the beast would have to be upon her, and nothing in the world of the living would be able to survive such a force.

The crown bear roared again, its lips sputtering out to reveal teeth as large as daggers.

"Roe, behind me. I'll distract it and that's when ye fly into the bush." She glanced down to Roe who remained motionless. "That's an order, damn ye, seaman!"

Mayadeen scanned quickly around for something big and decided upon what she was already holding. She swung the jug and threw it into the middle of the oasis where it made a sizable splash. "To me, ye stinkin' ball of matted shit! May the gods stick it in yer arse as I stick it in yer—"

The crown bear lunged into the water. Mayadeen fell back as she watched the grumbling storm of hair, spume and teeth half the distance between them.

The bear's grumble turned into a guttural yelp. It stopped and shirked to one side. Three spears now protruded from its lower back and side. The beast turned and stomped into a charge towards a group of armored soldiers with round shields that emerged from the grasses. Another group of soldiers—bulls as they appeared—pursued the bear from its flanks. A screeching roar and a swipe sent one man flailing over the prairie grass like a child's stitched toy.

With the fight moving away, Mayadeen jumped into the water to retrieve her jug. She still hadn't wetted her cracked lips and quickly cupped some cool refreshment into her mouth. She noticed Roe had disappeared into the grass as she commanded. That coupled with the water nearly made her smile.

She began to wade back to the tall grass when ten more bull soldiers with weapons drawn surrounded the pond.

Mayadeen sighed. Suddenly her whole body ached, and whatever surge of energy she'd felt before entirely subsided. She brought up the filled jug with two fingers and took a long swig. "Fie, ye glittering swabby cocks. Join me for a drink?"

"Captain Damned!" Roe peered out from willow grass between two of the soldiers.

Then something hit Mayadeen in the head.

#

When Mayadeen woke up, four dark-skinned bull soldiers wearing plate mail peered down at her with their long swords drawn.

"Give her some space," came a male voice with a thick accent. "And withdraw your weapons."

As the soldiers did what they were told, Mayadeen reached for her belt to no avail. It would seem she'd already been disarmed. The shard, of course, still remained a lump in her pocket. As she did with the witches of Valindrost, Shorsas must have masked the shard from a body search. There'd be no getting rid of that ghost of a splitty.

A bull wearing much nicer raiment of tooled leather and golden steel plate stepped forward, the same who spoke before. His raven black hair was pulled into a small ponytail. "Forgive me that I had to disarm you, Captain," he said. "I also thought it better not to disturb your rest. It appeared as though you needed it."

Mayadeen felt the egg on the back of her head. "That what ye call it?" She looked around from a patch of dirt beneath the large siclus tree, where the damnable Crown Bear had made its stand. She shifted sharply when she spotted Roe sitting by the campfire and gnawing on a piece of meat. Mayadeen salivated at the sight of it. She rose carefully to her feet, gaining at least five inches on all of the intruders. As to Laddy and Creyland's whereabouts, she didn't surmise.

"They have food and water, Captain Damned," said Roe with some sort of cooked fowl in his mouth.

"I am Siljan," said the leader. He revealed a water bladder and took a quick sip from it. Then he pitched it to Mayadeen.

She took a long drink herself then threw the bladder at one of the soldiers who took it hard against his chest. Mayadeen addressed Siljan. "Fuck is this and where are my bulls?"

"Your male companions are safe and were escorted ahead to our encampment," replied Siljan. "One of them went willingly while the other ... did not."

Mayadeen had a good idea of which one went willingly, the greasy peacock.

Siljan continued. "The boy there was rather adamant about staying with you. We gave him some meat off of a fresh kill."

"Well, Siljan, this is some desolate fucking main for me to keep running into everything on two legs. Who sent ye?"

Siljan raised a brow. "You are as astute as your reputation suggests, Captain Damned. Indeed, we have been tracking you since the Rullite incursion on the boy's tribe. Her Majesty, the King, wished me to personally intercept you."

"That so?" Mayadeen spit a thick one into the dirt just inches from the foot of one of the soldiers. She was surprised to find the stalwart little man didn't flinch. "Well if ye ain't with Lusul or Ursade as they're no fan of cocks, then ye must be with that one in the north, Bolora. Never figured she'd be so anxious to see me."

Siljan furled his brow. "I do not speak of Bolora or her false kingdom. I serve Leweln, King of the Scorprince and ruler of the great realm of Sundvane."

Mayadeen reeled. "That desert cunty?"

XVII
THAT DESERT CUNTY

There needn't be such disparity between the sexes. Men can take orders just as well as women, and loyalty begets uniformity.
~ General Tavilus of Edenvane

Leweln's Sundvanian army was bivouacked about four leagues northwest of where Mayadeen and Roe had stood off with the crown bear. Siljan and his men all had mounts, but he'd informed Mayadeen that upon hearing the great bear, they'd left their horses at another tiny oasis less than a league from the other. That watering hole was where the clawbacks had congregated after the fuzzback claimed the first puddle for itself. Siljan's bulls slaughtered four of the clawbacks, each about the size of a small reef seal, with little sharp talons protruding in rows down scaly backs.

Now Siljan and two other soldiers escorted Mayadeen and Roe through their primary encampment. The designs and aesthetic of the Sundvanians were different from anything else Mayadeen had come across in the Warlands. Vibrant reds and burgundies were used against whites, creams, and golds. Their flags and shields bore the sigil of either a star or a sun with what appeared to be the coiled tail of a scorpion within. The smells were also different here, with exotic spices wafting from scattered cook fires. The unique aromas of oils and perfumes that leaped from the tents reminded Mayadeen of the various desert lands she'd visited over the years, their climates fostering similar delicacies by the hot sands and arid winds.

Roe stayed close to her side, and his head strained to not lose sight of several bulls engaged in combat training exercises with wooden dirks. Unlike Lusul's, this was an army fashioned for a more regimental prerogative, though a slightly savage and undisciplined veneer still set these uniformed warriors apart from the traditional militaries found in the Meridian Isles, Edenvane, and the Soldrons. There were female soldiers as well, though far fewer than the men and most likely of higher ranks. The group of bulls they now watched, however, would be vanguard fodder. They strained and huffed like typical males striving for a cause, yet Mayadeen supposed they could prove formidable in swarms. When she seized the chance, she'd be sure to teach Roe how to kill like a Daughter born.

The five of them arrived at a pavilion slightly larger than the rest, with two guards stationed at either side of its draped canvas entrance. One of the guards slapped his hand against the tent flap upon seeing their approach, and out stepped a swarthy man with a tattooed bald head and a long, pointy beard. He wore burgundy robes with a tabard bearing the recurring scorpion sigil. He struck Mayadeen as being some sort of sorcerer, although male magicians were rare in the whole of Tabor.

"This is Sajar Premba," said Siljan. He gave Mayadeen an understanding smirk. "Yes, he's exactly what you think."

"Another witch," grumbled Mayadeen while sizing up the fancy bull. "Yer kind seem to be right plentiful in the Four-fuckin' Kingdoms."

Sajar Premba did not look amused. He glanced at Mayadeen's holstered rapier and daggers. "Siljan, why did you not remove her weapons?"

"We did," said Siljan. "But she demanded—"

"She *demanded?*" Premba scowled at Siljan and turned his granite brow onto Mayadeen.

"You'll need to relinquish those before entering."

"That so?" she replied. "The next time I'll be parting with these implements is when I'm stone dead and they're plundered."

Premba straightened. He looked at Siljan, who only shrugged.

"Mayhap the seven of ye bull cocks could manage that." Mayadeen lifted her eye patch for some air and spat in the dirt. "But by the gods high and low, six of ye couldn't."

She could flourish her rapier and impale the silence that followed.

"Wait here, if it please you," Premba said at last, and he ducked back into the tent. After a moment he returned. "As you wish then. But the child cannot enter."

Mayadeen was about to protest again, but then figured Roe might be better off with the bulls for the time. Other than the magician, she'd sensed minimal hostility from the Sundvanians, which could only mean that whoever had her—mayhap one of Leweln's generals or ambassadors—wanted something from her. Siljan seemed like he could think outside of his duties, and Mayadeen even found herself fancying the taught, sunbaked man. Of course, there was still the matter of where they'd taken Creyland and Laddy. Leverage was a master hard to defy.

She knelt to Roe's level, though even on a knee she stood three heads taller. "Ye stay with these soldiers until I return. Mayhap they'll dole ye out more vittles 'n' drink." She glanced up at Siljan who nodded at her suggestion. "And on my lee, don't ye try flyin' off, shipmate. I'll need ye to help crew my vessel. Aye to that?"

"Aye, Captain Damned."

Mayadeen tousled his wiry hair. She stood and turned to Premba.

"Follow me then," said the sorcerer.

#

Inside it smelled like a potent mixture of herbs and death. Embers glowed in a nearby fire pit, and Mayadeen at once recognized the stone contraption set above it. The device was similar to the one

Elona used in her private quarters back at Lusul's camp—an amplifier as Red had called it.

Sheer white drapes separated one side of the pavilion from the other. They were pulled back from within by two large servants, definitely bred of the natives, probably Rullites. Mayadeen wondered how many of Lusul's savage bitches had found themselves serving under a different Sister King.

At the center of the space sat a woman. Her features were bold and perfect, with eyes so large that the greys of her irises glinted and sparkled in the lowlight. Her dark, straight-combed hair formed a long ponytail, clamped off at sections all the way down, which fell to one side of her broad shoulders. Her robe was simple yet elegant—white satin embroidered in gold lace—with metallic fasteners down the trim that looked to be crafted from pure gold. She lounged on a chair constructed of large bones, leather and fur. Her feet were propped up with a blanket covering them.

And if not for her state of infirmity, this womaner would be one of the most handsome Mayadeen ever laid eye on.

"Thought Lusul would have painted herself with your innards by now," said the woman. "Your mettle definitely hails from the Island Realm. You pirates would survive the next Scourge of the Fallen." After a sudden coughing fit, she gestured for her servants. One of them brought her a chalice from which she took a long sip. She cleared her throat and pounded twice against her chest. "Do you know who I am?"

This was no jaded general or privileged emissary, and Mayadeen almost cackled in disbelief. "Ye're King Leweln, and I've the luck of an impotent bull on Seedus."

Leweln laughed and suffered more coughing. "I celebrated Seedus once while visiting Ateria many years ago. I never understood the allure of it."

Mayadeen glanced at each of Leweln's rippled womaner servants. "Nay, I don't suppose ye would."

Seedus was a fertility festival celebrated in many nations across

Tabor, usually on the last day of summer. In the Island Realm, the ancient holiday had devolved into an excuse to have barges of wanton sex rather than a convenient way for a Daughter born to choose seed for a child.

Leweln shooed away her servants with a couple half-hearted waves of her hand. "Leave us."

They each obeyed with a bow of their heads and glided to the tent's exit. Their scents of sweat and perfume wafted past Mayadeen. At least they attempted to smell better than Lusul's fermented twats.

"You, too, Premba. Go find out which of my generals wishes me dead most. I'll be sure to disappoint her for as long as possible."

"Your Majesty, this pirate is armed—"

"Leave us, I said." Leweln focused on Mayadeen. "Swords are of little use in matters such as these."

Premba glanced hard at Mayadeen before giving into a bow and then pivoting away.

Soon it was just Mayadeen and the King of the South. Although what she was doing in the north would be the first big question wanting to be answered.

"You seem confused, Captain. You can speak your mind with me. It would prove a refreshing change around here of late."

"Well, uh ... Yer Majesty?"

"Dispense with that. You know my name. Besides, I am a king only to those who serve me."

"Womaners for yer servants and bulls for yer soldiers? Almost seem Edish in yer ways."

"You accuse me of too much. I simply understand that men are useful beyond their third legs, though I've been so often disappointed."

"Mayhap." It was becoming difficult to believe that Leweln shared the same blood as her sisters.

Leweln scoffed at Mayadeen's unspoken thoughts. "As if you yourself don't insist on men to crew your ships? You and I have a lot more in common than you know, Captain Damned, not the least of which involves angering and vexing my sisters."

"I've only been trying to get the hell out of their lands. On my lee, that's the truth of it. And yer the only one of 'em I thought I wouldn't be meeting."

"And even that I'm afraid wasn't by chance." Leweln coughed and took the final drink from her cup. She turned it over in the air. "Fetch that bottle and we'll partake in the only decent wine for seven moons in any direction."

Mayadeen spied the roped bottle she referred to and retrieved it from a small end table. She undid the cork with her teeth and approached Leweln. The King of Sundvane held out her golden cup and Mayadeen tipped a generous pour.

"We drink to the end of the barbarian kings," toasted Leweln. "Myself included, and to our miserable lands opening up to the world at last."

Mayadeen waited for Leweln to drink first, and the latter did so with a smack of her lips. Mayadeen took a pull straight from the bottle. It was, indeed, good wine.

"Not by chance ye say?" Mayadeen pretended to be surprised. The various schemes she'd fallen victim to since Elona and Creyland's double-crossing conspiracies would make even the wind seem calculated against her.

"You and your friends travel north, do you not?"

"Aye. And not out of want."

"No, I would say not." Leweln smiled. "Not even the most adventuresome pirate would seek out Bolora's company."

"I need a ship, s'all, and I've had to traverse the whole of this fucking main to secure me one, if there's one to be had." Mayadeen took another pull from the bottle.

"A pity we hadn't drunk together before now. I would have given you any ship of your choosing. Unlike my sisters, I have a prosperous sea trade out of Tyrport—"

Another volley of coughs overwhelmed her, and Mayadeen shuddered to watch a good portion of wine fall from Leweln's cup to the dirt floor.

After tilting her head back with a languid sigh, Leweln continued. "But I'm not much longer for this life, and I couldn't swear to your safety once I am gone if you were to join our caravans on a return trip to Sundvane. Besides, we march forward, not back. That is why Premba, and a handful of his most trusted men, will accompany you north to Bolora's stronghold at Crinmarr Spire. As you say, if there is a ship to be had at Bolora's stronghold, you can secure it before my armies arrive and sack the entire wicked place."

Mayadeen couldn't help but huff, for the golden question always seemed to bring up the rear of a powerful person's generosity. "And what would ye be wanting from me?"

"That deal has already been struck. It would seem you yourself have a sister that cares deeply about your well-being." Leweln swished the wine around in her cup. "All three of my sisters want me dead." She shrugged and took another sip.

So Elona was alive. Although Mayadeen was relieved, she was equally roiled that once again her insufferable half-sister plotted an intervention. "Sister ye say? Ain't got a sister I know of."

Leweln smirked. "Very well. Then some delusional little witch who worships you secured an alliance between myself and Ursade for your safety and procurement of a ship in return."

"That so? Well then it seems once again I'm the smelly bait dangling from my own fucking line." Mayadeen nearly set down the wine bottle, but decided to guzzle the last quarter of it instead. Although it didn't have the same boot as rum, it eased her head just the same. "We're done here, damn ye. The sooner we set out the better, whatever deal ye struck."

"You're angry. I can understand that," assured Leweln. "But you're lucky to even be standing. Which brings me to other matters."

Mayadeen heard the tent flaps open and she turned to see Creyland Fenn thrown forward by two male guards. He barely moaned when his face hit the dirt, having been beaten to something resembling a slab of rotten meat. He was stripped of his breastplate down to a torn white shirt and ragged trousers. Even his boots had been removed. That was by the far the worst of it—Mayadeen liked to think that they would at least keep her boots on if she was to be subjected to torture.

She loved this man once, though it was a selfish and chaotic love—a forbidden and exuberant memory like a place that one has visited but will never see again. Mayadeen put a hand on the hilt of her rapier and twisted back to Leweln. "Where's the boy?"

"The child is fine. As is your other skinny companion." Leweln's face grew dark. "But why by the nectar of men would you be traveling with this Edish swineherd?"

Mayadeen relaxed. She and Creyland both had gathered many enemies over the years, but it would seem one of them reaped a reunion at last. What had seemed like an ambush turned out to be a simple comeuppance—for one of them at least. "So yer acquainted with this feather cock, are ye?"

"You'll answer my question, first," warned Leweln.

"Creyland Fenn and me go back a ways, aye."

"He's your ally?" Leweln suppressed another cough.

"Nay. He's my mortal fucking enemy, ye might say. But he can be a trump when put to proper use, and I need him for a particular venture."

"He's a reckless thief," scorned Leweln. "He pillaged at least two of my ships and nearly cost me my trade treaties with Marbane." ·

Mayadeen huffed. "*Reckless* is the word rightly chosen."

King Leweln remained unamused.

Mayadeen drew in a deep breath and wished she had more wine. "With all due respect, Leweln, and ye pocket mine twenty-fold, I'm the greatest bloody thief on the Nine. But unlike this idiot, I know who not to plunder." Speaking such a truth was a gamble, but since this affable Sister King already knew Mayadeen's own notoriety, it might serve to square the general lack of honor in the room. If not, well, at least she wouldn't die sober.

After an eternal moment and a final drink from her goblet, Leweln guffawed. She almost spoke but laughed some more.

Mayadeen glanced at the guards who'd dragged in Creyland. They appeared confused but stood at the ready with their own weapons, two with spear and two with sword.

Leweln gathered herself. "Two infamous pirate captains without ship, crew or water to put them in! The world is changing, Mayadeen Damned, and it's only a matter of time before your petty conquests become as isolated and meaningless as the Warlands Main.

"But, alas, you've done me a service, no matter your intentions. In less than a fortnight Sundvane will rule three of the Four Kingdoms. Lusul's forces will be broken, Bolora will be unseated, and that intrepid Ursade will have to agree to an accord on my terms. I only hope I'm around long enough to see it."

"For my own, I hope I'm out to sea fast enough not to see it, yer Majesty," said Mayadeen. "And I do speak the glittering title as ye're the only king I've ever met that might actually be worthy of it."

Leweln smiled wanly. Mayadeen could see the weariness in her eyes was winning one of its final battles.

"And this puddle of liquefied shit they call Fuckin' Fenn of Edenvane?" Mayadeen asked. Part of her felt for Creyland while part of her could care less. It is how it had always been between them.

"He's all yours and will be delivered to your quarters. I'll even have him tended to so that he's not too much of a burden. After all, you still have our business with Bolora. And for that, my friend, you'll need all the help you can gather."

#

That night, good as Leweln's word, Creyland was brought to Mayadeen's small, yet private tent. Two bull soldiers all but carried him to the rolled back flap entrance. Roe and Laddy were kept in a separate tent under guard, although Mayadeen had been allowed to see them briefly before shown to her own accommodations. Roe was sound asleep, and even Laddy seemed too tired for his usual protests. Four soldiers also stood watch outside Mayadeen's own tent. Leweln didn't entirely trust Mayadeen after all, but such could only be expected and Mayadeen didn't begrudge the ailing Sister King for her precaution.

The guards exited and Creyland promptly collapsed to the ground next to the small fire pit.

"A sad sight are ye, Fenn. If I were any younger and dumber, I might even give a rum 'n' piss."

Creyland moaned. "By the gods I've loved me an unjust woman."

"An unjust love deserves as much," retorted Mayadeen. "At least Laddy, I heard, put up a fight."

"Laddy? He all but waved the white kerchief." Creyland winced in pain and rolled to his side. "I'm the one who drew on them."

This was news, and Mayadeen could usually sense whether Creyland Fenn was lying, speaking true or prancing somewhere between. So Laddy was the one who, according to Siljan, had gone willingly. Perhaps the young bull had finally seen too much. Either way, his loyalty would now be in question. It was a high and swaying precipice to have to add to an already unsure scaffolding of shit that was the entire trip north.

She exhaled with the burden of eternal consternation and sat down beside Creyland. She gently moved his head to rest on her lap. His tongue could yield honey almost as well as it could turn a twat inside out. Having spent these past days with the scoundrel reminded Mayadeen of how comfortable he made her feel. It was as if she'd known him all of her life, like annoying twin siblings who could finish each other's sentences—a strange serenity born of a stalemate between the urge to fuck him and the urge to kill him.

"What's next, Emerald Eye?" Creyland grunted with closed eyes.

Mayadeen cleared away the greasy, blood-encrusted bangs from his swollen forehead. A thick salve had been applied to his wounds. The ceaseless feather cock was a survivor, and she'd drink to that.

"We go with the bull magician and a handful of escorts to Bolora's domain on the morrow," she answered. "To what true end, I ain't privy, though Leweln's army will follow anon."

"Sounds like she's sending the messengers. And you know what happens to them."

"Aye, aye. This Bolora sounds to be a demon bitch, sure as weeds in the sea. But Lewaln's on her way to the Bone Yard, 'n' I surmise she wishes us a fighting chance, if nothing more than as a final affront to her despised kin. She's no love for any of 'em."

The shelter of the tent, the soft crackle of the pit fire, and the warmth of Creyland's head on her lap made Mayadeen feel like she could finally succumb to a proper night's sleep. Her eyes grew heavy with her head propped against her bear skin travel coat and saddle. She'd grown accustomed to resting this way the past several nights, yet she would no longer need the saddle as she already knew the horses would not travel through a magician's portal. They would be requisitioned by the Sundvanians, although the wretched animals never belonged to Mayadeen to begin with.

Creyland's cough and another moan brought her away from the precipice of sweet slumber.

"Why Lewaln of all bloody people?" Creyland asked while barely moving his lips. "How'd she find us?"

Mayadeen sighed. "Elona."

Creyland's eyes opened slightly. He smirked and wheezed a laugh of disapproval.

"I've no trust for Lewaln and her fancy wine," insisted Mayadeen. "But I trust my... I trust Red." She caught herself, for now wasn't the time to start explaining cursed bloodlines and sad matters of family. "Ye should be thanking her, damn ye. She struck a deal 'twixt Ursade and Lewaln for my own skin. 'Tis the only reason we laze in a warm tent."

Mayadeen peered up to the smoke hole at the top of the tent. Faint stars shimmered through the rising haze. Those same stars, which looked to be part of the Flavus constellation, would always connect her to her home, to the Nine Seas, and to her sister. They even connected her to the Southern Isles, and soon her sight would set on those treasure-strewn lands once again. "As for yerself, Fenn," she said while still gazing at the misty cosmos, "they'd've stretched yer skin to the tanning rack. Mayhap I should've let 'em."

Creyland only replied with belabored snoring.

XVIII
A PROMISE AND A PORTENT

Sure. I once saw the future ... just before I saw the ground.
~ Dipson, *I'll Have Another*

Mayadeen at once recognized the dancing orb of spectral light in the golden-laced field before her.

They'd awoken at dawn to congregate in an area removed from the rest of the encampment. Mayadeen and Creyland were met by Premba, Laddy and Roe outside their tent. Whatever the magician administered Creyland for his myriad wounds during the night allowed for him to at least walk unassisted.

Roe now clung close to Mayadeen while holding onto the looped leather that also secured the scabbard of her rapier. She approved, as the pull of the magical doorway could be felt, and she didn't want the child to get caught unawares in its summons. For the first time she could make out a reddish hue to Roe's mess of hair. He and Laddy both had taken opportunities to bathe during the night, which sadly translated to Mayadeen only smelling herself. She'd traverse a hundred portals if they at last dropped her into something with water and a bit of soap.

Five more bull soldiers joined them at the field. To Mayadeen's curious pleasure, they were led by Siljan. The Sundvanian man possessed good, squared shoulders and legs that would carry him for days. She normally preferred the softer type, at least in build and stature. Of course, she knew well never to underestimate the power of carnality.

Mayadeen hailed Siljan with a chuckle. "The Good King decide to cast ye to the snakes along with us?"

Siljan only grinned. Mayadeen would have Siljan out of his raiment just as soon as the opportunity arose—a pun worthy of a shanty. She licked her tooth with an extra flip of the tongue.

"You have seen a thread rift before, have you not?" asked Premba, interrupting her lecherous thoughts.

"Aye. 'N' by the gods' gaping splitties I hope this'll be the last." She finally turned to the magician.

One of Premba's eyebrows rose. "It will spare us four days' journey on horseback. And unlike other magics you may have encountered, my castings are sound. You have nothing to fear."

Mayadeen wondered whether Elona could have made such a claim. Yet somehow she missed Red's inexperienced enthusiasm as compared to this tawny magician's cool confidence.

"Ain't about me, cock nymph. I've bulls to watch over. How might they fare yer thread hole?" she asked while tousling Roe's hair.

"The men will be fine. Most of our army traveled through multiple rifts to get here."

"That so? And Leweln?" Mayadeen already knew the answer to that one.

"Well, Her Majesty preferred to march ... as a show of strength for all the land to bear witness."

"Aye, Primbutt, and 'cause she's smart enough not to give herself to some charmer's infernal spellcasts."

"My name is Premba." The fire rose in his cheeks. "If you wish to stay—"

Mayadeen's hand shot up. "Nay, nay, damn ye. I'll go as I've little choice. As for the rest of my sea dogs, they'll choose for themselves. They weren't part of the pledge."

Creyland opened his mouth to speak.

"Ye're excluded, Fenn," added Mayadeen. "Ye're going through if it splatters ye across Bolora's portcullis. Not that ye could fare any worse."

Creyland rolled his eyes.

Mayadeen's concern was for Roe and whether or not she should allow the child to travel through the portal on his own accord. No matter what Primbutt the Bald assured, there always stood a chance of utter doom with forces unnatural.

"I'm with ye, Cap'n," said Laddy.

Mayadeen half nodded at him. Laddy appeared rested and sharper than he'd been in weeks. She decided not to press him about his questionable response to their ambush the previous day. If he was willing to risk his skin to travel through another portal only to risk his skin again at Crinmarr Spire, then a bonny trump he remained.

"One of ye swabbies be mum," said Mayadeen. She was talking to Roe, who only stared at the mesmerizing gate of pulsating light. She nudged her hip enough to jostle him out of it.

"Aye, Captain Damned," replied Roe.

"Aye? Aye what, ye budding cutthroat?"

"I'll go into it if you go into it."

She smiled down at him. "Ye're a sea pup worthy of the swells. On my lee, ye'll be riding 'em soon enough."

"Then if there are no further misgivings, we must ready ourselves," said Premba. "I have swaddled us within a curtain of the thread fire."

"That so?" Mayadeen scanned her arms and body. "Don't see or feel a bloody thing."

"It enshrouds you nonetheless," Premba assured. "Think of it as your own bubble, thin yet strong against the elements. Though it would not protect you from, say, an arrow, it can hold fire and water at bay."

The first time Mayadeen ventured through a thread rift, she hadn't even realized it. After piecing together a time line to account for the chaos of that fateful night that brought her to the main of Rul, she knew the *Sea Licker* passed through the large rift before the ship broke apart and before she lost consciousness. The traversal had been unnoticeable and instantaneous. She had no remembrance of whirling through space and time just as there was no flash fire from the void. Of course, with the *Licker* standing on its gunwales, the deluge of a massive storm, and the yawning rictus of a krode beast only ten flailing boot heels from Mayadeen's own, she wouldn't have known if she was on fire with a harpoon up her arse.

And yet now Mayadeen understood how she survived the shipwreck—more than just a fool's luck. Elona had conjured such a protective bubble as Premba's, which would explain how Mayadeen hadn't plunged to the cold, black depths along with her ship. As for the rest of her crew, although a few had made it to the beachhead, even a magical defense would have been worthless against a splintering hold and a two hundred ton sea monster grabbing for supper.

Then there was the second portal at Lusul's camp, which at the time Mayadeen thought to be her first. Once again, there was nothing to be experienced when she entered it. One moment she was running toward the gyrating blob of light and the next she was drooling face-first in a patch of weed grass in the Ragged Forest. That second time, however, she must've blacked out momentarily as she recalled neither leaving her feet nor hitting the ground.

"It is time," said Premba.

Mayadeen lifted her eye patch for a cool spot of air and drew in a breath. She watched as the five soldiers followed Siljan single file into the vague thread rift. No flash or showy exit. The radiance simply absorbed them.

Mayadeen took Roe's hand. "I offer ye a promise and a ..." She peered down at him, the shag of his hair and the young skin of his brow set aglow by the wonder before them. Those dark brown eyes yearned only for the adventure of life, and in them there was no death. There was no portent.

"A promise and a what, Captain Damned?" asked Roe.

"Just a promise," said Mayadeen.

And together they stepped into the light.

#

There was nothing beneath Mayadeen's feet. No ground and no sky above. Just a scent, old and musty, like a seaside shack with damp linens and tarps under a thousand days of salt and gray. She no longer felt Roe's small hand in her own, and she panicked.

A promise.

But then she floated past the hull of a most beautiful ship; its magnificent prow and figure head rising into the abyss. Flames rose to engulf it, the heat so intense that Mayadeen could feel her own flesh singe. And before she could scream it was gone—the sort of gone as if it never was. A pair of wings fanned out from the darkness, wings resembling those of a bat. A giant black spider bobbed upon clouds of impossible webbing. An equally ebon snake unfolded as tall and stout as a guard tower. Mayadeen saw her mother; an image not far removed from the others, and felt the crunch of Mabelia Damned's hard fist against her cheekbone. Her mother smiled and told her she loved her, and then cuffed her again in the nose. *That which does not kill ye ...*

A portent.

Something burned through Mayadeen's blood. It started in her stomach and flared out to her fingers, toes and head. Suddenly, she could see with both of her eyes. Thoughts and remembrances dashed through her head that were not her own—a parapet overlooking the masses of great city, a steaming pool with splashing children, a chasm filled with golden artifacts, bronzed statues and jeweled trinkets of every shape and size. The metallic taste of blood permeated her palate and olfactory while its warmth cascaded from her lips and down her naked body. She gurgled with joy, a perfect-sized shaft growing and receding within her. All around her gathered the dead, bloated faces of her sunken crew. Jagger, Yolton, Tyker, Stromm.

Their mouths moved to *a promise and a portent.*

Mayadeen cried out to them. Again she saw the leathery wings and scales and legs. Dark. Alive. Almost human. They were closer. They enveloped her. Then it all went away—a gut-wrenching emptiness in its wake, and the tomb of her right eye sealed once again.

#

Mayadeen was being held up under her arms. She gained her footing and let loose a backhand, which hit squarely into the side of a helmeted head. A soldier grunted as he staggered from the blow.

She recognized the Sundvanian, one of the bulls Premba brought along. More faces all at once came into focus around her—Creyland, Laddy and smallish Roe amongst them. Their voices faded in from dim to deafening. The pounding in her head forced her to one knee.

"Emerald Eye, you with us?"

"Give the Cap'n a berth, ye sand fuckers ..."

"Captain Damned ... Captain Damned ..."

The sharp stabbing behind Mayadeen's good eye subsided to a dull throbbing. She looked up to find Roe directly in front of her. She smiled and placed a hand on his shoulder, in part to assuage him and in part to find her balance. Sajar Premba loomed over them.

"You nearly did not make the transference," he said with certain awe in his voice. "I felt your peril ... but ..."

"But what, damn ye sorcerer?"

"Something ... beyond my abilities took over." Now Premba's incredulity seemed as though it troubled more than intrigued him.

Mayadeen knew bloody well the Crystal Cunty had something to do with it. Shorsas either took advantage of Premba's magic to further assert her dominance over Mayadeen or intervened simply to save Mayadeen's skin from dissolving into a witch's purgatory. Though the former was more probable, Shorsas had shown more than once that she'd wished to remain in Mayadeen's keeping—or for Mayadeen to remain in her keeping—for the time.

Creyland stepped in and helped her to her feet. Looking at him now, she wondered if their misadventure together would prove something more than a temporary alliance.

"You really need to turn around and take in the view," he said through a swollen, lacerated smile.

Mayadeen did so and because of the air itself, which already began to invigorate her, knew exactly what she would behold. Five or more leagues out, beyond the sprawl of a small city and the towers of a keep, the bluish gray waters of White Bay glistened beneath the glowing afternoon clouds.

Captain Mayadeen Damned, First Daughter born to Nine Master Mabelia Damned and heir to a seat at the Table of Corolon—unless her insufferable, bastard of a half-sister ultimately screwed that up— knew at that moment nothing born of nature would stop her from reaching the Jeweled Sea again. She rested a hand on the hilt of her rapier and considered her options. If she struck fast and hard, she might be able to take out Premba and two of the soldiers before the other two escorts and Siljan were upon her. For that to succeed, she would need Creyland's aid, and he was in no fighting shape despite having halfway healed overnight. Laddy, too, would have to be quick to exploit the coup, but the young bull wasn't known for being quick when it came to anything. Then there was Roe. The boy was resourceful, yet there was no denying he would continue to be a liability in dangerous situations. Mayadeen had made a weak decision in taking the child under her flag.

"Captain Damned?" Premba broke her concentration.

"Aye, aye, Primbutt ... I'm fine." She looked at all of them. Siljan seemed to be the most out of place with his own kind, and Mayadeen wondered if she should try to recruit the sturdy bull jack for her prospective crew.

"If ye were wise, ye'd let us part ways here," Mayadeen continued after ending her gaze upon Premba.

"And why we would we do that?" Premba sounded curious rather than rhetorical.

"Ye think this Bolora is going to let us walk in, tell her she's about to have the walls razed around her, 'n' let us walk out? Heh. On my lee, ye'd be a foolish fuckin' magician if ye thought that much."

"We act as emissaries to the Fourth Kingdom of Sundvane," assured Premba. "And I fully understand the danger of our task."

"Do ye now? Ken what happened when Ursade sent emissaries to Lusul? The High Witch of Valindrost received a box back with their drippin' heads."

"She's right," said Creyland. "There's no heraldry or parlay among the Four Kingdoms. There are just four sisters who despise each other, although I've heard Lusul is quite fond of Bolora, which makes our being here even more foolhardy."

To Mayadeen's surprise, Siljan also spoke up. "Sajar Premba, the two pirate captains speak true. This only seems a suicide mission."

"Our King has given us a specific task, Siljan, and I live to serve my King to whatever end. Last I knew, so did you."

"We could also use the opportunity to scout out the city's guard and barracks in preparation for our King's arrival," persisted Siljan. "That would serve Her Majesty far better than merely alerting our enemy to an attack."

"Enough." Premba threw up both hands, a gesture of which Mayadeen was all too privy, and she knew he could set the lot of them aflame with a quirk of his eyes. Alas, there was just no cajoling a zealot.

Mayadeen turned her palms to the stand down position for everyone to heed. This must have appeared strange to the four Sundvanian soldiers who, as far as Mayadeen could tell, never wavered from their duty to Sajar Premba.

"We're all on the same side here," she said. "I'll fulfill my end of the raw deal given me by yer benevolent king, whose cleverness only bows to her hubris. By the gods high and low and up my splitty, I know a little something 'bout that myself. But I ain't come this far being a complete soddin' idiot. If we all venture into the jaws of the beast, then we're all going to be eaten."

Mayadeen waited for Premba to lower his hands. "I only ask that we proceed with a plan, Primbutt. Surely ye gather the sound reasoning in that?"

Premba furled his brow with a sigh. "I'm listening."

Part Four

XIX
BOLORA

Thou art a perfectly crazy bitch.
~ Olnera, *She Who Allows Death*

They made their way through one of the saddest open cities
Mayadeen had ever encountered. The town itself was called
Gronsenlek, which according to Premba translated to the clever
name, Village by the Sea. Unlike the pristine yet desolate Valindrost,
the squalid, rundown shacks and cottages of this shithaven
overflowed with inhabitants. Womaners and bulls alike scuffled
about their dull activities in the muddy, fecal-laden streets. Many
looked sickly or pale with tired faces and permanent frowns. The
agrarian customs seemed minimal here, with some scattered farmland
on the outskirts, but little in the way of tilled soil or garden plots in
the town itself. There was food to be had, however, and Mayadeen
snatched a large radish right from a vendor's gunny sack. The sleight-
of-hand trick entailed holding up a different radish, one from the
hock box, and inspecting it in front of the merchant while her other
hand lifted its target from the sack below. Mayadeen mastered the art
of diversion by the time she was ten years old, and it had never failed
her with yokels and peasantry across Tabor.

The plan she devised for Premba's consideration was simple

enough. Only she, Laddy, Premba and his soldiers would enter the castle. Roe would accompany Creyland and Siljan to the docks in a separate effort to secure a ship on the probable chance that introductions and tidings of *ye're fucked* didn't settle well with King Bolora. Mayadeen had spied several ships moored in the small harbor set behind the castle upon her approach, so despite the legion of unknown elements working against them, availability would not be one of them. Of course, for any vessel with more than a single mast, some able hands to crew it would also need convincing. Premba had given Siljan a couple rings of considerable value that could be used for a purchase, or at the very least, a charter. Although Mayadeen nursed no love for the stiff magician, she appreciated his willingness to conspire in the name of simple survival.

Before they'd entered Gronsenlek, Creyland conjured the idea of raiding an outlying farmhouse to secure some proper clothing for the covert portion of their plan. The residents were elsewhere, and so Creyland and Siljan had been able to walk in and walk out with a couple of tattered old seal-hide jackets that at least covered the foreign fashions of their upper halves. Young Roe would be fine in the wild monkey outfit he already wore.

Mayadeen's parting with Roe had been difficult. The boy didn't want to leave her side, and she felt a strange charge to keep him close. By all that was sensible, her feelings should have provided little foundation. She'd never particularly liked children, with all of their sniveling and constant need for attention, and siring a bull rather than a lass would be about as useful to her as a ship without sails. What's more, Roe had only been in her ward all of three nights. If she grew that fond of everyone she spent three or more nights with, half of Tabor would be considered family.

Either way, sure as the damp hair under her pits, Mayadeen reckoned Crinmarr Spire would be no place for a child. Elona told of how Lusul had simply handed Bolora the North, and it was apparent the youngest sister had not rose to power through experience or popularity. Judging by vast disparities between town, castle and harbor, the region of Leth must have had another ruling influence at one time. Funny then that only Leweln was considered to be a usurper amongst the Sister Kings.

Mayadeen took a bite out of the plump radish, its spicy rawness coaxing a tear from her good eye. "So, magician," she said while chewing. "I ain't yet gathered yer story. Wouldn't think ye to hail from Sundvane."

"You would be correct," replied Premba. He continued to cautiously scan the streets and shoddy facades as they walked side by side.

"The Thresnare?"

"No. Unlike many I never studied in Thresnare. I came from a tiny realm called Qwilan, far south of this continent."

"Aye, off the Seraphim Sea near the Rim of Heldersten. I know it well."

Premba met her eye. "Then you truly *are* a woman of the world, Captain." He continued his wary amble. "But what would bring such an accomplished Meridian pirate to the Four Kingdoms?"

"Why, the natural splendor, boundless treasure and hospitable folk, of course." Mayadeen took another bite but spat out a mushy part.

Premba laughed, though it was more a series of controlled *humphs*. "Sundvane is very different, you know, from the rest of what you call the Warlands Main. Color and light abound by sun or stars in the Scorprince. It's as if the gods paint each day anew. And the same can be said for our people."

"That so? How'd Leweln ever come to rule 'em?" Mayadeen already knew the story of how Leweln had seduced a woman twice her age, the then ruler of Sundvane, only to convince the pliable fool to send her two daughters to war against the Rullites. The daughters never returned, the King fell to her death from a temple spire, and Leweln was able to convince her sister in the North not to come and wipe out Sundvane. But Mayadeen wanted to hear Premba's undoubtedly more noble take on Leweln's overnight rise to deific power.

"Her Majesty ran away from the savagery of Rul when she was quite young. She crossed the Bone Veil alone, seven days and seven nights as the story goes—"

Mayadeen held up a hand and halted.

A murmur of foreign tongues rose, and at first Mayadeen thought it was the four bull soldiers who had occasionally argued or jeered with each other.

"Trouble, Cap'n," said Laddy with a hand on his dirk.

The townsfolk now lined the dour streets on either side. They spoke a language different from Rul, Drost or Sundvane, yet their words took on ubiquitous insult when backed by raised fists and spitting sneers.

Mayadeen saw it enough times before. A mob was forming.

#

A tumbling cabbage bounced and unraveled in pieces onto the thoroughfare.

Premba's soldiers broke into a flanking defensive position around Mayadeen, Laddy and Premba. They held their spears at angles, but without shields they did little to form any kind of barrier against the assembling onlookers.

More food, mostly rotten by the look and smell, whizzed by until some root vegetable broke apart against Mayadeen's cheek. She reeled from the sting, annoyed she couldn't return the gift to the coward who threw it.

"Keep close," directed Premba above the din, "but do not draw your weapons."

"If comes down to us or them," assured Mayadeen while keeping one hand on her rapier and the other in front of her face, "I'll carve my way to the bloody keep."

A chant emerged from all the shouting, which sounded something like *Use ka left.*

Mayadeen watched a clod of soil explode over Premba. The

rhythmic chant grew louder. "What're they sayin'?"

"Food. Food for the devils," said Premba.

Mayadeen could find no immediate reason why an entire town would think strangers to be devils, although she'd learned long ago to never try to decipher the whims of a mob, particularly one so isolated and ignorant as lived in Village by the Sea.

As they neared the exterior wall surrounding the castle, two large gates—not a rising portcullis as Mayadeen had predicted—swung open and a group of guards clutching halberds and clad in white vestments ushered forth. Laddy's dirk was now drawn, and just when Mayadeen's own blade exposed half its shine, the white sentinels formed a defensive circle against the swelling onlookers.

One of the sentinels, a gangly womaner with a deep vertical scar down an entire side of her face, stepped forward with her halberd held back. "Atuksa salem." She gestured at them to move inside the gates. "Atuk!"

Mayadeen heard a cry and glimpsed one of the crowd being struck down by a crescent-bladed halberd. More screams and cursing followed before the iron gates shut closed behind Mayadeen's group and half the defenders, leaving the rest in the streets to continue the butchery. Mayadeen thought it odd when she spied one of them shouldering the fallen carcass of a townswoman and carrying her off. Odd or not, it was an extreme and morbid way to deal with a bunch of unfortunates whose only offensive entailed rotten vittles and profanities.

Mayadeen waited a moment to catch her breath and motioned for Laddy to put away his blade. They stood in a small courtyard of cobblestone that led directly to the arched entranceway of Crinmarr Spire. The keep itself was old and weathered, with several colors of moss creeping across its dark and salt-stained masonry.

Mayadeen wondered whether King Leweln knew about the welcoming they would receive before ever reaching her sister's castle.

"Yer precious Leweln must've really had it in for ye, Primbutt. A fine reception, that. At least they aimed to feed us."

Premba ignored her and commanded his own baffled soldiers to stand down. The white sentinels outnumbered them two to one, and the Sundvanian bulls looked like cowing children standing beside these womaners of Leth.

Mayadeen flinched and scrunched her nose as she noticed they stood on a wide bridge built over a flowing sewage trench. Seemed Gronsenlek smelled of shit no matter where one happened to be standing. The clamor from the villagers outside subsided to intermittent shouts and some heated exchanges. Amazing how quickly sharpened steel could dismantle an angry mob armed with root vegetables.

"I am Pila," said the scarred leader of the white sentinels. She eyed Premba up and down and sneered as if offended by his entire presence. "The magician and his ... servants ... from Sundvane will gain no audience with my Master."

Mayadeen didn't like the sound of that, and Premba appeared to dislike it even more.

"My name is Sajar Premba, and I have been sent by order of King Leweln specifically to seek audience with your Master and King, Bolora."

"It matters not who you are, magician," said Pila. "My Master receives who would please her." She turned her blank gaze onto Mayadeen and added, "She chooses the pirate."

Mayadeen raised her eye patch for some air. She got no reaction from the stone-cold Pila.

"Not to worry, Premba," said Mayadeen. "I'll relay the salt 'n' sentiments of one Sister King to the other." She reached over and pulled Laddy to her side. "But this one's with me, choice or not."

Mayadeen heard Laddy swallow hard. If throats begged to be cut in the courtyard, so be it, and nothing up until that point suggested it would be a rash alternative.

"Very well," Pila replied. She moved to the keep's entryway. Two of the sentinels flanked Mayadeen and Laddy while leading them away from the rest of the group.

Mayadeen called after Pila. "What about them?"

Premba appeared quite perplexed by the entire exchange, as if he'd never been treated with such disdain or disrespect. If that was true, then Sundvane was just as isolated as the rest of the Warlands Main, trade runs or not, for no threshold in all of Tabor would grant a bull magician a friendlier reception.

"They will be shown to temporary quarters," said Pila. "And we will ensure our guests from Sundvane are well attended to."

Mayadeen nodded at Premba. They hadn't really formulated a plan if they were to be separated, but she suspected he could relay a message via his sorcery if the need arose.

"Come," said Pila. "My loving Master awaits."

#

Mayadeen and Laddy were allowed to keep their weapons while escorted by a single male servant into the torch lit belly of Crinmarr Spire. Pila and her fellow guards handed them off to the odd-looking bull while crossing into a dank foyer. A strip fashioned of metal and cloth covered his mouth and tied off at the back of his partially shaved head. Other than that, he wore only a white drape hanging from his shoulders, simple leather sandals and a familiar bangle clasped to his left wrist: twin serpents encircling and ending with two fangs curved in. Once they moved beyond the grand entranceway, the natural light invading from fenestrae and portholes gradually receded. They passed beneath pointed archways lined with heavy, dark tapestries, some depicting faint symbols as strange as they were subtle. The masonry, too, appeared dark—even blackened—in the ringed penumbras cast from spiked sconces that resembled crude weapons.

A corridor twisted around to a set of stairs leading up.

They ascended to a large chamber with neither windows nor skylight. Tall braziers with galloping flames lined the walls, their combined glow making up for a lack of afternoon sunbeams. But the stale air ensured the space took on more the tone of a crypt than a throne room.

The woman seated at the chair behind the center of a thirty-foot long banquet table bore no resemblance to any of her sisters, with a petite stature more akin to Elona. Pale and pretty, Bolora did carry the same grey colored eyes as Lusul and Ursade, yet hers were large and disproportionate to the rest of her sallow visage. There was something not right about those eyes, and Mayadeen suspected the rumors might be true regarding this sister's sanity.

"Lakta tukasa ul okvol," said Bolora to their muted escort.

He bowed his head and hurried off through an antechamber.

Bolora focused her disturbing gaze on Mayadeen. "They tell me you speak the common tongue," she said with almost no trace of an accent.

Mayadeen answered, "Aye, and the only one at that."

"Excellent. Of the six languages I know, I far prefer the common tongue. Maybe that's why it's the common tongue? Oh, I humor my big sister and these idiots around me who were squeezed out in her fields, but I rather enjoy the words used by the ..." She licked her lips. "Sculpted women of the Island Realm." She scanned Mayadeen from head to boots and up again. "Eat. Drink. Fuck. Kill. Short words that thrust like daggers. Oh, I do like the common tongue." Bolora's eyes latched onto Laddy. She picked a cherry from a bowl in front of her and rolled it in her mouth before splitting it with her front teeth.

One of her servants, groomed for leisure and wearing naught but a shoulder drape that exposed her supple breasts, stooped to remove the cherry pit from Bolora's mouth, the latter sucking the tip of the servant's fingers in the doing of it.

Another servant stepped forward with a flagon of wine to refill Bolora's gold chalice, which was nearly as large as the flagon. This servant was an athletic, well-hung bull completely naked but for a red sash wrapped tightly around his mouth.

Laddy blushed and crossed his hands in front of his crotch.

Insane or not, Bolora enjoyed appetites that went far beyond wine and cherries.

"We're here on ..." Mayadeen hesitated. She was about to say *on our own accord*, but such would have sealed the already questionable fates of Premba and his bulls. And although she didn't feel like she owed Leweln so much as a mouthful of chum, she had given the at least reasonable Sister King her word. "We're here on behalf of King Leweln, yer ... Reverence," said Mayadeen instead, now regretting having taken the direct approach rather than braving the local black market with Creyland. After all, the inexorable Premba had been the only one of the entire group with a death wish.

"Reverence? Do I look like that shrewish old witch, Ursade? Now Leweln ... *she* was the beauty of our brood. Haven't beheld her since I was a little girl, and even then I wanted to lick her wet. But I'll be seeing her soon enough, as you've got all my dear sisters in a frenzy. Total war it seems. Exciting." Bolora said all of this without the hint of a smile, like a dog snarling while wagging its tail.

"Ye know about that then, yer ... uh ... Majesty? Eminence?" Perhaps Mayadeen wouldn't need to elaborate on Leweln's wry threats after all.

Bolora yawned. "I am neither reverent, majestic nor eminent."

"Bolora, then," said Mayadeen unable to conceal her irritation. "Ye know me as Mayadeen Damned and this one is Laddy."

"I know you as Captain Mayadeen Damned. Captain ... now there's a title I could straddle with satisfaction."

"Well, I ain't much a captain without a vessel. A ship's what I need, and I've come to ask ye for one. I was never meant for these lands, but yer sister, Ursade, conspired to bring me here. And Lusul's the one who found me. As for my part in all o' that, I did only what begged doing."

"Indeed, I heard all about your little adventure and I'm quite thrilled you've decided to call on me. A true Daughter born of the Nine Seas in my own abode. Visitors are a rarity at Crinmarr of late, and I find myself suffocating in the doldrums. I will grant you a ship.

I will grant you whatever you want ... Captain."

Mayadeen and Laddy exchanged quick sideway glances. Now it was time for Bolora to ask for something, and sure as moss on the twat it wasn't going to be a neck rub.

"I'd be grateful," said Mayadeen, "but I'll repay ye in whatever manner ye fancy ... gold, jewels, another ship or all three."

"No, no. None of that. Such trifles would only increase my boredom and make me very tired, I'm afraid." Bolora took a drink from her giant cup, not bothering afterward to wipe away the dark red liquid streaming down the corners of her thin, colorless lips. "But there is something you have that I want."

Mayadeen felt the Shorsas crystal vibrate in her pocket. Now wasn't the time for a possession or other show of magic, and if Shorsas was trying to tell her something, then the biddy spirit needed to hold her non-existent tongue. But if it was a warning, Mayadeen had been ready for action since the moment she stepped foot in Crinmarr Spire. She cupped her hand over her pocket and steeled herself for a challenge. Other than the play-toy bull servants, only two armed sentinels stood guard at the rear of the chamber. She could easily get to Bolora before they could muster a defense, and she'd have Laddy for backup, no matter how dumbstruck and agog he looked at the moment.

"Your presence. Your presence at dinner is what I want." Bolora grinned slightly until her lips sprang back to their natural frown.

Cursed lil' monster. It was the one request Mayadeen was hoping not to have to honor. If she didn't procure a small ship and at least twenty hands to set sail before the night was over, then she would never leave. Leweln's forces would surely arrive by nightfall, and who knew what other surprises might follow? There was no time. She and Laddy would have to steal out, find Creyland, Siljan and Roe, and take the first ship they found—

"Do I ask too much of you?" challenged Bolora while swirling the drink in her cup.

"Nay, nay," returned Mayadeen, wanting at that moment to pull her other eye out for not ending negotiations then and there. "A bonny proposition, that. And one we'll take ye up on." She felt something expand within her, rising like a bubble to burst at the surface. Her senses of late had grown more connected to the pelitite shard, to the little piece of soul-trapped witch that was her bedeviled talisman.

"What of the Sundvanians who accompanied us?" Mayadeen put a hand to her head. Her vision began to blur. Now was no time for Shorsas to take possession.

"Ah, yes, the magician and his cocksures," said Bolora with no change to the fast and apathetic cadence of her words. "I could smell them even beyond the castle walls. We most certainly will have them for dinner."

"Aye, but the ship ... I'll need ... me ... a ... a crew ..."

"Then it's decided. You, and your yummy pet, will be my guests tonight." Bolora took a long sip of her poison. "And then you can *cast off*—I believe is the speak?—from White Bay as early as tomorrow if you so ..."

After the windswept sensation of falling, Mayadeen thought the last word she heard was *desire*.

XX
BEEF

I'm not evil. I'm hungry.

~ Anonymous

Soon we will be one. The radiant woman stroked Mayadeen's hair. Her effervescence washed over Mayadeen in soft, tranquil bliss. It permeated her limbs and massaged her bones. Pounding chest. Boiling blood. The love of something sharp and the hatred of something devouring.

It was inside her.

Belok fuhz Sinbalak!

Mayadeen gasped awake. She peered around a lavish guest quarters with vibrant drapery and fine furnishings. The receding light of magic hour fanned through open doors to a veranda. Her head still ached although the pounding had ceased and her vision returned. Laddy snored on a sofa set against an opposite wall. Mayadeen forced herself out of the bed in spite of its indulgent comfort, which tried to hold onto her with giant, invisible hands. The smell of succulent, roasted meats wafted from beyond the room's sole entrance. Her bed served as the room's centerpiece, a grand four-post delight made of onyx, jade and serpent wood. All three materials fetched a good price on the black market. Ransacking profitable fixtures, however, would have to wait another day.

She bounded to the thick wooden door and tried it carefully. It was unlocked, and when she poked her head out to the thin corridor, six of Bolora's white sentinels stared back at her. They each held their cursed halberds, which would be of little use in such a tight space, yet dirks also hanged at their belts.

Mayadeen just smiled and nodded at them.

She fell back in and closed the door. It could only be locked by the turn of a key, so dual access to the room could not be avoided.

She rushed to the veranda. Other than a tower blocking her vantage to the left, she had a good view of White Bay and most of the docks. At least three two-masted vessels listed on the moor posts, and a large, three-masted xebec kept anchorage on the shoals. Any one of them would make a fine exit from the Warlands. Unfortunately, from four stories up with sheer, mossy stone on all sides of descent, they would be difficult to get to.

"By the nine gods 'n' their holy splitties..." She ran back in and pushed Laddy with the heel of her boot. "Wake up, damn ye sawing idiot."

Laddy gulped in some air and sat upright. His nostrils flared. "I was dreamin' of my supper."

"Aye, and it may be our last. I need ye savvy and sharp. I was hoping to be pushing off the harbor nigh about now. Instead we're trapped with fancy fittings, tempting vittles and a fucking lunatic."

"Ye sayin' King Bolora has it in for us, Cap'n?"

Bolora's glib reception was unexpected, but despite her offerings there remained something most singular about the Sister King of the North. She was mad as a bitch without breakfast to be sure, but Mayadeen couldn't gather if hers was a careless or sinister madness. Whatever Bolora's game, she would have spies everywhere, and Mayadeen had to send word to the others as to the present change in their predicament.

"I'm saying what we're smelling is covering what we ain't smelling—squid piss in the vinegar."

"We've our blades at least," said Laddy. He glanced down at his belt as if to make sure that was still a true statement.

Mayadeen still had hers as well, but there was one thing missing. *Shorsas*. This time the spiteful spirit hadn't eluded being filched.

"Bugger all bloody hell ..." Mayadeen patted herself down. "What happened when I fell?"

Laddy bumbled. "Them big gallies, they, uh, lifted ye right up and carried ye, Cap'n. Carried ye right in to where we linger, they did. I watched 'em put ye on the berth. Ye were breathin'," he added with importance. "I, uh… well, then I thought I'd lay down myself, and, well..."

"Enough, damn ye. They took the magic shard. Did the bitches say naught?"

Laddy thought for a moment and then nodded. "Sundown. Dinner at *sundown*, said one of 'em."

Mayadeen crossed to the balcony once again. The sun would indeed be down in minutes, and she imagined Bolora to be the punctual sort. She squinted and scanned the alleys directly behind the castle wall as well as the marketplace and wharf beyond. The citizens of the strange, isolated township were beginning to vacate the streets. Gronsenlek didn't look to be the sort of place one wanted to occupy after dark. If the deprived saps only knew what they were in for with the arrival of a Sundvanian army.

Mayadeen had no wish for her short stay to be a repeat of Valindrost. She'd been able to keep one step ahead of the war only to have it catch up whenever she'd stopped stepping.

"We have to assume the magician and his bulls are dead," she said while returning to Laddy. Her head was spinning from one unforeseen scenario to the next, and the stolen pelitite shard brought up even more questions. "That bracelet ye wear ... let me see it."

Laddy extended his arm. The silver bracelet with twin serpent fangs curved slightly inward fit snug on his small wrist, so it definitely was fashioned for a bull.

"Ye've had this bangle since the Ragged Forest, aye?"

"Aye, Cap'n. Prick dropped it and then ye gave it to me."

Mayadeen's memory was still a bit hazy on that subject with all of the manipulative magic that was involved, but she did remember giving the bracelet to Laddy after her trusty redgull swooped in to say hello.

"Every one of Bolora's bitted bulls wore the like, and don't think she didn't notice it on ye. I wager Prick lifted it from the forest, which means King Crazy and her gagged cocks had been there."

Laddy thought for a moment. "Mayhap they was trapped in there same as we?"

"Mayhap," said Mayadeen, more to herself. "And mayhap Bolora was looking for the pelitite shard herself." She peered around the room and pulled a blanket from the luxurious bed. "We need to fashion a rope with knotted linens and climb out—"

The door to the guest room swung open.

#

There was little to be done but to accept Bolora's looming invitation to supper. Mayadeen and Laddy were escorted back to the same throne room, which had been converted from a cold, crypt-like chamber to a garish pleasure nest. Satin pillows and exotic fur rugs now covered the large space directly in front of the sectioned banquet table. Golden torch urns were placed for a more even, warming light that reflected and danced off of the silver and bejeweled wares setting the length of the table.

At the center of all this, eight bulls and two women rutted and pleasured each other in naked savagery like it was their last night in Tabor.

"Mayadeen, I am so elated that you have decided to join me," said Bolora with all the elation of a snake. "And with your luscious little bull slave, what's more." She motioned to the grunting, shifting group before her. "Would you derive pleasure from watching him fuck?"

"Nay," replied Mayadeen. "He'll need his vigor for later, 'n' it won't entail watching for my own part." She gave Laddy the slightest nod to make sure he was following her lead. Either way, the longer she could keep them both unmolested, the better chance they'd have to survive the evening.

"I see you brought your stabbing implements," said Bolora as if she'd already lost interest in the cross-sexual orgy happening in front of her. "They might prove quite useful for cutting your meat."

Mayadeen thought to laugh although couldn't gather whether Bolora jested. She took another inventory of the exits at either side of the grand chamber, plus a third side double door. Womaner guards—not the gagged bull slaves that seemed to serve for everything else—stationed themselves, two at each of the three archways. These sentinels wore padded leather armor, despite still sporting the white coifs and capes. And their halberds in this large space, unlike the castle corridors, would serve as perfect weapons for fending and herding.

A naked womaner cackled while she reclined and allowed a gagged bull to separate her thunder mane. The bull seemed small for his lover's supple proportions, but that didn't hinder him from hugging her pillars with each arm and burying himself betwixt. Nothing extraordinary there until the womaner reached up and squeezed the thrusting bull's wrist by his serpent-fanged bangle. Two dark streams trickled from fresh puncture wounds down the bull's hand and into her mouth as if she had placed herself beneath a weeping wine spigot. More couples repeated the perversion in various ways, with some simply bathing in the dripping plasma of their driving partners.

Mayadeen had witnessed a similar bacchanalia in the Palgremen Isles, but those godless savages at least used pigs' blood. She lifted her eye patch for some air and noticed Laddy trying to desperately remove the snake bracelet from his wrist.

"Not to worry my trump," she whispered to him. "I won't be wringin' ye dry any time soon." Mayadeen huffed although Laddy's current pallor suggested his own blood had reversed its flow and leveed itself to a single pool deep in the center of his husk.

Bolora squirmed and gyrated in her black throne, which resembled the shriveled body of a dead, giant web spider, and let escape what sounded like a short yelp of glee. "*Now*," she commanded while throwing her head back with an orgasmic exhalation.

One of the muffled bull slaves in the orgy, his pole pushed deep into the arse of his groaning partner, brandished a small dagger from somewhere beneath the pillows. In a frenzy of vicious blows, the rider bludgeoned his mount repeatedly under the rib cage. Blood spurted in leaking clumps as the victim thrashed and contorted into positions unique to the human body.

"Cap'n..." Laddy's voice arrived from far away.

Mayadeen recoiled, hand behind her back and pressed firmly on the hilt of one of her own daggers. Soon the two rutting bulls were a red, glistening mess, yet none of the other couples seemed to notice. Their group enthusiasm grew all the more.

From beneath the draped banquet table in front of Bolora emerged a bald, naked servant, her long breasts brushing against Bolora's hand as she rose. Baldy turned to eye Mayadeen while licking away the wetness from her lips.

"Mayadeen, you look as though you feel left out," said Bolora with an amazing sincerity. "Let your slave play," she pointed to the carnal entertainment, "and come join me at my feasting table."

The cloying carcass of the unfortunate bull before her should have placed Mayadeen's appetite in exile. Instead, the tangy smell of blood mixed with the succulent aromas of what was about to be served made her mouth water even more. It was a vile clash of sensory overload, but instead of shuddering in revulsion, she'd use it to fortify her resolve.

"When do we eat, s'all that interests me," said Mayadeen while forcing a smirk. "As for this one," she gestured at Laddy, "he's right fine at my side."

"Of course," said Bolora. "It would seem your appetites precede you, Mayadeen Damned. We have much in common, you and I."

Mayadeen presumed that wasn't an accurate assessment and nodded anyway. While a bull couple wrestled out another growling climax of seed and joy, this one without mortal violence, Mayadeen and Laddy took their places at the L-shaped table. They were situated around one of the corners where Bolora could still study them while maintaining just enough distance to discourage an assassination attempt. It would take a good leap and stride to close the gap, and at least three of her topless tongue servants hovered about to provide added insurance.

"For example," continued Bolora, "we both would wish to leave this castle tonight before Leweln overtakes it."

The side entrance double-doors flung wide, and four gagged slaves carried in the main course on a steaming platter. Sajar Premba was cooked to perfection upon a bed of potatoes, cabbage and leafy garnish. Only his arms had been removed.

Mayadeen's heart raced as she forced a rising lump of bile back down her throat. That Sajar Premba had been a self-righteous pain-in-the-arse bull magician was true enough, yet such a loathsome fate befitted no creature who spoke and stood on two legs, bull magician or otherwise.

The charade was approaching a dangerous end.

Mayadeen readied herself and withdrew a dagger beneath the table. With her other hand she squeezed Laddy's thigh. He gasped and writhed in his seat.

"Ye speak true," said Mayadeen to Bolora's smug assertion. "Leweln's on her way to take yer stronghold apart stone by stone, and she'll take no quarter on this chum puddle ye call a *kingdom*. I was to be the messenger, but I just didn't have the heart to tell ye how buggered are ye."

The servants set Premba's roasted and basted remains in front of Bolora. A sizable portion of his torso was cut away with fork and knife and placed upon her plate.

"The magician, however, certainly had the *heart* to tell me," replied Bolora. "As well as the liver, the kidneys, the tongue ..." She trailed off while ripping away the first fleshy morsel with her fingers.

The servants came around to dole out portions of Premba to Mayadeen and Laddy. The drone-like bull cocks appeared uninterested in the taut conversation at the table, and so they would be of little consequence should Mayadeen decide to launch a quick offensive on her wanton host.

Laddy stared at his plate as if it were staring right back at him, for which Mayadeen couldn't begrudge him. She'd have to be starving, frenzied and half of wit before turning cannibal.

Mayadeen kept her sight firmly on Bolora and her four other senses on everything else in the stifling room. "I don't eat people, magicians or otherwise."

"Well, we won't hold that against you," said Bolora while masticating. She swallowed and began tearing away another greasy mouthful. "On the contrary, I am infatuated with you, Mayadeen Damned. And so is my Master."

Her master? She's out of her teats 'n' timbers. "Didn't figure a king to have a master."

"Oh, yes, we all have masters. Mine happens to be very selfish. And, alas, she wants you all for herself." Bolora reached into her tunic and pulled a silver chain from around her neck. Upon the chain dangled three crystal shards of deep purple.

Three shards of pelitite.

Mayadeen rose from her chair. She at once recognized one of the three stones as her own.

Bolora gazed at her. "The ways in which I would have enjoyed you." She placed the next shred of dripping meat into her mouth.

By a hard snap of the wrist, Mayadeen's dagger spun beautifully across the table to pin Bolora's chest just above the fabled crystals. Bolora retched out a mouthful of Premba only to guffaw and laugh at her own blood and spew.

Mayadeen felt her eye grow to the size of her forehead.

"Laddy—" She leapt onto the wooden table, rapier drawn.

Laddy brandished his short sword while nearly stumbling over his chair, which he ended up kicking halfway across the room.

The white sentinels at the doors did not advance. Their halberds were angled at the ready, but their faces showed restraint.

Bolora's laugh subsided to more of a chuckle, and she dislodged the dagger from her chest with a twist and a pull. Her face appeared different—bluish and wan—as if all the blood within her had already escaped from that single wound. But the blood was minimal. Instead, a redness filled her eyes and her smile now revealed the edgy teeth of some carnivorous beast. She lurched slightly forward.

Mayadeen thought she noticed something move beneath the purple velvet cloak on Bolora's back.

Laddy whimpered squelched words, to which Mayadeen hissed, "Keep yer fucking stones."

Bolora coughed up more blood and then smiled again.

"I was going to suggest I come *with* you. But I suppose you wouldn't want me along?"

Mayadeen readied her other dagger—this time she would aim for the barmy bitch's eye—when a great combustion rocked the main entrance to the chamber. One of the large wooden doors blew entirely off its hinges, pinning and half crushing a floored sentinel. The other door flung wide to knock another guard to her knees.

A figure stood above the downed guards and rubble in the clearing smoke.

Mayadeen beamed like she might have at the sight of a newborn sister all those years ago.

"Another *magician*," said Bolora. "I could smell her beyond every stench in this room." She pointed with a sharp finger at Elona. "Kill her. You may certainly kill that one."

All of the remaining sentinels ran towards Elona with the furious ends of their halberds.

Faster than Mayadeen had ever seen him do anything, Laddy launched to intercept the nearest charging guard. He ran his short sword through her side before she could turn to parry the thick blade. A surprised yell escaped her.

The next moment all of Bolora's lackeys, including the orgy participants, were rushing the Sorcerer of Prenn.

Elona's hands rose into the air and a pillar of hellfire swirled up and around her robed body. One of the gagged bulls crossed within mere feet of the spectacle and immediately burst into flames, gnarling and writhing to the floor.

Mayadeen jumped into the center staging area of fluid-stained cushions, her rapier finding the belly of a flaccid cock bull and her dagger driving under the jaw of another. Both blades retracted to a shower of blood and bile. She turned to face Bolora, who seemed thrilled with the proceedings. A fist sank into Mayadeen's cheek as she was blindsided. She held onto her blades until the fist was quickly followed by a foot to her crotch. The pain shot through her and the rapier fell from her grip. She recouped to face her opponent, Baldy, the same cuntlicker who had carved Bolora's canyon during the blood orgy. Mayadeen slashed her dagger upward. Baldy defended the blow with a forearm and Mayadeen followed with an uppercut to her sternum. The sinewy womaner folded, and Mayadeen landed an elbow under her nose. Baldy dropped to the pillows and Mayadeen's boot put at least one more dent in her dome.

Catching her breath, Mayadeen glanced around to see Laddy grappling in a far corner with a halberdier.

"The necklace, Mayadeen. Get Bolora's necklace!" Elona clutched a bleeding arm while another doomed opponent screamed and burned in front of her.

Mayadeen again turned to face Bolora. *The necklace, aye. Three shards for the ancient witch, Shorsas.* But what would that mean?

Mayadeen swiped up her rapier and stepped onto the table in front of the mad Sister King. Another bull slave rushed forward and found Mayadeen's heel with his chin. In a single motion, she skewered Bolora's hand to the table with the rapier and crouched with a dagger to her throat.

Bolora never flinched. Her eyes closed, and when they opened again their color had changed to silver.

"Run, Mayadeen," said Bolora with a tone quite different from her own. "Take the shards and run." The silver receded from Bolora's own glassy eyes of crimson and onyx.

"What in bloody hell are ye?"

"By and by," Bolora grinned. "By and—"

Mayadeen slit the grayish throat from ear to ear. Bolora's head fell forward. The gore came dark and thick. If she recovered from that, then Bolora was something not of the world, for no mortal could suffer such a fate and drink another daiquiri.

Shorsas. She had peered briefly into the eyes of the possessor. Mayadeen ripped away the necklace from Bolora's hanging head. When she did so something surged within as if a larger version of herself was trying to escape a prison of stunted thew and bone. She felt faint and nearly fell backwards off of the banquet table.

"Mayadeen!"

Elona's cry sobered her. She rolled from the table to the fuck cushions. Smoke and flame billowed up from the drapes and tapestries at the main entrance of the space. There Elona stood while pointing. She breathed heavily and wiped away blood from her nose. But Red was in no immediate danger.

Mayadeen followed her sister's finger to see Laddy through the haze clutching his side near a great stone pillar. He kept his dirk up in an effort to block the halberd that chopped at him in deliberate jabs.

Mayadeen dashed towards the wielder, one of Bolora's smaller bitches who'd already taken some scratches herself. When she noticed Mayadeen, she threw down her halberd with a yell of frustration. Mayadeen didn't stop and her rapier ran clean through the womaner's gut. The victim spewed and Mayadeen quickly withdrew the blade to topple the impaled sentinel to the ground. If she was given the order not to harm Mayadeen, then she obeyed it.

Smoke now loomed above the entire chamber and Mayadeen could feel the heat from the flaming tapestries. She helped Laddy to stand up straight, but he had taken a sizable gash to his side. Mayadeen ripped away some of the dead sentinel's white tunic and pressed a ball of it against Laddy's wound. "Hold it firm," she told him.

She noticed Elona behind her shoulder as she assisted Laddy. "Ye came back to admire more of yer schemes, did ye, Red?"

"How nice to see you, too, sister," said Elona. "Can you walk, Laddy?"

"Aye, methinks," he responded.

Mayadeen noticed him perk up. "Yer gushin' enough from the wound, damn ye." She looked around to make sure no more of Bolora's guards hovered with halberds. The three of them seemed to be the only ones left standing. Mayadeen gave Laddy a shoulder while he kept a hand on his makeshift bandage. "Let's sod off. Red, lead the way out."

"Where's Bolora?" asked Elona as they hobbled towards the main entrance.

"Ye mean the immortal psycho/demon/cannibal barely tickled by my blade across her throat and through her heart? That the one, Red?"

"She's not what she seems."

"Ain't what she *seems*? That fuckin' right?"

They came to a vestibule with gossamer overhangs, which led to another corridor connecting to the castle's main foyer. Shouting could now be heard from just beyond that area, and a few of the voiceless bull servants ran by in a stumbling panic.

"Leweln's forces are here," said Elona. "But I suppose you already know that."

"Aye, aye, damn ye. Piss on 'em. We need to get us to the docks."

They exited through to where the main entrance to Crinmarr Spire met with the small courtyard to the iron gates.

"Fenn should have a vessel waiting for us," Mayadeen continued. "If not, then we'll be swimming 'cause I ain't squandering another night in the Warlands."

Ahead of them, several of Bolora's people stood at the gate and atop the torch-lit battlements while peering out into the night. Something had them rattled, and Mayadeen would have guessed it was Leweln's bull army already taking the city and about to storm the castle. But then she spied a single hulking warrior, double-bladed axe in hand, climb onto the ramparts while vaulting to engage Bolora's sentries. This warrior was obviously a Rullite, one of Lusul's she-monsters, which could only mean the Rullites had arrived before the Sundvanians.

Regardless, there was no exiting through the gate. Mayadeen remembered a small waterway, probably for sewage, that cut under the short bridge before the main gate.

"There," Mayadeen gestured toward the bridge.

Laddy's weight grew heavier, but somehow he was able to keep up. All three panted like slobbering fox curs. They stopped at the edge of the drain crevice, which cut down into the cobble about six feet.

"Looks like we'll be swimming, anyway," said Elona.

Some clinking of steel and furious yells came from above. Mayadeen swore she felt some blood spatter on her. "Those aren't Leweln's," she said while glancing up the twenty foot wall at the violent combat now happening. "They're Lusul's."

"Then we really are in trouble," replied Elona.

Red had obviously devised a plan to get into the castle and not so much a plan to get out. Then again, neither did Mayadeen. And yet the creature, Bolora, didn't want her dead, for reasons undoubtedly tied to the insufferable Shorsas, unless Bolora was saving Mayadeen for Lusul. Traps sprung against traps, and for once Mayadeen was without traps of her own.

"Captain Damned," sounded a voice from over their shoulders.

Mayadeen whipped around with her rapier ready to bite.

It was the same lanky bitch who'd first greeted them upon their tumultuous arrival at Crinmarr Spire—Pila was her name—now with two short scimitars at either side of her slender hips. "I have been sent to see that you get to your ship."

Mayadeen kept her blade up. "Fuck would we trust ye, gut-eating bilge harpy?" The action on the battlements and just beyond the iron gates grew louder by the moment.

"Because my Master has ordered me to keep you safe," replied Pila.

"Where's Bolora then?" Mayadeen glanced around half expecting the leering Sister King hovering next to them with flapping devil wings.

"There is little time." Pila looked disapprovingly at Elona.

"Mayadeen, we should go," urged Elona. She crossed to Laddy and placed his arm around her shoulder. "Laddy, can you make it? Let me help you."

"Aye, Elona. I can 'n' will," said Laddy.

Mayadeen hadn't taken her eyes off of Pila. "Leave them scimitars."

Pila hesitated but then obliged. She unsheathed both at once, hilts forward, and dropped them to the cobblestone.

"Now ye lead the way to my ship 'n' hope I don't bridge yer arse to yer splitty with steel."

XXI
WINE DARK SEA, BLOOD DARK CHOICE

Responsibility is measured simply by how often your choices affect lives. Power is measured by the number of those lives.
~ High Vicar Gwethol,
The Unofficial Memoirs

By the time the four of them reached the docks, Mayadeen could smell the metallic tinge of battle and siege ravaging the air over Crinmarr Spire. They used a passage through the sewers after all, which ultimately led to an exit from beneath the main wharf. The rear of the castle sat atop many layers of stone, and so the boardwalks leading to the quay were raised high on this end of the harbor. Pila remained morose, even while navigating the stink and pitch darkness of the sewage tunnel with naught but a candle lamp plucked from a sconce. Once they spotted moonlight at the tunnel's end, Mayadeen briefly thought about running the creepy bitch through, but figured they might still need her to procure any sort of a ship. Instead, Mayadeen stepped to the rocks far beyond the point where the sewer drain met open water, thrust her hands into the ocean at high tide and brought a cool, pungent splash to her nose and lips.

The sea once again belonged to her. If some ball of flaming death found her at that moment, she'd be a happy ghost in the Bone Reef.

"We made it, Cap'n," cried Laddy. He choked briefly on warranted tears while Elona merrily embraced him.

"Aye, by the gods high and low we did at that," returned Mayadeen. Before she could stay Elona off, her sister grabbed her by the arm and kissed her on the cheek.

"I knew you'd find the sea again," said Elona.

"Aye, aye, very well, damn ye."

But now it was time to find Creyland, Roe, and Siljan, board something that floated, and leave behind the cursed Four Kingdoms forever. *Only that would be cause for celebrating.*

When they climbed two high ladders to the rickety dock planks, there still appeared to be a selection of seaworthy vessels, although the one large square-rigged xebec she'd spied from her tower balcony had already left the shoals—King Bolora's own escape vessel no doubt. Three ships remained: two corsair-rigged schooners and a two-masted brig. Some cutters and whaling canoes also were docked, but those were small boats not made to sail in open waters.

Mayadeen turned to Pila. "Ye have us a ship then, galley?"

Pila glanced down at Mayadeen's sheathed rapier, as if she was challenging her to draw it. Pila pointed to the second largest of the three ships still moored, a two-masted schooner.

"Your ship there waits."

A schooner, though swift, was not built for long hauls in open waters and, depending on its outfit and armaments, might prove useless in a skirmish. This one appeared sturdy and well cared for, but daring the winter storms of the Fire Hoof was not a venture fit for its calling. The other schooner was slightly smaller and looked as though it hadn't sailed in twenty years. No, the brig would be the choice vessel for continuing on to the Southern Isles. Mayadeen guessed him to carry about three hundred tons, and at half the size of Mayadeen's old ship, the brig might even prove faster and more maneuverable than was the mighty *Sea Licker*. The only problem was the brig would take nearly twice the crew than the schooner to operate with any efficiency.

"What about the brig—?"

"Mayadeen," said Elona, with an urgency her sister recognized.

"Eh? Spill it, Red."

Elona side-glanced at Pila. "Mayadeen, you ... there's something you need to know before we—"

Metal slid from hard leather as a dagger appeared in Pila's hand. The clever creature must've hid it. She lunged for Elona but lurched forward instead with a surprised gasp.

Mayadeen's dagger had been quicker. She twisted it upwards into Pila's chest, scraping past bone to the bulb of the heart. Empty eyes stared back, as if any and all pain and fear had fled them long ago. She pushed Pila off the blade, and the strange womaner toppled over the pier with a splash to the black water below.

"Cap'n?" It all happened so fast Laddy just now mouthed his alarm. He glanced over the wood-rotted edge.

Mayadeen faced Elona, her moonlit dagger still brandished and wet with blood.

Elona took a breath. "You're so fast. She would have killed me."

"Some sort of demon like her mad master, that one." Mayadeen huffed while scanning the lapping water where Pila landed. No sign of the treacherous minion. If she was anything like Bolora, then a beating heart may not have been her life's source.

"You can't leave the Four Kingdoms, Mayadeen. I can't let you."

"Fuck ye say, lil' nymph?"

"Bolora had other plans for you," came Elona's voice from behind. "She wanted you to leave on that schooner. And, obviously, she didn't want me to accompany you."

The yells and clinks of mortal struggle could be heard from the front and side yards of Crinmarr Spire. The invading force had not yet reached the wharf, though several torch lanterns now swung in the distant shoreline beyond the quay. Mayadeen turned back to Elona and sheathed her dagger. A part of her wanted to stick it up her sister's melodramatic nose.

"When I left you at the mountain pass, I journeyed back to

Valindrost," Elona continued.

"Valindrost went up with the Four Fuckin' Winds," growled Mayadeen. They didn't have time to stand around discussing fond destinations.

"No, the city never went anywhere. But that doesn't matter. I went to see Ursade, and despite everything, she agreed to receive me."

"Red, damn ye. We've no time to argue yer soddin' birthright—"

"Mayadeen, listen. I'm not talking about me ... I'm talking about *Shorsas*. I told Ursade about the pelitite shard you've carried since the Ragged Forest. She nearly melted the Throne of Pain in response."

Mayadeen hardly gave a thought to the Bitch in the Rock since swiping that one and two more from Bolora's gushing neck. The *Master* that Bolora so smugly referred to must have been the same witch of old. Indeed, Shorsas had even possessed Bolora for a brief moment with the warning for Mayadeen to take the shards and run, did she not? It had all happened in an instant, but it happened nonetheless.

"Ursade knew that Bolora already possessed two of the five imbued shards," continued Elona. "She ranted for hours about how Bolora sires a growing cult dedicated to bringing Shorsas back to the world of the living. They call themselves the Sinbalaksatha, and their ties extend far beyond the Four Kingdoms."

Such would explain how Laddy's serpent bracelet came into Prick's discerning little talons during their romp through the enchanted woodland. Mayadeen had seen the same bracelets on every one of Bolora's entourage of puppets. It would seem the wicked Sister King and her henchwenches had struck a raw deal of their own in the Ragged Forest with the Almighty Shorsas of the Rainbow Cunties.

Suddenly Mayadeen wasn't feeling very special, and maybe it was just as well. She reached in her pocket and produced the three pelitite crystal shards fashioned to a thick, gold chain. The necklace was expertly crafted to hang five charms, with two of the claw-like sockets empty. The shard Mayadeen had carried all the way from the far side of Rul was set into a claw, along with the two Bolora had already procured. She dangled the chain in front her as each of the violet crystals glowed in a perfect, sinister unison.

"The old nymph, Shorsas, fancies this world," said Mayadeen. "She wants to return."

"And she's already tricked both you and Bolora into bringing three of the five parts of her soul back together," added Elona. "Mayadeen, do not forget there was a reason her soul was spellbound to begin with."

Mayadeen remembered Elona's telling of the legend, of how Shorsas wanted to overthrow her king and claim power over all who did not possess the Sinbalak. It took two of her most gifted comrades to stop her, and even then they could not destroy the magician Shorsas, but merely rend her spirit to an eternal imprisonment.

"With those three little crystals you cling onto, Shorsas has the potential to triple her power. We can't let her get any stronger. There's a process, Mayadeen ... a transference that must occur between the shards and a living host—"

Elona's words stopped, as did Elona. A low humming sound took over and the air itself blurred around them to envelop their space, altering the background to a vision Mayadeen had only known after a bottle or two of strong rum.

And the shards grew brighter than ever.

#

A grayish phantom appeared before Mayadeen. Everything beyond bent and bled into everything else—the torch light along the quay, the stars, the rolling waves off of the docks, Elona, and Laddy—with no sound but for the low hum of this unholy, celestial sphere.

Mayadeen knew the phantom to be Shorsas, and the legendary magician of old now assumed a form all her own. Though ghostly and incorporeal, the spectral Shorsas reflected every shapely detail of a sculpted and most handsome specimen. Her flowing hair coiled around a tall neck and sharply pointed breasts to drape at broad hips. The hollows of her eyes sat deep and dark beneath a prominent brow. If her present stature showed true, then she'd most certainly been a womaner named and bred of the Warlands Main, maybe even ancestral Rul.

"What is this, ye ol' witch?" Mayadeen's words vibrated and rippled before her as if they skimmed the surface of an invisible soup.

"Do not speak," said Shorsas. "Only listen."

Mayadeen struggled to move her arms, but doing so reminded her of the time she waded through quicksand, every movement an effort toward loss instead of gain. She still clutched the glowing crystals out in front of her.

"You have arrived at a crossroads, Mayadeen. Your sister by half bears good intentions, but remains ignorant of that which has yet to pass."

"S'why ye tried to kill her and Laddy while sparing my own skin?"

"If I had tried to kill them, then they would have been killed."

Mayadeen forced one hand from her side to little avail, and her legs barely shifted in place. It was like trying to run away from some gibbering terror in a bad dream.

"Seems ye're only missing skin 'n' bone. Just two more of them shards ye need? Then ye can bugger everything that stands or crawls."

"More impudence?"

"What do ye want from me, insufferable cunt? Speak true!"

"Ursade has the power to send me back to eternal imprisonment," said Shorsas. "But not without a fight. For if she tries the Order of Prenn will be no more. Her pathetic lands will be no more. Your sister, Elona, will be no more. You, Mayadeen Damned, will be no more. I will see to that much before being dispelled back into oblivion."

Mayadeen growled in frustration as her movement continued to be hampered. In all her days at sea she'd never encountered so many things as unnatural as she'd weathered during less than a fortnight in the Four Kingdoms. "Fie, ye ancient devil! Threats ... s'all ye ever give me are threats. I've shouldered my part true to my word. What have ye done for me?"

"More than you can fathom. Our fates are intertwined, Mayadeen. I watched over you in Valindrost—across the mountains, in Bolora's domain—and I watch over you now. Do not forsake my gratitude and love for you."

Shorsas' words dripped with presage, and yet now they intimated far less sinister than when echoed from Elona's possessed tongue.

"We'd a deal, damn ye. Nothin' less and nothin' more. A deal for which yer true gain ye still remain mum about, and the same one besides ye struck with that flesh-eating crackpot, Bolora. Ye would use me and cast me off like a snake would its scales. Bolora flaunted two of yer cursed crystals around her own pale neck—without singe or sear to show for it. So ye'd favor the likes o' her the same as ye favor me?"

"It is true," admitted Shorsas. "Although King Bolora and her followers searched out two of the soul bind crystals by their own means, I honored their offerings. And yet they've nothing to do with our prophecy, Mayadeen, and the shard I bestowed upon you was ever guarded by the forest. Why, then, would I have trusted it unto thee? Why would I have spared your life, and the lives of those you hold dear, even now at the precipice of your return to the sea?"

"Ye're a wicked ghost. Don't ye spit me riddles that only ye know the answers to."

"Fate is the answer, Mayadeen—our fate."

"There's no time for words and prophecies!"

Shorsas' eyes seemed to narrow although her exact expressions were hard to glean in shadow and mist. "Time is of no consequence when I control it here." Shorsas gestured around. "But out there, time now works against us. One Sister King will defy all to get to me, while another Sister King will stop at nothing to get to you. All that you hold dear will perish if either or both come to pass. I believe fate, however, works in our favor. Don't you see, Mayadeen? As you well know, I did not bring your ship to crash upon these shores. And yet because of fate, it was no accident that out of all the places in the world, you would arrive at one of five burial sites of my imprisonment—those dreadful woods you call the Ragged Forest."

Though it did seem convenient for Shorsas, Mayadeen could not unequivocally connect the two plots. Elona had confessed to that part of the treachery with Creyland Fenn, who for his own part conspired with Ursade. Weaving both webs so tightly together with three other Sister Kings and the fate of the Four Kingdoms was Mayadeen's own doing. She could now either choose to navigate that web alongside a force far beyond her understanding, or burn it all down where it hung.

"I did only what you would have done, Mayadeen, which was to sieze the opportunity fate afforded me."

"Tell me then, damn ye, spirit. What would ye have me do?"

"I ask that you retain our alliance. Take the shards. Continue to the sea. Do not tarry here for all to be lost. I will help you get to the Southern Isles, that place of wonder you have sought for so long. The Sinbalak is strong within us. I realized my power long ago only to have it taken from me. Whereas, you, my most worthy Daughter of Corolon ... you have only begun to realize your power."

The apparition grew to threefold its size, a magnificent visage now just inches away from Mayadeen's own. A giant hand stroked the back of her mussy hair.

"Do you not know I would never betray you?"

Shorsas disappeared in a folding of space before her final words carried from beyond the nexus. "Would you ... betray ... *me*?"

Suddenly Mayadeen lurched forward and nearly fell face first to the wooden planks of the pier. The sights and sounds of the frigid night on White Bay at once returned. Shorsas' calling might as well have never happened. And perhaps it had not.

"Mayadeen?"

She swung around. Elona stood by, strands of her thin hair fluttering in the night's gales. Laddy was next to her, still firmly clutching his side.

Mayadeen adjusted her eye patch and spat into the darkness. To oppose an ancient force she knew nothing about only to have it destroy everything she gained was not an option, and she wasn't about to entrust such a gamble to Number Two Sister King Bitch, Ursade, no matter how much Elona regaled the pious witch.

It would seem that fate, for once, had a valid stake in her plans.

"I set sail tonight with or without ye, 'n' I'll drown in that sodding bay 'fore I'm buried in the Warlands Main. Ye're either with me, sister, or ye're with Ursade."

"What about the shards?" Elona referred to what Mayadeen still grasped.

"With White Bay on our lee and windward ho, together we'll parse how to handle the shards," said Mayadeen while again cramming them into her front pocket. "It's that or naught, Red. That or naught."

"Captain Damned!" The excited voice belonged to Roe. Mayadeen watched as he ran towards them with a hop in his step. Just the sight of the boy immediately made her spirits soar with a hope renewed.

She turned once more to Elona and Laddy, scanning them for a response.

"Hurry ... Captain Fenn got us a big ship," said Roe.

Elona nodded. "I'm with you, sister. I'll always be with you."

"Aye, Cap'n," added Laddy.

Mayadeen smiled. "Then we need to move with a shiny purpose."

Roe caught up and grabbed her hip belt. "C'mon, c'mon."

"Lead the way, my bonny sea pup."

#

Fires throughout the nearby village and castle cast the night sky aglow with smoky oranges and reds. Distant screams of panic would follow the occasional crash from a siege engine's projectile. But the real action had yet to reach the docks.

Just minutes down the length of the quay on the west side of Gronsenlek's wharf, the two vessels in question were moored one after the other. The schooner came first, and Mayadeen could just make out the letters, "C-O-C-K-S-W-E-L-L" on his hull. The ship was familiar, and so too was the captain that sailed him.

"Captain Damned," urged Roe. "That's not the one. Captain Fenn has a bigger boat ... I mean ship."

The two-masted brig that Creyland had apparently secured rose higher in its splendor than the *Cockswell*, but the latter vessel posed double the intrigue: once because it was the ship that Bolora had requisitioned and twice because Mayadeen knew well Captain Theren Bon Shemble, First Daughter born to Nine Master Sonner Bon Shemble and heir to a seat at the Table of Corolon.

"Avast there, sailor," said Mayadeen to Roe. She reached out and grabbed the scruff of his ragged hide shirt before he could run off toward the brig.

Captain Theren herself walked down a narrow gangplank to where Mayadeen, Elona, Laddy and Roe stood fast. Like Mayadeen, Theren was bred from the finest stock. She was slightly thinner and taller with short-cropped, rusty blond hair, razor-thin lips and brownish green, almost golden eyes. Her long, muscular limbs sprouted forth from her signature red Krode Beast-skin jerkin. Mayadeen had known the confident Meridian mariner ever since she'd trained under the tutelage of Theren's mother, the old Master of the Nine who still sailed the profitable side of Tabor.

"Well, well, if it ain't the one-eyed tongue robber herself," said Theren with a half-grin that crept to her ear. "Never thought I'd see yer ravenous splitty in the Warlands Main. How for, Emmy?"

They clasped forearms.

"Ther," greeted Mayadeen. "'Tis a long bloody tale 'n' no time to recount it."

"Aye to that," said Theren while glancing past to Elona, Laddy and Roe. "These belong to ye?"

Mayadeen nodded, and she was starting to get annoyed that Theren was the one asking all of the questions.

"Listen, damn ye. King Fuckin' Bolora sent us to this ship. Tell me true if ye be with her and her shirtless cunties."

"Gotta trade deal with Bolora, s'all. So nay to that." Theren mirrored Mayadeen's suspicion. "But she said ye'd be comin' and to wait to shove off with ye. Didn't think it would really be yer hide I'd be gatherin' though."

"Ahem." Elona cleared her throat.

"Who's the witch?" asked Theren.

"Charming," said Elona. "But my name is—"

"Bolora chartered yer ship to me, Ther," continued Mayadeen. "Privy to that, are ye?"

Theren guffawed. "I'd be buggered while drownin' 'fore that mad bitch gave me any orders. This look to ye like yer soddin' *Sea Licker?*"

"I ain't askin' to take yer charge," snarled Mayadeen. "Turns out I've gotta ship." She flipped her chin at the nearby brig. "But I'll need some of yer scalawags to crew it."

Theren guffawed again, and Mayadeen briefly thought about putting a fist through her bear trap of a mouth.

"Ye're lookin' to shove off in that barge? Bonny good luck with that, Emmy. Ye'd be in for one hell of a fight." Theren reached for her belt, and Mayadeen's hand snapped to the hilt of her rapier.

"Relax, ol' chum," said Theren while keeping her other hand in the air. She carefully withdrew a cylindrical object made of brass. With her free hand she pulled one end of the cylinder until it expanded to the length of a small baton. "New lil' trinket from Ateria. Let's ye see as well as a redgull, clear and far." She put one end of the cylinder to her eye and pointed the contraption toward the open end of the bay. Then she offered the eyepiece to Mayadeen. "Ye're in luck. It only requires one peeper."

Mayadeen snatched it from her hand. She put the small end to her eye. The enlarged face of one of Theren's female crewwomen filled Mayadeen's vision. She flinched back and saw the same fish-faced womaner lashing down some rigging.

Theren gently pushed the wide end of the looking glass to face the bay. "Point it to where ye would spy."

Mayadeen readjusted her position. After some fiddling with the vector, several tiny lamplights came into view. They belonged to ships—an entire flotilla of ships—about fifteen strong.

"Confound the Nine," grumbled Mayadeen. "Meridian?"

"Nay. Edish," said Theren. "How they knew the two of us would be afloat the same place 'n' time, I can't gather." Theren took back her nifty spyglass and collapsed it. "Not even a magician could help 'em with that."

A magician indeed. Mayadeen glowered at Elona. "Ye know anything 'bout this, Red?"

Elona stammered. "No ... no, but I'm sure Ursade is behind it. I told you she didn't want you to leave."

"Mayadeen!" Creyland now ran over from the adjoining dock. "For the sake of bleeding arses, we need to shove off."

"Fuckin' Fenn of Edenvane," said Theren with certain disdain.

Creyland barely nodded. "Bon Shemble."

"I tried to tell them," insisted young Roe.

"Roe, get ye on that schooner." Mayadeen pointed up the gangplank.

"But Captain Damned—"

"No butts, damn ye sailor pup." She picked him up and gave him a sloppy kiss on his cheek. "Captain Theren will put ye to work. Ye'll be the Ship's Lass ... eh, Boy."

Roe gleefully ran up the gangplank.

"Can the wee bull swim?" asked Theren.

"Aye, but ne'er in the open blue," replied Mayadeen. "So keep 'im in the hold and have yer scalawags watch over. Tell yer splitties I'll see personally to any who think otherwise." She hailed Laddy.

"On board with ye, my trump. Ye're in no fighting shape." Again she addressed Theren. "With a proper diversion ye think ye can sail close to the wind to sneak out of the bay?"

"What have ye in mind?"

Mayadeen pointed to the brig. "We'll set that one afire and cast it out."

Creyland snickered. Then his face dropped. "You can't be serious?"

"Aye, I'm that and more," returned Mayadeen. Creyland's wasn't the only flummoxed visage.

"But isn't that the superior ship?" Elona searched the others for affirmation.

"Not for what we want," said Mayadeen, annoyed that her sister even asked.

Creyland persisted. "That brig is what's going to get us to the Southern Isles—"

"We'd barely be able to crew it," said Mayadeen.

"We're fortunate to have bloody found it!"

Creyland never did have a mind for tactics. He was and always would be the dreamer. Nobody wanted a vessel worth its weight more than Mayadeen, but that brig, bearing the strangest name Mayadeen had ever seen for a ship, wouldn't be the one.

"We take the schooner, damn ye. Our chances of avoiding that blockade will be far greater, and ye know it well, Crey Fenn."

"We've three captains here," said Creyland while turning to Theren. "What do *you* say to this madness?"

Mayadeen was fairly certain Theren didn't consider Creyland Fenn a captain, and her derisive smirk lent credence.

"The *Hag Harpy*?" Theren looked to the valuable vessel with the doomed moniker and shrugged. "Burn the bawdy bitch."

XXII
THE CAPTAIN AND THE KING

I am resolved that this shall end with the destruction of worlds.
~ The Siah (Gladistia 3:1)

Just moments after deciding to send the *Hag Harpy* out like a floating torch into the night, the war cries of axe-wielding Rullites pierced the cool mist settling over the docks behind Crinmarr Spire. An explosion sounded in the distant orange glow of battle. The long deprived village of Gronselek would be no more come sunup.

"Shove off," said Mayadeen to Theren. "Look for a yawl boat a quarter league out when the decoy's aflame."

Theren nodded and whistled at two of her deckhands. "Bress. Wenda. Come ahead, damn ye!" The two hearty Meridian bloods ran forward. "These two'll help ye raise anchor. No need to be towed out as the wind flies favorably. The sails on that brig will gather fast."

"Just have me some rum waiting," said Mayadeen.

Theren grinned and ran up the gangplank to the *Cockswell*. Two more of her deckhands retracted the gangplank to the main deck.

"They'll be swarming the docks in minutes! Douse the lanterns and raise anchor, damn ye crippled cunties!" ordered Theren.

Mayadeen cinched her waist belt and took quick inventory of her implements, her twin daggers at the small of her back and the rapier she'd carried all the way from Valindrost. Creyland clutched a short sword; Siljan a fine, curved blade from his southern lands. Bress and Wenda each held sturdy cutlasses. Elona, of course, had her strange gestures and fire-flinging hands.

Mayadeen glanced at the docked *Hag Harpy*. They would have to run the length of two piers to get to her, and the approaching group of Rullites would have to do the same.

"Let's be quick on that forecastle to raise anchor. Fenn to the helm. Siljan with me to stave off the heathens 'til we're away."

"What about me?" asked Elona.

"On that vessel to ready yer flamin' twat," snapped Mayadeen.

"The sails are set for a bay wind haul to start," assured Creyland. "I'll steer her out. After that the wheel's got a locking mechanism to keep him steady. Of course, once those flames find the sails, the ship will be adrift."

Mayadeen threw him a nod and smiled. She brandished her rapier with a swift scrape. "Charge for yer lives then, my trumps!" She broke into a sprint and the others followed on her heels. The rickety wood creaked and moaned under every foot stomp. Some of the boards were slick with fresh spray from the slosh below. Mayadeen felt her pitted leather soles slide a couple times, so she slowed her pace just enough to stay sure.

The Rullite warriors, six in all and big even for their own beastly race, spotted Mayadeen running towards them from half the length of the adjoining dock. These were Elites, and Mayadeen thought for a moment whether their benevolent leader was amongst them. But that would be unlikely through the chaos of a thousand screaming warriors raining upon the firelit city.

Mayadeen and her launch crew reached the t-section of dock well before the Rullites, if only because they had less deck to cover. Her lungs burned, but her legs felt like they could clear the rails of the brig in a single bound from ten feet below. When she reached the base of the steep gangplank to the *Hag Harpy*, she stopped and swung around. Bress and Wenda kept up nearly to her flanks.

"On that capstan, damn ye. Raise anchor!" said Mayadeen while motioning for them to continue onto the ship.

Siljan came up next followed by Creyland.

"Cut away the lines," Mayadeen shouted at them.

Elona lagged behind with her shorter legs. The Rullite Elites would have an axe in her back in seconds. Mayadeen dashed back up the pier to intercept her.

"Red, damn yer pissin' twat—"

Elona screamed something in reply but not before Mayadeen lifted her and flung her over her shoulder. After a couple of strides she felt a blast of heat at her back followed by a yelp and a splash. Elona must have roasted one of the Rullites even from her precarious position.

Mayadeen threw Elona onto the gangplank. Too winded to curse, she grabbed her sister by her black leather greaves and pulled her forward while scrabbling up the incline herself.

Siljan and Creyland carried out her orders well as the final towline whipped through the air. Although Elona's pants split her arse like a string to rising dough, she made it to the deck. Bress and Wenda quickly spun the capstan into a pinwheel as the anchor chain raised.

"Fenn, on the rudder! Siljan, to me," shouted Mayadeen from where the gangplank met the main deck. The ship would be slow to cast away from the dock, and they'd have to fend off the unwanted boarding party.

The first Rullite upon them wielded a club. A deft swing just missed Mayadeen's knee, the latter having the higher ground of the incline. But the same Rullite stretched to catch Mayadeen's ankle and yank her back onto the gangplank. Mayadeen countered with a boot to the bitch's cheek. That hardly loosened the Rullite's grip until Siljan's scimitar found half of her thick neck. The hefty womaner growled and toppled off the side. The gangplank shifted again as the ship's sails hauled wind. Mayadeen kept low to maintain her balance while two other warriors snarled from the base of the plank. More

Rullites raced from across the pier.

"We're off anchor. To the deck, damn ye," ordered Mayadeen aside to Siljan.

The lithe Sundvanian bounded back to the main deck just as the gangplank gave way.

Mayadeen's hand reached for the same ledge and found purchase with just three fingers of her bad hand, the one that would never again be the same since her welcoming on the shores of the Warlands Main. She grunted as her fingers slipped, sending her to the ridged sills of archer porticoes six feet down to the *Hag Harpy's* mid-deck. This time she clung with both hands after dropping her rapier to the water below. She heard her name called from the main deck above when a shower of splinters exploded next to her cheek. The blade of an axe planted into the wooden frame just inches from her head.

Two Rullites made the leap from the dock as the ship cast off, and they both hugged to corniced sections of the brig's hull just aft of Mayadeen's position.

"Mayadeen?" Elona peered over the rails joined by Siljan. "We'll get a rope or something—"

"Nay, nay ... first light up these two creatures beside me!"

Mayadeen heaved herself up far enough to use the embedded axe as a step to the ship's gunwales. She heard an angry shriek and a splash from below. Never again would she deny Elona's usefulness in a skirmish. Mayadeen grabbed Siljan's hand for a final lift to the main deck. The little man was strong for his size. She didn't regret that she'd filched him from Leweln's pathetic bull army during her brief visit of that Sister King's encampment.

"Sweep the decks and sides and make certain there are no more bitches clinging to the ship," she said to Siljan with a slap on his back. Siljan nodded and stepped to it.

"You are stubborn, sister, and I am thankful for it." Elona gave Mayadeen a quick hug.

"Just get ye afore and be ready to make sparks, damn ye."

Elona hesitated. "Afore?"

"The bow, the bloody bow." Mayadeen turned Elona's shoulder and pointed to the front of the ship. "*That* way, Red. Afore!"

#

As the mainsails and topsails of the two-masted *Hag Harpy* gobbled up the westerly wind flying over White Bay, Mayadeen could now make out—without the use of Theren's brass eye erection—the hundred or so lamplights floating across the misty roll between the end of the bay and open sea. Mayadeen guessed the blockade to be ten to twelve ships strong. They would be war brigs with a galleon or two in their ranks, each equipped with armored hull rams, archers, and perhaps even some of those deafening bombard cannons. There was no sign of Theren's *Cockswell* on her flanks, which boded well for that schooner's surreptitious search for an exit. Mayadeen just hoped she'd be on it.

Theren Bon Shemble wouldn't double-cross her. They had been best of friends and more at one time, both serving under Sonner Bon Shemble, Theren's mother, who still refused to turn in her captain's chest for a coveted seat at the Elders of Corolon. The one thing Mayadeen and Theren each had in common from their first days swabbing decks and climbing ratlines was their hatred for the insufferable crone. Old Bon Shemble was as vicious as she was vindictive, and it came as no surprise that she and Mabelia Damned also were bonny chums at one time.

Piss on the both of 'em.

"Nice 'n' steady as she flies," Mayadeen called up to Creyland who still kept the helm. The stubborn rogue of a bull did well in already having the mainsails rigged and the ship prepared to raise anchor. It was all just enough to support the coming charade.

Time to put their plan into motion. Despite the *Hag Harpy's* doomed moniker—it was bad luck to name a ship after a woman, magical or otherwise—the brig Mayadeen was about to willingly destroy was already proving a fine vessel in shallow depths and at a speed of less than three knots. Mayadeen hated to toss away anything worthy of the sea.

"Red, time to set it aflame!"

Elona nodded and positioned herself facing the prow of the *Harpy* just under the foresail. Mayadeen watched her silhouette lift both of her gauntleted hands high into the air.

Mayadeen pointed to Theren's two pirates—she'd already forgotten their names—who lingered at the capstan. "Ready that starboard yawl," she ordered them.

A beacon of fire flared up from the prow of the *Hag Harpy*, starting at the bowsprit and trailing steadily back to the foredeck.

"Ha, ha," cheered Mayadeen. "We'll give 'em a show to damn their bloody eyes 'n' blistering cunts!" She swept her hand through the air. "Red, to the yawl boat! Crey Fenn, to starboard yawl. Siljan ..."

Mayadeen trailed off as she hadn't seen Siljan since after she'd made it on deck and sent him to scout for any unwanted barnacles of the seven-foot-barbarian-bitch kind.

"Siljan, damn yer bronzed arse..." Still no sign of the beautiful bull. The Sundvanian soldier most likely never stepped foot on a ship before now, and a landlubber falling overboard wouldn't be out of the question. She hurried to where the yawl boat was lowered halfway to the water with Theren's seasoned sailors loosing the davits' roped pulleys.

Creyland climbed down from the poop deck.

"I hope this wasn't for naught, Emerald Eye."

"For once we agree on something," returned Mayadeen. She slapped Creyland lightly on his cheek and followed with a lick and a bite on his lips.

"Until we meet again, Captain." Creyland grinned and vaulted himself over and onto the yawl. Mayadeen dropped a rope ladder, which Creyland grabbed onto for the next passenger's descent.

Elona ran forward out of breath. "That took more out of me

than I thought it would. But those flames will burn to the bottom of the bay."

Mayadeen stroked Elona's wavy brown hair that fell loose from a braid beneath a circlet. Her sister flinched and Mayadeen smiled. The orange light that slowly overtook the front of the ship danced and flitted across Elona's soft features.

"Yer a ranklin' lil' cunty if ever there was, but I do adore ye, my bonny sis."

Elona's eyes turned up with her smile. Then they grew wide as her chin dropped.

Mayadeen spun around to find a head tumbling and clopping across the main deck of the ship. It was Siljan's head, and his open mouth at last settled in a seeping puddle of spittle and blood.

Behind the severed noggin lurched the umbra of a seven-foot giant. The shape of her serpentine helm, jagged bone shoulder pauldrons, tattered cape fluttering behind just above her hips, and tree-sized great sword resting at her side were at once familiar.

Without pause, Mayadeen grabbed Elona and tossed her overboard to plummet and crash onto the yawl boat. She then snatched the davit rope from Theren's closest crewwoman.

"Into the boat!"

The hearty Meridian took the order and leaped over the railing.

"Let it go," yelled Mayadeen to the pirate who held the other line. They each did so at roughly the same time, and the yawl boat splashed stern first to the black water.

"Overboard, smartly now," growled Mayadeen at Theren's mate. She remembered her name now, it was Wenda.

The seadog shook her head in defiance and drew her cutlass. Wenda dashed forward, at first seemingly at Mayadeen, but rushed past to take on the monster with hell as its backdrop. Wenda led with a downward sweeping slash easily dodged by her towering target. She followed with a backslash that was blocked, her wrist then grabbed and twisted in the opposite direction for a bone-cracking disarm. Wenda yelped and the cutlass clinked to the deck. The same pincerlike hand that accomplished all of that now sprang to the doomed pirate's throat. It squeezed and shook and squeezed some more until Theren's woman expired, crumpling to the dais of the ship's mizzen.

And through the entire effort, King Lusul's other hand hadn't even left the hilt of her great sword.

The flames now curled and lapped their way to the foremast of the *Harpy*. They climbed the post, found the yards, and took bursting ecstasy in bringing the canvas sails into their fray. Heat from the devouring inferno could now be felt the length of the ship, though it would be minutes before it overtook the second mast to where the captain and the king now squared off.

Mayadeen considered her options. She felt for her rapier before remembering she had let it go to the drink, having nearly gone there herself. *One less option.* Her twin daggers were still sheathed at the small of her back, but they would be of little use in head-on combat with the most powerful and skilled warrior she'd ever faced.

She could always jump ship. Part of her enjoyed the idea of swimming away while leaving Lusul to burn alive on a floating pyre. But she had no doubt the Rullite king could swim, and if the feud didn't end between them tonight, it would never end.

Lusul removed her frightening helmet and tossed it to the deck where it hit with a single thud. Her thick, curly hair was styled as before, shaved on the sides and tufted to the top. A lock dangled loose to cake against beads of sweat upon her hardened brow. She kicked the late Wenda's cutlass to topple across the deck toward Mayadeen.

Lusul then reached behind her back and produced another implement, which she pitched forward to join the cutlass.

It was Mayadeen's own broken rapier, the very same that Lusul had shattered on the beach. The jeweled hilt sparkled in the firelight with almost a third of its clouded steel blade still jutting to a jagged point. The behemoth bitch had carried it all this way just to gloat.

Mayadeen looked at the weapons but didn't pick them up.

"Don't suppose ye can swim?"

Lusul stepped forward. A vile smirk folded her rectangular cheek.

"Would Meridian woman drown," she said in her most stunted, guttural vocalization, "or would Meridian woman burn?"

Mayadeen sighed. She flipped up her eye patch and spat off the gunwales, though she hardly had any spit to dredge up.

"Meridian woman won't be doing either, ye great, big cunt-dunking whore monkey..." Mayadeen's dagger was already flipping through the air. She shoulder-rolled to the deck to grab the cutlass and partial rapier, and emerged on her feet and into a charge.

Lusul grunted and held her right ear where the dagger had clipped bloody. She looked up just in time to parry Mayadeen's cutlass with the flat side of her great sword. Mayadeen followed with the rapier, but its stunted length fooled her and poked the air inches short of Lusul's ribcage. Lusul flinched back off her center, and Mayadeen pushed the assault with another slash from the cutlass. This time she gashed Lusul's upper abdomen, though it was as solid as if she was wearing light armor. Mayadeen knew she had to keep the fight between middle to close quarters to trump the great sword as much as possible. She took an elbow to the side of her head, but for some strange reason hardly felt the blow. Lusul snarled and trapped Mayadeen's left arm while Mayadeen locked the pommel of her rapier in her right hand against Lusul's sword-bearing left.

They struggled for a moment with near equal force, even with the bulk of Lusul's weight hunched over Mayadeen.

Surprised at her own strength matched in brute force against Lusul's, Mayadeen missed the forehead hammering down upon her nose. She reeled from the pain as tears flooded her eye, yet once again she recovered fast and sliced the top of Lusul's hand with the rapier's partial blade. Lusul cursed something in her native tongue. Mayadeen snuck a punch up to her chin with the hilt of the rapier. The beastly womaner roared in fury, lifted Mayadeen up with both hands and flung her backwards several feet aft of the second mast.

Mayadeen came to her elbows and patted her front pocket where bulged the three pelitite shards. *Shorsas.* The old devil nymph was giving her some sort of magical strength.

Lusul continued to yell, and Mayadeen noticed the primary source of her opponent's frustration. Lusul had backed too close to the impending flames, now having engulfed a third of the ship, and her cape had caught fire. With a single violent motion she reached across to her right shoulder and doffed the flaming cape, armor pauldrons and all. Her raiment was now minimal, with just a leather breast guard, cod piece and bone vambraces.

Although Mayadeen couldn't feel her nose, her muscles surged and her body was somehow lighter. Her cutlass and rapier had been disarmed for the moment, but Lusul had temporarily dropped her great sword just the same. Mayadeen bounded to her feet and once again launched an offensive. She came in low, drew her second dagger, slashed the inside of Lusul's thigh and planted the dagger at just above the knee. The warrior king howled, grabbed a firm wad of Mayadeen's hair and yanked it back. Mayadeen reached for the protruding dagger and twisted it. An angry fist cracked atop her spine and then Mayadeen was once again flailing in mid-air to smack hard against the post of the main mast.

She came to all fours in a daze. The Shorsas shards in her pocket vibrated and stung against her hip. Mayadeen looked up just in time to see the great sword arcing down, Lusul screaming in fury behind it. She rolled out of the way and the blade hewed a splintered canyon into the slightly raised dais. Lusul yelled again as she wrenched her sword from the wood to bring about another attack. The great warrior king now limped, her left leg cascading a dark sheen of blood.

A crash of embers came from the bow, the result of a burning yard falling from aloft the foremast. The fire now crept along the main deck to the middle of the ship.

Mayadeen shuffled to her feet. The ship canted slightly to starboard, causing Lusul's next two-handed attack to swing wide. Mayadeen countered with a kick to Lusul's granite stomach, which probably hurt her foot more than her target.

Despite Mayadeen's newfound strength and resilience, Lusul was still too enduring a foe.

"Let's see how well ye climb, damn ye colossal bitch," quipped Mayadeen as she scaled the ladder to the poop. From there she caught onto some ratlines, which led to the second mast above the spanker. She was always quick on the rigging, and like a spider navigating its own web, scuttled to the first yard arm in less than a minute.

To her astonishment, Lusul remained inches from her heels. The insufferable savage chose a more direct route by simply shimmying up the mast pole from the deck. Mayadeen thrust her foot down onto Lusul's fingers, which gripped a ratline directly below. Lusul only rose higher to grasp the yard arm. Mayadeen perched on the thicker part of the same yard with both feet. She hugged the main post and threw another kick to Lusul's face followed by a third and a fourth. Lusul absorbed each blow while never letting go, her face now as bloody as her leg.

If she could just reach the main topsail yard, Mayadeen knew she'd be able to balance out to the tip and dive to the black water forty feet below. The impending flames now encircled them. The heat from the blazing foremast sails singed Mayadeen's back. Embers flew all about and the smoke grew thick even in the open breeze. She grabbed a spar line and strained to pull herself higher. She was fairly certain Lusul had broken her nose and two or three of her ribs, and what once was numb now seared with pain. Whatever advantage Shorsas imbued her was wearing off.

Mayadeen looked down. The *Hag Harpy* was overtaken by Elona's magical inferno, and the heat and smoke from below and aloft would have already vanquished most living things. Soon the hull would rupture at a dozen points at once and the ship would be a piece-strewn monument at the bottom of White Bay.

Mayadeen yelled and with all her might pulled herself to the ledge of the topsail arm. She crouched into a half crawl and carefully made her way out onto the yard, its sail already starting to burn from errant embers.

"Coward," growled Lusul who found her footing on the first yard below. "Fight me, coward!"

Mayadeen glimpsed Lusul's hand shoot up to grab hold of the jutting wood in front of her. Another hand caught Mayadeen's boot and pulled her to slam crotch-first over the yard. Mayadeen cried out in pain so unbearable she almost let go. She roused with her drooling cheek against the hot wood surface. Half of Lusul's dead weight threatened to take both of them to a fiery doom at any moment.

Mayadeen reached into the side of her trousers. She inched Bolora's necklace out of the shallow pocket of her free leg. The three pelitite crystal shards of legend glowed like never before.

"I'm ... I'm no coward," Mayadeen said through short breaths. "But ... I am a bloody ... fucking ... pirate ..." In spite of dizzying pain, she snorted a laugh. She dangled the glowing necklace just above Lusul's rabid face. "And a cheat 'til the end."

She dropped the necklace across Lusul's eyes. The stones sizzled and seared into the warrior king's skull to a shriek so shrill and horrible it would best a banshee. Her eyes bubbled and blistered as the shards penetrated halfway into her head. Only then did King Lusul's voice go dormant and fingers surrender to the last anchorage of her existence.

Mayadeen watched as Lusul and the Shorsas shards plunged through the fire and canvas and wood that still separated them from the bottom of the bay and eternal damnation.

There was but one thing left to do as the entire mast cracked and popped. Mayadeen carefully lifted her knee back onto the yard. Though she'd years of practice clambering around ratlines and shuffling across spars in the days of Bon Shemble, she always did so either barefoot or with sandals. Boots were something else entirely. She stayed low and struggled to find her center. She believed the cracked bones in her chest would break with the slightest movement in the wrong direction, and yet the duress from that notion did little to counter the dizzying pain when trying to move her legs. The skin on her face and neck felt as though they were being filleted away, and the raw sting of it kept her from swooning. The heat of the inferno reached up for her—beckoning her to join what it had already taken. But the flames from the mast beneath her only acted as encouragement. Mayadeen clenched her teeth with a gasp and shuffled out another foot, just an arm's length away from the tip of the burning yard.

With a final free step she vaulted into the abyss.

XXIII
REQUIEM FOR A DAIQUIRI

A trump can understand your language and a better trump can speak it. But it's a rarer matey still who can cipher the meaning. Call her your first mate. Call her your sister. Call her your best ploughing friend.

~ Nine Master Mabelia Damned

The thing about the Jeweled Sea was its ever-familiar, refreshing embrace right around the autumnal equinox. During that seasonal window in the early years of her childhood, Mayadeen would set out each morning with her Pap from the fog-shrouded landing of Cleft Rock on their home island of Marpel, one of the largest of the Meridian Isles. Her Pap's sturdy, single-masted trawler didn't have an official name—such wasn't permitted on fishing vessels commanded and maintained by men—but they called the ship *Hooker*, and on a three-day run they could fill his stores with more than a ton of salted perry gill.

Now Mayadeen watched a different child who'd be forging his own memories of the bonny blue. She stood with her back against the prow railing of the schooner, *Cockswell,* her every breath devouring the cool wind of open waters. Roe clung to the ratlines of the foremast as he confidently negotiated each hand-sized square weave. Mayadeen had allowed him to practice his climbing aloft so long as he remained beneath the lowest yard. The boy wasn't afraid of heights, which boded well for his fledgling career as a sailor. In a few days, barring any clumsy accidents, she'd let him ascend to the second yard.

"Captain Damned," called Roe as he reached out and pushed a dangling spar. "Look at me!"

"Aye, my trump 'n' pearls. Eyes upon those hands, damn ye. Always mind yer hands."

Theren's mates had also kept a close watch on the young bull, perhaps more out of curiosity than concern. They were a dutiful lot of Daughter born, thirty-two strong with loose-fitted shirts and enough silver and gold crowding their mouths to fill a barrel. Many fancied their pates shaved, though a few kept their hair either knotted or scarved off. Mayadeen's own jungle of a mess, which usually resembled a rippling mound of angry black ants, would still need to be tended to, and cutting it all off humored an idea as tempting as any.

Elona emerged from the small cabin astern. Captain Theren had temporarily relinquished her quarters to Mayadeen, and so Mayadeen in turn allowed Elona to share with her the best berth on the ship. Such made sense considering her sorcerer sister insisted upon staying with her the first two nights while tending to her painful wounds. The infernal battle with Lusul had left Mayadeen plunging into the frigid water with three cracked ribs, a broken nose, more bruises and contusions than could be counted by the average scalawag, and raised burns down a good portion of her upper half. Although Elona hadn't access to her noxious salve, Theren's ship was well-supplied with medicinal herbs and ointments that at least could dull some of the sting.

As Elona strolled forward to the bow, Mayadeen thought for the first time her sister wore a handsome elegance that even their shared mother might have lacked in her early years. Of course, if Theren's mates eyed young Roe with simple intrigue, then they eyed Elona with ribald disdain. But such was the magicians' lot in a world that rarely understood them.

"You seem to be mending well," said Elona, at last reaching the bow. She raised a hand to shade her eyes and tilted her head back to find Roe on the rigging. "And now you're warden to the happiest boy on the Nine Seas. Guess that makes me an aunt."

"Aunty Red?" Mayadeen sneered. "By the gods that'll make ye a strumpet complete."

Elona rolled her eyes. "How are your bandages?"

Mayadeen grimaced as she slightly curled her shoulder while clutching her side. "Were my guts spilling out, they'd be right proper."

"The bandages had to be tight, Mayadeen, for your bones to heal properly."

"Aye, 'n' to bring my chest up to my chin, besides."

"Indeed," said Elona with a cheery smile. "You'll fit right in with us strumpets." Elona draped her elbows on the railing and sighed out over a calm sea.

"What's on yer pretty lil' tongue, sister o' mine?"

"The pelitite shards—the Shorsas stones. You said they're at the bottom of White Bay, but something doesn't feel right."

"Well, let me spin the lyrics for ye again, Red. The cursed brig's at the bottom of the sea. Lusul's bloated head's at the bottom of the sea. The sodding shards then being inside Lusul's bloated head, which were all on the cursed brig, so too, are at the bottom of the sea."

Elona's eyes searched her. Mayadeen could nearly discern the fire in those eyes, whether from a sordid life's beating or the boiling Sinbalak blood running through her veins. Whichever or both, her sister was a survivor.

"But how do you *feel?*" said Elona at last.

In truth, Mayadeen felt like she could start at the very same shore she washed upon that fateful day in Rul and retread every footprint, hoof mark and portal puke at a straight dash without break.

The wounds she'd sustained pained her, it was true, but prior to the events on White Bay such a beating would've had her bedridden for days. No, the old witch Shorsas had infused her—had given her a tactical advantage during her fight with Lusul. What, exactly, Mayadeen neither knew nor wanted to know.

"Right as the ocean breeze, is how I feel, Red. Right as the ocean breeze."

"I'm sorry about Laddy," said Elona after a pause. "I have to wonder whether or not he had other intentions. He didn't say anything ... only looked at me."

Mayadeen had learned that Theren's schooner found the drifting yawl boat on the dark side of White Bay with four survivors, including an unconscious Mayadeen who the others promptly fished out of the drink after witnessing her plunge. Elona and Bress climbed out with Mayadeen in tow, while Laddy climbed in. Creyland and Laddy then grabbed the oars and rowed the opposite direction, presumably toward the Edish flotilla. Theren told Mayadeen she had her archers fire a warning volley over the deserters' prow, but it did little to stop the two bulls from rowing off into the night.

Mayadeen was trying not to think about that little desertion and now understood what having a cursed, gossiping sister was all about. She watched the gentle seesaw of the horizon.

"Crey told me that Laddy had been the one to surrender without so much as an insult when Leweln's bulls found us in the grasslands," recalled Mayadeen. "I knew then the swabby's allegiance to his captain was waning. 'Twas a time he'd have followed me to the cold, black depths."

"Laddy would *still* follow you to the cold, black depths, sister. I know it."

Mayadeen frowned. The real reason Laddy left was that he'd glimpsed more than a few things to live for during his misadventure. Elona herself was not the least of them, and despite Laddy's ongoing mistrust of Creyland, the young bull obviously envied the Edish pirate who answered to no one. Apparently, Laddy wasn't quite as dumb as Mayadeen always thought. If she ever found him again, she wondered if she could find it in her heart not to end him.

"I was surprised to see that slimy rogue, Creyland, still around when we made it to the docks during the siege," added Elona with disdain. "I guess he figured he had a better chance to escape with us as opposed to without us."

"Crey Fenn'll never change. 'Tis why I loved him once. I'm sure he reckons the same. On my lee, that's the only understanding him 'n' I will ever have."

"I'll roast him to a crisp for you if I ever see him again," assured Elona.

Mayadeen faced her. "Humph. Aye. I bet ye would at that."

Roe finally climbed back to the main deck and now fiddled with a rope Theren's mates gave him. Tying sound knots and splicing lines would be one of his first and most important lessons in contributing to life on a ship.

Mayadeen started toward him, curious to see how he was faring.

"Wait," said Elona. "There's something else ... and it's best I tell you now."

Mayadeen sighed. Elona took her hand and tugged her back to the railing. She turned her body to block anybody who might spy them aft of the bow. From beneath her red and black spun silk tunic she produced a tightly rolled parchment.

"I returned to Ursade to obtain proof of my birthright. After quite the ... debate ... this is what she gave me." Elona hesitated. "Our mother had told King Akaranza, who once controlled all of the lands of both Drost and Leth, to burn this once she'd decided whether or not to take me in. Ursade was fifteen years of age at the time and already left her sisters for a life with the Order. Since Ursade was the only one who could forge a treaty with Lusul and the Rullites, she had immediate value and quickly rose to power with Akaranza's blessings. It turns out that Ursade looked after me as a favor to Akaranza. She kept this letter."

Mayadeen incredulously took the parchment. The greater

portion of Mabelia Damned's unmistakable personal wax seal—a swirl ending on an eyeball, the Eye of the Storm as she had always called it—still remained. She unrolled the parchment to find a letter dated 73~282 of Frehns, almost thirty years past.

For My Dearest Akaranza, Your Majesty of Drost,
 It has been too long, my bonny love, and the tides bring woe to the Isles at Cleft Rock ...

Mayadeen read the letter to herself. The scrawl had her mother's hasty edge, and what would have been a two or three page letter by any other hand was little more than half of one sheet. That the letter appealed to a lover was no reveal, although Mayadeen had never known Mabelia Damned to take the splitty over the splitter. Yet there seemed to be something more personal about Mabelia's request to King Akaranza.

After only a moment of brooding, Mayadeen focused back upon her sister.

"So the letter speaks of yer birth. But there ain't naught of who or how." She rolled the letter and pushed it back to Elona's bosom. "Doesn't prove much, Red. And 'tis no secret my Mum was the biggest soddin' rake this side of Tabor. S'pose a womaner or two could've been in the long line of bedders."

"Ah, but that letter wasn't for Akaranza. It was for Akaranza's brother, Tolis."

"Ye've said that name before, *Tolis...*"

Elona drew out her next words. "My father."

Mayadeen harrumphed, although knowing quite well her mother's cleverness; such discretion would have made much more sense.

"Akaranza helped keep our mother's secret," continued Elona, "whether for Mabelia's sake or my father's sake. What's more, she made certain I was kept safe. She charged Ursade with that task, and Ursade did her best to carry it out."

"That so?" Mayadeen jettisoned a good snot bird to the swells.

"Ye told me ye were whoring yerself out for food in Thresnare and Edenvane, then runnin' amok with Lusul and her bitch beasts. Seems Ursade shirked her charge."

"That, well... that was all my own doing," said Elona. "Unbeknown to Ursade or my father, I stowed away on a merchant vessel to Thresnare when I was twelve. When I returned five years later, my father had gone missing, and Ursade locked me in a tower for countless days." Elona leaned against the gunwales in thought. She smirked. "I must've read a hundred tomes and recited a thousand incantations in that old study room. Not one of them could breach Ursade's spell to keep me imprisoned there. I remember her telling me how important I was to the Order, how I had been chosen to fulfill a certain duty, one that she had to protect me from. She never told me any more than that, and honestly, I didn't care. I was such a fool. Only when I returned to Valindrost after we parted did I finally get the truth out of her and learn about the prophecy."

"Prophecy says ye?" Mayadeen tilted back her head with a snort. "By the salted cunts of drowned gods, I need a drink!" Elona frowned, her eyes pleading. Yet another sisterly understanding that Mayadeen could do without. She relented and collapsed her arms over the railing.

"Shorsas will rise again through the Sinbalak—through a Daughter born of Corolon—using the strongest bloodline of the last thousand years as her vessel. All this time, Ursade, and Akaranza before her, believed I was that vessel."

As Elona spoke, Mayadeen marveled at just how much she didn't know about her estranged half-sister. But even the bard's longest lyric couldn't fill the time they'd have on the sea to their next destination, and so time enough for a history removed.

"Hard way of it, that," Mayadeen conceded. "Tied by the tit to some silly nymph's prophecy of rainbows and unicorns. But ye're more the trump for it, Red." She gave Elona a hard pat on the back. "Glad we had this palaver." Again, she turned to leave, and again Elona grabbed her hand. If she'd been anybody else, Mayadeen would've put her fist through her nose.

"I know now that it's never been me who is the vessel, Mayadeen. It's you."

Mayadeen started, and then bit her lip. There was no denying her sister was probably right. Shorsas, the insufferable witch of old, had indeed chosen the Damned bloodline. But it wasn't Elona who the ghostly biddy had struck a deal with. Shorsas had picked Mayadeen, and shards or no shards, it was doubtful the legendary sorcerer was finished with her.

"No more on that, damn ye." Mayadeen took a deep breath. "We've plenty of time to talk about that which may or may not be so. Right now, give me what I can grab, squeeze and taste." She grinned. "Pride of the Day, Red. S'all that matters and that's what we call it."

"Pride of the day?" Elona smirked even after she questioned it.

"We saw the sunrise this morning, and so says I, Pride of the Day."

#

The magic hour remained calm and clear just before sunset, and Mayadeen, Elona, Roe and Theren took their repast in the aftercastle at a proper setting. Mayadeen had insisted her old friend take her captain's quarters back, but Theren would have none of it, relenting only to the invitation to dine there. In the two days Mayadeen had intermittently observed Theren, the latter's skill and command over her ship and the affairs of her crew would impress even the saltiest Master of the Nine. Theren's mates were all Meridian cunties but for two well-equipped bull twins, and although the scalawags were a reserved bunch, they carried out their duties with the jolly fervor of familial purpose. Such a life represented what every Daughter born captain strove for, and the admonition made Mayadeen miss hers terribly.

They supped on salted pork, roasted leeks and dumpling stew, with Roe already devouring his second helping of all three. Captain

Theren ordered a cask of wine opened for the occasion, and she'd given Mayadeen three fine bottles of the blackest rum from her personal stash.

Mayadeen raised her cup, filled with four generous fingers of terrifically tart daiquiri, to the opposite end of the rectangular, cherry wood table. "A draught to Captain Theren, a bonny ol' chum and soon-to-be Master of the Nine, for delivering my pale arse from the most godsforsaken main to ever plod above the water's edge."

"Hear, hear," Elona tapped her silver fork against her own cup of wine. Roe happily did likewise; himself allotted a finger of red wine for the occasion. Then they all imbibed.

Theren stood and thrust her twin-handled cup into the air. "I'll see yer toast and raise ye one better, Captain Damned, ye ol' troublesome rum trump 'n' sinker of ships and shafts alike!"

There was a swollen silence for a moment as all eyes shot to Mayadeen for reaction. A smile crept across her face and she guffawed. Theren laughed, too, and soon Elona joined in followed by Roe, though the boy had no idea what he was laughing at.

"Nay, nay ..." Theren resumed. "To Mayadeen, who ne'er needed the likes of me nor any for a rescue, as she'd quench the fires of four 'n' twenty hells before they consumed her. And when ye find that sparkling green eye upon ye," she mimicked one eye staring at Elona and then at Roe, "pray to 'em high and pray to 'em low it e'er be yer first and ne'er be yer last!"

Another clink of forks on cups. Theren had inherited her dramatic flair in earnest from her old piss of a mother. Sonner Bon Shemble could have an entire crew laughing, crying and wishing they were dead all in the same turn of phrase.

"Now," said Mayadeen after downing the rest of her much missed and favorite beverage, "let's palaver of things to come. But first, I've a right jolly secret to share with ye, Ther, my matey. That handsome lil' nymph sitting right there," she gestured to Elona. "She's my own true sister."

Elona's eyes grew the size of her pewter dinner plate. "Sister?

Gracious me ... Captain Damned's had too much of the grog—"

"I've had me two drams and remain as clear as the stillest tide pool, Red. It's okay. Ther can know our dirty lil' secret."

Theren leaned back in her chair and tipped a good drink. "A bastard sister, heh? What'd be the odds o' that? Right fuckin' thick, I'd wager. Yer Pap was known for the finest seed in the Island Realm. Surprised it's taken ye this long to meet a cock sister."

Mayadeen smiled knowingly. "Aye, ol' Ther. But Red here's a twat sister as my Mum's be the one that squeezed her out."

Theren's wine tumbler stopped halfway to her smirking lips while a single brow approached her cropped yellow hair line.

Mayadeen regarded Elona who stared down at her plate like it held the secrets of eternity, her hands readying themselves on the table's edge. Her sister had been made to feel ashamed of whom she was for far too long, and now her true plight would begin. But this time, she wouldn't be alone.

"Yuck," said Roe. "I don't ever want a sister." His innocent remark did nothing to break the tension.

"And here I thought ye'd simply taken to the tongue," said Theren over her cup before finally taking that sip. "If ye speak true, then ye'd be wise to keep that secret a bit closer, Emmy. A bastard Daughter born is one thing, but a witch's brood ... If word got back to the Isles—"

"Piss on the Isles," said Mayadeen. "I've the Sinbalak swimmin' through my veins, damn ye. Terse and true. Am I to cipher the Bone Reef over it? Lay me down to the Dream of Ghosts? Nay. I am what I am before as I am what I am now. Nothing's changed."

"What of yer Mum then?"

Mayadeen flipped up her eye patch for some air. "She'll deny it and so it won't make a lick o' difference. Or mayhap I'll get lucky and the ol' wicked cunty will set sail and come after me. She's been raising birds 'n' burying cocks for long enough in her fancy rags on Pelican Peak. The Elders grow soft as swollen sponges. They might rule the Isles, but *we* rule the seas. Yer own dear mother knew it ... 'tis why she sails still."

Theren considered for a moment. "All right then, if this madness be true, then I suppose ye've good reason to believe it so." She smiled at Elona and shoved the smaller woman on the shoulder. "I don't envy yer blood, but a sister of Emmy's a sister of mine."

Elona glanced up and tried to form a smile. Mayadeen knew she wasn't comfortable with their secret on the out, but she'd better start getting used to it.

"Now, with that drivelin' settled, let's speak of what we do best," said Mayadeen. "The Southern Isles hold treasure beyond naught gleaned by even our grandmothers. Before my galleon was shattered by storm and beast, I held ol' Bon Shemble's maps."

"And how would ye've gathered those?" asked Theren with a scowl.

"Minnow Baels had 'em, and I sent the lil' pisser and half his mates to the Bone Reef. But Crey Fenn assured me those maps were sham. The cursed peacock fessed up to stowin' copies of the real charts. He'd no reason to lie when I was about to drive a spike through his throat."

"Seems to me a fine time to lie," snapped Theren. "Was wondering what ye were even doing with the puffed up feather cock. Thought ye were a pair again."

"Nay to that. But don't concern with Fenn. The day he sprouts wings is the day he'd get beyond the Spread. 'Tis why he sought me out... for a joint venture." Mayadeen replaced her patch over her eye. "I say that joint venture belongs to us, Captain. Together we could not only reach the Southern Isles, but find every last crooked cairn and loot 'em proper."

"I can tell ye those maps would've done ye for shrimp shit," said Theren.

"That so?"

"That's so and some besides. There be fell magics lurkin' about those isles. Whenever my Mum charted a new anchorage, the shoals would take to the opposite side of the ploughin' compass the very next daybreak. Mum told how it kept up just like that for a fortnight and a moon, 'til one day the shoals trapped the ship."

"How did she get out?" asked Roe with a fair curiosity. He gnawed on the end of a broken cinnamon stick for his dessert.

Theren chuckled with a side glance. "Why she cussed at the shallows 'til they opened right up again."

Mayadeen finished her tangy grog. She'd taken it slow so as not to get too drunk too quickly. She wanted the post-supper palaver at least to be lucid.

"I don't aim to just chart 'em, and it'll take more than shiftin' shallows to stay me off. We've our own magician, besides." She nodded at Elona. "How 'bout it, Red?"

"You know I'm with you, Mayadeen."

"Just one more particular," said Theren. "The *Cockswell* ain't fit for the voyage. 'Twixt the swells of the Spread and the storms of the Fire Hoof, he'd be 'bout as sure as a fish floppin' through a flock of redgulls."

"Then it's nigh time for ye to start wearin' fancier boots," said Mayadeen. "We'll need twice the crew and twice the vessel."

"Aye, though we'd be wastin' a keg of time headin' back to the Isles." Theren poured herself more wine and offered the flagon to Elona, who humbly accepted. "I suggest we port in Clattercan. A three week's voyage, give or take some days of windward haul."

Roe had finally fallen asleep against the large, buckled back of his chair with cinnamon stick still in hand.

Mayadeen thought for a moment and nodded. A brief stop at Clattercan was a fine idea if they were to procure a new vessel or even reoutfit the *Cockswell* as a last resort. She reached for the bottle of fine rum, always wrapped in rope to protect the glass from cracking during the everyday jostle caused by a ship's motion. She uncorked the stopper with her teeth, but spit it out lightly upon her supper plate so as not to confuse Theren's cabin for her own. She grabbed half a lime—imported from the Thresnare, no doubt— preserved with simple magics to keep many months in most climates.

Mayadeen suspected a similar magic was used for protecting mates as they ventured through portals. In the past such trivialities eluded her, while now they brimmed in her head with curiosity and excitement. She squeezed the citrus to trickle into her cup, a zesty mist briefly inspiring her nostrils. After setting the lime aside, with the same hand she pinched up some sandy brown chunks of sugar and added to her concoction a generous sprinkle. The rum came last—a flowing sable gloss coupled by the stench of molasses.

"Mayadeen?" prodded Elona at last. "How then do you suggest we acquire a bigger ship?"

A squawk carried from an open portico on the far side of the cabin. Feathers rustled and soon the window was filled with a dark shape in the careening lamplight.

Mayadeen grinned and took a good pull of her daiquiri. Without turning, she extended her arm. With another rustle and a firm pinch, the redgull perched just above her elbow. Mayadeen caressed his chest with the back of her finger and lightly smacked her lips. She pried a golden ring from his curved talons, and Prick pecked at her hair. She held the ring up for better inspection. Fine tooling set a dark ruby atop brambles or thorns. She pitched the ring to Elona who caught it in one hand.

Theren laughed as the ring was too big even for Elona's gloved, middle finger.

Mayadeen pursed her lips again with a soft kissing noise, and Prick launched back to the open portico.

"Well, Red, unless Prick has me at least ten more of those rings and a fence to pay top coin for 'em, I propose we tie down to the nearest port, find or wait for the vessel of our choosing, and kindly take the fucking thing."

#

After she tucked Roe into a makeshift berth at the foot of her own bed, Mayadeen took to the decks. Just as the stars began to puncture a million tiny holes in the night's fabric, she found Elona on the foredeck gazing out at the final pink of sunset. Theren had at least five lookouts on picket, while a particularly jolly mate named Sweyda worked the wheel. With a crew never at rest in deep waters, the *Cockswell* continued to cut through the carry on the southern edge of the Jeweled Sea. A few large black shapes filled the horizon to the southeast. The smattering of isles would continue for many leagues until they ended at the great Sea Spread, the largest and most southern ocean of Tabor.

"Those are the first of the Forsatha Islands," observed Mayadeen. "Hundreds of 'em. Only the Meridian Isles claim more."

Elona turned and put a finger to her lips. "Shush ... listen. Do you hear that?"

The faintest melody of a vocal song flitted across the gentle waves. Mayadeen concentrated just enough to recognize what charmed them from the distant shoals.

"Sirens. Ye never heard their wailing?"

"It's beautiful," whispered Elona as if speaking any higher would stop the singing.

"Never did I love, ever did I live ..."

"Aye, all pictures and posies 'til they're ready to eat ye. They sing what ye'd want to hear and even resemble what ye'd want to fuck."

"The spider and the snake and the old mandrake ..."

"I've read about them, of course, and I think those tales are exaggerated. But like so many of Xinixelica's children, I assumed the sirens only to be another legend lost to the ages."

Mayadeen huffed. "There ye go with that cunty again. Ye call 'em her children. I call 'em fell creatures of a low god. Either way, a scalawag worth her salt knows to stay clear of sirens just as they know to keep wide of a sturdy vessel. So then there's nothing to exaggerate, Red." She cackled a bit under her breath and was actually relieved when the singing stopped. "Pirates from every corner of the Nine colonize those islands, Meridians among 'em. Many a crone and captain's retired there. Ol' Ther's idea is wise. We'll port at Clattercan by the next new moon."

Elona searched Mayadeen's face with a curious smile. "We've been through so much together, and yet we've hardly been together at all. It's strange, isn't it?"

Mayadeen just nodded. Her sister's voice was much more pleasant to the ears than those cursed sirens.

"Now that Lusul is gone, and most likely Bolora, I fear the Four Kingdoms will be in utter chaos, perhaps even worse than before," continued Elona as she stared off into the now pinpricked cosmos.

"Mayhap Leweln spoke true ... the time of the barbarian kings draws to an end."

"You mean you actually met with King Leweln of Sundvane? How—"

"'Tis a yarn, Red, and ye might say I even fancied the loopy bitch. But she was dying; on her last go of it. With no other kin to stymie the path, seems Ursade and her witch brood could now snatch the whole cursed Warlands Main for themselves."

"She doesn't want it. Never did. Despite what you may think, Mayadeen, her Reverence Ursade is not a bad person. No, the various chieftains and warlords across Rul and Leth will vie for the empty crowns. Ursade and the Order of Prenn will simply have to strike accords all over again with whoever comes out on top. Such is how it's always been in Valindrost and all of the Four Kingdoms."

Mayadeen didn't give three slippery shits off the scuppers about Valindrost or any of the Four Kingdoms, and yet she wondered if Elona knew they'd probably never return. The Nine Seas beckoned, and she'd take her sister over the glistening swells of each and every one of them.

"Are we really going to steal a ship, Mayadeen?"

"We'll do whatever we need to continue south. Clattercan

Island's the last colony before the Sea Spread. I know one or two shriveled old cunties who may be willing to barter their vessels and crews."

"Why not go back to the Meridian Isles to procure a new ship? Why not ask our mother?"

Mayadeen snickered. Elona's indoctrination into the family would be a slow and rude one.

"Our mother wouldn't give us the puddin' off her sop rag. And when she finds out about yer sugared arse exposed to the Four Winds as her bastard, the whole of the Island Realm will make the Warlands Main seem welcoming. She'll likely want ye dead, and she'll all but see I go with ye to make that happen."

"I've been thinking about that," said Elona. "I found what I came for. I found you, sister, and it's not necessary that I complicate your life any further. I belong with my own people, Mayadeen. Whether at Valindrost with the Order or back in Thresnare, I should be with them. I am one of them."

Mayadeen flipped up her eye patch. The crisp air felt cool and comforting on her fused and half-empty socket. She discharged a good one off the port side gunwales and returned the cover to its cavity.

"Persuasive words, those, sis" said Mayadeen. "Ye believe 'em?"

Elona sniffled and wiped away pooling tears. She shook her head. "No. No I don't. I believe there's so much more. For me, for you, for all of it."

Mayadeen placed both hands on Elona's shoulders, squaring her off. She cupped her sister's soft cheeks.

"Ye're a Damned—Damned if ye fancy and Damned if ye falter. So ye may as well fuckin' fancy. We're Daughter-born pirates of the Nine. Now ye're one of us."

Elona nodded with a suppressed grin, her glassy eyes now lights of their own.

"To the ends of this world's where we're going, Red. To the ends of this rich, rich world."

ABOUT THE AUTHOR

J. Lendell White (Jeff, to his friends) is a Northern California native-turned-mutant Los Angeleno. After a stint as an actor at Playhouse West and The Groundlings, he turned to writing as a more civilized expression of his creative impulses. Jeff is a sucker for old boats, ghost towns, roaring hearth fires, pinball and his omniscient cat, Khaleesi. After writing several short stories, he completed his first novel and dove headlong into the next. He enjoys writing fiction while combining genres and bending them to his twisted will.